RETRIBUTION

MABRY TURNER

SweetWaterPress
4 River Bend Circle
Little Rock, Arkansas 72202

FIRST EDITION

1 3 5 7 9 10 8 6 4 2

Cover designed by G. R. (Dik) Jenkins
Democrat Printing and Lithographing Company

Library of Congress Card Number: 00-190277
ISBN 0-9678528-0-3

Acknowledgments

Retribution required a great deal of research, dealing with some topics I knew little, if anything, about. I was fortunate to have the assistance of a number of people who gave generously of their time and considerable expertise to help me sort them out. Any errors in descriptions, depictions, or specifications are mine alone, and should be blamed either on literary license, or my own failure to understand.

For matters military I am deeply indebted to Lt. Colonel Dave Grossman, U.S. Army, Retired, whose book, *On Killing*, has become today's standard on the psychology of desensitization; and Colonel Lewis Magruder, U.S. Army, Retired. Lew's wartime experiences in Vietnam provided authentic background for my narrative.

Pulaski County Coroner Mark Malcomb was gracious to explain the duties of his office.

Inner workings of the Secret Service are courtesy of John T. Cook, Jr., retired Special Agent in Charge of the Little Rock field office. Without giving away any secrets, he painstakingly guided me through preparations for a Presidential visit. I beg John's forgiveness for liberties I may have taken with his information. WHLA Sykes-Smythe is wholly a product of my imagination, and should not be laid at his doorstep.

To Donald L. Holbert, Chairman of the Board of Central Flying Service, and Trooper Jim Moore, able helicopter pilot for the Arkansas State Police, I owe abundant thanks. Their first-hand knowledge of aerial combat, technique, and equipment proved invaluable. If they find themselves as thinly disguised characters in the pages of *Retribution*, it is because I couldn't have done it without them.

Bert Parke, CEO of Democrat Printing and Lithographing Company, championed my cause. It is through his efforts, and those of G.R. (Dik) Jenkins, who tutored me in the fine art of printing, that *Retribution* is being published.

Dr. Jim Burleson, Professor of English at Arkansas State University in Jonesboro, Kate Askew, and Ann Grimes, writers and scholars all, were kind enough to check the manuscript for content and mistakes, and offer critical advice.

And my especial gratitude goes to my good friend George Wildgen, who had the unenviable task of reading *Retribution* in installments as it was being written. George suffered through multiple drafts and rewrites with patience, wit, and unflagging encouragement. If there were times I doubted my abilities, his support kept me going.

Thank you one and all.

For
ROY

What would the past thirty years have been without you?

RETRIBUTION

CHAPTER 1

The steering wheel bucked in his hand as Boyd struggled to stay on course. Deep furrows gouged out of the hardpan by an army of logging trucks made the dirt lane tough going for the laden command vehicle. When the undercarriage wasn't scraping on crusts of mud, the axle cleared the center hump by scant inches. Staring through thermal imaging goggles, Boyd saw the ruts stretching before him in watery shades of green, a swathe through the jungles of Laos. The flashback caused a lapse in his concentration, and the van jolted to one side.

"Shit, Commander, watch it!"

Jerked out of his bitter reverie Boyd corrected, but not before the thorns of a honey locust raked pinstripes in the vehicle's ebony hide.

McKensie growled angrily, "What the fuck? You want me to drive?"

The mobile command post was McKensie's creation, and he was nervous enough without Boyd caroming all over the place, although negotiating the bumpy road without headlights was a bitch, McKensie'd grant him that. After eleven on a moonless night, it was pitch black, the gloom intensified by glimmers of distant sheet lightning. For the band of commandos traversing the countryside under mantle of darkness, night had assumed a palpable quality, the presence of a co-conspirator.

Boyd ignored McKensie's outburst, focusing his attention on driving. Now wasn't the time to spar with an edgy subordinate.

Ahead an abandoned double-wide loomed through a gap in the trees. The door had been boarded shut, one corner of the

1

roof peeled back like an empty sardine tin. Just beyond the mobile home lay the most dangerous part of the journey. The road
wound up a scalped hillside, scarred victim of clear cutting. On
the bare slope they would be naked, exposed from every angle.
Not that there were all that many people out here *to* see them.
That had been one of the criteria. Most of the land was national
forest land, or leased to one of several large timber companies.
Earlier that day during their last reconnaissance run, a six pack of
migrant workers had been planting pine seedlings over the dam-
aged terrain from canvas bags slung Santa Claus-style across their
backs.

There were holdouts. Here and there scattered homesteads
clung to small, privately owned plots that the lumber companies
hadn't been able to gobble up. Each house represented potential
witnesses. Fear of discovery had governed Boyd's use of NVGs
to cover the open stretch.

At the top of the hill the lane widened out, creating a passing
bay. Their turnoff was two hundred yards past the bay, over the
crest of the ridge. Once on Weyerhaeuser wood road 4827, they
traveled blind for another hundred yards to the protection of un-
harvested timber. Shrouded in trees, Boyd flicked on his parking
lights to help thread the rest of the way to the promontory.

At the end of the track he reversed, positioning the van back
the way they had come. He checked his watch. They were close
to schedule.

Getting out quickly, Boyd came around and unlatched the
cargo door. Immediately a large, thickset man clambered down.

"Okay Heavy, let's do it."

Heavy was an apt name for the eldest of the Bolin clan. A
huge man, big-boned, with massive shoulders hunched over a
square torso, he had been christened Eugene Claude Bolin, Jr.,
but he had never been called anything but Heavy. Willing and
complaisant, he was a gentle giant capable of prodigious effort,
whose physical prowess far outstripped less abundant mental resources. Guile and subtlety were unknown to him; his was, in

every sense of the word, a literal mind. Boyd didn't know why Daniel had chosen the simple man for his spy, but it was all right with him. In his long career he had been saddled with far worse.

Heavy nodded assent, reached back into the vehicle, and with Boyd's help, wrestled a bulky object to the ground. Together they half carried, half dragged the cumbersome piece of equipment to the edge of the bluff. With only the stars and a hooded lantern for guidance they had to be extremely careful. One slip too near the cliff face meant a thousand foot free fall to the river.

With the efficiency of long practice Boyd completed his preliminary tasks, bolting the carefully engineered assembly onto concrete support pilings sunk into the earth weeks before. The pilings had been covered with dirt and pine straw, and had he not known precisely where they were buried, he would never have located them. Heavy busied himself transferring their remaining supplies into position. When both men were ready they worked in tandem. One by one, Heavy lifted the weapons gently from their cradles, hoisting the hundred pound weights like they were toys. Boyd led the way, illuminating the path. With exquisite delicacy the men slotted their precious burdens into the waiting rack. They toiled in silence, broken only by an occasional grunt or muttered *Careful!* When he was satisfied that everything was in order Boyd returned to the vehicle. He rapped twice. The van took off.

Had it been eleven in the morning instead of twelve hours later, the view would have been spectacular, a broad panorama of dammed-up river valley forming the headwaters of Lake Dardanelle. That the Arkansas River, which formed the lake, was in flood stage wouldn't hamper their activity at all. On the contrary, it was a distinct advantage. With pleasure craft warned off by the Coast Guard, and commercial shipping at a standstill until the waters subsided, any chance they would be spotted from the lake was virtually nil. That was one of the reasons Boyd had pushed Daniel to carry out a dry run. No amount of drilling could ever duplicate the real thing. Coordinated on three separate fronts, timing of the assault was critical. Boyd was banking that a full dress rehearsal in the field would turn up any problems before the Independence Day strike. Axiomatic it might be, but glitches were better discovered *before* the fact. James was in place. He and Heavy were set. McKensie was a different matter.

McKensie's stomach was churning, his cocky attitude a veneer masking profound anxiety. If *he* botched things the mission was over. He steered cautiously, weak beams catching a raccoon crossing the trail, its eyes glowing orange like a goblin in a House of Horrors. When he reached the point where his lights might be visible from the main road he doused them, donning the awkward goggles Boyd had left on the seat.

The descent went faster. The road was neither as steep, nor its surface as rough as on the uphill face. In less than ten minutes McKensie was approaching his destination. Off to the right, the rusting hulk of a John Deere tractor grazed in a ruined pasture, restrained by sagging strands of barbed wire. Next to the pasture a rundown farmhouse, its picture window alive with the blue flame of television, sheltered under an enormous oak. A battered Datsun and a Chevrolet pickup huddled together companionably in the front yard.

The house was the final obstacle before the lake. He was almost there. Barely touching the accelerator McKensie crept forward, inching past the driveway. But before he could clear this last hurdle a piercing shriek shattered the bucolic calm, sending chills zinging down his spine. *Shi-i-it! What the hell was that?* Heart pounding he froze, gripping the wheel tighter as the eerie wail was repeated. *Come on Mike, don't piss your pants. It's just a screech owl. Another fifty yards you'll be in the clear—then you can breathe again.*

An eternity of several seconds ticked by before the ramshackle dwelling was behind him, screened off by a dense thicket of hardwoods and pines. In the center of the copse a deserted clearing opened to the lake. McKensie braked, coming to rest with the van's front tires positioned on the lip of a corrugated launching ramp.

Next came the diciest part of the exercise, and the subject of much debate. Given a choice, McKensie would have been happier utilizing an advanced wireless system for the modem of his computer. Had that been an option, it would have greatly simplified certain aspects of the mission, but it wasn't possible. He required access to a land line. Consequently, for a short period McKensie would be forced to leave the security of the command vehicle.

He opened the door, swung his legs outside before buckling on his spikes. No courtesy lights came on, no buzzer sounded to remind him to remove the keys, just as the brake lights had not flashed when he rolled to a halt. Those wires had been disconnected long ago.

A spool of insulated cable was clamped on a spindle inside the rear hatch. Releasing the clamp, McKensie grabbed the wire by a loop knotted in its end, playing out the cable over his shoulder. He still wore the NVGs as he trudged through the trees back toward the house. Rooted twenty yards from the foot of the drive was a telephone pole. McKensie would be vulnerable astride the pole, but he would really be pushing his luck sneaking up to the farmhouse. At the base of the pole he made a decision. Stripping off the burdensome glasses he climbed by the flickering light from the television. He climbed with grace, shinnying up to the cross bar like a veteran lineman. The splice was a piece of cake; he could have made the cut blindfolded. Once he had taped the joint he wasted no time getting down, picked up the discarded goggles, and made a bee line back to safety.

*   *   *

Addy hated her name. She really, really hated her name. It was plain and dull and old fashioned. How would she ever amount to anything with a name like Addy? In her fantasies she was a movie star or a talk show hostess, a pop singer, the darling of a TV sitcom, a prima donna of the tennis circuit. Sometimes she was even Miss America with a diamond tiara sparkling atop her regal head . . . Whoopi, Whitney, Oprah, and Vanessa . . . Venus, LaToya, Aretha, Queen Latifah. Childhood dreams where anything was possible if only she had a glamorous name to hang her hopes on.

Reality was ADDY. ADDY was a dilapidated frame house at the end of a dirt road going nowhere. ADDY was an unmarried African-American mother trying her best to keep body and soul together against the grinding poverty and racial prejudice of rural Arkansas. ADDY was a nine year old imp, quick, clever, lonely, and curious, who wanted desperately to grow up to be SOME-BODY, somebody *not* ADDY.

Furrowing her velvet brow, Starship Commander Seretha Willis trimmed the left rudder, correcting her craft's slight slew to starboard. Stability restored, the pilot began plotting a course for Jupiter. Actually she was going to Io, but she had to leap half the solar system before swerving away from the giant planet's gravitational pull to land on its sulfurous moon. The last party sent out from Earth Federation had vanished without so much as a distress signal. Space-ace Seretha Willis had been dispatched to locate survivors—or, finding none—to complete the aborted survey mission.

"Take the controls Smorg, your Captain will be right back."

The intrepid explorer left the bridge. Addy tiptoed along the passageway to the bathroom. When she had finished she washed and dried her hands and stole softly back down the hall, being careful not to disturb Maybelle and Earl, who were plonked on the couch in front of the television. Addy liked Earl okay; he was Maybelle's friend, but sometimes he brought Addy candy or a tape. One time, on her eighth birthday, he had even given her a black Barbie, which was awfully considerate, seeing as how Earl knew zip about kids, girls in particular. So she tried not to get in the way when Earl came over. Besides, it was Saturday night, and Maybelle had a midnight curfew on Saturday.

She and Addy *never* missed church on Sunday. Maybelle sang in the choir at the Trumpet of Zion AME Temple in Dardanelle, second soprano to that snooty Mrs. Hezekiah Ames. Mrs. Ames couldn't sing half as well as Maybelle, but she was sanctified, and had money to boot, since Deacon Ames had dropped dead, naked as a jaybird in Deneidra Shaw's bedroom, leaving Maybelle forever subordinate to the older woman in the choir's hierarchy. Maybelle wouldn't give the old biddy the satisfaction of seeing her more talented rival hung-over after too late a night, or even worse, of not showing up at all. So the rule was, all of Maybelle's Saturday dates had to be gone by twelve o'clock, period

Addy slipped back in her room, retaking the controls.

"You let her drift, Lieutenant. There's an asteroid dead ahead! Sound Battle Stations! Arrooogah! Arrooogah! Shields up!"

Bracing for the inevitable collision, Seretha didn't notice Boo growling at first. The low rumble remained background noise as the asteroid hit the ship head on.

"Damage assessment, Smorg!" Boo's growl grew deeper, gradually penetrating Seretha's engrossment with her stricken craft. Addy came down to earth.

Crossing to the window she peered out the screen. Nothing. Just what she expected. "What you fussin' bout, Boo? I don't see a thing. Hush up you silly ol' dog." Boo regarded the beloved face with moist brown eyes and kept complaining.

Addy unlatched the frame and scrambled nimbly over the sill. Dropping soundlessly onto the packed soil she wrapped both arms around Boo's neck; wriggled slim fingers under his collar; tickled the sweet spot until he curled, grinning, troubles temporarily forgotten. She lifted one floppy ear. "You gotta be quiet now. Maybelle catch us out here this time o' night she'll skin us alive. Ain't nothin' out there 'cept some ol' boys goin' coon huntin'. If'n you hush up, we'll go see." Mollified, Boo agreed.

It was a perfect summer night, lush and soft. Warm darkness enveloped Addy like a cocoon, a down caress against her skin. In late June the heat and humidity were usually oppressive, but this year all the rain and a dip in the jet stream had kept temperatures below normal. Fireflies flickered luminous come-hithers; cicadas thrummed their songs in the underbrush. Tree frogs joined in, rasping a strident plea for more rain. Above the western horizon, obscured by a leafy umbrella, heat lightning strobed a southern Aurora Borealis. Overriding a musky blend of earth, pine, honeysuckle, and water, the faint, acrid odor of pesticide stung her nostrils. Addy wrinkled her nose, became for an instant a daredevil crop-duster jousting the pylon windmills that led away in all directions from the power station at Russellville. Trouble was, sometimes the pylons won. She sneezed, sent the pilot packing.

Addy was comfortable in her domain, her world completely familiar. She and her canine companion rested easy in the night's embrace.

Fresh footprints cratered the path. Kineesha paused, alert, immobile, as the enraged leviathan bellowed an angry challenge. *"Have you got the tranquilizer gun?"* she whispered. He slipped the loaded rifle in her hand. Stalking the renegade T. Rex, world famous paleontologist Kineesha Willis and her faithful scout Boo followed the rampaging dinosaur's tracks toward the lake.

☆　☆　☆

McKensie had designed the mobile command post from scratch and done most of the conversion himself. After months of preparation, the time had come to prove himself. He flicked on the controls. The lights came up. *Yes!* Tapping a series of keys on the console, he heard the unmistakable bleeps and whines of numbers flying through cyberspace. He had done it. The connection was solid. With a self-congratulatory smirk he watched the program scroll across the shimmering screen. *God, didn't you love technology.*

McKensie's next order of business was the GLLD [Ground Laser Locator Designator: a self-contained, man-portable laser designation system]. He pushed a button to slide open the moon roof. Standing, he peered through the opening to orient himself. Then he set the exclusion code that would guarantee the missiles homed in on the pre-programmed frequency of his particular beam. He secured the laser in a pop-up holder and zeroed it on the target. With the computer on line they were ready to go. All he had to do now was wait.

Before things got hot the hacker had five minutes to kill. From a thermos at his feet McKensie poured iced tea into a plastic container. Sucking at the straw attached to the insulated bottle he thought he heard a sound, ill-defined, but distinct from the night music around him. He shook his head, as if to clear away not only the foreign noise but suspicion as well. It was his overactive imagination—nothing more than another raccoon or opossum conducting its nocturnal prowl for food. No vehicle had entered the clearing. A visual alarm would have alerted him to any encroaching conveyance. Glancing at the display reassured him. Everything was running normally. What was he worrying about? It could've been the engine ticking as it cooled. He took another long pull of tea, chasing away his unease. He was jumpy, that's all.

Damnit to hell! There it was again, a subtle vibration as the van seemed to shudder in the wind. Except there was no wind, only an erratic breeze, barely strong enough to riffle the spiky loblollies. A pulsing yellow indicator blinked frantically, silently screaming intrusion. Something had set off the sensors. The van's space had definitely been violated.

McKensie sat stock still, switched off the flashing alarm, and cupped a hand behind his ear, straining to hear. *Damn!* . . . Very close by . . . a muffled thump, scraping, and a funny hissing that sounded like *shsssh*. He reached down, found the haft of his knife, snug in its ankle scabbard. Okay. Looked at the time. The digital display read 11:56. He had three minutes max before he had to contact Boyd. And that would be cutting it awfully fine. *Shit. Shit. Shit.* Not much time to deal with a problem, but what the fuck, as if he had a choice.

9

Whoever or whatever it was sounded like it was coming from the front of the vehicle, still parked above the ramp. McKensie slid out of his seat and clicked open the latch. Padding soundlessly along the paneled side of the van toward the lake he heard a sharp bark, followed by a tiny clear voice calling, "Hush, Boo, hush! Come on!"

Rounding the front of the van McKensie encountered a stiff-legged black dog planted firmly on the concrete slope. Water was lapping at its feet. Six steps behind the snarling animal a small girl in pajamas, eyes wide in fright, was pleading, "Come on, Boo. Come on. Now! I mean it!" The dog didn't budge.

McKensie couldn't fool around. He had to get back to the computer before launch time. He backed up the way he had come, out of the dog's line of sight. Had he turned to run or made a sudden move the animal might have charged. But as long as it stayed between him and the girl he couldn't neutralize her. He reached the open door, eased it shut. In that instant the child decided to flee. McKensie rolled around the bumper and lunged, grabbing her arm as she sped past.

She started to scream then, a high-pitched keening as plaintive and chilling as the screech owl's wail. McKensie stifled her scream abruptly, clamping his hand over her nose and mouth. She writhed in his grasp, kicking and flailing, while the black dog raced toward them barking furiously. *Fuck it all!*

He broke her neck cleanly, a reflex action, no more difficult than swatting a fly. The child went limp in his arms, a Raggedy Ann, all protest spent. Carrying her to the edge of the lake he tossed her in. She was gone in an instant, borne away without a trace by the surging water.

Miraculously, the dog, too, was gone. It had turned tail and slunk away the moment Addy's neck snapped. Driven by some atavistic impulse to seek asylum in the encircling darkness, the child's guardian had retreated without a whimper.

McKensie *had* to get back on station. 11:58. His frigging watch read 11:58! He didn't have time to worry about where the kid had come from or where the dog had gone. He had to get back in the van and hope nobody had heard the commotion. He had one foot on the running board when a hammer crashed into the back of his skull. McKensie staggered, reeling, into the van. *Oh God, not now. Please, not now.* He pressed the heels of his hands to his temples, trying to stave off the incipient migraine, but the headache refused to go away, settling into the familiar throb he knew would escalate into incapacitating pain. He had to . . . had to . . . Catching sight of the monitor he forgot his headache, the child, the dog, everything but the task at hand.

His agile fingers sped over the keyboard. He was a virtuoso, an electronic Houdini slipping uninvited into the control room to take out the safeguards. He was a fucking genius, that's what. A fucking genius. If only his head would quit pounding. McKensie scrunched up his shoulders, trying to relieve the pressure, his eyes locked on the screen. Swiped a palm through damp hair. It was time to call Boyd.

Oh, shit! He had forgotten the laser.

Strictly line of sight, laser targeting is incredibly precise, and across the lake McKensie had an arrow straight shot at their objective. But what good would that be if he didn't turn the damn thing on, keeping the target painted until the missiles hit home? From their position on the cliff, Boyd and Heavy were also using a GLLD. Dual tracking beams would assure pinpoint accuracy. McKensie reached up and switched on the designator. Okay.

He fingered the transmitter. *Hurry up, Boyd. Hurry up!*

Seconds later, in response to McKensie's mental urging and the insistent clicking of the receiver, Boyd's baritone "It's a go," resonated through the ear piece.

McKensie sighed in relief. It was going to work. It *was* going to work! *Sweet Jesus.* They were in business.

CHAPTER 2

Humming a snatch of *I'll Fly Away*, Maybelle rapped softly on her daughter's door. It was eight a.m.

"Time to get up, honey. We don' wanna be late."

She hurried on to the bathroom, her mind on the choir's anthem. The choir master had assigned Maybelle a rare solo, and she wanted to strut her stuff in defiance of Arniece Ames. She brushed her teeth and hopped in the shower, filling the small enclosure with a riot of melody, every note absolutely perfect. Satisfied with her performance, Maybelle toweled off, smiling at her reflection. She'd show that hypocritical old bitch how to sing. Morning ablution completed, Maybelle swung open the door, fully expecting Addy to be waiting impatiently for her turn, but her daughter was nowhere in sight.

"Lord, that child will be the death of me." She strode with purpose to Addy's room, knocked firmly, and went in. No Addy.

Puzzled, Maybelle looked around, spotted the half raised window. The screen was unhooked, and a gaping crack yawned between the bottom of the screen and the window frame. Carcasses of gnats and mosquitoes dusted the sill.

A sudden shiver of apprehension raised goose bumps on her arms and legs. Where was her daughter?

"Addy! Addy! What you playin' at?" Maybelle yelled from the window. "Come in here, *now!*"

Maybelle shifted back to the door. Maybe Addy had gotten up early and gone out to play with the dog. She walked out on the porch, calling, "Boo? Addy? Boo? This ain't funny. Where're you at?"

From the crawl space under the floor boards Maybelle heard a muffled whine. She darted down the steps; peered into shadow. All she could see were mournful eyes blinking in the dark.

"Addy, are you under there? Boo, get out here right now."

The dog thumped his tail and stayed put.

"Damn." She hustled into the house, found a flashlight, and ran back outside.

Bending, she panned the beam along the ground, quickly illuminating the entire recess. No sign of Addy. Exposed, Boo wriggled out, tail limp, groveling at Maybelle's feet.

She was panicky now. Frantically she dashed back inside to her baby's room, foolishly convinced that Addy would be there; had been there all along. Her heart was a jackhammer, thuddering in her chest. The room was as deserted as before.

Although the sheets were mussed her child's bed hadn't been slept in. The patchwork quilt which served as Addy's spread was folded back neatly, her pillow propped against the headboard. On her TV tray nightstand the china ballerina lamp was lit, more insect dust speckling the tray's surface. Maybelle absently switched off the lamp. Her dazed glance bounced over the shabby furnishings. On top of a wicker chest-of-drawers her baby's favorite pair of white dress-up socks with ruffled lace cuffs lay on a clean slip and panties; her Sunday shoes were lined up meekly in the corner. Maybelle started over to pick up the shoes when her foot struck something hard. On the worn throw rug two Mighty Morphin Power Rangers were locked in mortal combat beside a dented space craft.

Maybelle knelt, scooping up the toys as if their plastic bodies held the answer. For several minutes she remained on her knees, clutching the figures while staring blankly at Addy's bed. What had happened to her child? Eventually she sighed, shaking off her temporary paralysis, and rose, automatically smoothing Addy's rumpled bed clothes. That was when she noticed one corner of the sheet, tightly knotted to ward off the devil. And then, with startling clarity, Maybelle remembered the banshee cry of the screech owl and understood. Some thief, some wicked demon had come in the night and spirited Addy away.

"Jesus, God. Jesus, God," she prayed over and over, rapidly dialing 911. "Please let my baby be okay."

*   *   *

"Shit, you stupid bastard! This is a little kid we're talking about, not some lard-assed deputy."

The explosive force of the epithet struck McKensie like a blow. Boyd must *really* be pissed. Naturally reticent, the Commander spoke only when necessary. McKensie had never heard him engage in small talk, either with his men or anyone else. And he was very, very rarely profane.

"What a cockup! Do you realize you've compromised the whole mission? Did she see you tap into the phone line? You say not. So what *could* the child have seen? Some funny gizmo shining out the roof? That's nothing. And if she told somebody later about the van? It's a public access area. What was there to tell?"

McKensie started to interrupt but Boyd wasn't having any of it, holding up one finger in admonition. "Don't. Don't say another word. Not one. I'll decide what to do about you."

Seething, the pain behind his eyes murderous, McKensie grimaced but kept his mouth shut. To say anything in his defense at this point would be suicidal. In operational matters Boyd had absolute authority. If McKensie wanted a reprieve he would have to take his protest to Daniel.

He ground his teeth and headed up the stairs to rack out. Not his finest hour. The migraine he'd had since he climbed back into the van had seized him by the scruff of the neck and was squeezing so hard his vision was splitting. McKensie grabbed a hand towel and wrapped it around his forehead, twisting as tight as he could to relieve the pressure. They had discussed all types of incursions and appropriate countermeasures, but nobody had speculated on a kid and a dog. It wasn't fair Boyd blamed him.

Besides, McKensie didn't think for one instant that some redneck cocksucker passing for local law in this God-forsaken backwater could ever connect the disappearance of a pickaninny with a plan to wipe out half the state. Where did Boyd come off laying it all on him? Without him there wouldn't *be* any plan. Hell, Commander Richard fuckin' Boyd wasn't even a true believer. McKensie couldn't figure out what they needed the sour old fart for anyway. Half the time he didn't go to the Tabernacle, and when he did go, the burr head just sat there like a dried up cow patty.

* * *

Seen from a distance the white building perched on a towering bluff overlooking the Buffalo River was striking, even awe inspiring. A motorist catching a first glimpse of the edifice might think it a mirage, a Greek temple transported through the ether to materialize on the rocky palisade. But the huge pile of bricks and columns was no atmospheric illusion. It was, instead, a modern Parthenon, the home of Brother Daniel and his Tabernacle of Divine Redemption.

In actuality, the building was a fine example of Greek Revival architecture, colonnaded on three sides in the Doric order, gabled, with a vaulted roof and denticulate pediments. Above the entry portico a mural of *Jesus Ascending into Heaven* marred the classic design, one of the architect's losing battles with an intransigent client, but on the whole, good taste prevailed.

Unlike its impressive exterior, the interior of the Tabernacle was Spartan simplicity. Polished oak pews rested on islands of burnished plank flooring, separated by rivers of azure carpet. The sanctuary held no windows of any kind. Neither paintings nor decorations defaced pristine, white-washed walls. With the lone exception of a ten foot tall, back-lit wooden cross mounted behind the chancel, there were no visible distractions whatsoever to deflect attention from the evangelist and his message.

Centered by itself on a raised platform beneath the cross, a gleaming walnut table served as both altar and pulpit. Carved in its apron gilded majuscules proclaimed:

I AM THE WAY, THE TRUTH, AND THE LIFE

A fair linen cloth was draped lengthwise over the table, sur-mounted by fat beeswax candles guttering in brass holders, the air redolent of their cloying perfume. Between the candles a brass lectern held the Bible. Suspended from arched beams, Gothic-style lanterns cast a dim glow over all.

On the last Sunday in June the church was packed. In the windowless, twilight world of Brother Daniel's religious theater, the closing strains of *Onward Christian Soldiers* dissolved to amen. The warm up was over.

An expectant hush fell over the assembly. A minute passed. Then another. Hymnals rustled, feet scraped, buttocks squirmed, sporadic coughing broke out. Finally the house lights faded and all nervous movement ceased, the congregation holding its collective breath. From behind a concealed door Daniel stepped into the vacuum, a commanding figure robed totally in white, illuminated by a moving spot. He strode to the lectern in incandescent glory, his flowing garment sweeping the floor.

"Daniel! Daniel! Daniel!" The crowd chanted enthusiastic approval.

Hate had brought Brother Daniel a long way.

*   *   *

Thaddeus Daniel Selestak was born in Philadelphia, Pennsylvania, in 1946, with three strikes against him. The tenth child of dirt poor Polish immigrants, he arrived two months premature, the direct result of an unsuccessful abortion. Found by some of her older children collapsed in a sea of blood, Daniel's mother was rushed to the hospital. Doctors took one look at the pallid, comatose woman and performed an emergency Cesarean section,

16

delivering a viable, two pound, thirteen ounce boy. Mrs. Selestak died moments after the baby was rescued from her womb. The tiny infant's cleft palate was a maternal legacy from an earlier botched abortion attempt. And Daniel's father, whose religious beliefs were equal parts superstition and rigid Catholicism, rejected the child outright, denouncing its malformation as a curse from God.

Daniel would grow up as a ward of the church.

*   *   *

A comprehensive search for Addy Willis began on Sunday afternoon and lasted fifty-two hours. By the time choir members left that morning's service at the Trumpet in Zion, Maybelle had managed to convince Yell County Sheriff Paul Pressler that her little girl had truly disappeared. A call went out for volunteers. By two o'clock more than one hundred searchers had convened under the oak in Maybelle's front yard.

They came from the sheriff's department, from the church, from the poultry processing plant where Maybelle worked. A dog handler arrived from the state police with his pack of bloodhounds, and a Little Rock television station's helicopter provided aerial coverage. Weyerhaeuser sent foresters to cruise the cut-over stubble leading into Maybelle's place, and the county judge, mindful of his next bid for reelection, authorized a fresh load of gravel from the maintenance depot and a dozer operator to grade the rough road.

One searcher was bitten by a timber rattler when he climbed over a fallen tree without first looking on the other side. Another slipped on some pine straw and broke her ankle. With so many people poring over the coarse terrain, assorted cuts, sprains, and bruises were to be expected, but none of the injuries was life threatening, although the snake-bite victim had to be hospitalized for two days.

Women from the church prepared meals for those involved in the hunt, putting on a bountiful buffet under the spreading oak. Even the frequently off-key Arniece Ames showed up in her nearly new Cadillac to contribute a fresh coconut cake. Maybelle couldn't eat a bite.

For all their efforts, no one could find a trace of the missing girl.

The cops hauled Earl in—worked him over pretty good. Sheriff Pressler had never been known to stand on ceremony when he wanted information. Bruised and puffy eyed after the grilling, Earl still proved a credible innocent. They let him go. He immediately rejoined the search.

In the absence of any indication of foul play, it was widely assumed that Addy had fallen into the lake and drowned, despite her mother's assurances to anyone who would listen, that Addy would *never, ever,* go near the water by herself. Especially not in the middle of the night. Maybelle's protests went largely ignored. There simply wasn't any other possible explanation.

At sundown Tuesday active participation was called off, although the Sheriff's office set up a local Hot Line, in case they might have missed something. The toll free Watts number was broadcast regularly over radio stations in the area, and carried nightly on the six and ten o'clock newscasts in both Little Rock and Fort Smith. Attempts to drag adjacent areas of the reservoir would have to wait until the flood waters went down. Rescue squads had combed the shoreline for miles in either direction with no results. In a few days Addy's body would surface—if it was going to. Sometimes they never came up.

On the Sunday following Addy's disappearance, Maybelle asked Earl to take her to church. Her only child had been gone for one solid week. During that week Maybelle had not left her house, persuaded, no matter how irrationally, that if she left, she would miss a call from her daughter. The call never came.

Maybelle had prayed hard. Throughout the long, desperate hours of the past seven days she had begged, implored the Almighty to return Addy. She had attempted to bargain with Him, promising anything, if only He would hear. Now, all she asked for was an answer.

Dry-eyed, Maybelle thanked the minister and congregation for their help. She was finished with church. Returning to her empty home, curiously forlorn under the mighty oak, Maybelle began packing up Addy's things. She knew she would never see her child alive again.

*   *   *

Daniel was positively livid, his face mottled with fury as he stormed down the ramp to his subterranean fortress. When he passed through the deactivated entry level air lock, the men sitting at consoles in the main ops chamber bent to their terminals with renewed vigor. No one wanted to call attention to himself by inadvertantly catching the evangelist's eye. Experience had taught it unwise when their leader was angry.

On the far side of the room a spiral staircase descended to a lower floor. Daniel clattered down the metal steps, halting before another air-tight door, this one engaged. He withdrew a laminated card-key from his pocket; rammed it into the electronic scanner. Above the door a blinking red bulb changed to green. Daniel thrust the card back in his pocket, grabbed the safety wheel, and wrenched. The seal broke with a sibilant *hiss*, and the slab swung outward.

Daniel had to talk to Laura. Boyd's terse assessment of the damage had sent him into orbit, and Laura was the only one who could calm him down. With the President due in less than two weeks they had been so close. He ground his teeth in frustration. All their careful preparation. And because it was McKensie's fuck up, Daniel was hamstrung, enraging him further.

He stepped through the lock, pulling the thick door closed behind him. When it was seated he spun the hydraulic control, once more securing her sanctum. Laura would know what to do.

*   *   *

In his entire life the cult leader had only loved two people. Laura was the second. His first love had been Sister Mary Magdalene, who had come to his defense at the orphanage.

Sister Mary had begun her vocation as a novice at St. Agnes when Daniel was four. An instant rapport fused the foundling and the fledgling nun. She did her best to draw out the shy, painfully self-conscious little boy; he responded to her kindness with a child's unconditional devotion.

Although his deformity had been surgically repaired, the scar marring his upper lip and attendant lisp had made Daniel the butt of vicious teasing at the hands of other orphans at St. Agnes. In the cruel way of children they were blunt in their torment, calling him hare-lip, reject, retard. They mocked his speech impediment, mimicking his lisped words, or, alternately, ignored him altogether, their pointed silence worse than their jeers. In short, they made his young life miserable. Sister Mary did what she could to deflect the abuse. It was only natural for Daniel to turn to the one sympathetic face in that hostile environment.

Funded entirely by charity, St. Agnes operated just above the poverty level, a no-nonsense institution dedicated to turning its charges into productive citizens. Hard work, stern discipline, and prayer were the rule. Not that the Sisters of Enduring Mercy were uncaring. It was more a matter of priorities. They were involved in a constant battle just to provide life's basic necessities. After spending his first three months in the sterile isolation of his incubator, Daniel was right at home in the chill stone halls of St. Agnes.

Aware that Daniel's scars were not all physical, Sister Mary made an extra effort to praise the child. She encouraged him to study, to use his mind to overcome his handicap. Under her tutelage his grades improved, as did his speech. Eventually he began bringing "A" papers for her inspection. The other children gradually left him alone, finding new, more vulnerable targets for their derision.

When Daniel turned eleven his world collapsed.

Sister Mary had joined a teaching order so she could become a missionary. St. Agnes was her proving ground. Each year she applied for a foreign posting. Each year the diocese turned her down. After seven years of apprenticeship her application was finally approved.

Losing her was too much for Daniel to bear. His mother had died, abandoning him at birth; his father flatly repudiated him. Now his only friend was deserting him as well. What was wrong with him? Why did God hate Daniel Selestak so much?

She stayed until the end of the school year. Through a peep hole behind the studded, iron-barred door of the orphanage Daniel watched a taxi carry Sister Mary Magdalene away. After hugging and kissing the children who had crowded around her, and loading her luggage into the cab, she had stared back at the entry, giving him time, hoping he would come, hoping he had forgiven her. He had not and would not. To save face he had feigned indifference at her leaving. The cold truth was that he could not trust himself to say good-bye, horribly afraid he would break down and weep, thereby earning himself renewed scorn.

Wretched, disconsolate, Daniel hid and watched her go, snuffling into his shirt sleeve as his hopes vanished with the nun's meager belongings. That was the beginning. In the void left by her departure, in the rank, sour soil of his broken heart, the healing kernel of hate began to swell.

Laura would never leave him. Reclining in luxurious, tucked and tufted satin splendor, in the finest, French-polished mahogany coffin money could buy, Laura wasn't going anywhere.

CHAPTER 3

McKensie didn't know why he bothered she was such an easy fuck. He would have preferred a little resistance. Hell, he would have preferred a lot of resistance. McKensie got his rocks off on pain—inflicting, not receiving. He wasn't one of those masochistic perverts who liked to crawl around on all fours while some bimbo dressed up like a Hell's Angel's wet dream beat his bare butt with a buggy whip. All that black leather shit was for the birds. McKensie could teach those phonies a thing or two about Pain.

As penance for his handling of the snot-nosed brat at the reservoir McKensie had been confined to the bunker for a week. Although his punishment was galling, it hadn't been time totally wasted: he had tweaked the system, installed a couple of refinements in an ancillary program, smoothed out a problem in the software. He was still Daniel's fair-haired electronic wizard, even if he had made Boyd's top ten shit list.

He glanced over at the dumb cunt sitting on the sofa. The things he'd like to do to her. But Daniel had categorically forbidden anything that might call attention to the faithful. Groups similar to theirs had come under increased scrutiny lately. And right now, with their mission hanging in the balance, he couldn't afford to give Daniel cause.

McKensie hadn't minded being bounced out of the army. Those stupid fuckers had their heads rammed so far up their asses they had balls for brains. The Tabernacle was different. He felt more at home there than any place he'd ever been, and he had been around plenty. Best of all, Daniel let him buy any new toy that came on the market so his set-up would remain cutting edge. No outmoded components for him. Jesus, he loved his computer. He could get in *anywhere*. McKensie was no ordinary hacker, in any sense of the word. The pun amused him, and he laughed out loud. The girl raised one eyebrow, questioning his sudden change of mood. Let her wonder. It was fortunate he was so good at his job. If he weren't, that asshole Boyd would've x'd him long ago. If his halo was a trifle tarnished at the moment it wasn't his fault.

Wendy was buttoning her blouse. She didn't have big tits, more like a couple of fried eggs, but her nipples were huge and erect, thrusting against the flimsy fabric of the cheap blouse. A picture of his knife danced in his mind, long and slim, and very, very sharp. It flicked out like lightening, kissing her left boob, circling the rosy areola. In its wake a faint line of red appeared, tiny beads of blood welling from the cut. He watched in fascination as the beads swelled, formed ruby rivulets, trickling down the undulating curve of her rib cage.

His eyes followed the liquid crimson squiggles snake lower and divide, skirting the exclamation point of her naval. The tracks flared wider, coursing over the gentle mound of her belly to reunite, submerge in her dark, curly snatch.

God. He grunted, feeling himself get hard again. Stretched out a hand to the girl. She brushed him away.

The knife was just out of reach, hovering above her short, dark hair. His penis chafed against the denim of his jeans, worn tight, slung low on his hips, with nothing underneath. Jesus, his dick needed to get out.

"Come on, Wendy. You know what you do for me. Come on baby, just one more time. Here. Put your hand over here. Look what you caused."

He hated himself. She was such a stupid twat. If he could just use his knife its blade would do the talking, and it sure as hell wouldn't be begging like some puling mama's boy.

"Ooh my, baby. You got magic fingers. Come on over here. Ooh, that's good. Come on, come on now. Gimme a little head."

His swollen penis rested in her hand. She bent down, licking it slowly, savoring the taut flesh. Caressing its tip with her cunning tongue, running it around the smooth head, up and over, licking an ice cream cone to catch the drips.

He arched his back, thrusting, wanting, craving the release of her mouth. Come on, hurry up, hurry up . . . eat me, eat me now you fucking whore.

But Wendy continued the torment, drawing it out. Teasing his prick with tiny bites, nipping him with her teeth, squeezing, massaging, coaxing him to come. Stroking the length of him with the soft pads of her fingers, then raking her nails s-l-o-w-l-y up the insides of his thighs, making his scrotum crawl. Starting all over.

The stiletto hung in space, quivering silver in the velvet dark. Oh God, if only he could cut her, cut her now, she was, sweet Jesus, he was in her mouth now and she was sucking, sucking, and he couldn't hold on, couldn't . . . with his fists balled and his mind focused on the gleaming knife he came in that warm, moist vacuum, spasms wracking his muscular frame as his seed spurted into her greedy mouth.

The knife began to fade as he drew his spent penis from the girl's grasp. She took a Kleenex from her purse and dabbed her lips, smiling at him like the cat that got the cream. McKensie wanted to kill her she was such a smug bitch. He'd show her who was boss—just as soon as they finished the mission. He didn't give a good goddamn what Daniel and that hot shit bastard Boyd had to say, he was going to flat nail this tramp.

Just because she was Heavy and Vonnie Lee's little sister didn't make her immune. That whole fucking family was dumber than a brick. In Boone county there was a standing joke, "How do you spell dumb?" And the punch line was B-O-L-I-N.

Driving back to town Wendy leaned against the passenger door, as far from him as the seat would permit. McKensie was furious. He needed to regain the upper hand, to impress her, to *make* her respect him. So he told her about the kid. And then, without quite meaning to, he found himself telling her how Boyd had blamed him unfairly, and about his dressing down, and his humiliating punishment.

Wendy wasn't privy to operational matters—she was your basic drone, slaving away to make money for the church and servicing the faithful in her spare time. McKensie knew she was safe. But having bottled up his frustration for an entire week of incarceration, he had an urgent need to tell *someone,* even if his confessor was a mindless slut he despised.

She didn't offer much in his defense. In fact, she seemed to hug the door tighter, visibly shrinking from his confidences. He vowed not to take her out again—knowing that he would, even as he resolved not to. That was all right. Wendy's day would come, and he could make *that* last.

*   *   *

They were in their eighties, Norman and Rhea. He had sold insurance to the military. She had studied for the stage, a black haired Texas beauty with flashing eyes and a temper to match. In their prime they were "A" list Washington, with a cruiser berthed on the Potomac and a stately brick home in Georgetown.

Retirement had settled easily on the old couple. Childless, they had sequestered themselves in Arkansas, where she had relatives. Rhea's health had declined in recent years, and while she still attended Trinity Episcopal Cathedral, and enjoyed dining with friends at the Little Rock Country Club, her main diversion was monitoring the comings and goings of her neighbors from the balcony of their three story condominium on the banks of the Arkansas River near downtown Little Rock. She was quite content with her life, lolling on a chaise longue behind a pink mandevilla that framed her own private window on the world.

On the Fourth of July the levee was buzzing with activity. Rhea studied the scene with interest, happy to leave the party preparations to others.

25

Every year their property association sponsored a gigantic barbecue in observance of the holiday. Invitations to the event were highly coveted, partly because it was always a swell affair, and partly because the condominiums afforded a front row seat for the municipal fireworks display that crowned the Arkansas Pops concert in Riverfront Park. This year the extravaganza was supposed to be extra special, with the President in town for the Clinton Library groundbreaking. The development's extensive grounds would soon host upwards of five hundred people.

At nine o'clock it was already hot, eighty-two and climbing. By mid-afternoon the thermometer would be pushing one hundred. Although the river had dropped, it remained much higher than normal. The rounded tops of wooden stabilization pilings barely protruded above the water, stitching the river to its bank in an irregular seam, as puckered and twisting as an old scar. Bright cotton candy clouds dotted the sky, threatening to clump together in an afternoon thundershower. Rhea fervently hoped it wouldn't rain. Entertaining such a large number of people at an outdoor fete was courting disaster.

She rose with some difficulty and moved to the iron railing. "Norman, try not to overdo. You're sweating like a stuck pig."

Her husband looked up and mopped his brow. Norman and Marcel, their pleasant, middle-aged handyman, were setting up rental tables and chairs around a koi-filled fish pond. The Rhodes had invited more guests than their patio furniture would accommodate, and while youngsters could plop down anywhere on the zoysia lawn, their vintage required proper seating to support the various indignities of age.

"We've only got two more tables," he answered. "Marcel can handle the chairs by himself and I'll come in and clean up."

Satisfied that things were under control, Rhea returned to the chaise. Outside their gate children and grandchildren darted about helping. When the adults had stomached all the help they could stand, the kids were paid up and packed off until dusk, when the festivities were scheduled to begin.

Rhea watched a detail of Bailey grandchildren advancing on the viewing platform, really a glorified deck, constructed at the end of a pier jutting fifty feet into the river. A willowy belle with waist length hair led the parade, trailed by three stair-step copies, all clutching bunches of red, white, and blue balloons. Bringing up the rear was a stockier, male version of the family's gene pool, carrying a large American flag.

The quartet turned onto a brick sidewalk which coursed between a pair of ancient cottonwoods guarding either side of the footbridge. Normally twelve to fifteen feet above mean water line, that morning the platform's weathered gray timbers rode just above the wave tops. Five days earlier, when the river had crested, the whole deck and part of the path leading to it had been underwater. During the height of the flooding a log had become wedged between the bank and the pier's underpinnings, forming a triangular-shaped enclosure clogged with debris.

Toby, the flag bearer, gazed with interest at the scum. He'd much rather gross out his sisters with some repulsive, dead thing than tie balloons on the corners of the dock. When he had guided the flag into a bracket fastened to the center railing he sauntered back across the footbridge. Ignoring the warnings of his older siblings he found a stick and began poking at the trash.

His initial probe was fruitless. All he turned up amid the broken limbs and organic rubbish were three plastic milk jugs, a Miller Lite can, a tennis ball, some nylon fishing line, one purple plastic flip-flop, and the crumbling lid of a Styrofoam ice chest. Rats! He flipped the Styrofoam out of the way, scraping a small opening in the glop. A whitish-green, squishy thing popped to the surface in the hole he had cleared. Hot dog! He'd get those girls now.

Toby dropped the stick and crawled out on the log. He could just reach the dead fish if he didn't lose his balance. If he fell in, he'd never hear the end of it. He got a firm grip on a protruding knot and leaned out precariously, bare inches above the water. Cupping his free hand into a scoop, he swiped at the fish. Yuck!

It sort of disintegrated in his fingers. He was going to have to get closer.

He eyed the prize longingly; decided it was worth it. Screwing up his courage, Toby eased out farther, lowering himself until his chubby body was stretched full length along the log. He ventured a quick peek to see if his sisters were watching. Only Alice, the youngest, was staring wide-eyed at her brother's exploit, thumb tucked securely in her mouth. Toby shook his head, cautioning the child to remain quiet. Then, holding his breath, he reached out as far as he could and grabbed.

Only, only, it wasn't a fish . . . it was . . . it was . . . oh help!!! Oh Mama! Oh *NOOOOO*!!!

⁕　⁕　⁕

Tendrils of smoke curled upward from a basin bristling with joss sticks, weaving their way through the glass-beaded curtain onto the sidewalk where Daniel was taking a break.

Following a bumpy ride over the Rockies, Daniel had arrived at Los Angeles International Airport both relieved and exhilarated after his first flight. He reclaimed his luggage and joined the shuttle queue for downtown. With no preconceived destination, other than that he wanted to see Hollywood, he threw his duffel into the bus's hold and climbed on board.

Forty-five minutes later, after washing up in the central station's men's room, Daniel stuffed his bag in a coin locker and hit the streets. He was twenty years old, had money in his pocket, and was setting off on a pilgrimage of discovery. Three hours of wandering brought him to Sunset Boulevard. Instead of being enervated by the rough flight and long perambulation through the bowels of Los Angeles, he could barely contain his excitement. The steaming miasma of sharks and swimmers was like nothing he had ever imagined.

Neon signs painted the night: GIRLS! GIRLS! GIRLS!, FIRST RUN XXX MOVIES!, TOPLESS A GO-GO!, MADAME WOO'S ORIENTAL MASSAGE PARLOR! Interspersed with the topless joints, head shops like the one he was standing outside catered to a different vice. They were all present, the seven deadly sins and then some, all residents of Hollywood's tenderloin, the exposed underbelly of southern California's sixties' counterculture.

A tide of vacant faces surged up and down the Strip, looking for one more trick, one more hit, one more score. Human flotsam borne on an ocean of desire: prey and predator, pimp and prostitute, Moonie and flower child. Grifters, drifters, drop-outs and hangers-on; has-beens and wanna-bes. Pushers and pot heads chasing psychedelic dreams in Day-Glo minivans. The dregs of society feeding on the weaknesses of man. And if there were those who mistook the slim, hare-lipped young man decked in soldier's khaki for an easy mark, one look into his smoldering eyes sent them scurrying away.

Daniel left his post to resume trolling. A graphic window display touting the wares of a corner sex emporium caught his attention. Dildos of every size and shape vied for attention with sadomasochistic paraphernalia. A variety of the "latest European" breast enhancers crowded shelves lined with nostrums. He gaped in disbelief at the centerpiece of the exhibit, an extremely realistic mannequin clad only in a luxuriant merkin—custom made, three days' delivery. He did not know such things existed—or why.

She was standing in front of a Thai restaurant, handing out leaflets from a brown paper bag. For an instant Daniel thought fate had played a cruel cosmic prank; that Sister Mary Magdalene had materialized from whatever heathen nation she had been proselytizing to halt his pell mell fall from grace. He quickly realized that was impossible. The slight blonde woman bore only a passing resemblance to Sister Mary. What she shared with the nun was an aura, a glow that spoke directly to him. Daniel was thunderstruck, the *coup de foudre* of myth. The radiant woman distributing handbills thirty feet away was the embodiment of all his desires.

*   *   *

Greetings. Daniel's ticket out of St. Agnes arrived in the spring of 1965, two months before his high school commencement. He had duly registered for the draft on his eighteenth birthday, but his summons had been delayed, allowing him to graduate. Now Uncle Sam wanted *him*. If he were lucky, he'd get posted to Europe. He was cognizant of the fighting in Southeast Asia, although he had no reason to suspect, in the summer of 1965, that he'd automatically be sent to Vietnam. That escalating conflict on the other side of the world was far away, and not well understood.

Any hope of a deferment on medical grounds was dispelled when Daniel presented himself for his physical. The attending physician passed him without comment, taking no notice of the thin scar distorting his upper lip. Apparently, if he could breathe, he was in. Thirty days later he was aboard an Army-chartered Greyhound ferrying Daniel and forty-nine other inductees to Ft. Leonard Wood, Missouri, for basic training. He would never look back.

Thanksgiving coincided with the end of boot camp and found Daniel posted to Ft. Benjamin Harrison, situated outside Indianapolis, for an eight week MOS assignment in Communications. By the time he completed the advanced training course, qualifying as a company clerk, he was intimately more knowledgeable about America's presence in the Far East. New Year's Day, 1966, saw some 184,000 U.S. servicemen stationed in Vietnam. Camp scuttlebutt had that figure doubling in the next twelve months.

Orders to report to Camp Stoneman, at McClellan Air Force Base in Sacramento, confirmed his destination. Camp Stoneman was the army's main staging area for flights to Tan Son Nhut, the principal airport outside Saigon and gateway to Bien Hoa, at that time the major redeployment depot in South Vietnam. Europe was out.

Private Selestak had eighteen days of accumulated leave. He had an airplane ticket to Sacramento, courtesy of the Military

Transport Office. He also had the balance of his pay, a whopping $132.00 a month, which he had saved since first being drafted. Aside from an occasional beer at the PX, he had found no need to spend his government scrip.

Studying a large map mounted on the adjutant's wall, Daniel decided he'd like to see more of the country that was sending him to war. He was curious about Dallas, smarting from prolonged notoriety in the wake of President Kennedy's assassination. On the base bulletin board he found a ride-share notice that would get him to Texas. Then he wangled an exchange on his airline ticket, so that he could fly from Dallas to Los Angeles. Daniel planned to spend several days in each city, then hitch-hike to San Francisco for a taste of the Bay area before reporting to McClellan on March first.

He was disappointed in Dallas. Having grown up in a city of monuments, at the site of such a cataclysmic event in American history Daniel had expected something more dramatic than a nondescript building overlooking an ordinary intersection.

From Dealey Plaza he roamed the streets of metropolitan Big D, checked out the lobbies of the Baker and Adolphus hotels, toured fabled Neiman-Marcus, noted the discreet plaque marking the entrance to the Petroleum Club. He observed the languid cadences of speech, the unhurried grace of movement that characterized Texas utopia. In twenty-four hours he was bored and ready to move on.

☆　　☆　　☆

The soldier stayed out of sight, keeping a covert eye on the blond woman until she had emptied her sack. She lingered in place a while longer, glancing across the wide thoroughfare and speaking occasionally to passersby. Then she abruptly quit her post and hurried toward him. He withdrew into the shadows. The woman swept past, intent on someone or something Daniel couldn't discern. At the corner she darted across the street just as the lights changed. He followed her progress back along the opposite walk until she reached a bearded man also carrying a paper bag. They embraced, strolling off together.

When the woman and her friend? lover? husband? partner? had moved beyond his field of vision, Daniel hailed a cab for the return trip to the bus terminal. He was ravenous, settling on a stool at the snack counter and ordering a #4 breakfast. When he had sopped up the last bit of egg yolk with the last scrap of pancake, he retrieved his bag from the locker and canvassed the immediate vicinity for a cheap hotel, falling in bed in his underwear. He slept for ten hours, oblivious to the daytime world outside his door. At dusk he showered, dressed, and headed for Mecca.

Daniel stationed himself outside the Thai restaurant, an ever changing sea of faces swirling around him as he waited. Where was the woman? Would she reappear? She *had* to come. He had never wanted to believe anything more.

At length she did come, weaving through the crowd to 'her' spot on the sidewalk. Elated, Daniel ducked into the eatery to continue his vigil. He might as well have been dining on cardboard as the spicy Thai curry he ordered.

On some level Daniel understood that his preoccupation with the woman was dangerous. It made him as vulnerable as other consumers of the Strip's tawdry wares. He chose to ignore the risk.

There was a lull in the pedestrian flow when Daniel exited the restaurant, isolating the woman in a pool of ambient light. She turned at his approach, extending a leaflet. Daniel couldn't speak, couldn't look at her. Mouth dry, face hot, hands sticky with sweat, he accepted her offering without a word, certain his deformity would repel her. Eyes downcast, he could sense her turning away, sense the rejection.

Then suddenly he convulsed in amazed laughter, freezing the woman mid-turn. She stared at the soldier uncertainly, her smile slipping in Daniel's high-voltage gaze. Fate had proved to be a practical joker after all. When Daniel glanced at the tract clutched in his damp fingers, anticipating some esoteric come-on, some ad for carnal services, it was printed with Bible verses.

"Is everything all right?" she asked, in the flat, nasal drawl he had come to associate with the Ozark hills of boot camp.

"Everything's fine. Thank you very much. And thanks for the pamphlet. I'll be sure to read it."

She relaxed a little, the lost smile creeping back over her countenance. "Jesus loves you, you know, so see that you do. Look, do you mind telling me what was so funny? Since I've been working the Strip I've gotten all kinds of responses, but you're the first person who's laughed."

He laughed again. "It's a long story."

"Then tell me. I'm a good listener."

Daniel shook his head. "I don't think so."

"I'd really like to know," she persisted.

They were being jostled by the crowd. "Some other time. We're blocking the sidewalk."

"Come on. Please."

He capitulated, unable to refuse. What did Daniel care if she were Lucifer's messenger or God's? "How about I buy you a drink?"

"Make that a cup of coffee and you've got a deal."

He held her chair. She repaid his courtesy by extending her hand, empty this time, her sack of religious propaganda deposited under the table.

"Let's start over," she said. "My name is Laura."

CHAPTER 4

Mickey Harmon stood up to his elbows in foetid water. It sloshed over the bib of his waders, soaking his green polo shirt and trickling inside his Dockers. Mickey was the Pulaski County Coroner, and he was recovering the body that Toby Bailey had uncovered earlier that morning. In atypical casting, Mickey was also a hunk, drop dead, movie-star handsome. With his aquiline profile, wicked green eyes, and disarming grin, his looks were some compensation to his wife for the irregular hours his profession demanded. Unfortunately, that attribute was woefully wasted on the mortal remains which were his stock in trade.

Blue crepe paper streamers fluttered in the hot breeze; bouquets of balloons tugged at the corners of the platform at his back. A gaggle of voyeurs had collected on the paved walkway, careful not to come too close—morbid curiosity tempered by queasy apprehension. News of the grisly discovery had sped like quicksilver through the complex, drawing a crowd and halting the party preparations. There was nothing like the intimation of mortality to dampen a festive mood.

Mickey maneuvered the corpse within range of Arvil, his assistant, waiting on the bank with a collapsible stretcher. From a discrete distance one solitary Little Rock cop kept an eye on the proceedings, gratefully sipping a Coke with Rhea and Norman Rhodes. Closer to the action, two sheriff's deputies lounged near the brick stairway in a patch of shade. Hard driving punk rock blared across the turgid water from a boom box on the North Little Rock shore, lending a surreal quality to the proceedings, as though they were all actors in a gritty television drama. Farther down the levee a hyper dachshund barked non-stop, racing back and forth on a fenced patio. From time to time one of the specta-tors would detach herself from the group and yell at the dog to shut up. It didn't. For Mickey Harmon it was a standard, run-of-the-mill Fourth.

The coroner had been home mowing his back yard when Arvil bleeped him. He slipped out of his cut-offs and into the khakis that constituted his uniform before hurrying to meet the assistant investigator stuck with duty on a holiday that death never took. As he was backing out of the driveway, Mickey en-countered his wife pulling in.

He rolled down the window. "Sorry, babe. When you gotta go, you gotta go."

Marcy was used to it. She unloaded three sacks of groceries, iced down a cooler of drinks, and made a big bowl of spinach/cream cheese dip for that night's party. Then she cranked up the Lawnboy to finish his chore

Arvil was waiting for him inside the walled compound. When Mickey turned his Acura off Riverfront Drive onto the private road bearing the development's name, the ornate wrought-iron gates were standing wide open. An LRPD blue-and-white, the white coroner's van, and a beige Chevy with sheriff's decals were parked at the bottom of a wide brick stairway scaling the levee between a double row of townhomes.

Rhea Rhodes had phoned 911 upon confirmation of Toby's gruesome find. When the Little Rock police arrived and deter-mined that the body was still in the water, they happily forfeited jurisdiction to the Pulaski County Sheriff's Department, whose Water Patrol was responsible for river rescues. It was a fine dis-tinction, since this particular body was a bare five feet from shore trapped in a log jam, and much easier to reach from the bank than by boat. In any event, the sheriff's dispatcher had called the Coroner's Office, reaching the investigator on duty. Arvil had paged his boss.

The body was a real mess. It had been in the water a week, minimum. After that it was difficult to calculate the duration of immersion without forensic testing.

While the coroner stripped off his waders, Arvil conducted a preliminary survey of the corpse. Given its size and weight it was almost certainly the body of a prepubescent child, probably female, although he couldn't be sure. The outer layer of skin had sloughed away, exposing the dermis, which was a mottled green. Since pigmentation occurs in the epidermis, without that covering he couldn't visually determine the cadaver's race. Most of the hair was gone, as were the toes, and several fingers. The left earlobe was missing as was the soft nasal tissue. A gaping wound on the right thigh was so deep that the femur was exposed through a rend in the quadriceps. The body's left clavicle appeared to be crushed; its left shoulder dislocated.

The child was naked, save for a circle of elastic cutting into its bloated mid-section, shreds of orange and white print fabric adhering to the band. Rigor had long since come and gone; the head drooped at a peculiar angle.

Mickey joined his assistant in inspecting the victim. He was anxious to finish the initial examination and deliver the quickly decomposing corpse to the morgue. In July's noontime heat the stench of rotting flesh was becoming unbearable. Those die-hard gawkers who remained had moved back to the top of the levee, upwind of the tableau.

Mickey tried to express the child's lungs, searching for telltale white froth that would indicate pulmonary edema, a natural consequence of drowning. None appeared. The absence of the foam was puzzling, but it wasn't necessarily significant. When a body had been in the water as long as this one, it would take a forensic pathologist to sort things out.

The perspiring men coaxed the child into a bright yellow body bag. When it was securely zipped, the two deputies sidled over, sheepishly inquiring if they could be of service. Little Rock's finest had already completed his report and taken off. The coroner didn't blame them. Next to crispy critters, floaters were often the hardest to take, even for professionals enured to death in all its grotesque forms. It was worse when the victim was a child.

In an unusual arrangement the Pulaski County Coroner's Office keeps a key to the State Crime Lab's morgue, which is normally locked on weekends and holidays. Because they are both located in Little Rock, this eliminates the need for a separate county morgue, since all autopsies are handled by the State Medical Examiner anyway.

They delivered the body to the back door of the laboratory, Mickey trailing the meat wagon in his car. When the yellow bag had been locked safely in the cooler, Mickey Harmon washed up and headed over the Broadway bridge to his house in Lakewood. Maybe he'd get the grill cleaned out without another interruption. For some reason, Marcy didn't like to do that.

Arvil was left to fill out the paper work. Back in the van he opened his laptop and began to type.

Name of Decedent: JANE DOE

Age: UNKNOWN

Date and Time of Death: UNKNOWN

Manner and Cause of Death: UNKNOWN

Disposition: PENDING INVESTIGATION

---

*   *   *

It was not until they sat sipping coffee in a sleazy diner off Sunset that Daniel noticed the thin gold band on Laura's left hand. How could he have missed that? Nor, in the brightly lit ambiance of the cafe, was she as young as she had appeared on the street. Night, and the filter of infatuation had erased tiny crow's feet and smoothed wrinkles that were now apparent. That didn't matter. Nothing mattered except that she was sharing a table with him, seemingly oblivious to his imperfection.

Daniel had no way of knowing that by the time he encountered Laura distributing flyers on the streets of Los Angeles, the metamorphosis that would transform Ruby Jean Gravis into Laura Van Horne was ninety-nine percent complete. Only the stubborn trace of Ozark soil clinging to her accent remained of the girl from Redfern, Arkansas, and she was working hard on that. Neither did he have any inkling that the self-possessed evangelist had just wed a third husband to go with the twelve year old daughter she had from her first marriage. He would find that out in due course. On their initial encounter, it was Daniel's turn to talk.

Prodded by her gentle questioning he let the hurt flow, venting a lifetime's pent up rage and frustration to the sympathetic stranger patting his arm in encouragement. As the hour latened and their coffees grew cold a waitress approached, but Laura shook her head and the woman left them alone.

Finally, a coin dropped in the jukebox shattered the spell. *Broken Hearted Melody* swelled from a gleaming Wurlitzer. Laura brightened. "That's one of Larry's numbers," she informed the smitten soldier. He nodded dumbly. Laura looked at her watch. "Look, Daniel, I'm really sorry, but I've *got* to finish handing out tonight's lesson." She clasped his hand. "Come help me."

That was the furthest thing from his mind. "I don't think so."

"Sure. You can do it. It's not hard," she squeezed his hand, "and I'd like the help."

"No. You go on if you need to. I'm not good at things like that." Then he added hopefully, "Maybe I'll see you tomorrow?"

"You're coming with me right now. It won't take any time with both of us doing God's work." Taking Daniel firmly by the arm she led him outside. He didn't resist. "Don't worry," she assured him. "It's easy."

Surprisingly, it was.

*　　*　　*

Arkansas county coroners exist in a symbiotic relationship with the State Medical Examiner. They supply the bodies—the M.E. performs the autopsies. Because the Medical Examiner's office is closed on weekends and holidays, and Death is seldom a respecter of these man-made distinctions, Monday mornings are frequently hectic at the morgue. Given a pool of seventy-five counties to draw from, coupled with the fact that Friday and Saturday nights are prime time for crime, the cooler is often full at the start of the work week.

Three pathologists share responsibility for post mortems on a revolving basis; the pathologist on duty completing his roster of autopsies if there aren't too many cases stacked up, requesting assistance from his colleagues if there are. Nonetheless, cadavers occasionally have to be held over a second day before they are cleared. That is what happened the first weekend in July.

Two bodies that came in late Monday from out in the state were left over until Tuesday, but Tuesday was the Fourth and the office was closed, so they had to be delayed until Wednesday. Meanwhile, a bloody holiday brought a fresh harvest of fatalities to the morgue. Addy had plenty of company.

When Dr. Peter Zoellner clocked in for work Wednesday morning he was in an ebullient mood, having just enjoyed something rare for man in his line of work: four consecutive days off. At his wife's insistence he had taken a personal day on Monday so that they could join other couples whose distaff spouses were members of the Order of the Eastern Star, on a weekend bus tour to Branson, Missouri, the polyester Las Vegas devouring Ozark hilltops like a giant PacMan. In three days they saw five shows and went to four outlet malls. At dusk on Monday their chartered scenic cruiser deposited a load of enthusiastic worthy matrons and worn-out husbands back in Little Rock.

On the Fourth Peter fertilized his tomato plants and played a round of golf. After a leisurely afternoon nap, the Zoellners cut across the twelfth fairway from their two story colonial to the Pleasant Valley Country Club, for P.V.'s annual holiday blowout. They came home in high spirits, which carried over into the bedroom.

Yes indeed, Dr. Zoellner was feeling fine when he looked over Wednesday's scheduled cases and started to scrub up. Peter Zoellner was Arkansas's Chief Medical Examiner. By day's end, his mild euphoria would be a thing of the past.

Autopsies are slated not on a first-come, first-serve basis, but by established protocol. Homicides take precedence, followed by jail deaths, then children. In descending order of importance are accidents, suicides, and suspicious "natural" causes.

Dr. Zoellner began with the carry-overs from Monday. After lunch he was ready to process Tuesday's crop of decedents. A revenge shooting by a spurned lover at a Ft. Smith trailer park had yielded two bodies from Sebastian County. At last it was Addy's turn.

She was weighed, measured, and wheeled to X-ray, where complete body exposures and dental films were taken. Then she was transferred to a stainless steel examining table for autopsy. When he was through, Peter Zoellner knew everything about Addy but her name.

Mickey Harmon had been right. The child hadn't drowned. Her death had resulted from a violent sideways wrenching of her neck. Fracturing C1 and C2 had caused severe compression of the spinal cord, resulting in instant paralysis, including paralysis of the diaphragm. She literally had stopped breathing the moment her neck snapped.

The Medical Examiner stared at the small corpse. This death was no accident. Someone who knew exactly what he was doing had killed her. Quickly and quietly. Professionally.

Wearily he pulled off his latex gloves.

"Martha," he turned to his assistant, "get me the sheriff."

*   *   *

Daniel's war was over in three months. He had drawn a lucky assignment, clerk for B Company, one of three communications companies of the 523rd Signal Battalion, expanding radio and telephone capability across South Vietnam for the U.S. build-up. In March, 1966, Chu Lai, on the South China Sea ninety miles south of Da Nang, was burgeoning, slated to become a division headquarters. In August, 1965, when it was still a remote outpost, three battalions of Marines had defeated Viet Cong troops in the first major engagement of the war between American and enemy forces. As the base expanded, the VC would lob a few rockets into camp just to keep the Americans on their toes. They would whistle in after dark, the first crump sending everyone diving for cover. Racing across the duck boards to his sandbagged defensive position, Daniel didn't dive fast enough.

"Daniel?"

Laura couldn't keep the shock out of her voice. Could the gaunt, bearded man on crutches be the same infatuated soldier who had poured out his inner anguish to her just four months before? For a week he had tagged along, her self-appointed protector while she ministered to the prodigals on the Strip. Each night when it was time to join Larry he had refused, excusing himself despite her invitation to accompany them home. Her eyes took in the scraggly hair, hard eyes; traveled down to the stump where his left leg had been.

"Daniel, is that you?"

To augment her street crusade Laura had been volunteering at the West Los Angeles Veterans' Hospital. As body bags came home and casualties mounted, the war in Vietnam was becoming increasingly unpopular. Laura didn't hold with angry protesters who felt if the conflict were bad, then those who fought it were equally to blame. Reviling wounded soldiers was not the Christian way. Rather than acrimony, the bitter men languishing in VA facilities needed a healthy dose of God's healing grace, which she could provide.

The man hobbled off without answer. Laura followed, put out a hand to stop him. "Daniel."

He turned. "What's left of me."

She came every day. When his prosthesis was fitted and the therapists had done all they could, she took him home. He had no where else to go.

CHAPTER 5

The home Laura took Daniel to was a sprawling ranch in the desert outside Los Angeles. Laura had big plans for the spread, envisioning a secure retreat where she could rehabilitate drug addicts, shelter runaways, and counsel drop-outs uprooted by society's anti-establishment revolution. In those early days of the Foundation, their *ménage à trois* was short lived. It became in rapid succession a *ménage à quatre, onze, cinquante,* until Laura's followers were counted by the hundreds, and their commune had grown to one of the largest in California. Laura's unique gifts lured the disaffected by the score, to the safe haven of the Foundation of Eternal Life. Her converts were cleaned up, fed, weaned off drugs or alcohol, and put to honest labor in the vineyards of the Lord. Daniel soon became a willing partner in the triumvirate that ran the Foundation of Eternal Life.

Laura saw herself as the emissary of a disappointed Father, sent to rescue His children from a corrupt, Godless society. Hers was an old time, Cotton Mather religion of hellfire and damnation. Redemption was possible through discipline and hard work; sins expiated by God's love and forgiveness, funneled through His handmaiden Laura. In the drug-drenched, sixties' heyday of free love and rebellion, sinners were crying out for discipline and authority. At the Foundation they would get it—in spades.

*   *   *

"Won't you come down? Won't you come down and be saved? Make your decision today for the Lord. Won't you let Him into your heart? Take that first step for Jesus. Come right

43

on down, folks. Jesus Christ is asking you to accept Him as your personal Lord and Savior. Come right on down and be saved."

Reverend Gentry was warmed up and going good. The spirit was flowing, energizing the jam-packed crowd. It was the third night of a week's tent revival, and judging the size of the collection from the stream of bodies pouring down the aisle, the good Reverend rubbed his hands. He was raking them in, and there were still four nights to go!

Sister Lily Josephine, a fine looking woman with a little meat on her bones, the way he liked them, was cranking out a moving rendition of *Jesus is Calling* while he delivered the invitation. He wondered if she'd have a late supper with him back at the motel. The Reverend Gentry could feel lust raising its ugly head. Damn that old devil.

A small commotion at the back of the tent drew his eyes away from the pianist's cleavage. A sweet young thing of thirteen or fourteen was engaged in an argument with a gray-haired harridan, who was trying to make the tender flower of youth take her seat.

"Sister," he called out. "Jesus said, 'Suffer the little children to come unto me.'"

The old bat wasn't going to give in without a fight. "You don't unnerstan', Rev'rend. She's already *bin* saved. Ain't no need for her to come pesterin' you with her foolishness."

In the plummy, sanctimonious tones cultivated by those in his trade, Cecil Gentry insisted, "It's no bother. I'm sure God would be interested in anything she has to say."

It was an uneven contest, stacked against the older woman. With all necks craned in her direction she gave up with a glower, releasing her hold on the girl's wrist.

Ruby Jean paraded down the aisle, head high, radiating determination. When she reached the altar she knelt in front of the Reverend Gentry.

"What is it, child?" He laid his hands on the sleek blond head. She really was a toothsome creature. "What burden lies in the fullness of your heart?"

"Will you help me, Rev'rend?" she asked, tilting her head back and looking him squarely in the eye.

He raised her up, fanning his private demons. "Tell me your troubles, child. Lay your heart bare. What is it that you want?"

The hillbilly virgin stood, facing the packed house, her budding bosom heaving provocatively. The good Reverend's bald pate was shiny with sweat. Whooo, damn! So close.

"I want," she said, "to be a preacher. Just like you."

The daughter of a jack-leg carpenter and a sharp-tongued housewife with a fondness for cheap whiskey, Ruby Jean had a hard row to hoe growing up. Work was scarce, and they moved around a lot, her father taking odd jobs to get by. Eventually the family came to roost in Redfern, a small town in north Arkansas, near the Missouri border. The eldest of five, Ruby Jean often found herself in charge of the brood, especially if her father was working out of town and her mother was sauced. Things weren't much better when her daddy was home, her parents' frequent screaming matches just as frightening as her mother's benders.

When Ruby Jean was twelve her dad was killed in a sawmill accident. With no income and no formal education, Sadie Gravis was going to have to find a way to make a living. She didn't need three younger rivals in the same house. Ruby and her two little sisters were packed off to their paternal grandmother. The boys were allowed to stay with Sadie.

MeMaw was a foot-washing Baptist. Every time the church doors swung open, she was waiting on the steps with her granddaughters in tow. Some of Mrs. Gravis's excess devotion must have rubbed off, accounting for Ruby Jean's announced choice of vocation. Not long after the embarrassing incident, however, Ruby's inchoate ambition was temporarily forgotten in a rush of hormones.

She married at seventeen, fresh out of high school, as much to alter her situation as from any deep affection for the pimply faced quarterback who groped her up in the balcony of the Joie theater during Saturday afternoon matinees. Pregnant shortly thereafter, she gave birth to her own daughter three months shy of her nineteenth birthday.

Laura never talked about the chain of events that brought her to southern California. Neither was she forthcoming about her second marriage to Ike Sippowitz, a minor hoodlum in the Jewish mafia. When Daniel pressed her, she would say only that her days as Ike's wife had provided a home in which to raise her daughter, and enough funds to begin rescuing God's wayward children off the streets.

* * *

The problem, of course, was Larry. A two bit hustler who had seen Laura as his main chance and latched on, he wasn't about to step aside for Daniel. Hiding behind his ever present dark glasses, he made business decisions for the Foundation, while Laura garnered converts. Daniel ran the office.

Bright, canny, Daniel could have left the Foundation at any time, but he couldn't bear to leave Laura. As long as he stuck around, there was always a chance he could supplant Larry in her affections. In fact, Laura often preferred Daniel's company to Larry's. They would stroll around the compound laughing and talking, furtive conspirators in search of minor mischief. At night, she always returned to her husband.

Larry's past was as checkered as his wife's. Born Solomon Lazarus Green to a respectable Jewish family from Missouri, Sol headed to California when he finished high school, enrolling in UCLA to secure his parents' blessing. Fancying himself a country music singer, when he hit the west coast Sol's name was the first thing to go. College classes followed soon thereafter. He picked up bad habits and bad friends, getting into a series of escalating scrapes with the law. Before he could make it to the entertainment big time he was arrested and sentenced to six months in a California jail. He was paroled after three.

Larry van Horne was the petty hood's second reincarnation. A few playing gigs came his way, rekindling his musical aspirations. At length he met Laura, who had been traveling in overlapping circles, and Larry was set.

Under Larry's stewardship the sect prospered, amassing a substantial portfolio of stocks, bonds, and real estate holdings. Although neither he nor Laura was an ordained minister, they registered for, and were granted, tax exempt status. Using a simple formula based on unpaid labor and no taxation, profits soared. Isolated from outside influences, cult members worked as virtual slaves, existing on subsistent rations. Fourteen to sixteen hour days were the norm, followed by prayer sessions often lasting all night. And no convert was ever left by himself. Privacy was the ultimate no-no: the devil could snatch a person who was alone.

The Hornites (as they styled themselves) were subjected to incessant ranting about enemies of the Foundation, whose number included any worried relative trying to persuade a daughter or son, niece, nephew, husband or wife, to leave the commune. They were told that if they left, they would be cast into perdition, cut off from God. Only through Laura could they be saved.

But it was Larry's greed, not Laura's brand of religion, that ultimately doomed the cult. As the van Hornes' fortunes rose, persistent questions about commune practices began to crop up. With the defection of deprogrammed twins, stories of food deprivation and forced labor surfaced—charges which brought the Foundation under investigation by some of the same California state agencies which had previously awarded it citations. In the increasingly hostile atmosphere of official scrutiny, Larry and Laura decided to repair to a more salubrious location. What better place than her home town?

Property was cheap and abundant in northern Arkansas. Larry began liquidating the Foundation's western assets and buying up parcels of land in the Ozark foothills. In 1971, leaving their California complex in the hands of lieutenants, Larry, Laura, Daniel, and a nucleus of two hundred Hornites moved to the cult's new Arkansas Jerusalem.

Sequestered on a hillside five miles from the nearest town, the van Hornes began construction of their little kingdom. When they were finished it contained their personal dwelling, swimming pool, office, cafeteria and print shop, a pig farm, workshop, dormitories, cabins for married couples, garages for their many cars and limousines, a worship center, and a marble mausoleum.

Larry invested wisely, purchasing local businesses and staffing them from Foundation ranks. Drawing on his sojourn in Hollywood, he established a dinner theater in Arkhola, booking top name performers from Memphis and Nashville to standing room only audiences. In addition to the thirty or so businesses they owned in Redfern, Larry built up a hugely successful market for his clothing designs—elaborately painted, rhinestone-studded denim jackets which commanded prices starting at a paltry five hundred dollars. These were sold at a Foundation-owned retail outlet in Nashville, and in boutiques in Saks Fifth Avenue, Neiman Marcus, and other upscale fashion emporia. Since the jackets were being fabricated by volunteer labor in Foundation workshops, Larry was coining money.

In another move to solidify his hold on the local economy, Larry sent a flood of Hornites into Redfern to register to vote, thereby assuring the election of his candidates for aldermen and mayor, and preferential consideration of Foundation-sponsored proposals.

The Hornites were paid a token weekly wage of $5.00. Larry begrudged them even this pittance. If the Foundation supplied all their earthly wants, why should they need money? From this five dollars, fines were deducted for violations of compound rules, and there were *beaucoup* rules. One hapless follower was fined a million dollars by an apoplectic Larry for inadvertently walking across his private lawn. Where the man was supposed to come up with the money is anybody's guess.

Unnecessary conversation between the sexes was frowned on, hanky panky strictly forbidden.

Sick cult members were prayed over before receiving medical treatment, on the outside chance that God might heal them first, saving the Foundation the expense of a physician's care. Mental cases were unceremoniously driven to town and dumped on the hospital doorstep.

Somewhere over the great divide between Redfern and Los Angeles, Laura had gotten rid of Ruby Jean. Somewhere on the return journey, she had lost Ruby Jean's humanity as well.

*　*　*

It had been a particularly grueling day. A Jeep full of Larry's stewards had been bombing around Redfern, collecting receipts from the Foundation's businesses when a trio of local lovelies in short shorts had come parading down Main Street. The sight of so much thigh must have offended the stewards' delicate sensibilities, because they jumped en masse from the Jeep, stripping heavy belts from their trousers, and proceeded to whale the living shit out of the three teenyboppers, calling them sluts, harlots, and worse. Now Daniel was trying to diffuse a situation where he found himself in complete agreement with a very angry sheriff.

Larry slammed down the phone. "Daniel, get the hell down to the front gate! We got a problem."

"You wanna tell me what it is, or keep me in suspense?"

"How do I know what it is? Chester says the sheriff's down there with a warrant, and some state cops for backup. Go see what's going on."

"Why me? Why can't you go?"

Larry had been stretched out on a padded sun chaise when the call came in. He had just swum twenty laps in the heart-shaped pool, and was catching some late rays prior to suiting up for the night's show at the Van Horne All Star Dinner Theater in nearby Arkhola. Dolly Parton was the headliner, and the show had been sold out for weeks.

49

"Don't be such a dumb fuck. Just get the hell down there, like I said."

So there he was, promising to turn over the transgressors, as soon as he could find out which of the bodyguards were guilty. Probably some of the same ones holding loaded shotguns inside the locked gate, scowling at the show of force arrayed behind the sheriff.

"You've got until tomorrow morning," the peace officer was saying. "After that, we're coming in, one way or another."

This one wasn't going to go away. No wave of Larry's magic wand was going to cause three separate families to drop charges. Shit. He'd have to think of something. Larry and Laura were too tied up with the theater and their celebrity houseguests to be bothered.

Disgusted, Daniel got back in the golf cart, motioning for Chester to slide open the iron gate, and putted up the winding driveway to the house, a 14,000 square foot mansion with interior decoration patterned after Graceland.

"We have to hand them over. It's the only way."

Larry had almost finished dressing. Zipping his fly, he fastened a wide snakeskin belt with chased gold buckle around an expanding waistline. His tapered, white whipcord trousers were tucked in monogrammed, ostrich-hide boots. A gold nugget ring set with a gaudy, $50,000 diamond sparkled on his finger. After brushing a nonexistent bit of fuzz from his custom-tailored, white, western-cut jacket, Larry donned it carefully, then stood admiring himself in the floor length mirror.

"Okay," he said. "Do what you gotta do. But offer those kids' folks some salve to soothe their pain." He glanced at his ring. "Fifty grand should be enough."

* * *

Larry had called that afternoon with the good news. "Porter's gonna help us out. Get on to the station in Ft. Smith and make sure that ad man fixes our spot. And tell Nelson to print up some new flyers quick. We wanna make sure everybody hears about the change. I'm gonna stay over another day. Willie's in town, and I'm takin' him to dinner. Tomorrow I'll go by the store before I start back. Laura there?"

"No, she's gone to Ft. Smith. Said she might be runnin' late. You wanna leave her a message?"

"Nah. Just tell her I love her. And Porter sends his regards."

"Okay. Anything else?"

"Nah. That's about the size of it. Gotta go."

"Bye then. Have fun."

"Don't I always?"

Daniel was delighted. He'd have an evening alone with Laura while Larry played big dog in Nashville. Larry had driven over to the Tennessee house when the diner theater's next scheduled performer had dropped out at the last minute. The sect's image would suffer if they had to cancel a show, and Larry was loath to refund revenue from advance bookings. He was sure he could get a replacement artist if he popped in on some of his old friends. Fortunately, he had caught Porter Waggoner between engagements, and that took care of that.

Laura had been unusually quiet as they wandered the grounds, nodding to followers going about their appointed routines, then stopping by the chapel for a few minutes of prayer before heading up the staggered crosstie stairway to her private inspiration point, an off-limits shelter overlooking the valley, with the lights of Redfern winking on in the distance.

Tucked behind a curving windbreak, two chairs and a low table rested on a broad rock shelf, set back a dozen feet from the precipice. But Laura didn't stop at the chairs. She walked almost to the edge of the bluff before folding gracefully to a sitting position on the sandstone ledge.

"Come sit down, Danny. We need to talk."

He bent, balancing on his good leg, then lowering himself with arm strength alone, until he was seated next to her. It was

51

twilight in late October, the air crisp with the clean, evergreen scent of fall. But bleeding through the seat of his trousers, Daniel could feel the warmth of the Indian summer day stored in the stone. This was what he lived for, these stolen, quiet times with Laura. For nearly sixteen years he had loved her, waited for her to come to him. He had no illusions left. In those sixteen years he had seen her change, falling more and more under Larry's influence, until she became a willing participant in his rape of her following. The furs, the diamonds, the expensive clothes, all the trappings of wealth had taken a toll on the idealistic woman he had met healing the lost and wounded on the streets of L.A. And still he loved her, as helplessly as he had the night they met, without reservations, although the amorous aspect of that love had gone unrequited.

"I'm dying," she said simply. "I have cancer and it's already spread."

The words were a knife in his heart. "You can't be," he said, "I mean, are you sure? How do you know? Can't there be some mistake?"

"No, Daniel. It's hopeless. I spent the whole day at the clinic in Ft. Smith, and the doctors weren't encouraging at all. Now it's just a matter of time." She reached for his hand, squeezing hard. "They gave me six months."

He could tell she was exhausted. Why hadn't he noticed the dark smudges under her eyes? How she tired so easily? Her loss of appetite? In his lurid imagination he could picture the tumor gnawing away her flesh.

"Does Larry know?"

"He knows I haven't been feeling well. But he passed it off. If it doesn't directly concern Larry, you know how he is."

"We'll get another doctor," he said. "You can go to Houston, to M.D. Anderson. They're the best in the world. Or to Mayo's. Or the Cleveland Clinic. Somewhere. Surely somebody can do something."

She shook her head. "It's too late. I waited too long. All we can do now is pray."

She was trembling. Daniel put his arm around her and pulled her to him, holding her while she cried. "It's never too late, my love," he whispered. "It's never too late."

He kissed her then, the most natural thing in the world, their salty embrace culminating years of longing. Drawing back, he touched her cheek, gently wiping away the teardrops with quivering fingers while his own flowed unabated.

"Don't stop," she whispered. "Oh Daniel, hold me and don't ever stop."

It was the invitation he had waited for all his life.

CHAPTER 6

Milo grabbed the receiver after the first ring, glad of the diversion. For more than fifteen minutes he had been locked in a battle of wills with a pack of Marlboros. When the phone rang, the cigarettes were on the verge of winning.

It had been a brutal week, with normal law enforcement problems associated with every Fourth quadrupled by having the President in town. Milo had gotten through the ordeal, but not without lighting up. He was honestly trying to quit. When the legislature banned smoking in all state office buildings he had promised himself to break the habit, a promise thus far observed mainly in the breach. Aside from the physical benefits of abstention, Milo hated making the trek downstairs to join other nicotine addicts shifting restlessly about in the parking lot. It was too much like sneaking a fag in the locker room in junior high. On the slippery side of fifty, he should be beyond that.

Part administrator, part detective, Milo Thomas occupied a unique position in the top echelons of the Arkansas State Police. From his post at headquarters he served as chief liaison between the State Police and other law enforcement organizations in Pulaski County, as well as numerous federal agencies operating out of Little Rock. But that was the least important aspect of his job.

He was also the capital's investigator of last resort, although no one called it that. On his desk landed the cases that no one wanted—or had given up on. The bizarre, the outré, the ones that had fallen through the cracks. The dead ends. Milo loved his work, and he was very good at what he did.

"Thomas," he answered, dropping the unopened pack in his desk drawer.

"Howdy, Milo. Leslie Hanks. How're they hangin'?"

Leslie Hanks was the Pulaski County Sheriff, and a damned good lawman, except when exposed to the media. Then the innate politician surfaced. Sheriff Hanks had higher office on his mind.

"Doin' fine, Leslie. How about you?"

"Can't complain. Sun's still risin' in the east. Listen, Milo, I've got somethin' you might be interested in."

"Yeah? What'd've you got?"

"Three days ago LRPD called us to fish a floater out of the river; stuck in some debris at a fancy condo development close to downtown. Matter of fact, right down the hill from you. Mickey Harmon actually pulled it out—a little kid by all appearances, but it was hard to tell, the body'd been in the water a good while. We all thought it was a drowning, even though Mickey said at the time he wasn't so sure. Well, to make a long story short, when the M.E. finished with her, Doc said the coroner knew what he was talking about—that the kid hadn't drowned.

"Now this is the strange part. We got her identified. Some little black girl missing from up at Dardanelle. Been in all the papers. Though how the hell she got all the way down here is beyond me . . . we just don't know. Lucked out on one thing, though. Nobody picked up the call. Came in on the Fourth, and I guess the reporters were all down at the ground breakin'. The President's better copy any day, so right this minute there's no one breathin' down our necks. But Milo, I swear to God, it's the damnedest thing . . . "

Cigarettes forgotten, Milo wished Leslie Hanks would drop the hyperbole and get on with his tale.

"Okay, Les, I'll buy. What's 'the damnedest thing?'"

Sheriff Hanks wasn't going to be hurried. "Well, that's just it. Trouble is, I don't think it *can* be what it seems. Although Doc Zoellner's not usually wrong. Look, this is what happened:

somebody broke her neck. And the M.E. says, off the record, it was a professional job."

Milo vaguely remembered reading about the search for the missing child, but he had been preoccupied at the time and it hadn't really registered. Now he couldn't believe what he was hearing. "Are you trying to tell me somebody ordered a hit on this little kid?"

"No. That's not what I'm saying. Whoever killed her knew what they were doing, that's all. Doc says it was a completely clean kill, wham, bam, thank you ma'am. No muss, no fuss, no bother. And that's the weird part."

* * *

There wasn't much to see. Encircled by trees, the isolated clearing was nothing more than a graveled turn-around at the edge of the lake. A corrugated concrete ramp angled into the water from the center of the loop, and a few parking spaces had been scraped smooth on either side. At the top of the incline a metal garbage can was tethered to an iron post.

Milo backed his green Bronco into one of the slots and sat at the wheel, trying to get a feel for the place. There was nothing even remotely sinister about it, yet here, or somewhere very close by, someone had snapped a little girl's neck and dumped her in the water like so much trash. Why? What had drawn the child to this spot, and why had she been killed? Leslie Hanks was right when he said it was a mystery.

Milo had to pee fiercely. He got out, stepping behind the Bronco to relieve himself against a sapling encroaching on the parking area. It was hot, high nineties, July's sultry temperatures replacing the unusually mild weather of June with a vengeance. A cloud of gnats surrounded him, forcing him to close his eyes. He batted the air in an effort to disperse the swarm. When the gnats moved away Milo opened his eyes to find a black coon hound smelling the puddle of urine. The dog turned toward him, baring its fangs.

"Hey, boy. Where'd you come from? What're you doing here?" Milo stood very still, speaking in a calm voice.

The dog regarded Milo with suspicion, hackles raised.

Cautiously the man knelt, extending an unprotected hand toward the wary creature.

"Hey, now. It's okay. I won't hurt you."

The dog approached stiff legged, sniffing at Milo's out-stretched palm. Remaining immobile, the investigator let the dog smell him over. Earlier, Milo had seen the hound lurking under Maybelle's front porch, a darker silhouette against deep shadow. Watching him mount the steps, it had growled a low-throated objection to the invasion of its territory. It must have followed him to the clearing.

After what seemed like ten minutes to the kneeling man, but was probably closer to one, the dog appeared satisfied that Milo posed no discernible threat. With a feeble wag of its tail, the hound first licked the man's fingers, then laid its muzzle in his upturned palm.

Milo's intuition clicked into warp drive. It wouldn't hold up in a courtroom, but the investigator was sure he had found an eye witness. Whatever had befallen Addy, the unhappy creature had seen the whole thing. He was absolutely certain that the scruffy black dog with its head in his hand could identify Addy's killer.

Milo petted the hound, rose, and took a pair of Zeiss, wide angle binoculars from the truck. Together man and beast walked across the gravel loop to a shady spot with an unobstructed view of the lake. Milo settled comfortably on a bed on pine needles with the dog at his feet, and extracted the field glasses from their leather carrying case.

In the distance a lacy plume of steam rose from the cooling tower at Nuke One. The plume topped out around a thousand feet, then dissipated in the humid air. Overhead a flock of gulls wheeled in unison, their graceful wings achingly white against the summertime sky. A light breeze sent ripples skittering in all di-rections, while numerous pleasure boats trailed frothy threads of wake across the sparkling surface. Although still higher than normal, the receding lake was no more threatening than a Sunday afternoon.

Milo tried to imagine what conditions had been like two weeks earlier when Addy had disappeared. She had vanished at the height of the flooding, when the voracious river clawed at the land, ingesting anything that got in its way. In mute testament to the water's fury a broad band of rubbish rimmed the lake shore, marking the apex of its upward progress. Milo studied the littered bank as if it might yield a clue.

Without warning the dog jumped up and ran to the water's edge, cocking its head to one side in response to some silent summons. Milo felt his skin prickle, the eerie sensation of being watched. He whipped around. No one was there, but the uneasy feeling persisted. Turning back, he followed the dog's point to a dazzling patch of sunshine some thirty feet from the bank. Milo squinted at the brilliant reflection in utter disbelief as the child materialized. He could see her quite clearly, as tangible yet elusive as breath—bright, quiet, inquisitive, shy—a lot like Amy. The dog stared transfixed while Milo blinked rapidly, aware that his mind was playing tricks on him. But despite his denial, the illusion was still there, hovering above the glistening water. Addy Willis, a pigtailed wraith in Garfield pajamas. Beckoning to *him*.

Like a sailor to the Sirens' song, unlashed from the mast, Milo was incapable of resisting her spell. He felt himself being drawn closer and closer to the smiling apparition, until the electric clasp of a spectral hand tugged him beneath the waves.

* * *

Dotting the hills and valleys of northern Arkansas lie the scattered remains of one of the American military's most controversial projects. They are forgotten now, filled in with gravel, their mighty birds dismantled and rusting in salvage. But in their prime the raft of MIRV tipped, Titan II missiles nestled in case-hardened silos across the country's midsection represented the

United States' first line of defense against nuclear holocaust during the Cold War. Arkansas was home to eighteen Titans. Kansas and Arizona also had eighteen apiece.

The policy of interring ICBMs aimed at the Soviet Union was called "mutual deterrence," which was military-speak for "anything you can do to me, I can do to you better." In spite of all the angry protests and demonstrations, it actually worked quite well. Neither side ever resorted to the use of nuclear Armageddon, and the prospect of mass annihilation appreciably dampened the ardor of the Super Powers for global conflict.

With the coming of détente, even President Reagan deemed the Titan obsolete, and in 1982, he ordered the decommissioning of the missile fleet, to be effected by 1987. After the rockets and warheads were removed, the silos were filled with masonry and rubble, and left open for six months so that Russian generals could verify, via satellite, that they were inoperable.

An integral part of each missile site was its command control center, located thirty-five feet below ground, adjacent to the silo. The three story structure was mounted on springs above a thick concrete pad, which allowed it to float, insulated by tons of earth. Engineers theorized that this *shock isolation cage* could absorb all but a direct nuclear hit and remain functional.

The closest real life test of that theory came in 1980, when a mechanic doing routine maintenance on a Titan at Damascus, Arkansas, dropped a #3 wrench from access scaffolding. The wrench fell seventy feet, piercing the huge rocket's fuel cell. The silo filled with noxious vapor and exploded fourteen hours later, dislodging the seven hundred and fifty ton concrete hatch cover, and severely damaging the missile. Its multi-megaton, nuclear-tipped warhead was ejected from the silo, coming to rest intact two hundred yards away. No radiation leaked from the site, although the accident killed one person and injured twenty-one others. While the blast was hardly the equivalent of a hydrogen bomb, the command bunker withstood the accident unscathed.

In addition to demolishing the missile silos, plans for dismantling the sites called for the removal of all toxic substances; excavating buried storage tanks, and filling in the resulting pits and diffusion ponds to level grade; clearing head-works; and sealing entrances and ventilation shafts after salvaging electronics and secret material. They did *not* call for destroying the entire command module.

Through a local follower fronting for the Tabernacle Daniel acquired six hundred acres of scrub land in the Ozark foothills, abutting the northern-most deactivated missile site. The area is a sparsely populated, scenic wonderland of verdant forests, rocky hills, white water rivers, low mountains, and crystaline, unpolluted air. Along with a thimble-full of stubborn Arkies, a few hillbillies and hard core survivalists share the craggy terrain with deer, raccoon, opossum, and a variety of Nature's less benign creatures, including black bear, mountain lion, and the wild boar that has given its name to the state's preeminent sports team. Those entrenched nesters are neither curious, nor sociable.

Despite the isolation of the site and the reclusive nature of the region's inhabitants, Daniel needed a legitimate enterprise to disguise his activities. He had some of the land cleared, and a series of chicken houses constructed on the property. Raising chickens for a multi-million dollar Springdale conglomerate had become a third viable occupation for rural die-hards, joining tourism and lumbering as the area's other profitable industries.

Once the poultry operation was up and running, the whole shebang was "donated" to the Tabernacle. Daniel could concentrate his energy on renovating the buried command center, using the chicken farm as cover. Later, when the bunker had been fully restored, the farm would serve the added purpose of masking power demands for McKensie's computers.

Over a period of years Daniel's dream materialized. With the guidance of a disgruntled engineer newly discharged from Little Rock Air Base's 308th Missile Wing, and a small cadre of cult members who were plumbers and carpenters by trade, the air-shafts were unsealed, a reserve fuel tank buried, a new entrance tunneled in from under one of the long chicken sheds, and the interior refurbished to Daniel's specifications.

The lower floor remained much as it had under Air Force command. It was the mechanical heart of the bunker, home to diesel generators, water purification equipment, electrical systems, and a host of auxiliary appurtenances designed to keep the underground fortress humming in a worst case scenario. Medical supplies were stored in a locked closet; a cache of munitions in an adjoining compartment. The major change was the addition of Laura's chamber, fashioned from the former blast lock cableway.

If the lower floor was the heart of the bunker, the middle level was its brain. Where technicians had once monitored the Titan's vital signs the most dramatic retooling had taken place. Gone were the implements of nuclear war, hot buttons and failsafes, replaced by a small mainframe, linked by modem to PCs in the Tabernacle, van, and dwelling/office headquarters above ground. Four terminals accessed the hard drive from a console in the center of the room. Skilled operators manned the terminals daily in two eight-hour shifts, with one geek drawing graveyard duty, insurance that the system never had to be taken down. It was a slick, sophisticated set up, comparable to those in many large scale businesses and financial institutions.

But the real kicker lay in the software. Through McKensie's brilliantly structured programs, the Tabernacle was bilking the federal government to fund its illicit activities. A complex series of highly profitable social security scams kept taxpayers' money funneling into hidden Tabernacle accounts. It was a conceit that delighted the modern messiah. In addition, the computer kept tabs on the cult's legitimate enterprises, as well as maintaining the bunker's physical environment.

Vying for attention with the VDTs, a bank of television screens displayed images of the outside world. Security cameras panned the poultry farm and missile site. Other screens carried news programs and data from major financial markets, gathered by high resolution, digital satellite dishes hidden in feed bins and out buildings.

Reached by spiral staircase from the main level, the top story held accommodations for computer jockeys and security. Working three days on and two off, they were all single, male, and Daniel's most trusted disciples. Most had accompanied him from the Foundation, and had served Laura as well. Individual cubicles held bunk beds, much like quarters on a submarine, with a communal toilet and bath.

A kitchen and pantry occupied the balance of third floor space. The kitchen was basic—small refrigerator, double burner gas stove, sink, and microwave. The pantry was more extensive, stocked floor to ceiling with canned goods, survival rations, cases of bottled water, and other non-perishable commodities. Canisters of butane, kerosene lanterns, heavy duty flashlights, candles, batteries, and boxes of matches rounded out the provisions.

When all the work was complete, Daniel had an undetectable operations' center crammed with top notch technology housed in the most impregnable bomb shelter the U.S. government knew how to build. No more than a score of people had ever heard of the subterranean hide-away. Not more that fifteen had ever been there. For what the cult leader had in mind, it was dead bang perfect.

*   *   *

Daniel wasn't sure when he had decided to blow up Nuke One. He had been toying with the idea so long it was as much a part of him as his hare lip. Perhaps the notion had originated as far back as 1979, with the near meltdown at Three Mile Island. He remembered wishing at the time that Middleton had been a suburb of Philadelphia, not Harrisburg. If a portion of Pennsylvania were to be laid waste by radioactive fallout, what better place than the Cradle of American Democracy? The Liberty Bell was already cracked. A little U235 would be icing on the cake.

Steam rising from Arkansas Nuclear One's cooling tower dominated the skyline for miles along Interstate 40. For years the column had tantalized Daniel, a latter-day pillar of cloud guiding him to some metaphorical, twenty-first century promised land. Traveling between Arkhola and Little Rock on Foundation business, he had once detoured over to it, and been amazed by the lack of security. Absolutely anyone could drive right up to the reactor's front door. Fishermen lined the banks of the intake and exit chutes, and families picnicked in the park-like setting. It was as though the electric company were inviting him to destroy it.

Then Chernobyl exploded on the world's consciousness in 1986, and Daniel began to look more closely at the prospect. Utilities were clamoring to point out that the blown reactor was different from American installations, a more volatile design, with fewer safeguards. Intrigued nonetheless, Daniel pored over accounts of the disaster, learning as much as he could about the immediate devastation and its projected long-term effects.

Hard on the heels of the Russian tragedy came the United State's announcement that it was mothballing its missile fleet, and with that announcement, the genesis of Daniel's plan. Acquisition of the bunker had been the first step.

With Bill Clinton's election to the Presidency the hate and resentment that had been festering since long before Daniel's experience in Vietnam came to a head. Daniel had lost a leg for his country, and been spit on by his own countrymen, while Slick Willie, the Arkansas snake oil salesman, cavorted in safety in the English countryside, smoking dope and burning the flag. But it was the White House sexcapades that sent him over the edge. Clinton had finally been exposed for a liar and cheat and *nobody cared*. The worse the revelations, the higher his approval ratings. The public's attitude infuriated Daniel, fanning his smoldering rage to combustion. A draft dodger as Commander in Chief was bad enough, but the whole country writing off moral degeneracy as executive privilege? Because the economy was good? It wasn't Bill Clinton who needed a lesson. It was the American people.

*   *   *

When Milo came out of his trance he was dripping in sweat, his muscles cramping with fatigue. He had no idea how long he had been away. Accompanying Addy on her terrible ordeal down eighty miles of river must have taken days, surely, but that couldn't be right. The bright afternoon had faded, replaced with stonewashed dusk. Crickets were tuning up for their evening serenade. A mosquito buzzed his ear; stung the back of his neck. He slapped at the insect and the real world gradually came back into focus. Noticing his binoculars, Milo retrieved them, then pushed himself up on unsteady legs. The dog, which had waited patiently throughout the afternoon, trotted over. Milo scratched the animal's flank, surprised to find it still there. Together they headed for the Bronco, wading through lengthening shadows. Milo's sense of foreboding had vanished, replaced by determination.

At the truck he addressed his newfound friend. "She's gone, fella, dead and gone. And I can't bring her back. No one can do that. But I promise you, I'll find the sonofabitch who killed her. Then we'll see." Not much, but it was the best he had to offer. "You go on home now. Go on. Maybelle'll be looking for you. I won't forget. I give you my word."

The dog listened intently, judging from Milo's tone the depth of his commitment. Milo located his keys and unlocked the truck. When he turned back the hound was nowhere to be seen. Satisfied with the man's pledge, the dog had melted into the underbrush.

CHAPTER 7

McKensie rode in the cab beside Boyd, grinning hugely, high on success. Smacking a triple stick wad of Big Red in time to a paradiddle he was drumming on the dash, he could barely contain his elation. Even Boyd had a smile tugging at the corners of his mouth.

"Hot damn! We got 'em. We really got 'em. Slick as shit through a goose."

Boyd cast a sideways glance at the hyped-up killer. He despised McKensie's filthy mouth, his mercurial disposition. Mike McKensie was a vicious psychopath barely under control. He was also a computer whiz whose hacking abilities were instrumental to their mission and Boyd was stuck with him, like it be damned. It was an uneasy alliance, rankling both parties.

Boyd reached behind his seat to rap on the paint-speckled drop cloth. A solid *thwok* reassured him that the crates were still there.

McKensie stopped drumming. "Hey, Commander, haven't we come far enough? I gotta take a dump."

The adrenaline was bleeding off rapidly and they needed a break. "Okay. First place we come to I'll stop."

Five miles up the road Boyd turned into a McDonald's off Mena's main drag, parking under a crape myrtle. The men got out, stretched, and locked their vehicle. When they reached the entrance nearest the toilets, Boyd looked back. The innocuous Blazer slumbered peacefully, a sprinkling of crimson blossoms gracing its hood. No one could have guessed that it contained a half million dollars in cash and four Hellfire missiles stolen from the Red River Army Depot, in Hooks, Texas.

Dawn. Master Sergeant Jerome Stackhouse had specified a dawn delivery, and since Boyd knew the sergeant to be punctual, he and McKensie had to reach the rendezvous first. They slipped off State Highway 41 twenty-six miles south of DeQueen well before the sun rose, doubling back on a timber access road that dead-ended at Cotton Creek. Boyd backed in, killed his lights, and settled down to wait. McKensie got out, hid the knife; then he rejoined Boyd.

Jerry Stackhouse hadn't wanted to hazard transporting the missiles too far, so the exchange was to be effected fewer than thirty miles from New Boston, straight up Texas 8, over the state line. He had nearly been caught in 1992, when someone discovered that nine Stingers had been moved from their normal location, and alerted the Army. A frantic search had turned up the weapons before they could be smuggled off base. That incident had spurred drastically tightened security at the arsenal. It had taken the promise of an exorbitant amount of money to ensure the sergeant's cooperation.

Twin halogen beams washed over the Blazer, painting its occupants a sickly yellow. A faint rose glow suffused the sky, but under the trees it was still night.

Boyd climbed down, assumed an unthreatening stance, arms extended, hands empty, skewered in the high beams.

"Come on, Michael. Get out. He wants to see both of us."

McKensie got out, blinded in the bright lights like a startled rabbit.

The sergeant came toward them, wielding a custom, chrome-plated Colt 45 automatic Boyd recognized as the gunny's trademark sidearm. Boyd was also well aware that Sergeant Stackhouse knew exactly what to do with it.

"What's up, Jerry? You don't need the gun. This is a simple business transaction between old friends."

"Who are you kidding? We were never friends, Boyd. You were never anybody's friend. It was always 'Yes, sir. No, sir. Eat shit? Certainly, sir.' Where's the money?"

"In the truck. Michael can get it."

Overhead the little bit of open sky was brightening to pale lemon, presaging a scorcher. Holding his pistol loosely in one hand, the military man frisked Boyd expertly. Upon finding no weapon, he turned his attention to Boyd's companion. For once McKensie did as he had been told, submitting to the search without reaction. When Jerry Stackhouse assured himself that they were both unarmed he ordered McKensie to get the cash, holding his former commander hostage with his Colt screwed to Boyd's temple.

The transfer went smoothly enough under the supervision of the cautious serviceman. It wasn't until the heavy crates had been stowed safely in the Blazer that McKensie retrieved his weapon from its hiding place. Boyd would have to concede the bastard knew how to use a knife. It was highly unlikely that the M.P.s would ever find what was left of M.Sgt. Stackhouse, but if they did, they weren't going to have much to work with.

After obscuring the license tag, McKensie drove the sergeant's muddied Tahoe to a truck stop near the Summerhill Road exit off Interstate 30, on the Texas side of Texarkana, with Boyd following at a safe distance. It irked Boyd that only 321 miles registered on the SUV's odometer. It was just like Jerry to have bought a new truck on the come. Stupid. But just like him.

McKensie parked away from the diesel plaza behind a yellow J. B. Hunt rig at the very back of the yard, near a dingy, two story bunkhouse. The motel provided inexpensive accommodations for long-haulers, and other, unadvertised perks on demand. Hookers who worked the truck stop did a thriving business. The ladies of the evening were also well acquainted with personnel from Lone Star Ordance and the Red River Arsenal. It would not be a bit unusual to find an SUV ranged among the big rigs.

McKensie stuffed the keys under the driver's floor mat, a noticeable bulge, leaving the Tahoe unlocked. Striding briskly across the tarmac to the waiting Blazer, he stripped off a pair of inexpensive, plastic-studded work gloves. Without a beat the duo pulled onto the access road, across the viaduct, and back onto the Interstate. If they were lucky, someone would take the bait and drive off with the sergeant's brand new Chevy. If not, it could be days before anyone got too curious about the mud-caked vehicle parked at the truckers' haven. Either way, by the time Military Police came looking for Master Sergeant Jerry Stackhouse, Boyd and McKensie would be long gone.

*   *   *

Boyd had spent a lot of time in jungles. From the swamps of Florida and Louisiana to the rain forests of Southeast Asia and Central American banana republics, Boyd had got his fill of jungles. In his mind's eye they all ran together, a blur of fecund soil, strangling vegetation, noisome insects, the pervasive, coppery, sweet compost of decay. Heat, sweat, fear. Rot. Rot everywhere —in the close, stifling, humid air; in the dank, spongy carpet of humus laid thick on the jungle floor; in his feet. In his brain. Boyd knew jungles. Green was the color of his nightmares.

Boyd had survived three tours of duty in Indochina, beginning in Vietnam in 1961. His posting as an instructor with an American Special Forces battalion of military advisors preceded by six months the arrival of the first American combat troops in Saigon. Boyd was stationed at Vung Tau, tasked with training South Vietnamese army personnel in the use of U.S. supplied weaponry and equipment. The dinks were apt pupils, eager to learn the finer points of modern guerrilla warfare. Teaching survival, field hygiene, first aid, and battle tactics to indigenous peoples who had been fighting the Japanese, the French, the communists, and each other for four decades was an easy ride for the snake eater.

68

He transferred out in the fall of 1963, one month before the assassination of John Kennedy. After spending nearly two years in country, Boyd's flight departed only days before the ouster and execution of President Ngo Dinh Diem by members of his own ruling party, with the tacit consent of the U.S. government. The similarity of the two events was not lost on the Green Beret major.

Two and a half years later, in Laos, the jungle became the fodder of his worst dreams.

Shots barked from the hut, the rapid fire chatter of an AK-47 on full automatic, followed seconds later by the flash/bang/crump of a stun grenade. Men in jungle fatigues ringed the site, advancing cautiously in a tightening noose. Boyd trained his binoculars on the action, searching for some indication that the surrounded communist officers were going to surrender.

A whistle was his only warning. The shell took out the hut and its besieged occupants in a direct hit, spewing a deadly circle of fire and shrapnel outward. Boyd's entire cordon of troops was caught in the blast. Those who had not been killed instantly were writhing in flames on the edge of the crater where the hooch had stood. Deafened by concussion, Boyd couldn't hear the screams of the dying; couldn't hear himself screaming along with them. Then the anesthesia of shock wore off and he could smell the men burning.

He had witnessed the immolation of a Buddhist monk in Saigon in 1962, staring in fascinated revulsion while the religious protester, through some supreme act of will, remained immobile as his body was consumed by a ball of fire. Oily ash had coated the fine hairs of Boyd's nasal passages with the reek of burning tissue, a stench he had never been able to purge. It clung to the lobes of his memory like napalm. Now it was his own troops.

The awful scene was scorched on Boyd's retinas. His eyelids blinked spasmodically, the shutter of a camera recording images on the reel of his mind, so that he could play them over and over again, accompanied by the sickening odor of charred human flesh. It was that odor that usually woke him.

Boyd and the Meo tribesman serving as his guide stole like ghosts through the jungle, spectral beings outfitted with forty pound kits to weight their spirits to the earth, sneaking deeper and deeper behind enemy lines. Pouang Tak held the point. He gestured for Boyd to drop. Fifteen minutes ground by . . . half an hour. Gnats pasted themselves to Boyd's eyes, invaded his ears, filled his nostrils. He could hear the staccato patter of Charlie's conversation above the pounding of his own heart, smell the sweet, opium-laced tobacco smoke as it drifted downwind. Their voices faded, trailing away down an unseen path. Pouang remained motionless. Another quarter of an hour ticked by before the mountain man tapped him on the shoulder. They resumed their trek.

Technically, Boyd and Pouang *didn't* exist; at least not in conventional military terms. They were part and parcel of Colonel Murphy's irregulars, an off-the-books army operating out of Vientiane under contract to the CIA. The phantom corps was made up of ten thousand Army Special Force troops and Agency operatives, controlling a militia of thirty thousand guerrillas, composed mostly of Hmong tribesmen and Thai mercenaries, funded entirely from the deep coffers of Langley, Virginia. Boyd understood his employer's fiction of secrecy. He had worked for the Central Intelligence Agency before.

Initially, the Company's involvement was geared to recruiting hill tribesmen to resist not only the insurgency of the Pathet Lao, communist backed rebels seeking to topple the legitimate government of Laos, but the Vietcong as well, who were using eastern Laos as a staging area and supply artery for their incursions against the South. The scope of their brief widened to encompass clandestine operations of their own. Colonel Murphy specialized in sending South Vietnamese spies into the North to infiltrate the Vietcong and bring out intelligence. They were routinely caught and killed.

One agent who had managed to escape returned with word of a proposed meeting between Colonel Tran Hoac, a top level strategist from the NVA, Hanoi's Communist-backed regular army, and bigwigs from the National Liberation Front, the political wing of South Vietnam's opposition movement.

Was it a setup? Possibly, but once the Company got wind of the meeting it was hot to trot. If the Colonel could get his hands on any of the participants, information extracted (by whatever means) from such highly placed sources would be invaluable, and a prodigious coup for the spooks. Boyd drew the short straw.

It took the pair of infiltrators six hours to travel the last ten klicks. In the waning light they picked a careful route down the heavily timbered ridge, scolding monkeys tracing their descent. The rendezvous site was little more than a glorified hooch tucked in a natural depression halfway down the slope. A single track led to its door. Two hundred meters behind the structure the land fell away sharply, forming a deep gorge. Hard as hell to get to, and virtually undetectable by air, if their information proved reliable, Boyd could understand why the commies had picked this place.

Pouang stood guard while Boyd scouted the surrounding terrain for a suitable observation post. They dug in behind an outcropping of boulders with a view of the hut, and set up the radio. Night fell, engulfing the exhausted men in muggy darkness. Boyd stifled a yawn, bone weary; Pouang already asleep. Fat, honey-scented drops of rain began to fall, as big as quarters, splattering arrhythmically on the rock overhang. Boyd shrugged on his poncho, hunching up his shoulders against the rain. He was standing first watch.

"Incoming at ten o'clock." Time to rock and roll.

Boyd and Pouang ducked behind the boulder for protection as the daisy cutter burst, whizzing off the tops of trees like a buzz saw. The coordinates were smack on. Before the dust had time to settle, the whup, whup, whup of a Hook's rotor carried over the ridge. Boyd picked off Charlie's dazed sentries while Pouang manned the radio. The big Chinook 47 hovered over the newly opened clearing, disgorging Boyd's troops. As the men dropped to the ground, small arms fire broke out from the hut. The Hook took off.

Part of a platoon he had trained himself, Boyd was proud of this squad; they were handling the assault with the precision of a drill. Then the machine gun sprang to life. Boyd dropped his binoculars, started down the trail toward the hut . . .

The shell burst and there was nothing he could do.

*　*　*

Laura's death did not liberate Daniel. It took him two more years to quit the Foundation. The rift with Larry, however, began immediately.

"Come on Larry, be reasonable. This is monstrous. You *cannot* do this."

"Just watch me," Larry Van Horne hissed. "If you think you can tell *me* what to do you've got another think coming. I can do anything I damn well please. And," he pointed a manicured finger at Daniel's chest, "there's not one friggin' thing you can do about it."

They were closeted in the chapel vestibule, where Daniel was trying to talk some sense into Larry before he made another big mistake.

"Listen to me Larry, Laura's *dead*. I'm just as cut up as you are, but this is not going to help. We've *got* to bury her. *Please.* Let her have a decent funeral. It's been over a week now. We're already getting bills from the hospital. The damn press is sitting on our doorstep. Listen," he gestured to the closed door. Inside the chapel the babble of voices was getting louder. "Even the faithful are getting restless. You've got to stop this shit *now*."

When word first spread about Laura's illness, the van Hornes had summoned Foundation members to a marathon prayer session, announcing that Laura's cancer was Heaven-sent, a trial to prove their faith. If they prayed hard enough and long enough, if they *truly* believed, God would heal Laura. Her miraculous cure would catapult the Foundation of Eternal Life into worldwide prominence.

It hadn't worked. Now Larry had a new bright idea. They would raise Laura from the dead. That feat should garner the sect even more attention than curing her cancer. It was this lunacy that had Daniel and Larry at loggerheads.

Laura had been the divine spark, self-declared instrument of the Almighty. Without Laura, Larry was afraid the Foundation would crumble, taking with it his money making machine. If it took using her dead body to bind cult members to him, that was what he would do, and nothing Daniel said was going to stop him.

When the undertaker had plied his craft, Laura was installed as the centerpiece of a shrine Larry had set up in the mansion's dining room. Then he convened the membership to announce his latest interpretation of God's Holy Will. It was at this point that Daniel tried to intervene.

As usual, Larry prevailed.

Larry commanded the faithful to keep vigil at Laura's bier around the clock, two disciples at a time, in two hour shifts. She was *never* to be left alone. The Foundation of Eternal Life would resurrect Laura through prayer. Two years later they were still praying and she was still dead. It was only after God commanded him to remarry, a long-stemmed, Swedish beauty he had met in Nashville, that Larry finally agreed to lay Laura to rest.

As long as Larry held Laura hostage, Daniel could not bear to abandon her. Outwardly, he mended his fences with Larry. Inwardly, he was seething. How could that mercenary charlatan defile Laura by making her an object of derision, a laughing stock outside the Foundation? Daniel had anticipated public reaction to Larry's ploy, but Larry didn't care, so long as he held onto his corps of willing workers. There was, however, mounting dissatisfaction among the troops with Larry's autocratic rule, so much so that defections were becoming more numerous. Cracks were beginning to develop in the Foundation.

Larry needed a new gimmick. Egged on by Daniel (who had set about to orchestrate Larry's demise), the Foundation began publishing virulent anti-Catholic screeds, which found their way under windshield wipers from coast to coast. As a matter of policy, the Roman Catholic Church ignores such scurrilous attacks. But the charges were so outrageous that the Church did so at its peril.

Even more alarming was Larry's proposal to woo unwed mothers.

From the Foundation's inception, premarital fraternization was taboo. To deal with their hormonally ravaged converts, the van Hornes staged mass weddings, pairing followers arbitrarily. Because Daniel had consistently declined Larry's offers to take his pick of the batch, Larry harbored suspicions about Daniel's gender preference. The van Hornes routinely denounced homosexuals as deviants, perverts and scourges of the Devil. Privately, Larry was comfortable with his perception of Daniel's sexuality. The man was a valuable tool, and if Laura wanted to pal around with him, that was okay—he wasn't a threat. It was only Larry's arrogance that kept him from seeing the truth.

Married couples, if they were lucky, were eventually assigned a cottage and moved out of the sexually segregated dormitories. It was understood that if they conceived children, the upbringing of those children became the responsibility of the Foundation. But Larry's widespread appeal for babies was something else.

He took out ads in numerous publications, protested in front of abortion clinics, bought time on radio and television to tout his latest brainstorm.

If you are pregnant and unmarried, The Foundation of Eternal Life is the answer. Do not have an abortion. The Bible commands,

"Thou shalt not kill." We will pay your expenses. Your unwanted babies will have a safe, stable home, run by caring, Christian people. We will educate them according to strict religious principles. Come to us and let us help.

The prospect of fanatics indoctrinated from the crib was chilling.

These two campaigns, coupled with a California indictment over the severe beating of a follower's child, and the scandal of the cult's attempt to raise Laura from the dead, brought a stream of adverse publicity to media outlets around the country. Alarms were finally beginning to sound about the true nature of the sect, piquing the government's interest in revoking its tax exempt status.

At the same time he was handing Larry the knife to slit his own throat, Daniel was consolidating *his* strength. He had run the office, kept the books, done the purchasing from the start. When the sect prospered he had written the checks for Laura's designer clothes, paid for Larry's Cadillacs and silk shirts. He had filed the documents obtaining the Foundation's status as a non-profit organization, and cooked the books to support that claim. He, better than anyone, knew where the money came from, and where it went.

Moreover, he drew the unpleasant assignments neither van Horne would deign to handle. When dismayed parents tried to prise their children from the commune, Daniel was sent to reason with them before Larry's goons were unleashed to scare them off. If a problem cropped up with a local business, Daniel was the one delegated to work things out. He was the Foundation's anchor in reality, indispensable to the smooth running of the organization. And, he was observant. In sixteen years of being Larry's understudy, Daniel had the words down pat. But his was a far different agenda.

Many of Laura's original recruits, some having worked their way up to positions of importance over the years, were still active in the Foundation. Most had been devoted to Laura and deplored what Larry was doing. Daniel was counting on these loyalists to form the core of his splinter sect. But in the eighties Fundamentalism had become both more political and more militant. The far right blamed a government run amuck for society's ills. A disparate group, the movement was composed of survivalists, white separatists, environmental extremists, right-to-life fanatics, rabid gun enthusiasts, para-military militias, neo-Nazis, and a panoply of equally fractious factions, including remnants of the Klan and CSA. Espousing themes of Christian Identity and Patriot Movement ideology, these were the followers Daniel wanted to attract, and the people he would have to con.

After meeting Brigida, Larry was in a bind, keeping up the pretense of Laura's pending resurrection. He finally agreed to an interment.

The very best grade of white marble from a quarry in Tate, Georgia, was the material of choice for Laura's sarcophagus. Although prayers for God's handmaiden continued undiminished, once Larry determined to close her coffin and place it in the vault, the danger of her reemergence was nil. A period of several months ensued before the local monument company fitted custom, double hung marble doors to the mausoleum. That interval provided Daniel the opportunity to spirit her away.

Taking advantage of one of Larry's trips to Nashville, Daniel paired himself with Heavy Bolin, who had been Laura's personal gofer, for the graveyard, two to four a.m. prayer vigil. Working surreptitiously, the two men removed Laura's body, replacing it with sandbags before resealing the tomb. Then they secreted the corpse in a delivery van, which Heavy drove the next morning to a prepared hideaway. Laura would remain there until a permanent refuge could be secured.

Daniel stayed on for Larry's nuptial celebration, which broke the last bond between them. Then he was free. FREE. He was thirty-eight years old. He had learned many things. Daniel's turn had finally come.

*   *   *

Early on the morning of April 23, 1991, federal marshals, accompanied by FBI agents and the sheriff and deputies from Cromwell County, broke down the iron gates barring the only way into the Redfern Compound. Their authority was a federal warrant to seize all property, real and personal, belonging to the van Hornes and the Foundation of Eternal Life.

When things started to go south for Larry, they had gone in a landslide. Under the auspices of the Department of Labor, a family of disenchanted followers sued the Foundation in federal court citing unfair labor practices stemming from their years of unpaid, "volunteer" work. They were awarded a judgment of over two million dollars actual and punitive damages. It was time to collect.

In 1985, the Internal Revenue Service had revoked Larry's tax exemption on the grounds that he was running his religion for personal gain. A tip from an anonymous source intimately familiar with the inworkings of Foundation affairs had prompted the action. Without Daniel to straighten things out, Larry failed to file returns for the four consecutive years, in defiance of the government's revocation. Threatened with a summary judgment, he did file the next two years, but grossly underestimated his income.

The child abuse warrant from California was still pending, coupled with another for unlawful flight to avoid prosecution. Larry had disappeared in 1989, and was running his empire in absentia, after making telephone threats against a federal judge who had ruled against him in yet another civil suit.

Larry remained a fugitive from justice until the fall of 1991, when he was apprehended without incident living in Florida. In a nicely ironic twist, an alert viewer, after seeing Larry portrayed on a tabloid TV program, recognized him as the man next door and phoned authorities.

Assets of the Foundation in Arkansas, Tennessee, and California, were sold at government auction to satisfy court-ordered settlements. Most of the Redfern Compound went to the family who had brought suit against the van Hornes in the labor dispute. A stockpile of Larry's gaudy jackets was bought piecemeal by a curious public. Thanks to a coalition of anti-defamation leagues, reputable stores had dropped his merchandise cold when word went out about the cult's vicious propaganda attacks on Catholics and Jews alike.

A squib about Laura, who had merited so much media attention while the faithful were praying for her revival, made a bizarre postscript to the raid. When the marshals made their way to the mausoleum, they found her tomb had been violated, its marble doors lying in ruins. Behind the broken seal, the crypt was empty. Forewarned, Larry had ordered lieutenants to make off with the body, so that Laura's power would remain in his possession. What the grave robbers could not have known, and the federal lawmen never suspected, was that they were both too late. Larry might have the coffin, but only sandbags slept in its lavish interior. Its erstwhile occupant had new quarters, and her spiritual authority had devolved upon a new Messiah.

CHAPTER 8

The Eagles were screaming in War Memorial Stadium. Banks of amplifiers hurled the sound up and out of the arena, so that it assaulted the ears of anyone living within a mile radius. That included Hillcrest and part of the Heights. And Milo's condo.

Three quarters drunk, for some reason Milo had been trying to coax the title of a J. D. Salinger book out of the fog of his memory. The Eagles weren't helping. Their grating music made it difficult to concentrate on anything but wishing they'd shut up. Neither was the whiskey; it was only making him maudlin.

For christssakes you dumb shit, why can't you remember the name of the friggin' book? It was only your Bible when you were growing up. Now you can't even think of the fuckin' title. Shit. How could you have gotten so old so fast?

Wait, wait, it's almost there . . . almost . . . Catcher in the Rye, *that's it,* Catcher in the Rye! *Holden fuckin' Caulfield in* Catcher in the Rye. *Thank God. And* Franny and Zooey. *George Orwell's* Animal Farm. *Anything at all by Ferlinghetti. Op Art, Pop Art, cunnilingus and fellatio. Joan Baez and the Kingston Trio . . . "I went down to Boston on the something, something, something" . . . How could I not remember? And geez, what about "Where Have All the Flowers Gone?" And "Michael Rowed the Boat Ashore".* He put his hands over his ears. *Not like this crap.*

For christssakes. I was in North Beach when it went topless. I saw Carol Doda dance. I went to the Black Orchid and the Purple Onion. I knew hippies who slept on Fisherman's Wharf, who fixed me chicken hearts flamed in Tabacso. I was in the fuckin' CIA.

Milo needed another drink. Or sex. Or both. Anything to staunch the flood of memories unleashed by Addy Willis. He could not get the little girl out of his mind. Worse, he could no longer suppress the past, which he had kept successfully at bay for nearly twenty years. At least until the midnight hours, when Morpheus, summoned as often as not by Jack Daniel's, came to call, accompanied by the twin succubi of guilt and remorse. In that drugged stupor he was tormented by dreams of Amy and Angélique, dreams he was impotent to banish.

But if he had exiled, by force of will, his wife and daughter from conscious thought, his encounter with Addy Willis had changed that, scraping the scab off a wound he had thought long since healed.

Milo had bought the lye. Milo hadn't put it away. Milo had killed his daughter as surely as if he had poured the caustic liquid down her throat. The accident was his fault. He could not accept that Angélique did not blame him: he blamed himself. In the end he turned her away, unable to live with his guilt and her forgiveness.

Milo poured another drink and cranked up the volume on a Miles Davis album. He wasn't sure which he was trying to drown, the caterwauling or the pain.

*　*　*

Armed with files from both the Perry and Pulaski County Sheriffs' offices, Milo waded through the reams of paper work produced by the search for Addy and the discovery of her body. He was looking for something, anything that would help. So far he hadn't found a crumb. He stretched, left his desk and got a Diet Coke from the machine in the canteen. He held the can to his forehead, relishing the cold. He'd kill for a cigarette.

Reseated, he dialed Paul Pressler. A deputy put him on hold, then patched him through to the sheriff's patrol car. After exchanging the usual pleasantries, Milo got down to business.

"Paul, have you guys got a transcript of Hot Line calls on the Willis girl? I haven't come up with jack."

"Yeah. Farned finally got it typed up yesterday. Sorry we're a little slow, but we ain't got the staff you state boys have. Don't think there's anything there though. We checked out all the good stuff. But go ahead on. You're welcome to it."

"Thanks. I'd appreciate it if y'all could fax me a copy?"

"Sure thing. I'll get 'em to send it right now. Anything else we can do to help you out, let us know." Pressler was glad to have the death off his hands. They weren't ever going to find out who did it. Let the state cop take the heat.

When a child goes missing, an 800 Hot Line is often set up to handle information from the public. In cases of suspected kidnapping the FBI can be called in. The Bureau can also waive its mandatory twenty-four hour waiting period, setting in motion its Rapid Response protocol if sufficient evidence exists to suggest foul play. While no one seriously believed that Addy had been taken for ransom, other, more sinister motives always existed. Even though the Bureau was exquisitely sensitive to the plight of an imperiled child, in Addy's case the complete absence of any indication that a crime had been committed made the Feds reluctant to enter the picture.

Prodded by Maybelle and the black community at large, the Yell County Sheriff's Department had then agreed to establish and monitor a local Hot Line, with money for the hardware provided by Maybelle's corporate employer.

Perusing Addy's case files, Milo was irritated to discover that the Yell County documents contained no comprehensive transcript of these calls. He had read and reread reports of several follow-up investigations generated by the Hot Line, looking for anything the investigator on the scene might have missed. But nowhere could he find a complete list of all the Hot Line hits. Maybe something had slipped by the dispatchers.

Ten minutes later Milo was leaning over Marilyn's shoulder, as pages of fax rolled off the printer. If he spotted anything of interest he would ask Sheriff Pressler to dupe him a tape. Meanwhile, he would have a place to start.

"I know how to do this." Marilyn, the department's long suffering clerk, pushed him back.

"I know you do. I just thought you could use a little help." He was kidding, eager to get the document, and she wasn't put out.

"Milo, if you wanna help, why don't you take Tommy Lee off my hands (her rebellious, tongue-studded, teenaged son), or persuade the Colonel to give me a raise? That's the kind of help *I* need." She straightened the stack of papers and handed it to him.

He bowed, "My gratitude knows no bounds."

"You idiot," she laughed. "So, what about my raise?"

"Now Katy Scarlett," he said, "I'll have to think about that tomorrow."

Marilyn watched him go, still smiling. She'd been more or less happily married to the same man for twenty years, but she had a soft spot for Milo. He was so—so—vulnerable. Marilyn was a lot more perceptive than most of Milo's colleagues. They would have been astonished at her assessment. Milo would have been mortified.

He wasn't making much headway with the list of calls. The log consisted of the date and time the call came in, the number it came from, and a transcript of the conversation. Caller ID made it unnecessary to keep someone talking in order to run a trace. The number was automatically displayed at the operator's terminal as soon as the connection was made. Addy had vanished on Saturday night; the hunt had begun in earnest on Sunday afternoon. By Tuesday night as manpower flagged and the intensive search for the child or her corpse wound down, the Hot Line was up and running. Local radio and television stations had broadcast the number each time a news program aired, blanketing the state.

Over the next three days a flurry of calls had yielded a lot of speculation but nothing substantial.

Milo kept it up all afternoon, the slow, methodical process of double checking each entry against its disposition. In many instances no action had been deemed necessary. Dozens of tips were dishearteningly similar—variations of *"The kid's in the lake."*

A deputy on duty would ask for identification. Invariably the reply was, *"You don't need my name,"* or, *"my name's not important,"* followed by a broken connection. Many times the informant would simply hang up. But with the exception of occasional "unavailable" mobile numbers, Caller ID had matched each incoming call to a subscriber. At the time, these nuisance tips hadn't seemed worth pursuing. Milo resolved to check them all.

It was after five o'clock, but with only a couple of pages left Milo wanted to finish. His eyes were tired, the lines starting to blur. Toward the end of the week, fewer and fewer calls had come in as people's interest waned with the coming of the Fourth of July holiday. He scanned the next-to-the-last page, five hang ups and one legitimate call, all recorded on Monday, July 3. Addy's body had surfaced on the Fourth, but since it hadn't been identified until the following Friday, the line had stayed open for three more days. Even so, into the holiday weekend calls had really petered out.

Milo thought about a cigarette. He thought about a drink. He thought about Amy. He went back to the printout. Rifling through the Yell County file, he located a follow-up report for the lone valid phone tip received on July the third.

At the request of Sheriff Pressler, a state police officer had been dispatched to the Holiday Inn in Conway, whose manager reported a white couple keeping a black child confined to a room at the motel. The couple, driving a car with out-of-state plates, had checked in late Sunday afternoon. The man requested a room on the back side of the motel, away from the Interstate and swimming pool. Monday morning they had refused to let the maid clean the room. On Tuesday they again refused maid service, but the woman asked for clean towels to be handed to her through the door. All the publicity about Addy aroused the manager's suspicions. Since the drapes remained drawn and the child hadn't so much as stuck a nose out the whole time, the manager was sure he had found Maybelle's missing daughter.

Of course it was all innocent. The little girl turned out to be a Guatemalan orphan, legally adopted through an international relief organization. Her father, a professor of history from the Boston area, had recently accepted a position at Hendrix College. The family had driven to Arkansas to look for a house, but the child had gotten sick on the way. Her mother thought she might be coming down with Rubella, which had been going around in their Cambridge neighborhood, and wanted to keep her quiet and away from the light. She hadn't let the maid in because she didn't want to expose others to the disease. All of this had taken time to check and document, and it was all a colossal waste.

Shit. Not one useful piece of information in the whole goddamn mess. God he needed a cigarette. Milo picked up the final page of the transcript. Dropped it, grabbed the one he had just been holding. There. Right there at the bottom.

Monday, July 3   5:27pm   501-524-8786   49 sec.

"Yell County Sheriff's Department."
"Uh . . . uh, that little girl you're looking for, she's in the lake."
"Yes ma'am. Would you give me your name please?"
"No. No. You have to, you have . . . listen, she's in the lake."
"Which lake, ma'am? How do you know she's in there?"
"Uh . . . Lake Dardanelle, she's in Lake Dardanelle."
"Ma'am, how do you *know* she's in Lake Dardanelle?"
Silence.
"Ma'am, can you tell me *why* you think she's in the lake?"
Silence.
"Do you have anything else you want to report?"
"No. Uh . . .Yeah. No. But you better look in the lake, 'cause she's in there all right. And she sure didn't drown."

connection terminated   no action taken

* * *

On the red-eye into Dulles, Milo made up his mind. Ten years was enough.

The United 747 hit an air pocket at 38,000 feet, dropping abruptly before finding stable air and leveling out—springtime thermals yielding their standard bumpy ride over the Rockies. Milo had been dozing, lulled by the steady drone of the four huge, Rolls Royce engines. Seated on the upper deck in First Class, he had gratefully accepted a couple of bourbons and a late supper from an attractive stewardess. Misreading his gratitude for interest, she had been eager to chat, until he politely cut her off, saying a nap was what he really needed. The precipitous drop had jarred him awake, but he had logged too many miles to be bothered by a little turbulence. He closed his eyes and went back to sleep.

* * *

Milo leafed through the mail, hoping his check would be there. He was flat broke with the weekend fast approaching and he desperately needed an infusion of cash.

Damn. No envelope from the bank.

A cryptic note from placement caught his attention.

> Milo:
> Meet Tom. Friday, 4:00 p.m. Joey's Cafe.
> Loma Plaza Mezzanine.
>
> *P. Arledge*

What the hell did that mean?

Four weeks away from his master's degree at Stanford, Milo was facing an agonizing decision. Classified 1-A, with his student deferment due to expire in a month, he'd have to choose soon.

He could try to get into law school, three years and hope the war would be over; join the Arkansas National Guard like his cousin Richard had done, which would mean two years back in Helena; get married—forget it; or try the Peace Corps. Canada was out of the question, and he was not into self-mutilation.

At the time, Milo was leaning toward the Peace Corps, an option which would send him for two years to French speaking Cameroon. He'd be twenty-three on June 22, and the war in Vietnam had his life on hold.

Jamming his hand deep in his chino's pocket he fingered a solitary quarter. If he could cadge a dime from his roommate he could buy a pack of cigarettes. Milo hoped Tom, whoever the hell *he* was, would pick up the tab at Joey's.

In the decade of the sixties the Central Intelligence Agency was changing. No longer the exclusive preserve of moneyed Ivy Leaguers, it had widened its search for the best and the brightest—male, WASP—to include the South and West. Emphasis was shifting away from human intelligence to the technical aspects of intelligence gathering, made possible by mind boggling leaps in technology. Men of letters were still in demand, but engineers and scientists were increasingly sought after to staff the rapidly expanding DDS&T.

Recommended by a friendly academic (read Company talent scout), Milo's background and education put him squarely in the ranks of the former. While a career in espionage had never entered his head, he was not the first graduate in the spring of 1965 to see the advantage of serving his country in the CIA.

Tom explained that joining the CIA would not exempt Milo from compulsory military service. Under aegis of the Agency he would complete one year of training, rewarded by an officer's commission. Then he would be sent to a military intelligence unit (G-2) for another year. Following an honorable discharge, Milo would enter an eight months' course for junior officer trainees, held jointly at CIA headquarters in Langley, Virginia, and Ft.

Peary, the Company's rural Virginia retreat known simply as "the Farm."

From the batteries of psycholgical tests to which he was subjected, his recruiters must have predicted what Milo did not anticipate when he signed on: that he would turn out to be such a happy camper.

*　　*　　*

It was impossible to talk over the Huey's clatter without headphones. No matter. Milo was content to survey the variegated emerald carpet scrolling by beneath the chopper. Leaving behind the sooty urban sprawl of Saigon with its factories and tank farms, they flew northwest over flooded fields which gradually gave way to hillocks, growing increasingly higher as they approached their destination.

Milo had been in country for ten days. He had arrived on a commercial flight, the PanAm 707 from Don Muang escorted over Cambodian air space by Air Force fighters off either wing. Bangkok had been a terrific posting, but he had requested the transfer to Saigon in a calculated career move. All the action was centered in Saigon—by 1967 it had the largest CIA station outside of Washington. Milo thought he knew what he was getting into. He had been thoroughly briefed by his new boss, William Colby, who had returned to Vietnam just a month before to take over Operation Phoenix, a joint project of Robert Komer's Civilan Operations Revolutionary Development Staff (CORDS) and the Central Intelligence Agency.

Lacking sufficient manpower to run paramilitary ops aimed at VC infiltrators, estimated to be about 30,000 strong, from goat herds to generals, and to combat the 25,000 member *Ban-an-Ninh* (North Vietnamese Secret Police), who conducted terrorist raids in all forty-four Southern provinces, CORDS and the CIA had delegated the actual, day-to-day, nitty gritty of the operation to MACV and ARVN. Phoenix was devised to capture, coerce, turn, or kill Vietcong spies among the south's civilian population. Translated, that meant slipping into a hooch at night, slitting the suspect's throat, and taking some small souvenir as proof of mission accomplished. Any raw intelligence extracted from the captives was turned over to CIA for analysis. Overall, results had been less than triumphal.

Milo was taking a reconnaissance tour of one of the provincial interrogation centers, in the misguided notion that a first hand look would provide insight into information forwarded to his desk. He also wanted to satisfy his curiosity.

The pitch of the rotor changed. They were swooping down on a clearing, a vast linear scar slashed across a wooded plateau. Barracks dominated one end of a dirt street lined with flimsy buildings. The soldiers' quarters had been thrown up on the far side of a paved runway, running perpendicular to the road. The near side was fronted by a concrete apron.

Situated like a cork in a bottle, a squat edifice that looked like it had been put together from Lego pieces blocked one end of the street. Behind the building, coils of razor wire looped the perimeter of a stockade. A handful of detainees hunkered down in the shade, their backs turned to a lone guard carrying an AK- 47. Various military vehicles were parked haphazardly next to the building. As the helicopter descended, Milo saw a Jeep back out and head for the airstrip.

"Jesus H. Christ! Is that what I think it is?" Milo gestured at a suspicious item dangling from the key chain the major tossed casually on his desk.

"You bet your sweet ass it is. An' I got hundreds of 'em." Major Joshua Prine hefted a canvas tote from the floor, untied the cord, and offered the contents to Milo for inspection.

Milo had heard the rumors. Even in Bangkok. But this was his first encounter with the actual, bald fact. He didn't want the MACV officer to think he was a wimp, but he bigtime did *not* want to look in the bag.

"Thanks. I'll take your word for it."

Mildly offended, Prine shrugged. "Suit yourself. First time in the boonies?"

"Pretty obvious, hunh?"

"Sure as hell. Nobody's been here two weeks makes any fuss about fuckin' ears. Now this here's more like it." His voice carried a hint of grudging praise; a reluctant father acknowledging his bastard's accomplishment. "These dinks are fuckin' A crazy."

The major reached into a burlap sack, brown and crusty, producing an object of such unparalleled horror that Milo experienced a momentary illusion, a subtle shift in the time/space continuum, as though he had been sleeping and awakened to find himself twelve again, camped in his own backyard. In the darkened tent he was reading *Lord of the Flies* by flashlight, scaring the bejesus out of himself and his buddies. He closed his eyes, trying to dissolve the image. When the mist of imagination evaporated, the severed head was still there.

Milo gagged, grabbed a metal waste can and threw up over an assortment of paper wads and pencil filings, shame rising with the bile.

"You'll get used to it," Prine stated in response to Milo's discomfort. "We generally keep one around for a day or two—helps with the questioning. After that they get a little ripe, but hey, Charlie's got plenty."

Milo sucked in a lung-full of humid air, wiping spittle on his shirt sleeve. Someone was snickering in the background, obviously delighted at the Company rep's reaction to reality in the field, *fuckin' city boy don't like meetin' the natives.* Milo stared at the forty-something American officer in charge of the Agency's provincial outpost. The man had to be certifiable.

Prine looked normal enough. Glossy skin, clean shaven. Ebony, polished with a fine gloss of sweat. Muscular forearms extending from rolled up fatigues, the lightening runes of a Special Forces' patch decorating his left sleeve. Web-belted camouflage pants neatly tucked into mesh-top combat boots, the army's attempt to defeat jungle rot, a constant complaint in the hothouse that was Vietnam. The major was a recruiting poster in the flesh: hard, handsome, authoritative. Until Milo saw the madness leaking from his eyes.

"They bring 'em in from the hills to collect." Prine nudged the rucksack with the toe of his boot. "Mostly it's too hard to get prisoners down to the center. So they just kill 'em, slice off an ear, or whatever strikes their fancy, and bring that in as proof. In the beginning, we'd pay 'em for one, but two days later the same slope'd be back expecting us to pay him for the other one. So now they have to hand in a matched pair for their *piastres*, kinda like poker. Or," he directed his foot to the burlap tote, "just take the whole damn thing. That way we know they ain't cheatin'."

✴   ✴   ✴

Milo had been summoned to Washington by the Church Committee. He didn't want to testify, although he could hardly do more damage that the Director was doing himself. Milo could not imagine what religious conversion Colby had undergone that could transform the cold, calculating head of Phoenix into the born-again, confess-all DCI gutting the Company by laying bare its darkest secrets. What in God's name was the man thinking about?

Milo was not prepared to acknowledge his sins to Congress. He had stuck out the dirty work when more squeamish colleagues had requested reassignment, taking advantage of Colby's promise that they could do so without prejudice. If he were honest, Milo would admit that Angélique Ky had been a determining factor. But so what? He had done his job well, and his tenacity had paid off. He had gotten Amy and Anqélique out.

Now he *would* quit, before those bastards on the Hill got in their licks. But his dreams were still troubled.

A hand tapped his shoulder lightly. He woke with a start.

"Sir? Sir." The stewardess was holding a napkin and cutlery. "We'll be starting our descent into Dulles shortly. Would you like some breakfast before we land?"

90

*   *   *

The pages of fax from Yell County lay curled across his desk. Lost in the past, Milo hadn't noticed night creeping up outside. The first drops of a summer shower rattled against his windowpane; streetlights winked on, haloed by the rain. If he could find Addy's killer, would that lay his own ghosts to rest? At least he had a place to start. Tomorrow he'd get an address to go with the phone number; he'd drive up to Sheriff Pressler's and listen to the tape.

Tomorrow. Now it was past time to go home.

CHAPTER 9

Southwestern Bell listed 501-524-8786 as the number of a pay phone at Lester's Pit Stop, a combination truck stop/convenience store on Highway 65, just outside Turner Falls at the junction with Highway 62. Which meant that the call could have come from anyone. Undaunted, Milo walked into Paul Pressler's office at ten o'clock the next morning.

"Hey, Milo," Pressler boomed jovially, "you find anything on that printout?"

"Depends on what you'd call 'anything'," Milo replied noncommittally. "What I'd really like is to listen to the tapes. And talk to the deputy on Hot Line duty on the third."

"Well, the tapes ain't a problem—they're in the property room. I'll check to make sure who was answerin' the phone that day, but if mem'ry serves it was Chalkie Best, and he's off at his sister's weddin'."

Milo ensconced himself in an idle interview room. From a cardboard box labeled "Willis" he extracted the audiocassette of calls monitored on July third, loaded the tape in his Walkman, slipped on the headphones, and punched Play.

The first call was a hang up, as was the second. He pressed Fast Forward, skipping to the end of the tape and the call that had raised his antennae.

"Yell County Sheriff's Department."

"*Uh . . . uh . . .*" Milo closed his eyes, trying to fashion a mental image from the voice. The woman sounded young, local, and decidedly nervous. But voices were deceptive, and he was no expert. He played the brief call through, rewound, and listened again. Although clearly ill at ease, her tone carried conviction, an almost defiant sureness. By the time he had played the tape a dozen times, Milo was convinced the woman *knew* what had happened to Addy. He would take the cassette back to the State Crime Lab. Staff forensic audiologists would be able to confirm (or deny) his layman's conclusions about the speaker. Then he could devote his energy to locating that person. In the absence of any other lead, the mystery caller was truly his last hope.

Milo pumped ten bucks' worth of super unleaded into his Bronco, then entered the station. On the way to Lester's he had burned up the road between Danville (where Pressler's office occupied a floor in the Yell County courthouse) and Turner Falls, making what was ordinarily a two hour drive through some of Arkansas's most scenic countryside in under one hour and forty minutes. A sign taped to the door warned: *No shoes, no shirt, no service.* Milo entered and wandered around inside, casually examining the layout.

Half of the interior was taken up by a cafe. A steam table separated the seating area from automotive accessories, rows of snacks, toys, and shelves crammed with Razorback gewgaws and cheap, cracker-jack souvenirs of Turner Falls. Among the scarves, ashtrays, and figurines, a goodly number of religious items were for sale. Hand-crafted cedar boxes with crosses burned into the lids were filled with Bibles. A stack of brightly colored tee shirts with JESUS IS COMING! AND BOY IS HE WONDERFUL! stamped across the front caught his eye. And plates, coffee mugs, and still more tee shirts were decorated with images of the Tabernacle of Divine Redemption.

Milo evaluated the food in the buffet. He decided to pass. A short order board listed hamburgers, hot dogs, fries, and ham and cheese sandwiches.

Tucked in a short hallway behind a wall of refrigerated drink coolers he discovered two pay phones mounted side by side between doors to the restrooms. Neither phone was visible from the checkout counter. He picked up a receiver, dropped a coin in the slot, and dialed his office, more for the feel of it than from any need to communicate with headquarters. Someone using *this* phone had stood in *this* spot to call the Hot Line. Milo had to find that person.

He selected a package of snack crackers, got a bottle of iced tea from the cooler, and took his place in the checkout line. Stuck to the back of the cash register, a placard in block letters said STAND UP FOR JESUS. He had to wait while two truckers paid huge diesel bills with company credit cards. The man running the till seemed agreeable enough, chatting with one of the drivers whose Arkansas Best rig had pulled off the highway just in front of Milo.

"Think Houston's gonna have 'em ready this year?

"Don't know why not. Course last year was a roller coaster, but anytime you can knock off the defending national champions, *and* beat Texas in the Cotton Bowl, you got somethin' to crow about. Guess there's still some question 'bout the defensive line, and who'll start as quarterback, but hell, Houston's got 'em so pumped them Hogs jest might go all they way."

They were discussing the Arkansas Razorback's energetic young coach, Houston Nutt, and the upcoming football season. Milo wasn't in any hurry, content to linger in line, studying his surroundings. When his turn came, he dropped the Nabs and a twenty on the counter, holding up his drink for the cashier to see. "And that green Bronco's mine, so that's ten for the gas."

At that moment a girl pushed through swinging doors at the back of the cafe and bustled across to where Milo was waiting for his change.

"Trampas, can you cut me a check? There's some old coot out back with a bunch of Hope watermelons and he wants to get paid before he unloads 'em."

Milo's blood pressure shot off the scale. It was the same voice. The *SAME VOICE!* He couldn't be that lucky. He gathered his money from the tray and moved over to a rack of newspapers and magazines, keeping the girl in view. She was dressed in the uniform of the nineties, jeans and a tee shirt. A laminated plastic badge pinned to the tee shirt said **WENDY**. Her hair was a disaster, unevenly cropped black spikes striped with purple. Discounting the awful hair, Milo thought she might be pretty, but it was difficult to tell through her caked makeup. She had brown eyes, heavily rimmed with black eyeliner, and long lashes crusted with mascara. Magenta eye shadow matched pouting lips slicked liberally with wine glosser. Half a dozen small gold hoops marched up the side of one ear, punctuated with a diamond stud; a filigreed gold and silver cross dangled from the other lobe. He concentrated with all his might, trying to catch every word she exchanged with the man called Trampas. The entire conversation consisted of no more than a dozen sentences, but it was enough. Wendy took the check and flounced off through the kitchen door, but Milo was certain—it *was* the same voice.

He resisted his knee jerk impulse to confront the girl on the spot. There were too many imponderables. Why had she used the pay phone, when Lester's had a direct line? Did the business have a policy about personal calls or was she being furtive? What was her living situation, that she didn't use a phone at home? And why had she waited so long to respond? Addy had been missing for more than a week when the girl called. More importantly, she had adamantly refused to leave her name, meaning she didn't want to get involved. Milo's innate caution had saved him from mistakes on numerous occasions. It was his considered judgment that he needed more information before approaching her, and he also wanted expert confirmation of the girl's identity. Since she represented his one and only lead, dog excluded, he didn't want to spook her.

In a couple of days he'd make a return trip to Lester's wearing a wire, order lunch, and try to engage the girl in conversation. Then he'd take the tape to the technicians in Little Rock and let them make the match. Voice prints were as individual as fingerprints, and just as reliable. Meanwhile, he'd talk to colleagues in that part of the state and ferret out what he could about the girl, her background, and her employer. It would have to be done discreetly so he didn't sound any alarms.

From all reports, some branch of the Bolin family had lived around Turner Falls for years, hard working country people who were honest, if a tad slow. (A tad slow was putting it kindly. The general consensus was that they were all a couple of bricks short a load.) Mavis Bolin, widowed in a hunting accident, kept a tight rein on her brood. After her husband Claude was killed deer hunting with his youngest son, she was supported entirely by her five children.

Ranging from Heavy, the eldest at forty-one, down to Wendy, age nineteen, none of the Bolin progeny had ever married. Heavy worked for the Tabernacle of Divine Redemption, a fundamentalist sect with a large area following, whose majestic church rose on a bluff overlooking the Buffalo River about ten miles from town. The second son, Vonnie Lee, also worked at the church, or did odd jobs around Turner Falls. Billy Ray, the last boy, had joined the army, and from all anybody knew, was still in service. He hadn't been home since he graduated from high school. Billy Ray had been recruited by half a dozen major college football teams, but there was no way he could pass the SATs. Betty and Wendy, Mavis's two daughters, both worked at Lester's Pit Stop, a business wholly owned by the Tabernacle, as were many in those parts. Local gossips liked to speculate about Wendy's paternity, both because she was born nine months to the day after Claude Bolin's unfortunate mishap, and because she was smaller, prettier, and a good deal smarter than her siblings.

"I'll have a grilled ham and cheese on whole wheat, please ma'am. And a glass of milk, 2% if you've got it."

"Sure. You want fries or chips with your sandwich?"

"Nope. Neither one, thanks. But what about some dessert? Are those pies and cakes homemade?"

"Every morning. And they're good too. You wanna slice?"

"I don't know. What'd'ya recommend? I really like carrot cake. Y'all got any of that?"

"Yeah, we got carrot cake, but the chocolate's better."

"Okay then, I'll take your word for it. Bring me a piece of chocolate."

When Milo had finished the sandwich and polished off every crumb of his dessert the waitress sidled over.

"How'd you like that cake mister?"

"It was fine, awfully good. I'm glad I took your advice."

"You want anything else, some coffee or somethin'?"

"No thanks. Just a check, please. Hey, wait a minute. Can I borrow your phone book?"

"Our phone book? There's one out by the pay phones in the hall."

"No, there isn't. I looked just before I sat down."

Of course there wasn't one. The investigator had removed it.

Milo was sitting at a console in the State Crime Lab, listening to the tape of his encounter with Wendy Bolin. Yell county's Hot Line tape was turning simultaneously on another reel. He watched fascinated as Lois, the state's best audiologist, fiddled with an array of dials and switches, lining up fluctuating waves and spikes on the computer screen. Her forehead was creased in concentration as she fine tuned the instrument, drawing the undulating green lines closer and closer together. Then she visibly relaxed, pointing confidently at the overlapping patterns.

"You got her, Milo," the attractive brunette said with a grin. "In the ninety-eight percentile range. That's damn near perfect."

He had asked Lois's help in drawing up a list of questions, trying to get the girl to repeat 'look' or 'lake' in casual conversation. He had failed to elicit either of the key words, but he had done the next best thing: gotten her to say both 'book' and 'cake' in response to his preplanned queries. And the results were unequivocal. Wendy Bolin had made the suspicious call. Now to find

out why she had called, what she knew, and how she had gotten
her information.

Milo'd made three trips to Lester's in the course of a week
—he was getting to be a regular. The girl grinned at him when he
slid into the booth; she really *was* pretty, if she'd scrub that gunk
off her face.

"You come back for some more of that good chocolate cake?
Or the company?" She was flirting with him.

"The company, definitely. No cake today though. Just a cup
of coffee, please. Black."

It was mid-afternoon, and the small cafe was practically
deserted. A leathered driver in overalls and a plaid shirt, probably
belonging to a log truck parked outside, was Wendy's only other
customer.

She brought the coffee and set it on his table with an airy
insouciance.

"Thanks. If you've got a minute, I'd like to talk to you,"
Milo smiled at the young woman, taking her in. She had no idea
who he was, or what he wanted. He hoped she'd think he was
hitting on her.

"We-e-ell," she eyed first him, and then her empty tables,
weighing her options. Laughing, "Sure. I always got a minute for
a big spender." She perched on the edge of the seat opposite him.
"What'd'ya wanna talk about?"

"I want to know why you called the Yell County sheriff to
report that Addy Willis's body was in Lake Dardanelle, and how
you knew she hadn't drowned." He got it out fast and smooth,
blind-siding her.

The girl's jaunty air collapsed faster than a pricked balloon.
"I never," she said in a flat voice.

"Yes," he said gently. "You did. And I have the proof, so it
won't do you any good to deny it."

A measure of her confidence reasserted itself. "You got no
such thing. Who are you anyway? And what's it to you?"

Milo laid his badge on the table, turned so she could read his name. "I'm the law," he said. "And it means a great deal."

His shield lay like a challenge between them. Wendy looked around nervously, her foot tapping the tile floor. "Sheesh," she said. Her hand came up in an involuntary effort to redefine her space, exclude Milo. "Look mister. Please don't do this in here. I can't afford to get in trouble."

At that moment a fat man and blowzy woman came around the steam table and stood staring up at the sandwich board. "I gotta go," Wendy said desperately. She tried to rise, but he held her wrist.

"I need to know, Wendy. You have to tell me."

"Not now," she pleaded. "Lemme go. You don't unnerstand. *Please* mister." Milo could tell she frightened. He loosened his grasp and she jumped up as Trampas entered the cafe.

"What's goin' on?" the manager walked over to Milo's table. "You gonna' take their order?" Wendy's boss indicated the new customers. "Or do I have to?"

"I'm comin'." She scurried behind the counter.

Trampas glowered at Milo, who had hastily picked up his identification and slipped it in his pocket. "Everything all right in here?" he demanded.

Milo didn't press it. He didn't know why Wendy was afraid, but there wasn't any point in taking a chance. He would leave quietly, keep a covert eye on the place, and catch her when she went home. "Fine," he answered. "Everything's just fine."

Trampas studied Milo's table. "You can pay up now. That'll be fifty cents for the coffee. Plus tax."

Milo laid a quarter by his cup, handed a dollar to the angry manager, and walked out the door.

Most cops are accustomed to waiting—waiting is a big part of the job, so it was no hardship for Milo to park his Bronco with a good view of the Pit Stop, and settle down in anticipation of Wendy's departure at the end of her work day.

The afternoon passed; a steady stream of customers patronized the business, buying gas, food, divers items. Dusk fell, and headlights came on; still Wendy hadn't appeared. If it got completely dark he wouldn't be able to identify her in a passing car. Milo started his truck, slowly circling Lester's several times, peering into the well lighted interior. The girl wasn't there. He went around back, parked, knocked on the service door. When no one came to let him in he tried the handle. Locked. Something was wrong. Could she have gotten by him? He had had an unobstructed view of every vehicle entering and exiting the station, and he hadn't seen her leave.

He walked around front and opened the door, going directly to the checkout counter. A slender, older woman had replaced Trampas. He flashed his badge.

"Is Wendy Bolin here? Or Trampas?"

She seemed flustered. "Uh . . . um, I haven't seen Wendy. But Mr. Morgan's in the back."

Through a glass partition he could see Trampas sitting at a littered desk shoved against one wall of a cramped office.

Milo went to the end of the counter, raised the gate, and ducked through, ignoring the "Hey, you can't go in there!" protest of the new cashier.

He entered the office, his credentials extended. "Where'd she go?" he demanded.

Trampas was ice. "Where'd who go?"

Milo grabbed the manager's collar, lifting him out of the chair. "Cut the crap, buster. You know who I mean. What'd you do with the girl?"

With the ferocity of a tormented dog who has slipped its chain, Trampas broke Milo's grip. "Wendy finished her shift and went home, dickhead. You got a warrant? That badge don't mean jack shit without one. Now get your fuckin' hands off me and get outta here, before I have you arrested for trespassing."

Milo was batting a thousand. He he'd been to Lester's twice that day and been thrown out both times.

CHAPTER 10

Boyd needed to talk with Daniel. He had just gotten word from inside the administration that a date had been set for the President's next homecoming. Clinton had belatedly accepted an invitation to his Hot Springs High School reunion, slated to start Friday of the third weekend in September. The reunion coincided with the Arkansas-Alabama football game in Fayetteville. As the President billed himself the nation's number one Razorback fan, the game was an added draw.

That gave them roughly six weeks. Barely enough time. What he needed from Daniel was an okay.

The cult leader was talking on the phone when Boyd opened the side door, bypassing the outer office. Boyd motioned for him to hang up.

"It's important."

Daniel glanced at the cheap Timex he habitually wore, a far cry from the diamond studded Rolex sported by Larry during the glory days. *His* jewelry was limited to a pigeon's blood cabochon ruby, set in a plain gold band, which he wore as a constant reminder of his beloved.

He picked up a sheaf of papers. "I have a meeting at five. Let me give these to Nell and I'll meet you outside." Discussing the mission inside Tabernacle precincts would have been a dangerous breakdown of procedure. Tabernacle and bunker affairs were kept strictly segregated. Only Boyd and Heavy shuttled regularly between bases, and McKensie when he was needed at the church PC. The hardcore Foundation loyalists toiling in the bunker attended Sunday services, or prayer meeting on Wednesday night,

101

if their schedules permitted, but Daniel had absolute confidence in them not to talk.

Boyd sat on a bench in the rose garden, absently watching robins splashing in the bird bath. When Daniel joined him, the men strolled the grounds on immaculately tended paths, out of earshot of the church buildings.

"He's coming," Boyd said. No need to explain who *he* was. "Sooner than we'd figured. We've got five, six weeks, tops."

Daniel's pulse quickened. "You know this for certain?"

"Yeah. He's coming to his high school reunion. Good press, schmoozing the homefolks before the election. Pulling out all the stops for Gore. Barring some unforeseen calamity, that is." It was the closest Daniel had ever heard Boyd come to cracking a joke.

"And you still believe our original plan is compromised?" They had talked this through ad infinitum, the repercussions of McKensie's rash act.

"It's just our bad luck they found that kid's body. Without its turning up, everybody would have forgotten in no time. There's nothing to connect us, not a single thing, but I wouldn't want to give anyone a reason to come nosing around."

Daniel was silent, ruminating. He valued Boyd's opinion, but six weeks wasn't much time. The destruction of a nuclear power plant wasn't as simple as detonating a crude fertilizer bomb. Any media-hungry half-wit could get directions for that on the Internet. He hadn't thought Clinton would return to the state so soon. Not that they were planning to blow *him* up, although that might have been a good place to start. Bill Clinton personified everything Daniel hated. Timing the mission to coincide with ground-breaking ceremonies for the Clinton Library was meant to underscore the connection. And what would have been more fitting than to exact his revenge on the day America celebrated her independence? McKensie had bungled that.

*　　*　　*

Nuclear power is about heat. Heat to drive steam turbines, which generate electricity. If the technology is incomprehensible to a layman, the principle is simple. When an atom splits, a phenomenon called fission, it produces heat. Heat equals energy. Harness the heat of fission and you have an unlimited supply of energy. In Light Water Reactors, the only type licensed in the United States, the energy is transferred from the nuclear core to turbines by ordinary water. Nuclear One is a Pressurized Water Reactor, which means that the cooling pipes circulating water in a closed loop through the system are under tremendous pressure, which prevents the superheated water from boiling. Through the use of heat exchangers, the radioactive water, or primary coolant, passes its energy to a secondary loop of uncontaminated water. This is allowed to turn to steam, which powers the generators.

A small charge of Semtex, strategically placed, would blow the main cooling conduit. Pressure would do the rest. McKensie would hack into the plant's controls, overriding backup systems that would automatically shut down the reactor and keep the rods of enriched uranium from going critical after the loss of their primary coolant. But it was Boyd's master stroke of using missiles to breach the containment building that had transformed hypothesis into nuclear disaster.

For the venture to succeed a suitable launching platform was essential. There was no way to hit the reactor vessel from the front of the complex. Too much building intervened. And they were a couple of years too late for a shot from the rear. Growing from a concrete pad midway between Nuclear One and Nuclear Two, like a colony of giant sea anemones sprouting from the ocean floor, was a field of dry casks, thirty-inch-thick, concrete and steel silos designed to hold spent fuel rods for future disposal. (Two reactors are housed at the Russellville plant, but the installation is commonly called Nuke One. It didn't matter a damn to Daniel which of the reactors they took out.) A sprawl of houses, commercial buildings, and heavily trafficked roadways blocked access from the north. That left roughly a 30° arc, west-

103

south-west of the reactor, across open water. Since the missiles had to be fired from an elevated position, the possibilities were narrowed even further. And while the target could be lased from almost any spot, McKensie had to have access to a land line for the modem of his remote terminal, slaved to the main frame in the bunker. Finding an acceptable alternative was proving to be a tall order.

"And you haven't found another site? Damnit Boyd, surely there must be one somewhere."

"Maybe there is, but I haven't found it."

Daniel's eyes narrowed to slits. "Don't screw with me Boyd. You assured me if I provided everything you asked for you could deliver. Now you want me to believe the whole goddamn mission is stymied because you can't find a fucking *launching* site?" He bit off every word. "That · is · totally · unacceptable!"

"You're absolutely right," Boyd acknowledged. "But maybe there's another way."

"I don't give a good goddamn *how* you do it. You can shoot the fucking missiles from the moon for all I care. I just want the *fucking · reactor · destroyed!*" Daniel screamed, giving free rein to his fury. Then his voice dropped, taking on the menacing timbre of banked hellfire. "Do you understand me?"

Boyd certainly did.

The military strategist also knew when to retreat. He walked briskly along the path to an overlook near the edge of the bluff, turning his back on both the Tabernacle and its irate master. Far below, trout fishermen waded along the banks of the first-ever, federally designated "scenic" river. A solitary oarsman in a kayak paddled by, followed by a string of happy rafters. Light-hearted laughter floated up to him, amplified by the water. When Boyd heard Daniel's footsteps on the brick path he turned.

Brooding and hostile, the evangelist contemplated his second in command. "What other way?"

"It'll take a while."

"Okay," Daniel said. "Why not? I've got all the time in the world. Those shitkickers at the church can wait. Suppose you tell me what you have in mind."

＊　　＊　　＊

Her place was out from town, six miles past Picken's store. Go out the County Line; take Fielding Road at the fork, the first fork—if he saw a blue and white pre-fab he'd gone too far; hers was the fourth house on the right. He couldn't miss it.

Three sagging steps led to the porch. Supporting the steps, a truncated brick pillar, which most places would have worn a pot of petunias, geraniums, or mother-in-law tongues, was crowned with a wilted plastic bouquet. In the anemic glow of a forty watt bulb Milo could see layers of paint peeling from the faded door. The doorbell had succumbed to extreme old age. Milo knocked, listened for a moment, then knocked again.

Eventually the door opened a crack, revealing without doubt, one of the homeliest women Milo had ever seen. He guessed she was in her mid thirties, but it was impossible to tell. Bangs might have disguised the abnormally high forehead, but no stylist had wielded scissors near this woman's head. Falling straight from a center part, her lank brown hair was anchored behind protruding ears. One eye wandered lazily, while the other tried to steady itself on his face. Her nose must have been broken at some time, for it descended at an angle, as if trying to compensate for the restless eye. Thin, colorless lips exposed crooked teeth.

Milo extended his badge. "Is Mrs. Bolin at home? I'm Captain Milo Thomas, Special Investigator with the Arkansas State Police." When the woman didn't move or reply, he added, "May I come in? It's about Wendy."

Aiming her good eye into the house, the woman swung the door wide, standing aside in invitation. The smell hit him first, the acrid stench of something dead. He stifled an impulse to gag and entered, holding his breath. Having admitted him without a word, the troglodyte shut the door, crossed the room, and retreated through a door on the far side, closing it behind her. Milo was stranded.

Spider webs of cat hair festooned the backs and arms of the Bolins' living room furniture, fur variations of the crocheted anti-macassars in his great Aunt Annie Lou's parlor. A fifty-two inch Sony played soundlessly to the empty room. Next to the TV, a plastic litter box rested on several thicknesses of stained, yellow newsprint. From the godawful odor it was evident that the paper and litter box hadn't been changed anytime recently. He caught another whiff and gagged again. That did it. He would not stay there any longer. At that moment the woman reappeared, waving him toward the door she was holding ajar. Milo was through it in a flash.

One glance at the amazon presiding over the kitchen told Milo that she was Mavis Bolin, the redoubtable matriarch of the clan. The ugly woman must be Wendy's sister, though there certainly wasn't much family resemblance. Mavis had to be sixty at least, but her plump face was unlined. Enormous arms, balloon breasts, and a bulging belly stretched her white tee shirt beyond decency. She had on jeans and new Reeboks, and a wide leather belt cinched what must have been a fifty inch waist. Her hair had been permed, or perhaps it was naturally curly, wiry gray tendrils escaping from a woven leather headband. She looked, he decided, in the vernacular of the Arkansas delta, like a bale of cotton tied in the middle.

Mavis stood at a butcher block, an honest-to-God, old fashioned, heavy maple square, rooted on thick, turned maple legs. Round brass escutcheons decorated the sides, and its center was hollowed from years of use. A dish towel smeared with reddish streaks hung from a brass hook tacked to one corner. Holding a carving knife in her right hand, and a matching, bone-handled fork in her left, Mavis was slicing glistening strips from a raw beef liver splayed on the block, pausing periodically to wipe and hone the blade.

"Kitty, kitty, kitty," she called as she carved. "Here, kitty, kitty, kitty." A discordant chorale of anxious mewing filtered through a screen door leading to the back yard. Outside, cats of every size and description were pushing and scratching at the screen, prevented from clawing through the ragged mesh by an aluminum grid covering the door's lower half. Leaving Milo to fend for himself, his guide resumed her post as gatekeeper.

Periodically the dominant male, a battle-scarred yellow tom, would launch himself at the screen. Hanging on defiantly, he would claw his way to the top of the metal barricade. When he reached the upper, unprotected portion of wire, Mavis's offspring would knock him back. Milo caught her roving eye; detected a glint of vicious pleasure as she whacked the screen with the flat of her palm, sending the old tom sprawling. Apparently undeterred, he would regroup and try again. Milo judged the contest to be a regular ritual.

"Dinner's almost ready," Mavis crooned, expertly severing the last of the liver. The younger woman opened the door, and more than two dozen fluff balls burst across the threshold, all bent on the slimy mound heaped on the chopping block. Mavis stood her ground, even as two or three of the bolder felines tried to climb her legs to get to the food.

She dropped morsel after morsel into the roiling mass. When the block was bare she moved away, allowing the cats to jump up on its bloody, gelatinous surface. While they scoured the maple board, Mavis rinsed off her carving utensils and washed her hands.

"Tuesday's liver," she explained without preamble. "Wednesday's chitlins. Friday's fish. They look forward to their mama's little treats." She dried her hands on her rump. "I'm Mavis. You must be that cop that's lookin' for Wendy. She ain't here."

So much for catching Wendy's mother off guard. Trampas must have called. "Yes ma'am. I'm Milo Thomas, with the State Police. I just want to talk to Wendy." He glanced from Mavis to the other woman. "Do either of y'all have any idea where I might find her?"

Mavis ignored his question, following his gaze. "That there's Betty. She's the dumb one." She cackled at the tired joke, pleased to have someone new to spring it on. "Know'd soon as she were born she warn't quite right. Twenty-nine an' ain't never said a word. She kin work, though." Betty drooped her head, staring blankly at the filthy, brick-patterned linoleum. "She cleans up an' washes dishes mos' days down at Lester's and brings home the scrapin's for my babies."

Abruptly, as if she had somehow slipped up, Mavis turned and headed for the odoriferous living room. *Oh no. No way.* The thought of conducting an interview in the reeking chamber made Milo's stomach heave.

"It's such a pleasant evening," he said quickly, "why don't we talk outside."

Mavis seemed surprised by the request, squinting at the investigator for a moment in indecision. He could see the wheels turning. *What was he up to? Was he trying to trick her?* Milo smiled his best smile to reassure her.

She made up her mind. "Okay, if that's what you want. Betty kin git us a beer."

Trailing a comet's tail of sated, purring animals, Mavis led the detective to a group of lawn chairs near a tumbled-down shed. Cats twined around her ankles, licking their chops. Their "mama" lowered her impressive bulk into a glider.

"Set," she instructed.

Milo sat.

Sipping beer with Mavis while the feline menagerie frolicked at his feet, it didn't take long for Milo to tell he wasn't going to learn anything from that quarter. Slow, maybe. Stupid, no way. Mavis had no intention of telling Milo squat. But what was she covering up? And why? And who or what was Wendy afraid of? His only lead had taken a powder, but he wasn't going to find out anything from her mother. The scene in the kitchen should have told him. Mavis was a predator.

Milo rose. "Thanks for the beer, Mrs. Bolin. If you hear from Wendy, please give me a call. Here's my card. I just want to talk to her, that's all." He left, walking around the house to his truck. Mavis creaked back and forth in the glider, Jabba the Hut in drag, boring holes in his back until he rounded the corner.

As he neared the Bronco, out of sight of the back yard, Betty shambled down the front steps. She came straight to him, thrust a folded piece of paper in his hand, and went shuffling back in the house. In the dark Milo couldn't make out what was written on the scrap. He got in his truck and flicked on the reading lamp. A single line angled across the paper. In neat, precise script, it said:

Heavy come an took her away.

CHAPTER 11

"Where're we going?" Wendy wheedled, hoping Heavy's attitude would change, but it was no use. He kept staring straight ahead and wouldn't talk to her.

They turned off 65 and for a few minutes she was afraid he was taking her to Mike's, and she *really* didn't want to go there. He'd be so pissed no telling what he'd do, but she relaxed a little when her brother drove past McKensie's trailer. She tried again. "Com'on Heavy, please don't be mad. Please. Please. I didn't tell that cop a thing. Honest. You can ask Trampas. I didn't say a word. Just take me home. Com'on. Please Heavy. Why can't we just go home?"

Several miles later he turned onto the gravel lane that led to the chicken farm. It was the end of the road. "You wait here," Heavy directed, getting out of his truck in front of the manager's house. Wendy twisted anxiously on the vinyl seat, picking at a hangnail until it bled.

He wasn't gone long, reappearing with a doughy, fortyish woman wearing sturdy shoes and an apron over a housedress. "Bring her in the office," she said, giving Wendy the once-over. "We'll keep an eye on her while you talk to Brother Daniel."

While Wendy squirmed Mrs. Williams hastily emptied the medicine cabinet and unplugged the bedside phone. Heavy talked in low tones to her husband, leaving Wendy to wonder what she had gotten herself into. *Why, oh why, hadn't she kept her mouth shut?* She'd never seen Heavy so mad before. But then, she never expected some dumb policeman to come looking for her either.

Flora emerged from the inner room, carrying a cardboard box. "I reckon that's everything," she said. "Heavy, you kin go on now. She'll be all right."

Flora Williams might look like a frumpy housewife, but she was tough as a nickel steak. She had taken one look at Wendy's hairdo, makeup, multiple earrings and scowled with disapproval. No sooner had the men gone than she hissed at the girl. "I seen you paradin' around church, you little hussy, painted up like a two-bit whore. Well, it ain't gonna do you a whit o' good here. Now git in that room and keep yore trap shut and maybe we can kin git along."

"Fuck you, you old bitch," Wendy blurted defiantly.

Mrs. Williams slapped her across the face, a stinging blow that made Wendy's eyes smart, pushed her in the tiny room, and turned the key.

Next morning Heavy brought his sister clean jeans and a sack of tee shirts and undies from home, thrusting them at her as though she were a stranger. She asked for toiletries and was given a comb, brush, toothpaste, toothbrush, and a tube of Vaseline. The old biddy had left shampoo and soap in the bathroom, but that was all.

After two days in the cramped space Wendy swallowed her pride and offered to help in the kitchen as a temporary expedient to get out of her cell. Her face was scrubbed and her hair freshly washed, curling every which way without gel or a blow dryer. Mrs. Williams understood what she was up to, but she could use the help, and there wasn't anywhere the girl could go. So at noon and again at suppertime, Wendy was frog marched through the house and into the kitchen. She noticed the location of two telephones, for all the good that did her. Her third day as scullery maid Daniel surprised them, throwing a violent hissy fit when he found her at the kitchen sink. After that Wendy stayed locked in her room.

Mr. Williams—Harlan, had "donated" the chicken farm to the Tabernacle and stayed on as its manager. He ran a profitable operation, as were all the church's business ventures. Mrs. Williams's primary function seemed to be cooking for the men in the bunker. Flora was a good cook. Her food was better than Mavis's and much better than the slop they dished up at the Pit Stop. Wendy was getting fat sitting around feeding her face, watching television, and reading crappy magazines. Mainly, she alternated between being bored out of her gourd and scared to death.

*　　*　　*

Grady Davenport rolled a soggy, unlit cigar over to the corner of his mouth, scratched his fringe of sandy hair, and grunted, "See ya two and raise ya five."

"Too rich fer my blood." His opponent, a rail thin man with a nervous twitch, wearing the orange jumpsuit of a jailbird, laid his cards face down on the bunk. "Dammit, Grady, you took all my smokes fer a week. What'm I s'posed to do now?" Loose cigarettes were piled in front of the balding jailer, along with sixty-three cents in change and an unopened pack of Camels.

"Cain't pay, don't play." Grady was scooping the tobacco currency into a plastic bag when someone came up behind him, to the obvious delight of the loser.

"Davenport, you fleecin' the inmates again? Thought I told you they was off limits."

"Aw com'on Marshal, it's jest William Harold, an' he don't count."

"Give him back his cigarettes and get out here," the Marshal said firmly. "Somebody wants to talk to you."

Grady grudgingly handed over the plastic bag and followed his boss out of the cell, locking it behind them.

Milo needed to locate someone who could tell him more about the Bolin clan. Somehow he had so threatened Wendy that she had disappeared, and according to Betty, with her brother's complicity. But against her will? Or by her own design? Milo had known the girl was frightened, but *why* and *of whom* remained mysteries. Surely she had been trying to help when she made the anonymous Hot Line call. If she had been directly involved in Addy's death, it didn't make sense for her to have notified the authorities. Therefore Milo had to assume that she believed herself endangered by whatever guilty knowledge she possessed, but he was at a loss as to whether Wendy felt threatened by him, in the guise of the law, or some outside force he had yet to discover. Whichever, he *had* to find out what she knew. Mavis would do him no favors, and thanks to his own poor judgment, he was persona non grata at Lester's, so that was a dead end.

Milo had slept fitfully after his encounter with Mavis Bolin, his dreams peopled with both the quick and the dead. There was something out of kilter in that household, something *dark*. A creepy sensation that had nothing to do with the stench or the family's horde of cats. Maybe it was the casual cruelty with which Mavis put down her daughter, or the ill concealed glee Betty exhibited repelling the old tom. He couldn't put his finger on just what was bothering him, but *something* was off. And Milo knew better than to discount the feeling.

He was up well before dawn, drank a cup of tea, skimmed the morning paper, and left Little Rock at first light, headed back to Turner Falls.

Atop a column at the foot of Main Street, a Confederate soldier stood frozen at attention, forever awaiting a battle lost a hundred and forty years earlier. Milo circled the monument and turned left. Down an alley two streets off Main, backing on a vacant lot, sat the Turner Falls jail and Marshal's office, a two story concrete block building painted lime-sherbet green. Even without the sign out front, bars on the second floor windows indicated its primary function. A morning glory-covered trellis screened the entrance from the alley, effort of a City Beautiful campaign, and an American flag hung limply in the heat.

"What can you tell me about Wendy Bolin, and her brother Heavy?" Milo didn't waste time, once he had introduced himself to the town Marshal.

"Not a whole lot I reckon you don't already know," Marshal George Hildebrand answered. "But I got me a sergeant, Grady Davenport, he's the jailer here, grew up with Heavy. Them kids used to be inseparable. Started to school together, but Heavy just couldn't keep up. It's a shame about them boys. Strong as oxes, and about as slow. Got their mammy's looks and their pappy's brains. All but the little one. In Wendy's case 'twere t'other way around. A right smart number o' folks hold Claudie *weren't* her pa at all, but I ain't one of 'em. A bit on the wild side that one, an' sly as a fox. She'll get out from under Mavis's thumb one o' these days."

"She and Mavis're not so dumb then?"

"No siree. Not by a long shot. Claude had the wooden head. Folks 'round town used to call him 'Knothead' Claudie. Sawed off little shrimp. Don't know why on earth she married him, big strappin' gal like that. It boggles the mind, thinkin' about that couplin'. No accountin' for people's tastes, though."

Hearing the Marshal vindicate his take on Mavis Bolin partially restored Milo's battered self-esteem. "Is Davenport here, Marshal? If he is I'd like to talk to him."

"Sure thing. By now he should've just about finished cleanin' out William Harold's cache of cigarettes. Wanna cup a coffee or somethin'? I'll go get him."

"Me an' Heavy go way back, Cap'n Thomas. We been friends all our lives. It's just I don't see him much anymore, not since he got religion."

"How is that Grady? You make it sound like some kind of disease."

"I guess that's what it is with some folks. Though I wouldn't hardly have thought to put it that way. A disease." Grady pondered the notion. "Kinda affects their reason, if you know what I mean. Go right off the deep end. Times o' trouble, folks jest natur'ly turn to the Lord, or away from Him. Seed lots of both kinds. Some of 'em get over it; some never do. Near as I can tell, Heavy's been treadin' that path goin' on fifteen years. Since right after Billy Ray up an' joined the army."

"Was Heavy in some kind of trouble?"

"Not hardly. At least, none I ever heard about. An' I think I would'a heard. See, Heavy was the oldest, so the responsibility fell on him to see to his Ma and the younguns after their daddy got hisself kilt. He would a bin twenty-one, two, somethin' like that at the time. Then come Vonnie Lee, then Billy Ray, then Betty, an' nobody even knew about Wendy. Fer a while after Claudie died, four or five years, everythin' was okay. Then all of a sudden, Wendy wadn't hardly outta diapers, Heavy jest up and lef."

"Well, if he wasn't in trouble, something must have set him off. Can you think of anything that happened to upset him? Was he worried about his brother's enlisting? Girl trouble? Something at home?"

"Nosir, Cap'n, I ain't got no idea. An' I give it considerable thought. It jest wadn't like him to go off like that. The war was over by then, so he wadn't worried about Billy Ray. An' Heavy was awful shy, never really had a girl friend. Didn't want nobody to fix him up, neither. See, the thing was, somehow he got mixed up with them folks over at Redfern, that Foundation of Eternal Life. A whole bunch of 'em come through here one day, witnessin' and handin' out leaflets. Some of 'em hung around fer a while, camped out next to the Exxon station where Heavy was workin', bummin' meals an' preachin' to anybody'd who'd listen. Next thing you know, Heavy'd up an' lef, an' moved in with them people."

"So that really surprised you, Heavy's joining the cult?"

"You better believe it."

"What about his mother? She must have resented his going off and leaving her high and dry."

"Well now, that's another funny thing; Mavis never said much one way or t'other. An' she warn't never one to hold her tongue. With Billy Ray goin' off t' the service an' all, that jest left Vonnie Lee t' put bread on the table. Betty had dropped outta school by then, an' she did what she could t' hep out. An' Wendy was jest a tiny little thing. Mavis had a right hard time there fer a while. Then one day Heavy come back right as rain, like nothin' never happened. An' he's been here ever since. Though it ain't like it use t' be. Nowadays he spends all his time workin' fer that preacher, Brother Daniel, got that fancy church out there off 65, overlookin' the Buffalo."

"So since he's been back you and Heavy don't get together much anymore?"

"Well, you know how it is. I got me a wife an' fam'ly now. An' Heavy's tied up with the Tabernacle." Grady shrugged apologetically. "An' truth be told," he lamented, "ain't neither one o' us young bucks no more."

"Thanks Grady," Milo said, hiding a smile at the sergeant's obvious paunch and natural tonsure. "I really appreciate your telling me about Heavy. Do you mind if I ask, do you go to church there too, out at the Tabernacle?"

"Nosir. I'm a Baptist born and bred. But there's a heap o' folk around here goes there. An' a lot of 'em runnin' biznesses here in town. They ain't like that bunch from over at Redfern though. They ain't never caused nobody no trouble, from what I kin tell."

"Well, I'm sure you're right Grady. Listen, since you know the family so well, is there anything you can tell me about Betty, or Wendy, before I go?"

"Lor, pore Betty. Ugly as a goat's butt sewed with grape vine, with a few saw briars throwed in. Mavis tried to send her t' school, but the kids picked on her somethin' awful. She ain't deaf, ya know. She jest cain't talk. I reckon that jest about broke her heart, listenin' t' all that cacklin'. She finished sixth grade, but she wouldn't go back. County sent a social worker around, but it didn't do no good. Heavy said she didn't haf t' go, so that were the end of it."

"And Wendy?"

"Shoot, if she ain't a piece o' work. Pretty as a picture, when she was little. But got up somethin' awful now. Kinda went boy crazy, I guess. Finished school a couple o' years ago, bin workin' at Lester's ever since."

"Do you know if she has a boyfriend? Someone special? Or somebody she likes to hang around with? It's really important."

"Nobody in partic'lar comes to mind, Cap'n Thomas. I seed her with a half dozen diff'rent fellas. Now don't hold me to this, I may be talkin' through my hat, but I 'spect Trampas, that's the fella runs the Pit Stop since the Tabernacle bought out Lester Campbell, is stuck on her. Stop in there fer coffee, he's always moonin' around, lookin' over her shoulder. Don't think she gives him the time 'o day though. That little missy's lookin' fer bigger game."

✻   ✻   ✻

Milo took the stairs to the second floor, which housed the Newspaper, Government Publications, and Genealogy Room of the Little Rock Public Library. He signed in. The clerk on duty, an elderly woman with an untidy mass of upswept gray hair and a pair of spectacles dangling around her neck from a beaded chain, led him to a double row of back-to-back metal filing cabinets and showed him how to thread the microfilm scanner.

It would be nice if Milo knew what he was looking for, but he didn't. He began sorting through boxes of microfilm, searching twenty-year-old copies of the *Arkansas Gazette* and the *Arkansas Democrat* for some clue to Heavy Bolin's bizarre behavior.

For that's what it had been: bizarre. Without provocation, no grown man, no matter if his elevator did stop a couple of floors short, left a paying job and family responsibilities to run off and join the circus. Heavy had to have been running *from* something, or *to* something. Odds were on *from*. Because from what Milo

117

had gleaned about the Foundation of Eternal Life, Heavy had only traded whatever demons he had been fleeing for different Furies.

Before turning to the library, Milo had combed State Police archives in quest of data on both the Bolins and Brother Daniel's Tabernacle of Divine Redemption. The Bolins were remarkably unremarkable. He found that one Eddy Albert Bolin, (a cousin of Claudie's?) had been sent to the pen for bigamy, but his sentence had been commuted after wife number one agreed to a divorce, and wife number two decided she didn't want 'the little weasel' either. That was all he had come up with.

Intelligence gathering on the Tabernacle proved to be more rewarding.

Founded in Turner Falls in 1984, by a Reverend Daniel Selestak, the newly minted religion was registered with the state as a non-profit organization. During the first three years of its existence, an ever increasing membership had held services in an empty Magic Mart. Purchased at rock bottom after the discount chain went out of business, the commercial building sheltered Brother Daniel's flock while construction was underway on his ministry's fantastic temple going up off Highway 65. [The availability of the large space was one determinant in Daniel's selection of Turner Falls as his headquarters. Before making the final break with Larry and the Foundation, he had scouted northern Arkansas for a suitable location to set up shop. Buying the defunct store was Daniel's first investment on his own.] When his neo-Greek temple was ready, Daniel had a brand new tenant lined up for the Magic Mart property, a processor making kiln-dried hardwood squares for the furniture industry. More real estate transactions followed. Then the Tabernacle began buying up local businesses and staffing them with converts. Lester's Pit Stop was on the list, as were a dry cleaners, a Sonic, a chicken farm, a hardware store, an FM radio station broadcasting inspirational programming and religious music (KTDR, 89.7 on your radio dial), a Buffalo River guide service and float trip outfitter, and a video rental franchise. Up to that point, Daniel had duplicated Larry's practices, but there the similarities ended.

Milo could find no record of any legal actions or tax claims against the Tabernacle. It boasted no fenced compound guarded by gun-toting followers. No sweat shops turning out high priced, specialty clothing. No bands of stewards patrolling the streets of Turner Falls. While the Reverend *did* occupy a nice house on his church grounds, positioned to take advantage of the superb view, the dwelling was by no means pretentious. That distinction fell to the Tabernacle. Brother Daniel's organization paid its taxes, paid its employees, paid its bills.

Milo nearly put his eyes out scrolling through all of 1980 and 1981 without seeing a single article that would explain Heavy's sudden conversion. In three days of non-stop reading he came across absolutely nothing that he could connect to Heavy Bolin, or to any of the Bolins, for that matter. He did read a series of contemporary stories about the Van Hornes, wry footnotes in the aftermath of Laura's death and Larry's crash and burn.

Still searching, he started on issues from 1982. Milo ran the *Gazette* film first. Nothing. And then he found it. Not what had sent Heavy running to the Foundation, but the tie-in.

On April 17, 1982, the *Arkansas Democrat* had run a story on the front page of Section D, reporting the Foundation's inability to keep Laura alive through prayer. Accompanying the article was a photograph. Front and center were a smiling couple, she fair and blonde, he bearded and heavy set wearing wrap-around dark glasses, posed under the marquee of the Van Horne Dinner Theater in Arkhola. In the background, but clearly in focus, stood a younger version of Daniel Selestak.

*   *   *

The Federal Bureau of Investigation keeps files on many people—just check with the White House—but Milo didn't think folks at the J. Edgar Hoover Building would be receptive to his request, so he asked Quentin instead.

By virtue of alphabetical placement, Milo had found himself seated, during a joint briefing a couple of years back, next to an articuate FBI agent named Quentin Thomasino, Q.C. for short. The two lawmen had hit it off immediately, in spite of quantum differences in background and personality.

Thomasino had been posted to Arkansas after Bill Clinton's reelection to the Presidency, and he was not overjoyed with the assignment. A black graduate of Yale Law, he had attended college courtesy of Uncle Sam. Following an uneventful tour in the Navy, Quentin enrolled in NYU so he could live at home while pursing his undergraduate studies. He finished in three years, working part time as a bouncer in a ballroom dance parlor. His grades were good enough to get him into Yale. Completing law school at twenty-seven, he was actively recruited by the Bureau, which had come under intense scrutiny for its conspicuous lack of minority faces. Little Rock was his second posting. Quentin planned to make it to Washington by age thirty-five. He was hip, single, loved bright lights, hated the great outdoors.

Milo and Quentin's friendship was cemented the day a drug bust they had both been working was blown because another agent, on Bureau instructions, tipped off the main suspect. Milo's politically incorrect protest had earned him a reprimand. When he got home, angry and disgusted, Quentin had been waiting on his doorstep.

"I didn't know, Milo, you gotta believe me. I'm as hacked as you are. I've been dogging those motherfuckers all day, and they ain't sayin' beans." Quentin rose, a fifth of Jack Daniel's in one hand, a six-pack of Beck's in the other, and stood aside hopefully while Milo fitted his key in the lock. "So, you gonna ask me in or what?"

"Yeah, Q.C. Come on in. I know it's not your fault. Both of us got screwed. Anyway, I hate to see good booze go to waste."

Their commiserations morphed, over several boiler-makers, into shared confidences, forging bonds of mutual respect. If the chips were down, Quentin was one person Milo could count on.

*   *   *

If Brother Daniel's religious empire was squeaky clean, he himself was certainly known to the Bureau. He might have distanced himself from the van Hornes, might even have tried to discredit Larry after Laura's death. Might, in fact, have cooperated with authorities trying to close down the Foundation. But he had kept the books, his signature was on Foundation checks. That Daniel had never been charged with the crimes that brought Larry down, Milo discovered, reading through copies of the files Quentin had handed him with a "you've never seen this" admonition, was precisely because he *had* furnished evidence against his former partner.

That was the link, the one Milo was certain there had to be. Why hadn't he realized that Daniel had emigrated from the Foundation? Heavy was back home not because he had left the Foundation of Eternal Life, but because part of the Foundation, scrubbed up and dressed in new clothes, had come with him.

It had been sixteen years since Daniel had left the Redfern complex, and the public watchdogs had quit growling. Brother Daniel was not a carbon copy of Larry Van Horne. He was a disbled veteran who eschewed the trappings of celebrity, maintaining, as far as Milo could tell, a celibate and law-abiding lifestyle. If the preacher's theology was reactionary, geared to the ultra rightwing, that wasn't a crime—at least not in America. Above all, he appeared to be a smart businessman.

There was no denying that the dynamic minister had a wide and devoted following. To those of a certain mindset, Daniel was, indeed, a modern savior.

CHAPTER 12

On the Sunday morning sidewalks, wishin', Lord, that I was stoned,
'Cause there's something in a Sunday makes a body feel alone;
And there's nothin' short of dyin' half as lonesome as the sound
On the sleeping city sidewalks; Sunday mornin' comin' down.
—Kris Kristofferson

Milo came out of the Tabernacle in a throng of families heading home to fried-chicken Sunday dinners, lawn mowers, softball games, and naps on the couch. He couldn't equate the cheerful babble of Daniel's parishioners with their preacher's apocalyptic message. The happy sounds got to him. He did *not* want to go back to his empty apartment.

Yellville, Evening Star, Big Flat, Fifty-Six. Little towns with names like poetry, iambic stops along Arkansas Scenic Route 14 between Turner Falls and Mountain View. Milo got in his Bronco and turned toward Fifty-Six, seeking an anodyne to the loneliness. He hadn't toured Blanchard Springs Caverns in years, not since the Forest Service had opened a second, lower trail. In the underground labyrinth it would be cool—and dark.

He had slipped quietly into one of the back pews just as the service was getting underway. The Tabernacle was crammed with people, but a couple had scooted down, making room for Milo on the aisle. No sooner had he entered the church than the massive doors swung shut on oiled hinges, blocking access to further stragglers. Then the lights dimmed, and in the semi-darkness he could actually feel the crowd's excitement.

Milo had not been to church in a very long time. He could count on the fingers of one hand how many times he had sat through a religious service in the past twenty years. In 1980, he had gone, of necessity, to his mother's funeral, and seven years later, his father's. He had knelt in the small Episcopal church in Helena the year after his father's death, listening to the Bishop consecrate a new Sunday school wing provided for in his father's will. And once, in a moment of weakness during the Persian Gulf War, Milo had sought the precincts of Little Rock's breakaway Anglican congregation, which, like himself, still clung stubbornly to the comforting language of the old prayer book, to pray for the deliverance of America's servicemen and women.

The congregation was standing, leafing through hymnals as the majestic strains of *A Mighty Fortress is Our God* reverberated through the sanctuary. Milo thought back to Grady Davenport's homespun wisdom: in times of trouble, people turn to God, or away from Him. Milo had turned away. Whatever had befallen Heavy Bolin had caused the opposite effect. Milo had spent all the past week trying to discover what that might have been, and so far, he had been unsuccessful.

But he would keep digging. For he was slowly coming to suspect, based on gut instinct triggered by Wendy Bolin's abrupt disappearance, that somehow this fundamentalist sect, or some of its members, were mixed up in Addy's death.

He just could not fathom why.

*　　*　　*

Monday morning Milo had to get back to the office. He had become so obsessed with the Willis case and its strange permutations that he was letting his other work slide, leaving Marilyn to cover his ass.

A pile of mail had accumulated on his desk, capped with a stack of message slips in Marilyn's scrawl. Topping the stack, a yellow Post It in the same hand bitched: *Don't you ever check your voice mail?*

He bent to the task of catch-up, answering letters, returning phone calls, logging on to the computer to update files. At noon he ran out to Park Plaza, found a parking space in the lower deck, inhaled fries and a Chick-Fil-A, and hurried to Dillard's candy counter, where he blew a quick twenty-five bucks on chocolates for Marilyn—Fudge Love, truffles, and plump glacéed apricots dipped in milk chocolate. Thus armed, Milo was back at head-quarters in less than an hour.

Her back was turned when he got off the elevator. He tip-toed in, sneaking up behind her. "Gotcha," he said in her ear.

She swung round, startled, saw who it was and took a swipe at him. "Milo, you idiot, you nearly scared me to death."

Milo doffed an invisible hat, bowed, and presented the box of candy. "Mea culpa," he said. "You have my heartfelt apologies."

A small audience had gathered to watch the show. Marilyn accepted his offering, untied the gold string, and examined the contents. He knew he had her. She selected one of the apricots, broke off a piece of chocolate, and popped it in her mouth.

"Ordinarily I can't be bought," she said, slipping a fingernail under the chocolate and peeling another sliver from the golden fruit. "How-e-v-e-r, since the surgeon general says a chocolate a day will keep me from having a heart attack over your antics, I *will* make an exception."

Applause broke out from the gallery.

"Thank you, ladies and gentlemen." Milo was feeling a mite foolish. "You may crawl back into your cubbyholes any time."

"Hey, Marilyn," one of the diehards persisted, "aren't you gonna pass it around?"

"Yeah, give him a piece, Marilyn," Biggers sang out from the back. "He ain't had any in ages."

Someone else leered, "That's right. Let him have a piece."

Another took up the chorus. "Me! me! I wanna piece too."

"All right, that's enough. Watch your mouth Biggers. The show's over."

As their snickering colleagues drifted away, Marilyn handed Milo a manila envelope. "This came up from the mail room last Friday while you were gone. It got mixed in with a bunch of other stuff. I'm sorry. I just now found it again." She paused, "And thanks for the candy. You didn't have to."

"I know I didn't and you're welcome. I'm sorry I've been such a pain."

Milo's phone was ringing. He sprinted for his desk.

"Thomas."

"You want to get up here right now." The Colonel wasn't asking a question.

Milo didn't exactly hotfoot it to his boss's office, but he knew better than to tarry. Burton was upset about something. *Shit*, he thought, *what have I done now?* Earlier in the day he had dodged one unpleasant interview, grateful to find that the head of his review board was out of town. While many of Milo's duties were discretionary, he was required to give regular updates to the committee of department heads responsible for keeping him in line. But the committee was a polite invention. Basically, Milo was responsible to the Colonel.

It didn't take long to find out what the trouble was. What he had done was tromp all over the toes of the special investigator in the first district.

"What's this about Milo? Is there some reason you're gallivanting all over Terry Weltlich's territory asking questions about some religious group up on the Buffalo? You haven't got enough problems here to handle? I cut you a lot of slack because you're good at what you do, better than anybody in the department, but lately, you've been off on a tangent. Just what the hell is it with you?"

"Burton, believe me, I am *not* trying to horn in on Terry's patch. What I've been doing is following up the investigation on that little girl's death, the one from Dardanelle that got fished out of the river here in Little Rock. There's something strange going on there, and I think some members of that church may be involved. Terry's a good man. I'm sorry he got miffed."

"You mean to tell me that all this time, for two solid weeks, you been running around chasing your tail over *one* case? What have you got?"

So this wasn't just about Terry. "Nothing I can put a finger on," Milo admitted. He tried to explain. "It's got a bad smell, Colonel. I just need more time to figure out what's going on."

"Nope. That's it Milo. You're wasting your time, and ours. And you had no business poking around in Terry's backyard without consulting him. Turn the case back over to Pressler, drop it, or write it off."

"I can't," Milo said simply.

"Then you'll have to do it on your own. Take a week. Take two. You've got the days coming. But when you get back here, this department requires your undivided attention. Is that clear?"

"But . . ."

"No buts. That's an order."

Milo went back to his desk in a blue funk. What was he going to do now? Take off, that's what, just like Burton had told him to, as soon as he could clear out all the crap he had allowed to pile up. What made matters worse was that Milo knew the Colonel was right. He wasn't acting responsibly. And he would have been mad as hell if one of the other detectives had infringed on his space, without even a courtesy call.

Staring at him from the top of the heap was the buff colored envelope Marilyn had handed him seconds before the Colonel's angry call. He had forgotten all about it.

The envelope bore the return address of the Department of the Army. Covering all his bases, Milo had petitioned the Army for background information on Billy Ray Bolin. If Billy Ray had been a high priority, he could have pulled some strings to have his request expedited. But the Bolin boy had been gone a long time. With no reason to believe he was mixed up in anything happening now, Milo had been content to let his request percolate through channels.

Given the ponderous nature of the military bureaucracy, he had not expected an answer to his inquiry for God knows when. Milo was agreeably surprised at the speed of the response.

He slit open the flap. The letter was a bombshell.

DEPARTMENT OF THE ARMY
National Personnel Records Center
9700 Page Boulevard
St. Louis, Mo. 63132-5200
July 31, 2000

Captain Milo Thomas
Arkansas State Police
1 State Police Plaza Dr.
Little Rock, AR 72209
Subject: Bolin, Billy Ray

Dear Captain Thomas:

This is in reply to your letter of July 17, instant, re
Billy Ray Bolin, born 10-11-62, in Turner Falls, AR.
We are authorized to inform you that according to our
files, no service record exists for this person. As far
as we can assertain, he is not now, nor has he ever
been, a member of the United States Army.
If we can be of further assistance in this matter, please
contact Earl. G. Blankenship, Special Inquiry Branch,
at the above address.

Sincerely,
David L. Butts
David L. Butts,
Director

---

*   *   *

"I had to, Miss Laura. Had to. Couldn't do nothin' else. He was gettin' at her, see." The big man was sobbing. "What am I gonna do? I've got the mark of Cain on me fer sure."

Laura put her hands on his shoulders, let them rest there while he cried himself out. When his tears had subsided she urged gently, "Tell me about it Heavy. Tell me and the Lord will hear. I am His representative on Earth; I will intercede on your behalf. God loves you. If you confess your sins and have faith, if you will put your trust in Jesus, He will heal your wounds. Now come sit by me and tell Laura what happened."

It had been tearing him up, killing his brother. Heavy was so guilt ridden he couldn't eat or sleep, was wandering around the Exxon station in a daze. Mavis warned him to snap out of it, said he had to act normal or people would start to talk. She'd taken care of everything; told everybody when Billy Ray's scholarship had fallen through that he'd gone off to Little Rock and joined the army. But that didn't lighten Heavy's burden. Once he and Vonnie Lee had buried their brother under the shed out back, covered him over with potash and lime and put all the hoes and rakes and junk back in, Vonnie Lee avoided him like the plague. And Betty acted like she was afraid to be in the same room with him, when he had just been defending her. Only little Wendy was unaware that her big brother had committed an unforgivable sin, had broken God's fifth commandment. When Heavy dragged back to the house every night after work she would crawl up on his lap and sing her child's songs to him; play patty cake, putting her tiny, rose petal hands against his rough slabs. Wendy was the one light in his life, the only thing that kept him from joining Billy Ray. Then the contingent of Hornites came through Turner Falls. Heavy believed God had sent them to save him.

"He would sneak in her room at night, Miss Laura, late, when all the rest of us had gone to sleep. Pore Betty never had a chance. Never could say a word from the day she were born. I reckon he threatened her too, told her he'd kill her if she told.

And there was baby Wendy, jest four years old, right in the same room. What would he'uv done to her if she'd waked up and seed what he were up to? She might've blurted somethin' out without knowin'. It scares me now to think about." Suddenly a look of horror flashed over his face, as if in the telling, his fears had been realized. "You don't s'pose . . . I cain't hardly believe . . . but you don't reckon . . . she might've already said?"

Laura patted his hand. "Would it have made a difference, Heavy? If someone else had known? Would you have let it go on? Of course not. Don't worry about things you can't be sure of." But even Laura couldn't put that genie back in the bottle.

He sank deeper into despair. "Then Ma would'a bin the one. If Wendy saw an' tol', she would'a tol' Mavis." The tears welled up again, slid down his cheeks. "How could she let it happen, Miss Laura? How *could* she? Her own flesh an' blood. Billy Ray were always her fav'rite, always goin' on about how he was gonna be a hotshot football player in the NFL, play for the Dallas Cowboys, buy Ma a Cadillac an' a big fancy house when his ship come in." The big man's anger was surfacing, rekindled by the enormity of his suspicions. He sat up straighter, his voice deepened, leveled out. "It could'a been *years*," he said. "Ain't no way to tell *how* long he'd bin at her 'cause Betty wouldn't say." And then slowly, like the sun breaking over the mountain, the final realization dawned, poleaxing him. With a cry he sank to his knees, uttering one agonized word: "Pa."

Laura knelt by his side, wrapped her arms around the broken man. "I'm so sorry, Heavy. So sorry."

They stayed that way a long time, neither moving. Eventually Heavy became aware that she was crying too. He pushed himself to his feet, took her hands and pulled her erect. "Don't, Miss Laura. *Please* don't cry. It ain't yore fault. I'll be all right now, now I know."

They were in Laura's private office, her sanctuary really, a cozy, windowless space in the main building, accessible only to those privileged few who could get past Daniel. She paced the room, an avenging angel. "It *is* all right Heavy. You did what had to be done. God saw the blackness in Billy Ray's heart. He understands." He watched her stride, as mute as his sister while she worked off her rage. When her anger had finally dissipated Laura returned to the couch. "So how *did* you find out, Heavy?" She demanded. "You must tell me exactly what happened."

It was his turn to pace, alternately clenching and flexing his ham fists as he relived the traumatic event. When he had wrestled his emotions into submission, he lumbered over to the couch and sat back down.

"Well, Billy Ray'd had the big head fer a long time. Ever since he were a soph'more he'd bin a football star. All the girls was chasin' after 'im, callin' the house all hours. His senior year, the coaches started callin' too, an' comin' to the games. Arkansas first off. An' Texas, an' Baylor, an' Oklahoma, an' a whole bunch o' other schools. Billy'd always bin a Hog fan, loved them Hogs, but they was gettin' tough on grades up'n Fayetteville, an' they wanted 'im to go to junior college fer a couple o' years. So he picked Oklahoma, 'cause they said they'd take 'im straight off, signed a letter an' everything.

"Then one day right after graduation he come down to the station in a terrible state, fightin' mad, sayin' they'd changed their minds, that they wasn't gonna take 'im after all. His grades was jest too low, an' the NCAA was raisin' a ruckus, talkin' bout probation. He stormed around, cussin' an breakin' things, an' I had to set 'im down 'til he cooled off.

"He left that night right after supper, went out with a bunch o' other kids, joyridin', drivin' around drinkin' beer an' gettin' into mischief. Knowin' what a state he'd bin in earlier, Mavis were worried bout 'im, sent me out to bring 'im home, see to it he didn't do nothin' couldn't be fixed. But it weren't no use. I looked ever' where, an' I never could find them boys.

"When I finally give up an' come home, Mavis had gone to bed. I figured Billy Ray must've come home too, fer her to turn in, so everything was all right. The house was dark an' I took off my shoes on the porch, tryin' not to wake 'em up. Goin' down the hall, I heard some bumpin' noise comin' from the girls' room. I stopped an' listened. It kep' on, like somebody were jumpin' up and down on the bed, but it were the middle o' the night. I couldn't guess, so I eased open the door an' peeked in. An' there he was, on top o' Betty, humpin' to beat the band.

"I swear I thought he were the devil. Or the devil had got into Billy Ray. I pulled him off'n her, but he jest laffed, axt if I wanted some too. Said there was plenty to go around. He was all likkered up, but he shouldn't ha' said that, Miss Laura.

"Betty was cryin' somethin' fierce, but Billy Ray, he said she liked it, said she was so pug ugly she'd never get any anywhere else, so he was just heppin' her out. Then he tried to climb back on.

"That's when I hit 'im, ma'am. And I kep' right on hittin' 'im, 'til he didn't fight back no more."

CHAPTER 13

After digesting the Army's shocking dispatch, it required an enormous amount of discipline for Milo to stay put. But before he could hit the highway in pursuit of Wendy and Heavy, he still had a ton of things to take care of, which was part of what had called Burton's wrath down on him in the first place.

Milo worked like a Trojan to clear his desk. Twice he started down the stairs to smoke, twice he grabbed a Coke instead. His nerves were frazzled, he was hyped on caffeine, but he hadn't had a cigarette in over a week. When he finally put down the phone, signed off the computer, and strode past Marilyn's station, the clock was striking seven. She was gone for the day, the chocolates with her, and Ector, the night clerk, had taken her place.

Stepping outside was like walking into an oven. A group of shorts-clad, sweating cops was shooting baskets at the back of the parking lot, practicing for Hoop Fest. Milo rolled down his windows and watched the action for a few minutes while his truck aired out. The ball slipped through the fingers of a chuffing lieutenant, bounced at Milo's feet. He scooped it up, gauged the distance, and let fly. It rimmed off the front of the iron, not even close.

Reggie, the troopers' best athlete, a black forward who had played college ball with Scottie Pippen at UCA, yelled across the asphalt, "Hey, Milo, don't you know captains can't shoot worth shit?"

"Up yours, Reggie," Milo responded good naturedly. He got in his truck, disposition greatly improved.

Milo picked up a rib-eye and baking potato at Heston's, but he didn't feel like cooking. Gambling that Quentin hadn't eaten, he rang his friend.

"You wanna go to Brave's, or grab a pizza, or something?"

"Sure. I'm watchin' the ballgame. The Yankee's are beatin' up on the White Sox. How about the Town Pump? They'll have the game on."

"Meet you there in fifteen minutes."

The Town Pump made the best burgers in Little Rock, hands down. Juicy patties, lots of trimmings, and the addition of pepper jack cheese and grilled onions elevated the humble hamburger to gourmet status. It didn't help someone trying to quit that the sports bar reeked of tobacco, a constant pall of smoke hanging over the pool tables like tule fog over a swamp. Whatever. The beer was cold, the burgers terrific, and Milo would be glad of the company.

Only a handful of curly fries was left in the bottom of a shared basket when the waiter cleared away their empty plates and long neck bottles. "Y'all need another beer, or is everything all right?"

"Another beer sounds good to me." Quentin looked to Milo for confimation. Milo raised his thumb in accord. Once the new round had been served, the men resumed their conversation.

"What I think," Milo opined, "is that Heavy killed him. He or Mavis. And then his conscience couldn't stand what they had done. That's the only thing that makes any sense."

"But why would he kill his own brother, Milo? I mean, if it was an accident or something, why not just fess up? Why hide it all these years? And what about his mother? Surely you don't really suspect her, do you?"

"I don't know why, Q.C. I just know they did it, and now they've got Wendy, and I've got to find her before something happens to her, too, if it's not already too late."

*   *   *

Milo was correct. Wendy *was* in danger, but it wasn't from Heavy. Daniel would let Wendy live only as long as Heavy could guarantee his sister's silence. If she somehow managed to escape, or get back in touch with the authorities, Wendy would be fair game, and Heavy wouldn't be able to do a thing about it.

Getting back in touch with the authorities was the last thing on Wendy's mind. Locked in the spare bedroom at the chicken farm, Wendy knew she was in trouble. Frankly terrified following McKensie's revelations, she hadn't breathed a word to anybody about what he'd told her. She wasn't supposed to know what he was involved in; didn't want to know. Why couldn't the horny fool have kept his mouth shut? She was kind of afraid of him anyway. If it weren't for the sex there was no telling what he'd do. He had that look. She'd only called the Hot Line to put that poor·mother out of her misery, let her know her little girl was dead so she wouldn't go on hoping. And she'd been really careful about that, calling when Trampas was occupied and the station virtually empty. How in the world had that cop gotten on to her?

Wendy couldn't understand her brother. They'd always had a special relationship. Except for the time he'd gone away, he had always looked after her, been a lot more understanding than her mother. Heavy might be big, and not think very fast, but inside, he was a cupcake. Mavis was mean. She was mean to Wendy, and even meaner to Betty. Sometimes Wendy thought all Mavis cared about was those damn cats. If she got in a jam, she never asked Mavis for help, it was always Heavy. But this time her brother had surprised her.

*   *   *

"Yes, ma'am, that's right. The State Police."

She held his badge with two fingers, as if it were poison. "Well," she said, squinting at his ID, "Captain Thomas, is it? The Reverend is terribly busy. It would be impossible for him to see you without an appointment."

134

"I'm sure he *is* busy," Milo said agreeably, "but I won't take but a few minutes of his time. Would you please ask him?"

Tuesday morning, hoping to catch the proprietor of the Tabernacle off guard, Milo had showed up without warning at Daniel's office, and run smack into Nell Draper, the preacher's prickly secretary, who had no intention of letting Milo bully her.

"You can sit down right over there and wait if you want. But it's customary to call first," she lectured, frowning through her bifocals. "Brother Daniel has an extremely heavy schedule today. I don't think he can fit you in." Final.

Milo tried what was left of his boyish charm. "But you *will* ask, won't you please."

With a "humph," she got up and tapped lightly on the oak door, quickly disappearing behind it.

Milo didn't know the cult leader's status vis à vis what was going on with his aide. Was the preacher involved? Or was Milo constructing a convoluted plot out of whole cloth, when it was strictly a family matter? He could drive a Mack truck through the holes in his theories, largely because he had been unable to come up with any kind of plausible motive. What could this sect be doing that would have gotten Addy killed? Other than Daniel's rantings from the pulpit, he had no indication. Which was why he needed Wendy so badly. Which was why he was sitting here with a shit-eating grin on his face, waiting for Daniel's pet temple dog to plead his case.

Waiting for Nell to reappear, Milo leafed through stacks of pamphlets distributed around the anteroom. They were copies of Brother Daniel's sermons, annotated with Biblical references. He folded one and put it in his jacket pocket. At that moment Nell resumed her position behind the mahogany barricade.

"He will see you," she said primly, "as soon as he is off the phone."

Ten minutes later Nell coughed, more a throat-clearing-for-attention hack than a real cough. "You may go in now."

Daniel rose, came around his desk with his hand extended. "Captain Thomas? Nell says you need to see me. What can I do for the State Police?"

Milo shook the outstretched hand. "Thanks for your time, Reverend. I won't keep you long. Actually, I'm trying to locate a couple of your parishioners. I believe Eugene Bolin works for you."

"You mean Heavy? Yes, Heavy's been a valuable member of the Tabernacle staff for many years." He indicated a sofa and pair of chairs in a corner sitting area. "Won't you have a seat?"

"Thank you. Is he here now?"

"Heavy? No, I'm sorry. Right now he's out of town, taking care of some church business."

"When do you expect him back?"

"Is that important? I really couldn't say. A week, maybe two. May I ask what this is about?"

This wasn't accomplishing anything. Whatever was going on, Daniel had no intention of helping Milo figure it out. However the pastor's glib responses confirmed that he *was* involved. Milo plowed ahead.

"How about Wendy Bolin? Do you happen to know where she is?"

"Heavy's sister? I have no idea. The church has many communicants, Captain Thomas. I can't possibly keep track of every one. Why do you ask? Is she in some kind of trouble?"

"No, no trouble. I just need to talk with her."

"Well, I seem to recall that Heavy got her a job at one of our support facilities when she finished high school. I think it was Lester's, or maybe the video store. I can have Nell look it up, if that will help."

"I'd appreciate anything you could tell me about her."

"Tell you what. Let me put you in touch with Trampas Morgan, he's the manager at Lester's. He'd be the one to ask."

"I don't think that's necessary, Reverend. She's not at work. She's missing."

"Missing? That's dreadful. Her poor mother. But you must be mistaken, Captain. I'm sure I would have heard from Mrs. Bolin if there were a problem."

"Maybe so. I don't doubt your information is more accurate than mine. But if you should talk to Heavy, would you please ask him to get in touch with me. Here's my card. He can call anytime."

Daniel dropped the card on the coffee table. "I'll be happy to tell him, Captain Thomas. And now, if there's nothing else, you must excuse me."

Milo stood. "Thank you, Reverend. Oh, one more thing. Did you by any chance happen to hear about a little girl, Addy Willis was her name, who disappeared from her home near Dardanelle? Her body turned up later in Little Rock."

"Tragic. Just tragic. Of course we heard. Who in the state did not? At our Wednesday evening service we prayed for her safe deliverance. Crime has touched all of our lives, Captain Thomas, but it is especially difficult to understand when the victim is a child. There are some very wicked people in this world. Here at the Tabernacle we are dedicated to stopping the violence so prevalent in our society today. You really should join us some time. It would seem we have a common cause."

Bad vibes was putting it mildly. The man had given him the willies. Milo crossed his arms, rubbed his biceps, trying to shake off the malaise. Seated in the comfortable easy chair talking with Daniel in his study, Milo could have sworn the temperature had dropped ten degrees. There was no denying the cleric's hypnotic power. It had been like talking to a cobra, waiting for the snake to strike. The preacher had been courteous, attentive, concerned, and lying through his teeth.

Some wicked people? He'd get no argument from Milo. And no matter how smooth the pious poseur had been, after meeting him in the flesh, Brother Daniel would rank right up there near the top of Milo's list.

*   *   *

Daniel went ballistic. No sooner had the dectective left than he hurled a heavy paper weight against the far wall, denting the paneling and chipping a chunk out of the crystal hand cooler. Nell scurried to the connecting door in response to the thud.

"Get out of here," Daniel yelled when she peeked in. "Get out and leave me alone." He picked up a book and started to fling it after the paper weight.

Daniel was so mad it took him three tries to punch in the right number on his private line. Heavy and McKensie had both been restricted to the bunker until after the mission. The girl was locked up tight. But Boyd needed to be warned that the fucking lawman was still nosing around. Double damnation! McKensie's compounded stupidity could ruin everything. First he'd killed the kid. Then the dumb sonofabitch had bragged about it! Jesus! Before anyone could answer he slammed down the receiver. Forget the phone, he was going to the farm. To Laura.

During the twenty minute drive Daniel got his anger under control. Because even though he wanted to rip McKensie's balls off and feed them to him for breakfast, he needed the little asswipe too much. And that's what really kinked Daniel's tail. Like it or not, the mission's success depended on the hacker. Without McKensie, he could kiss his retribution good-bye.

CHAPTER 14

A deer bounded out of the brush, sailing across the south bound lane directly in front of Milo. He slammed on the brakes and swerved hard right, skidding across the shoulder and down a gradual embankment. A jagged outcropping rose to greet him. He wrenched the wheel left, but his fender grazed the rock, sluing the truck sideways. The Bronco's externally mounted spare caught the bluff next, separating from the cargo hatch with an agonized metalic shriek. Now canted up the slope at right angles to the road, the truck's grill plowed into the graveled berm, rupturing the radiator and sending a geyser of steam, pebbles, and dirt spewing over the windshield. Blinded, Milo hung on for dear life, hoping he wouldn't roll. The truck was rapidly losing momentum. It finally shuddered to rest, half on the pavement and half off, facing back the way he had come. Bruised and shaken but mercifully intact, he had missed the deer by inches.

Milo's safety belt was cutting painfully into his chest, but it had probably saved him from severe injury. His Bronco was an older model, and wasn't equipped with air bags. Milo undid the clasp and slumped against the steering wheel, his legs jelly, his breathing ragged and shallow. But he was all right, and that was what counted.

Highway 377 between Snowball and Witts Springs is a lonely stretch of secondary road, seldom traveled and remote. Milo had been taking a short cut from Turner Falls to Dardanelle when the deer interrupted.

Eventually he thought he could stand without wobbling.

With a little banging Milo got his door open. His Bronco was a disaster. He was studying the damage when an old pickup with a camper shell pulled off and stopped. A woman in khaki shorts and blue chambray work shirt tied at the waist got out.

"You okay?" she asked amiably.

"I think so. All the parts seem to be working."

"Good. Have a blow out, or trying to miss a deer?"

"A deer. How'd you guess?"

"Saw your skid marks. Clear day, straightaway. Either that, or," she shrugged, waggling her fingers, "you were drunk." And then, as if more explanation were required, "I'm staying around here. Deer all over the place. Worse at night though—you were lucky."

He agreed.

"Can I take you some place? The closest wrecker's in Marshall, and it doesn't look to me like that Bronco's goin' anywhere soon."

"Thanks," he said, "but I have a phone and a radio. I can call somebody to come."

"Okay," she acquiesced. "Just tryin' to help. You sure you're all right?"

Milo's head was clearing. He took another look at his would-be rescuer. Late thirties or early forties, tall, tanned, good body. Shining, shoulder length dark brown hair with red highlights. No make up and she didn't need any. In addition to the shorts and cropped top, she wore socks folded down over laced-up hiking boots, and a serious sports watch. He checked her fingers. No rings.

"Look," he said sheepishly, "I didn't mean to sound churlish. I guess I'm still a little shook up. You don't happen to have any water, do you? I could use a drink of water."

"Sure," she grinned, pleased there was something she could do. "Hang on a sec. I've got a bottle in Homer. Be right back."

She was back in a trice, carrying a plastic cup and a quart of Mountain Valley. "Say when," she said. She poured the cup full, handed it to him. "Sorry I don't have any ice, but it's better for you this way."

He drained the cup, held it out for more.

"You shouldn't drink too much. You might get nauseated. Delayed shock, or something."

He nodded, relinquished the cup. "I'll be fine," he said. "I'm feeling better already. I really appreciate your stopping. By the way, my name's Milo. Milo Thomas."

"I'm Betsy Wilmarth," she said. "Glad I could help."

Suddenly he didn't want her to leave. "Did you say you live around here?"

"Sort of. I've got a cabin a couple of miles back toward Snowball. Why?"

Another car was pulling off on the far shoulder. They waved the new Samaritan on his way.

"Well," he said, "I was thinking. Maybe we could call the wrecker and go to your house to wait. It'd sure beat standing out here on the side of the road." As soon as he got the words out of his mouth Milo realized what a clumsy come-on it had been. He wasn't out of practice, he had forgotten how. He tried again. "I'm okay," he said. *Dumb*, Milo. "No, not like that. Well, maybe like that too. What I mean is, I won't hurt you. I'm a cop. Really. With the State Police. You don't have to worry."

She wasn't worried. "Come on then, Milo Thomas with the State Police. Let's put out some emergency markers and get you off your feet."

✳   ✳   ✳

Milo rolled over gingerly, trying for a position where some part of his anatomy didn't hurt. A long soak in the Jacuzzi, half a dozen Motrin, and a generous amount of Jack Daniel's had taken the edge off, but his body still ached all over. His Bronco was totaled; he wasn't any closer to finding Heavy or Wendy—all in all it had been a great day. Why then, when the sky was falling, did he feel so optimistic?

Milo's defenses were weakening. He could not remember when he had been so attracted to a member of the gentler sex. Not since Angélique. And that had been a long time indeed. Not that it was going anywhere. He needed a romantic entanglement now like a root canal. Besides, she'd only be in Arkansas another couple of weeks. But he had to admit, Betsy Blair Wilmarth was something special. Forty-three, divorced, two dogs, no children. And smart. *Doctor* Wilmarth, if you please, a tenured professor of cultural anthropology at the University of Cincinnati. But what had Milo going went deeper than brains and an attractive package. Betsy was, he struggled for the right word, *comfortable*. Their easy conversation relaxing in the all-purpose space that served as her kitchen/study/dining room was the genial patter of two old friends, not the wary sizing up of newly-mets. When the wrecker had finally driven up, he had hated to see it appear.

Milo didn't know it yet, but the two hours he had spent with Betsy Wilmarth was the first step toward a long overdue exorcism of his past. For the first time in over three weeks, when he finally drifted off to sleep, his last conscious thoughts were not of Addy.

*   *   *

Scrambling over the crest of the ridge, Betsy trained her binoculars on a granite ledge half a mile away, beyond the horseshoe bend in the river. Below her lay a narrow valley, carved into the hills by the serpentine meandering of the White River. Interspersed with patches of weathered stone, tufts of corn and hay sprang from small pockets of fertile soil, latticed with broader bands of trees. This was one of Betsy's favorite spots. If she held her head at just the right angle, so that she didn't see the microwave tower astride Heller's Leap, she could have been studying a scene unchanged for a thousand years. In the late afternoons of summer, when the last rays of sun slanted across the valley floor, tipping the crowns of sycamores, ash, and hickories in a rich, Venetian rose-gold, the sheer beauty of nature made her heart sing. At other times, over Thanksgiving or the Christmas holidays, when those same trees stretched skeletal branches toward the thin, tensile light of winter, and a gossamer mist lay tucked in the folds of the mountains, she could almost see the people of that forgotten time, shadow figures going about their familiar routines in a parallel universe.

Not today. Today she couldn't get her mind off the bunged up man she had rescued from the side of the road. Rescued and impulsively taken home with her. Geez, she chided herself, that was a damn foolhardy thing to do. What if he had been a mad rapist? But he hadn't been. In addition to being handsome in a rumpled, unkempt kind of way, he had turned out to be bright, even articulate, and sexy—sexy, sexy, sexy.

Betsy had supplied rudimentary first aid, with Merthiolate and Band-Aids, to a nasty scrape above his left elbow.

He winced as she daubed on the Merthiolate.

"Sit still," she commanded.

"Yes mother," he retorted immediately. Laughing, she blew on the cut to lessen the sting.

It had been an odd, intimate moment, touching and funny at the same time. And that had set her juices flowing. But a *cop* of all things! How had she managed that?

Betsy had been celibate far too long. Doggy kisses in the morning were all well and good, but a man in her bed would be a damn sight better. She sighed. In this age of Aids and herpes, casual couplings were taboo. But her response to the state cop had been intellectual as well as physical. She could talk *to* him, not *at* him. And laugh, again *with*, not *at* him. His wry, self deprecating humor had been contagious.

Oh shit, she thought, I hope I didn't blow it. Well, too late now. She gave herself the benefit of the doubt. Maybe he'd call; he had taken her number. On that positive thought her spirits lifted, and she continued down the steep trail.

* * *

Tuesday morning had started out exactly like most of Betsy's mornings in the Ozarks. She had gotten up at six, taken the dogs for a three mile run, and returned to the cabin for breakfast and a quick shower. By eight, she was dressed and on her way, systematically combing the hills and vales of her adopted state in pursuit of the elusive indigenes of prehistory. Betsy's particular interest lay in the society and culture of native Americans of the late Mississippian period. Working in conjunction with the Arkansas Archeological Survey, she was helping to gather and collate archeological data from open habitation and special purpose sites in north central and northwest Arkansas, a region of the Ozarks that had been neglected by all but a few, stubborn archeologists and anthropologists.

Betsy had been hooked on the subject since graduate school, when, as part of a field seminar, she had been impressed labor at a dig along the banks of the Buffalo River in Newton county. In the seventies so little had been known about the early Indians of the Arkansas Ozarks, in comparison to their contemporaries in Missouri and Oklahoma, that Betsy had settled on that topic for her own research. She had fallen into a tailor-made niche. This was her fifteenth summer in Arkansas. Now a recognized authority, she remained passionate about her chosen field.

Just as she started out the door her phone rang. She paused on the stoop, listening, heard the answering machine pick up, heard the whine when the fax clicked on. She could leave, the message would be waiting when she got back, or she could turn around and see if it was anything important. She turned around.

The dogs, who thought they'd been abandoned for the day, were ecstatic at Betsy's change of heart.

"Calm down, you nits," she shushed the animals. "I haven't come back for you. It's too hot to leave you guys in the truck."

Three hours later, fuming at the time she'd lost, she finally got on the road. Five minutes after that, the sight of the dejected man and the battered Bronco stopped her again. It wasn't Betsy's day to get much work done either.

* * *

Milo creaked out of bed, marveling that he could still move. Stiff joints and a panoply of bruises aside, his first priority was transportation. He rarely used a state car, preferring to drive his personal vehicle, submitting monthly time and mileage sheets with his expense account. His Bronco's untimely demise, however, put him at the mercy of the motor pool. From a fleet of unmarked state cars, Sergeant Rasco delivered a gray, four door Chevrolet sedan to his doorstep. Adequate, but not Milo.

After a morning spent hassling with a snotty claims adjuster and filling out the necessary insurance and police forms, he began calling Ford dealers, looking for a new truck. Before the accident, Milo had decided to trade in his aging Bronco in the fall, when the new models came out. The deer had taken care of that. By the close of business he had located a black, Eddie Bauer Expedition, with an optional V6, loaded with all the goodies, including dual air bags. Next morning he'd take it in to have his phone and radio installed; then he'd be back on the road.

* * *

"If you've reached this number by mistake, please hang up. If, however, you think I might want to hear from you, you may leave a message at the tone, or begin transmitting a fax immediately."

Nonplused, Milo couldn't think of anything to say. He hung up.

Okay, you jerk, try again. It can't be that hard. What do you want to say? Milo fixed a bourbon, rehearsing his speech until he thought it sounded pretty good. Easing himself into his chair, he pushed redial.

"If you've reached this number...'Hang on, I just walked in.' *... by mistake,...*'I'm trying to turn the damn thing off.'*... please hang up...*'NO, **don't** hang up!'*...If, however,...*'Wait a minute, I've got it.'"

"There." There was a lot of loud barking in the background. "Betsy?"

"Sorry about that. *Hush guys!* This is Betsy Wilmarth. What can I do for you?" More barking.

"Betsy, it's Milo. Milo Thomas, from yesterday. If this is a bad time, I can call back later."

"Milo! No, wait; hang on a sec. I just came in and the dogs are going nuts. Let me," he heard her put the phone down, heard *'I'm glad to see you turkeys too, but that's enough. Be quiet now.'* The barking stopped. "Okay, I'm back. How're you feeling?"

"Like somebody ran my clothes through the spin cycle with me in them. Seriously though, I'm fine. A little stove up, but that'll pass. Actually," he said, "I called to thank you for all your help. And to offer a small reward." Milo was perspiring. "I was wondering, if you're not too busy, in the nature of recompense, could I interest you in a picnic tomorrow?"

She was sitting on the porch when he drove up. "Wow," she greeted him, skipping down the steps, "Did you ever land on your feet! I'd give anything for such a terrific set of wheels."

"You really think so?" he asked, ridiculously pleased. He got out and came around to stand by her. "It's a little bigger than I had planned to buy, but I got a good deal."

"Absolutely," she assured him. "I covet it already. Homer is positively geriatric, a new ailment every day. Let's see inside."

Milo held open the passenger door. Betsy peered in, inhaled, relishing the new-car smell. Ran her hand over thick leather seats. "I'm ready," she said, stepping up on the running board. "Let's go try this beauty out."

He hadn't intended to start on the case. She was so easy to talk to that it was almost like thinking out loud. Sated, leftovers packed up and trash deposited in a garbage bin, they took a lazy stroll, wandering hand in hand along the river bank.

Out of the blue, Betsy asked curiously, "Where were you headed the other day when you cracked up? Three seventy-seven isn't exactly a major thoroughfare."

Milo didn't discuss his cases out of school. It was unprofessional and in some circumstances, dangerous. Outside of other law enforcement officers, he kept his work to himself. But he saw no need for evasion with Betsy. She had asked an innocent question; he might as well answer.

"I was going to a crime scene on Lake Dardanelle," he told her. "Maybe you remember, about a month ago a little girl disappeared from her home on the lake. Her body turned up a week or so later, in the river near downtown Little Rock. I've been trying to find out what happened."

"You mean like she was murdered, or kidnapped, or fell in, or what?"

"Something like that."

"So what was it? Was she murdered, or kidnapped, or fell in, or what?"

"Betsy," he said, "let's not talk about this."

"Okay," she said. "So, what were you doing in *my* neck of the woods? If you hadn't noticed, Snowball isn't on a straight line between Little Rock and Lake Dardanelle. It's in the middle of nowhere."

He studied her before answering. Under his scrutiny Betsy almost blushed. She could hear alarm bells, her fairy godmother scolding: *There you go again, Betsy. Don't be such a pushy broad. I've told you a thousand times, men don't like pushy.*

"I'm sorry, Milo," she apologized hastily. "I didn't mean to pry. Excessive curiosity is a natural characteristic of a cultural anthropologist. And," she admitted, "I'm a pushy broad. I should have known better. It's been a great day. I've had a wonderful time. Don't let me spoil it now."

"You haven't spoiled anything, Betsy. Come on," he said, turning around. "If you've got time, you can go with me, and I'll tell you on the way."

"It was right around here," he said. "By the time I got here there wasn't much of anything to see." His arm swept in a broad arc around the clearing. "Hundreds of searchers tramping around pretty much obliterates any physical evidence there might have been."

Having Betsy along was something of a relief for Milo. Her no nonsense attitude dispelled any lingering reservations he had about returning to the site of Addy's murder. Milo hadn't been back since his initial visit. He wasn't exactly apprehensive—he wouldn't admit that, not even to himself—but he had convinced himself that he had seen all there was to see. Yet following his interview with Daniel, Milo had turned instinctively toward the clearing. Unless he pursued the fifteen year old disappearance of Billy Ray Bolin in an effort to force Mavis's hand, he was going to have to come up with something else, and in short order. With Wendy and Heavy absent and unaccounted for, there remained only the clearing for inspiration.

All the old questions were still unanswered, plus a new one: what was unique about this place that would attract the Tabernacle of Divine Redemption?

Betsy pointed out the patently obvious. "Well," she said "there's Nuke One, for starters."

Omitting any reference to the nuclear power station was like ignoring King Kong clinging to the Empire State Building. Milo had worried about the electric plant from the beginning. One of his early theories, since discarded, had been that a cabal of international terrorists might attempt to sabotage the nuclear reactor. When he approached Entergy with the idea, company officials assured him that the facility could withstand any threat short of an atomic bomb. Inherent in the design were so many redundant backup systems that a melt down was impossible. There was no such thing as the China Syndrome anyway—that myth was an anti-nuclear scare tactic.

There was a certain logic to their arguments. Why would terrorists pick Arkansas, a sparsely populated, rural state? What would they stand to gain? If a reactor were the target, why not choose one in a high density corridor, for maximum collateral damage? To the electric company, it didn't track.

After the barrage of denials from corporate experts, Milo had filed the notion under 'highly improbable.' Then, when mounting evidence focused his attention on members of the Tabernacle, it had gotten relegated to bottom basement. There must be something else he was missing.

Betsy didn't think so. "I'm an authority," she said. "I've read every Agatha Christie and Arthur Conan Doyle mystery ever written. Look around you. What else is there? If you strip away everything that doesn't fit, drugs, sex, Satanism and the occult, some sort of accident—what have you got left? You *have* to go with the obvious. That's elementary, my dear Watson."

"Elementary, maybe," he replied, "but in this case, a little far fetched. Can you imagine a religious group, at least any supposedly *Christian* religious group, no matter how crazy or fanatical, wanting to blow up an atomic power plant?"

Put that way, even Betsy was stymied.

When they returned to her cabin it was just getting dark. "You wanna come in?" she offered. "I'll fix us a drink as soon as I spring the dogs."

"Sure," he said. "I'd love a drink."

She lay on her side, face turned away, her naked body damp from their exertions. Her shoulders rose and fell peacefully as she dozed. She had tossed a scarf over the lamp on her dresser, and in its dim light her skin had taken on a soft sheen, like the luster of fine pearls. One knee was bent on top of the covers, the other leg extended under the scrunched up sheet.

Sitting up, Milo gazed fondly at her dimpled buttocks, remembering. Years ago he had won a bottle of champagne for identifying the correct chorine from a line up of nude, masked beauties by the dimples in her ass. Spectators seated around the stage at the Moulin Rouge had roared their approval as the cork popped on a magnum of Veuve Cliquot, and he had taken a tipsy bow to raucous applause.

"You are so beautiful," he murmured, tracing the graceful curve of her hip with his hand. He bent over, brushing away strands of auburn hair from her flushed cheek, burrowing his nose behind her ear, "and, you smell good."

"Mmmmm," she purred, without moving. His hand stole around her waist, slid up until it found her breast. His fingers toyed with the nipple, working the flesh until it was erect. His tongue tickled the inside of her ear, sending shivers through her body. Stretching languorously, she arched her back, responding to his touch. Then she rolled over. "You were saying?"

"How did I ever get this lucky?"

In his eyes she saw gratitude—and pleasure—and desire. "Don't tell me you're ready again, an old geezer like you!"

"Wonders never cease, but it certainly looks that way." He smiled at her teasing, then lifted the covers, indicating proof.

She took his head between her hands, drawing him to her, and kissed him. Then she guided his lips to her breasts. "We'll just have to do something about that now, won't we?"

Later, as he lay spent inside her, their post-coital cuddling was interrupted by a mournful yowl, begun in bass register and rising in pitch until the hairs stood up on his arms and his flaccid penis shriveled from her vagina.

"Oh God," Betsy exclaimed, "the dogs!"

The unholy noise grew louder, accompanied by scrapes and thumps. Sharp, excited woofs joined the eerie howls in an off-key, syncopated duet, followed by a tremendous crash.

"Oh lord, not now, dummies!" Betsy sprang from the bed.

Too late. Milo was pinioned by a forty pound basset, slobbering and licking his face. He turned his head, trying to get away from the onslaught of bad breath and wet kisses, and found himself staring into the inquisitive eyes of a yellow lab, nose twitching, tail wagging a mile a minute.

Betsy collapsed on the floor, hand over her mouth, trying unsuccessfully not to laugh. "I'm sorry," she managed to hiccup through giggles. "I thought the barrier would hold. They're not used to having anyone up here but me and them. I guess they were jealous."

"Get him off me," Milo grumbled, yanking the sheet over his head in a futile attempt to ward off the dogs. But he picked up quickly enough on her revelation that visitors to her sleeping loft were few and far between.

"Come on, Milo, please don't be upset," she begged, genuinely dismayed. "I'm really sorry. I'll take them back downstairs. Its just they felt left out. They wanted in on the loving."

His mood changed, farcical nature of the situation sinking in. And then the laughter came, a great tide of mirth that started in his belly, rumbled up through his chest, and exploded in convulsive gouts, shaking his whole body so that tears ran down his cheeks and the basset hopped off the bed in alarm.

"I have never," he tried to say, but the laughter bubbled up again, and he spluttered, coughing, face red, gasping for breath. She brought a wet washcloth, wiped his face and patted it dry with a corner of the sheet.

"Oh, what the hell," he tried again, "I give up. Who could top that?" He patted the center of the bed. "Come on back up here buddy, I guess this is your territory. But Betsy, I gotta tell you, in all my fifty odd years, this is a first."

During the next two weeks Milo returned to his apartment twice, both times to drop off dirty clothes, pack clean ones, and collect his mail. He called Quentin. He called Terry Weltlich to apologize and solicit his help. He did not call the office. The days he spent shadowing the Tabernacle, talking to residents, checking out the church's various business ventures. Looking for Wendy and Heavy. The nights and weekends he spent with Betsy. He was happier than he had been in years.

CHAPTER 15

The auction barn sat well back from the road, surrounded by several acres of graded parking. Pickups, cattle trucks, semis, and trailers overflowed the lot and spilled out onto the right-of-way. Boyd slowed, stopping on the shoulder behind a dung-splattered flat-bed. When he got out a dry wind plucked at his sleeves, hurled grit in his eyes, sang the dirge of lowing, frightened cattle. McKensie came around the truck into the teeth of the wind, muttered a vehement *sonofabitch*, and yanked his cap lower on his forehead. Heads tucked, they made their way toward the hub of activity.

Inside the main entrance the pair paused to get their bearings. A group of steers was being herded around the center ring to the tongue-twisting patter of the auctioneer. At nine in the morning the stands were full.

Boyd and McKensie had taken Interstate 40 three hundred miles due west from Fort Smith, to the outskirts of Elk City, Oklahoma, spread out on a windy plateau not far from the Black Kettle National Grasslands. They spent a quiet night at a Ramada Inn across the freeway from town. Next morning they gassed up, bought donuts and coffee at a nearby E-Z Mart, and followed the clerk's *"just go on up the way,"* to their destination.

It had taken him the better part of a month to locate Wynne. Chris Wynne was the best pilot Boyd had ever met. Not a hotshot, top gun jet jockey flying aerial combat at twenty thousand feet, but a guy who could get you in to or out of a sheer-walled box canyon; drop your supplies on a dime in the middle of the jungle; home in on a transmitter, then hoist you up and haul ass before Charlie got you first. Chris Wynne could keep you alive.

And had.

Boyd hadn't seen him since the Fall. Not since Boyd's own hand picked, Special Forces had been reduced to schlepping pallets of smack out of the Golden Triangle for General Thieu. At the time, Wynne was flying under contract to Air America, the CIA's not-so-covert air force operating out of Vientiane. Instead of ferrying doomed men out of the killing fields, Wynne's handlers had him transporting a more lucrative cargo to safety. In a world of treachery, deceit, and death, they were a pair of weary warriors who had been squeezed through the same ringer and survived. Boyd had spent the last quarter century reliving those days. It was in no small measure thanks to Chris Wynne that he was still around to do so.

Boyd studied the stands, hoping that neither of them had changed too much. He had sent McKensie off to prowl around, check things out, get lost. The last thing he wanted to do was to confront Wynne with the little psychopath right off the bat. If things worked out, Chris would have that pleasure soon enough.

Wynne was sitting on the top row next to the cattle chute, his elbow resting on the guard railing. Chris must have spotted them when they first entered the arena, for he simultaneously caught Boyd's glance of recognition and raised his hand.

Boyd wondered if he looked as worn to his old comrade as the pilot did to him. Chris's features were the same, but the years had taken their toll. His skin was burnished leather, stretched mummy-like across prominent cheekbones, eyes no more than slits in cognac folds. The hawk nose too, seemed thinner and longer, maybe because Wynne's Pancho Villa mustache was gone. Always lank and lean, Chris seemed shrunken inside his clothes. Like most of the other men filling the stands, he was dressed in a plaid, western cut shirt, and faded jeans over old cowboy boots. A battered Stetson occupied the seat to his left.

Boyd climbed the grime-caked stairs and sidestepped a dozen bodies murmuring "sorry" and "excuse me" as he worked his way to the end of the row.

"Hi ya, Richard. It's been a long time," Wynne greeted him. "You look almost as old as I feel." So it was mutual. They shook hands. Wynne picked up the Stetson and settled it on a shock of thick, still dark hair. Boyd took its place on the bench beside him.

"Chris," he said, "it's good to see you."

Wynne continued conversationally, as though Boyd hadn't spoken. "You had to have some mighty powerful reason to track me down after all these years. I'm not all that easy to find." A masterpiece of understatement.

When Boyd had called to set up the meet, their first contact in two decades, Wynne hadn't registered surprise, hadn't asked him zip. There was only one way Boyd could have gotten Chris Wynne's number. With his permission.

"So, what's so important you'd drive all this way to talk to an old, broken down fly boy?"

Tex Ritter's burnt-out voice rasped from the jukebox, *"if the ocean was whiskey and I was a duck, I'd dive to the bottom and never come up."*

Chris had ordered for them, the house special. A three inch thick sirloin slopped off the sizzling platter, hot juices dripping on the red and white checked oil-cloth. Their salads had been cleared away, and a second pitcher of beer had swiftly followed the first. A top-heavy waitress poured into a skimpy rawhide costume cut down to there distributed steaming potatoes around the table, then refilled their mugs, and brought a third, foaming pitcher of draft. She snuggled her scantily clad butt next to Chris and bent over, giving them all a good look. "Anything else you want, hon?"

"Not right now." He patted her on the tush. "Maybe later, all right?" Sexual harassment wasn't an issue at Wylie's Steak Out Saloon.

As she sashayed away, Chris informed his guests, "Donna Jean's got great tits, but she's also got three kids, and her ex is one mean hombre."

McKensie had zeroed in on the woman the minute he sat down. He was chafing mightily under Boyd's tight leash. Wendy was out of bounds, under constant supervision at the chicken farm, and he was back in deep shit. The little bitch had pointed the finger at *him*, but *he* hadn't called the fucking cops. Stupid, stupid, stupid. Why'd she have to open her mouth, blab like that, the dumb, flat-chested cunt? Not like the hooters on this babe.

McKensie got amped thinking about the things he could do with Donna Jean. Wynne and Boyd were talking old time shit, maybe they wouldn't notice. He slipped his hand under the cloth napkin, furtively massaging himself until his erection was rock hard and throbbing, trapped inside his jeans. In his mind's eye he pictured the waitress, boobs naked, waiting for his stiletto.

When McKensie blinked the pilot was staring at him like he had x-ray vision. "You'd be buying yourself a mess of trouble, Mike. Whatever you're thinking, I'd forget it."

Sh-i-it. Another self righteous bastard, just like that friggin' asshole Boyd. McKensie scowled daggers across the table. These prune-faced motherfuckers couldn't get it up for shit. Well they could all go take a flying fuck. He stretched his fingers; his hand slid down his leg to caress his knife, then it found his penis again, rubbing urgently. McKensie clenched his teeth and thought good thoughts. Maybe this over-the-hill, bush league birdman would opt out. Aahhh.

A slow smile transformed the hacker's sullen countenance. "Sorry, Chris. I didn't realize she was a friend of yours."

✴   ✴   ✴

"What'da *you* want?" Trampas growled at Milo when the investigator entered the Pit Stop.

It had been nearly three weeks since Wendy had vanished. Betsy was gone, loaded up and on the road for Cincinnati. Milo

155

had helped her cram a summer's worth of clothes, books, research material, and miscellaneous odds and ends into Homer the night before, so that she could get an early start. Because she had the dogs she needed to make the drive in one day. With a lunch break and potty stops, the trip should take fourteen hours. She had promised to call as soon as she got in.

Milo was going to miss Betsy. She would write, she would call, she would be back at Thanksgiving. He could fly up weekends. Catch a Bengals game, she had tickets. Also for U.C. basketball, great seats. And the theater, if that was his bag. It was the kind of relationship most men dream of. Nothing permanent, plenty of space, terrific sex, no strings. Except . . . except, when Milo saw the back of Betsy's camper disappear around the curve his heart plummeted.

He went back inside the cabin to tidy up. It was 6:07 on Monday morning. His last day with Betsy. His last day of leave. His last day trying full time to solve the Addy Willis case. Too many lasts.

They had shared a hasty breakfast, orange juice, tea, and toast.

"I'll lock up," he said. "You go on and get started. That way you should get home by dark."

"Funny," she said. "I feel more like I'm leaving home than going there."

Milo knew what she meant. He had lived in the same condo in Little Rock for fourteen years; he had spent fourteen days in her cabin. The cabin felt more like home than his apartment ever had.

"Betsy, I . . ." he started, but she pressed a finger to his lips, shushing him.

"Don't. Please don't, Milo. I'm not good at good-byes. I look yucky when I cry. Just give me a hug, will you? It's not like it's forever."

He wrapped his arms around her, not wanting to let go.

"Mmmm," Betsy said, "that's nice. You get a gold star." She broke the clench. "Okay, time to hit the road. John Cato, Menga, you guys done all your business?" She opened Homer's door. Menga, the lab, jumped in. Betsy bent down, hoisted the basset onto the seat. She looked around. "Well, I guess that's everything. No wait, where're my sunglasses. I think I left them on the table. Milo, will you go see?"

"Be right back." He took the steps two at a time. Her glasses weren't on the table. He checked the couch, coffee table, bathroom. No glasses. Ran up the stairs to the loft. Heard the motor wheeze, kick over. Ran back down and out the door. Betsy was pulling out of the drive. She looked back, waved, and was gone.

"Keep the key," she had told him. "Use this place whenever you want. The utilities stay on all the time."

He rinsed and dried the dishes. Put them away. That was all there was to do. She had stripped the bed when they got up and tossed the dirty linens on top of the rest of the stuff in the camper. He walked around, turning out lights. Went back upstairs. Her scarf was still draped over the table lamp where it had been since their first night. He folded it, opened a drawer to put it away, changed his mind. It still smelled faintly of Joy. She would sprinkle a few drops on the cloth before they made love. The heat from the bulb released the scent, perfuming their bower. He buried his nose in the soft challis, sighed, and tucked the square in his briefcase. He went out, locking the door behind him. Milo was going to miss Betsy a lot.

"I'm worried about her Trampas. Three weeks and not one word. I thought you might be worried too."

The man snorted contemptuously. "You're trouble. Nothing but trouble. If it hadn't been for you, she wouldn't have left."

"I can't argue with that," Milo said, "but I'm not the problem. Listen to me Trampas—I think Wendy is in danger. Real danger. Maybe I can help her."

"Get outta here cop. You can't help anybody." But the hostility had gone out of his voice.

Milo was banking on something Grady Davenport had said: that Trampas might be in love with the missing girl. Over the past two weeks he had visited all of the other Tabernacle-owned businesses. Reactions to his inquiries varied from puzzlement to guarded cooperation to outright antagonism, but he was still no closer to locating the Bolins than he had been following his interview with Brother Daniel. No one knew anything, or if they did, they sure weren't telling. And Mavis was a dead end.

"Look," Milo said. "I know Heavy took her away. But I can't find either of them. Do you have *any* idea where they might have gone? Any idea at all? Is there someplace special, someplace she might have mentioned? Try to think."

"Why don't you just go away and leave me alone. Haven't you done enough already?"

"Trampas, can't you get it through your head? It's her *life* I'm talking about. Her *life* that's in danger."

And then the most amazing thing happened. Trampas began to cry. He was a big man, crying silent tears, sniffling against his will. Milo sat still, mouth shut, eyes averted. Finally Trampas blew his nose on a crumpled bandanna. When he spoke, there was a note of desperation in his tone.

"I've been lookin' for her too. I thought she'd be back in a couple o' days, thought she was just tryin' to dodge you. I didn't know what was goin' on. Still don't. But when she left here with Heavy she was plenty scared, I can tell you that. Then Brother Daniel called, himself, said if you came pokin' around I should say I didn't know anything. That was the truth. A week went by and she didn't come back. I pestered Betty, thought she might know, but she said she didn't have any idea. So I went out to the Tabernacle, talked to Brother Daniel. He said it was all right, she was doin' somethin' for him. But another week passed and she still didn't come back. So I asked again. This time he told me it was none of my business, to get back here and run the Pit Stop and quit askin' questions. Then I *knew* somethin' was wrong. That's when I started tryin' to find her. Man, I can't sleep at night. I've been sick, worryin' about her."

Milo wanted to reassure the man, offer him something for his cooperation. "She's not in trouble with me, I can promise you that. I think Wendy was a witness to something, a case I've been working on. That's what I wanted to talk to her about. And I guess that's what upset her. Is there anybody you can think of she was close to, palled around with, anybody she might have told? If we can figure out *what* she knew, maybe we can figure out *why* they don't want us to find her. But we need to be quick about it. We're running out of time."

The buzzer in the cramped office rang, indicating the manager was needed out front. He got up slowly, like an old man. "I have to get that," he said. "Keep your seat."

In five minutes Trampas returned, wiping his hands on the same dirty handkerchief. " . . . doesn't care anything about me. Won't go out with me. Runs around with all sorts of crap but I can't even take her to a movie." He was mumbling to himself.

"Sorry," embarrassed, Trampas seemed surprised to see Milo. He stuffed the bandana in his hip pocket. "Okay, here's the only thing I can think of. There's this one guy, some sort of computer geek, nasty little shit, hangs around here a lot. Really has the hots for Wendy. But lately, he hasn't been by. In fact, I don't think I've seen him since she's been gone. Hasn't asked about her or anything. Wouldn't you say that's kinda funny?"

"Yes," said Milo. "That is definitely kinda funny. What's his name and where I can find him?"

"His name," Trampas spat, with a touch of venom, "is Mike McKensie. And he works for the Tabernacle."

"Do you know this guy, Marshal?" Milo had gone straight from the Pit Stop to the Turner Falls' police station. Trying the Tabernacle would be pointless. But Marshal Hildebrand was a little warier this time around.

"I'm afraid I have to ask why you're hassling the good citizens of Turner Falls, Captain Thomas. We've had a number of complaints about you. There are some people who don't enjoy your meddling in their business." The genial, cornpone lawman was gone, replaced by an all business police officer.

"I suppose Brother Daniel is one of them."

"You need to understand that the Tabernacle is one of our largest corporate employers. I'd guess that their various enterprises make up fully a third of our tax base. This is a small town, Thomas, not a city like Little Rock. I'd like to help you, but I need to know why."

It was a reasonable request.

"Let's say that Wendy Bolin is a material witness in a case I'm working on. When I came in here before, looking for information, I had reason to believe that she'd ducked out on me, probably with her brother Heavy's help. Now I'm not so sure. There's a strong possibility that she's been abducted, or is being held against her will."

"And you think the Tabernacle's involved."

Milo would have to be careful. "I don't think anything about the Tabernacle, one way or the other. I asked for their help because both Wendy and Heavy are their employees. The preacher out there told me Heavy was away on church business, and that he didn't know anything about Wendy. That was over two weeks ago. Neither one of them has showed up since, and nobody seems to know where they are. This morning someone suggested I might talk to Mike McKensie, who is also a Tabernacle employee. Apparently he and Wendy had a thing going. I thought you might know where to find him."

The Marshal took out a pocket knife, opened the small blade, and began reaming his pipe. The operation took several minutes. He deposited the carbonized gunk in a large ashtray, filled the bowl with a fresh plug of Granger, and held a match to the briar. When the tobacco caught, he had decided.

"McKensie is a bad piece of work," he said through a cloud of smoke. "He's been here six or seven years, maybe longer, since right after Daniel moved out of K-Mart to that place on the bluff. There's something not quite right about him. Used to scare some of the local ladies, starin' at 'em funny. As a matter of fact, some time back, maybe a year or so after he showed up, a couple o' squirrel hunters found a body out in the woods. A woman, stark nekkid, carved up pretty bad. Had her tits cut off, and her genitals. Body's all there was, no clothes, no nothin'. She was pretty rotten, out there in the weather, so there weren't any fingerprints or anything to help with the identification. Course the sheriff sent her to the state crime lab, but that was before DNA and they couldn't find a match. We thought for a while she might be a lady realtor from North Little Rock, the one who went to show a house and never came back. Found her car abandoned—you remember. Left a three year old kid. But the height and age were wrong.

"Anyway, I brought him in, asked him a few questions, general stuff mostly. Smart mouth bastard. Would've turned him over to the sheriff if there'd been anything there. But there was nothin' to hold him on and Daniel vouched for him." He fiddled with the pipe, tapped it on the ashtray's cork knocker. Looked directly at Milo. "I still have my doubts. I see him from time to time out at Lester's, but he don't come to town much anymore."

"But you know where he lives."

"Lives in a trailer half way between here and Marshall, off a dirt road outta Yardell. Got it from another fella works for the Tabernacle, Joe Lacey Funderburk. You pro'bly met him when you were scoutin' around town. Joe Lacey ain't a bad sort, operates the church's video place and has a TV repair shop in back. And he does a pretty good trade on the side, hookin' up VCRs and stuff. Joe Lacey was about the closest thing we had around here to high tech before the computer craze. I reckon . . ."

"Marshal, can you show me how to get to the trailer?"

It was a long shot, but Wendy had to be somewhere. Why not the mobile home? According to Trampas, McKensie's conduct was curious enough to warrant taking a look. Milo brought in his atlas of Arkansas counties, showing every pig trail in the state. Marshal Hildebrand selected a printed dot. "Right there," he said. "That's it."

"I know that road," Milo said. "I was out there the other day when I drove out to the Tabernacle's poultry operation. I must have passed right by his place."

"Not much traffic out that way now, not since they closed down the missile silo. Not that there ever was very much; the Air Force was picky about letting folks on their property."

"One of the Titan silos was located around here? I thought they were all farther south, closer to the center of the state."

"Nope," the Marshal said. "There was one out there all right. Number eighteen. Never caused us any trouble, no accidents or anything, like at some of the others. That's pro'bly why it didn't register. If you went all the way to the end, out to Harlan's place, you were right next to it."

CHAPTER 16

James Coltrane stuffed a handful of popcorn in his mouth, chasing it down with a swig of Bud. He belched, ate more popcorn, then drained the can, crushing and dropping it with a thunk on the floor, littered with similarly crushed cans. Sean Connery's weathered face stared from the TV, wreathed with scraggly white hair. James pointed a greasy finger at the image. "You tell 'em."

Ambivalent, James was watching *The Rock* for perhaps the eighth time, rooting in turn for Ed Harris and the troops who had taken over the citadel, then for the forces marshaled to stop them. Since transferring to the graveyard shift on Daniel's instructions he was having trouble sleeping. He'd been on nights for over six months now, since right after Lorene took off, and still his biorhythms wouldn't adjust. So he drank—beer—lots of it, and watched action movies on the VCR. And hoped Boyd didn't catch him 'cause he'd vowed he'd sworn off the booze.

He got up with some difficulty, detoured by the john, and retrieved a fresh brew. It wouldn't do to think too much about Lorene. Where'd she get off running out on him anyway, after he'd married the rotten bitch? Now she was garnisheeing his friggin' paycheck, a prime example of what was wrong with this country, when some lyin' tramp could go and *legally* take the bread out of a workin' stiff's mouth.

Good thing Lorene didn't know about the Tabernacle deal. Because even though James was doing this for God and country, nobody ever said God couldn't reward those who helped Him out. Once he'd set the charge and blown the cooling pipe, he'd have pots of dough, so he wished they'd get the hell on with it.

*   *   *

177.00

320.68   741.01   368.33   195.58   326.16

[mm]

SEEKER SECTION   WARHEAD SECTION   PROPULSION SECTION

GUIDANCE SECTION GROUP   CONTROL SECTION

HELLFIRE MISSILE

At 64 inches and 100 pounds, with trajectory shaping features and ballistic/glide mode options to optimize the angle of impact, the Hellfire packs a potent wallop. In its original form it was the principal weapon system of the Army's AH-64 Apache and the Marine Corps's AH-1 Super Cobra attack helicopters. Proven to have superb anti-armor capabilities during Operation Desert Storm, it has since been modified into its present form, Hellfire II, an updated, improved system capable of defeating reactive armor configurations projected into the 21st century, and the complementary Longbow Hellfire Missile, a millimeter wave radar fire-and-forget version.

For Boyd's little band of terrorists, the older model was quite sufficient. Intended to take out tanks and similar tank-type targets, with a fuzing action specifically designed to penetrate the target before detonation, four missiles timed to fire at eight second intervals with laser precision at the steel-reinforced, concrete containment building would have a devastating effect, knocking a huge hole in the reactor's shell. Internally, the hole would be even larger, the exit spall into the core producing a lethal fragmentation shower of high-velocity shards, shredding the complex maze of pipes and condensers. Depending on wind velocity and direction, the resulting cloud of death could reach Little Rock in two hours, or be over Memphis before daylight.

Firing and air-to-ground missile from the bluff was not as tricky as it sounds. Boyd's launch position was well within the 2.8 mile effective range, and almost a thousand feet above the reactor. Although designated as helicopter armaments, Hellfire missiles are so dependable the military has done extensive studies to broaden their potential, utilizing both different aircraft and ground vehicles as alternative launch platforms. In test situations the Hellfire has been successfully fired from everything from a jet fighter to the broad back of a humvee. Boyd had extrapolated data from those test results, replacing the mobile launch vehicle with a transportable firing rack, stabilized on pilings countersunk into solid ground. Using the pair of GLLD targeters, he had calculated the firing mode as a direct, rapid fire, LOBL (Lock On Before Launch) engagement. It was a fixed-site, one time only deal, but then, he had been running a one time only operation.

McKensie had botched that brilliant scheme.

*   *   *

Coming down out of the hills on U.S. 65, they hit I-40 at Conway, exiting eighteen miles later on Military Road. Looping over the freeway through Burns Park the Jeep stayed on Military, driving onto the base through the main gate, which was not a gate at all, but a marked extension of the same thoroughfare. A

165

billboard picturing the base layout signaled the boundary, complete with red star indicating **YOU ARE HERE**. Affixed to the sign, a small notice said Camp Robinson was closed to the public from 2200 hours to 0600.

Boyd and Wynne were on their own. After dropping them at the corner of 26th and Nebraska, the Jeep, with Vonnie Lee at the wheel, headed immediately back to Turner Falls, well before the ten o'clock civilian curfew. Carrying flashlights and tool kits, they followed a dirt track into the woods, past a sign that said without the express consent of the base commander what they were doing was a federal offense. In the dark, nobody saw them. Had anyone been watching, dressed in woodland camos bearing 224th Maintenance patches, the two men would not have merited a second look.

After half a mile the road played out, terminating at a weather station, but the men kept walking. It was not until they had penetrated around the far end of the runway did they dig in.

Camp Joseph T. Robinson is a sprawling complex of 32,896 acres, filling the V between U.S. 67 and Interstate 40. Timbered in scrub oak and pine, it is rugged terrain both hilly and marshy, with strata of slate and moss-encrusted boulders, intersected by a dozen creeks. Camp Robinson serves as state headquarters for the Arkansas Army National Guard and Air National Guard. During artillery practice, mortars exploding on the firing range can be felt across the river in downtown Little Rock.

On a compass heading of 040°/220°, roughly parallel with the runways at LRAFB, the 5,000 foot strip at Camp Robinson culminates in a dog leg, bent right toward dense pines. Protected by a six foot chain length fence topped with three strands of barbed wire, and widely spaced floods, this angular extension of the runway serves as a storage pad for aircraft not in daily use. That night, with Wynne and Boyd secreted in the woods barely a hundred yards away, sixteen Cobra attack helicopters lodged single file on the auxiliary pad. Fully fueled at all times to avoid condensation in the tanks, the choppers were locked, their keys hanging on a pegboard in the Maintenance Supervisor's office.

Chris didn't need a key.

The closest structure to the helicopters was a maintenance hangar, with a passenger turboprop parked in front. Across the runway, letters on the main ops building identified Robinson Army Airfield. By quarter of two, all activity had ceased. The men in hiding hadn't seen any movement of any kind since a mechanic wandered out of the hangar shortly after midnight, lit a cigar, and drove off. Relatively sure the field had been secured for the night, Boyd stole out of the trees, hitting the fence directly opposite the last helicopter in line. There was minimal backwash, the floods directed inward to illuminate the tarmac, not the perimeter. Crouched at the edge of the spill, Boyd used wire snips to cut a two by three foot, hinged flap in the chain link.

"Now."

With Boyd covering, Chris rolled through the gap, sprinting to the Cobra on the end. Shielded from the maintenance building by fifteen other choppers, he expertly jimmied the latches, then waved for Boyd, who holstered his weapon and wriggled through the fence, lowering the flap behind him. Darting to the copter, Boyd settled in the front seat, clapping the cans over his ears. Chris was leaning through the pilot's hatch, head down, fiddling under the steering column. With a blue spark, a sizzle like grease popping, and the odor of singed flesh, the engine caught—as easy as hot-wiring a car. Chris spat on his fingers and swung up into the cockpit. He goosed the throttle, starting the rotor and revving engine power to 100%.

"Dick?"

Transported by the olfactory trigger, Boyd didn't respond.

"Dick? Okay?" insistent in his headphones. Boyd wrenched himself out of the jungle, grunted assent. Seconds later they were airborne.

They took off west, a menacing black bird swooping into the night. With no control tower to spot them, there was only noise to give them away. But what of it? With everything shut down tight at the airfield, who was there to follow?

Staying below radar, Chris picked up the river and traced it northwest, scanning the airwaves for signs of pursuit. There were none. After skirting Morrilton without incident, they decided they were in the clear. In the morning when the theft was discovered there would be a real brouhaha at the airfield, but for the time being, there was not one soul on their trail.

They had planned to cut north up the Pope/Conway county line, a course that would take them across large tracts of uninhabited Ozark National Forest. But the sky was theirs, and the opportunity to overfly Russellville and do a quick aerial recon of their target was irresistible. Then Nuclear One loomed beneath them, red warning lights flashing intermittently from the cooling tower. Hovering briefly, they examined the reactor from directly overhead. It was a chip shot.

* * *

Milo tried to keep his hopes down as he hurried out the winding road to McKensie's trailer. It was a long shot, but after two weeks of disappointments, his luck was due to turn. As 3.9 rolled over toward 4.0 on the odometer, Milo slowed. There it sat, as advertised, a nondescript, older mobile home, set amid the shade of pin oaks and hickories. Milo pulled into the drive, dirt ruts running two hundred feet to a free standing porte-cochère. Behind the parking structure a large capacity butane tank was mounted on struts. Stepping stones led to the front door, which was shielded by a rusting metal awning, and a mini-satellite dish sprouted from the roof.

The trailer was deserted. But Milo had known that before he rapped on the locked door. Five newspapers, their yellow plastic sleeves coated in dust, lay scattered under the tubular paper box. Another filled the cylinder.

Milo felt a mild pang of disappointment, but he hadn't really expected the girl to be there. In the Marshal's office, grasping at straws, it had seemed possible. But Trampas Morgan suspected the techno-nerd, and undoubtedly Trampas had been there before him. Still, he had to make sure.

Milo prowled around the exterior, looking for trip wires or anything that hinted of a booby trap. He was extremely cautious. Subversive nuts were notoriously paranoid about privacy, and he didn't relish getting blown to smithereens by a rigged shotgun blast.

The back door, aluminum-clad particle board with three glass panes, was locked too. The locking mechanism was a simple push button, not a dead bolt. After peering through the center pane, Milo pulled out a credit card and deftly popped the spring. Then he picked up a stick and pushed back the door. When nothing exploded he went in.

The place was clean.

Milo had been looking for Wendy for three weeks, two full time. The manager of Lester's had implicated a third member of the cult, who, by all indication, appeared to be missing too. For all his efforts, the investigator had no idea where the girl, her brother, and now this guy McKensie, might be. Addy was dead, people connected to the Tabernacle kept disappearing, and Milo didn't know why. It was driving him crazy.

*　　*　　*

James Coltrane eyed one of the fat Canadian geese asleep on the promenade. He drew a bead on the sleeping bird with his Glock. "Blam!" he said, "Got you, you dumbass motherfucker." James hated the geese, they were a messy nuisance, crapping all over the sidewalks, but the company wouldn't run them off. He pivoted smoothly, aiming at another bird, and another, wiping out a whole platoon of the suckers.

On break, James was taking a turn outside to shake the lead out. "Fine," he scolded himself. "Coltrane, you are one fucked up piece o' shit. You lie awake all day and soon as you go on duty you can't keep your eyes open. What would Johnny O' (his pa-

169

trol supervisor) have to say if he caught you out here with your gun drawn, poppin' a bunch o' friggin' geese?" James looked around guiltily and put the pistol away. "Just wait," he told the honkers. "Just you wait. A little while longer and you sons o' bitches are history."

In the distance he heard the drone of an approaching helicopter, scanned the sky automatically to see if he could spot it. Maybe it was a Medevac, or a TV SkyCam, or maybe even the state cops, on a manhunt. If he could just see the bird, he could probably figure it out. Three a.m., it sure as hell wasn't somebody out for a Sunday drive. One thing though, all that racket was disturbing the geese. They honked an angry alarm and took flight in unison, circling out over the calm waters of the lake.

And then in the downdraft he caught it, a moving silhouette, blacker than black, blotting out a section of stars.

"Hot damn," James whooped. "Hot damn. A gun ship. The Feds. Somethin' goin' down and they're bringin' in the heavy artillery. Wonder whatever the hell they're up to?" He saluted the helo, chopping his left palm into the crook of his right elbow and raising a rigid hand skyward in a universal gesture of contempt.

✳   ✳   ✳

"A band of low pressure is sagging down from the plains, setting up a broad trough aloft. Centered in eastern Kansas, the front is expected to reach northwest Arkansas around dawn tomorrow. Ahead of the front, showers and thundershowers will be breaking out across the state . . ."

Milo snapped off the television. He had been listening with half an ear to the ten o'clock news, waiting for Betsy to call. He was getting antsy—she should be there by now. *Don't be a damn fool. She's a grown woman, she's perfectly capable of taking care of herself.* Still, it was time he heard from her.

If he only had a cigarette. Milo was rummaging through untidy drawers in search of a stray Marlboro when the phone finally rang.

"Saved by the bell," he answered, relieved that she was all right.

"From whom or what?"

"Quentin." He couldn't hide his letdown.

"Well, excuse me. What's up?"

"I was expecting another call, that's all. And I *am* glad to hear from you, but will it keep?"

"Oh ho. Could it be that you have *cherche*zed *la femme* and found one? Well glory be."

"Q.C., wha'd'ya want? If it can wait I'm gonna hang up so she can get through."

"Fine, hang up, I can deal with rejection. Tell her I said hello. I'll talk to in the morning."

"Thanks, Quentin. First thing."

Milo didn't subscribe to any of the optional services offered by Southwestern Bell: no call waiting, call forwarding, or caller I.D. His home number was unpublished, and save for voice mail, mandated by the office, a single line and an answering machine were adequate for his needs. Nobody called Milo he didn't know, and know well.

He had no sooner put down the receiver than the phone rang again. He snatched it up. This time it *was* Betsy.

"Hi, guy." She sounded tired. "Had you given up on me?"

"I was startin' to get worried," he confessed. "After the way you took off this morning, I wasn't sure you'd call at all." That wasn't what he'd meant to say; it just popped out.

"Don't be a ninny. I told you I wasn't good at good-byes. Anyway, I just got in. What a day. I think everybody and his brother was on the road."

They chatted idly for a few minutes before she said, "Look, Milo, I'm dead on my feet and I've got stuff stacked up here out the wazoo and there're a couple of things I've got to unload that won't keep 'til morning. If you've got a minute, give me a buzz tomorrow. I have to be on campus for a faculty meeting at two, but I'll be here until then, tryin' to sort through this mess. Right now, I feel like I could sleep straight through until the bell rings for my first class."

"Okay, Bets. You get some rest and I'll call you tomorrow. Betsy . . ."

"Un-unh. Say goodnight Milo."

"Goodnight, Milo."

"Goodnight you doofus."

When the phone rang for the third time Milo was fast asleep, Betsy's scented scarf draped across his pillow. He was dreaming, and his brain resisted the intrusion, the bell insinuating itself into the dream. Repeated trills broke through the mental barrier, and he fumbled groggily for his portable.

"Unh, what?"

"Thomas? You with me?"

"Wha? Who the hell is this?" As his mind cleared, the numerals of the clock on his nightstand swam into focus. 3:12.

"We met some time ago . . . in Saigon."

Milo sat bolt upright, shivering involuntarily. A face materialized, formed out of pixels of memory. Holder. *Jesus!* No need to wonder how *he* had gotten Milo's number.

"Yes," he said. "I remember."

"Then listen up. There's something you need to know."

"I'm out of it Holder. Have been for years. But you know that."

"Come off it, Mister fuckin' Holier Than Thou. You may be born-again, risen from the ashes as it were, but underneath, you're the same as I am." Holder's not so oblique reference to Operation Phoenix had the desired effect. "Now shut up and listen. I'm taking a risk even telling you this. But there's something happening outside the loop, and it looks like it may be goin' down on your doorstep."

"Why are you calling me? Have you got any idea what it is?"

"If I knew I *wouldn't* be callin'. There's a big flap over at Red River an' the Army's sittin' on it tighter'n a virgin on a cherry.

172

Rumor is, four of their Hellfire missiles up and flew away, and there's an old Green Beret gunnery sergeant missing in action. Found his Tahoe abandoned at a fuck stop in Texarkana, dug some splinters o' what could be missile crate outta the carpet."

It was the end of August and Milo was foundering in a blizzard, arctic air playing tag with his vertebrae. He did not doubt Holder for an instant.

"And you think they're in Arkansas."

"Wouldn't surprise me any. Lotta old timers don't care much for your native son."

"Shit Holder, that's a real stretch. Those missiles could be anywhere. You gotta have more than that."

"Did you ever run across a fellow name o' Chris Wynne in your travels with Charlie? Company chopper jock, some say part Indian. Made so many dicey extractions they started callin' him Crazy Horse. Came over to Colonel Murphy right after Tet."

Milo's body might be encased in a block of ice, but his mind wasn't frozen. The name was familiar.

"What about him?"

"Word's around somebody was tryin' to locate Wynne, somebody he'd been hooked up with way back. He'd stayed on the payroll see, 'til he got shot outta the sky over Salvador with a load of Colombia's finest. He spent sixteen months as a houseguest of the Sandanistas before we could spring him."

"What the hell's that got to do with Arkansas?"

"Didn't I say? The person digging around, lookin' for the big chief, was a real hard ass, a three-tour Special Forces major who worked with our guys on the Bay of Pigs and ran errands into the north for the Colonel. He resigned in '77, went private. But all that's history. What should be of concern to you is that Major Richard fuckin' Boyd's last known address turns out to be in Ozark cracker country, some hick dump called Turner Falls."

CHAPTER 17

Any further rest after Holder's revelations was impossible. Milo got up, pulled on a pair of trunks, and headed for the pool. At three thirty in the morning he'd have the water to himself.

Rhythmically, with economy born of habit, he traversed the forty meter enclosure, again, and again, and again, until he lost count of the laps, swimming on auto-pilot while his mind floated free. An hour later when he dragged his water-logged carcass up the ladder and toweled off, he was still perplexed.

From the beginning Milo hadn't been able to figure out what Addy's killers had been doing in the clearing. For her to have been a threat she had to have seen something that would put them at risk. But what? (Which was exactly what Boyd had asked McKensie.) Betsy was so sure it had something to do with Nuke One that Milo had reexamined that possibility. He had spent another day in conference with the utility's engineers, and again they had taken great pains to allay his concerns. Because of safeguards demanded by the Nuclear Regulatory Commission, even if it *were* technically possible, an act of sabotage was unlikely to result in damage to the reactor's core. And if some undreamed of, catastrophic breakdown did occur in all of the fail-safe systems at once, radiation leakage would be confined to the containment structure.

Holder's tale dramatically changed any scenario Milo had previously envisioned. If the terrorists (he was now thinking of Brother Daniel's followers in those terms) possessed extremely accurate, high-powered missiles, nothing in the state was immune. Leaving only one question of any practical consequence: *In the mind of the charismatic evangelist, what target would be worthy of his spleen?*

Milo's thoughts filled with scattershot images of Arkansas's people and places. Would Daniel want to take out four separate targets, or would he use the stolen weapons against a single objective? The only indicators Milo had were the location of Addy's murder and the sermon he had suffered through. He kept coming back to the nuclear reactor. Given the inherent characteristics of the missiles, was using the lakeside clearing to blast Nuke One even feasible? Or was he so obsessed with the little girl that his reasoning was impaired? Was he viewing everything in terms of her death, when it might not be connected? Plenty of investigators had made similar mistakes, clinging to some cherished *idée fixe* while ignoring the obvious. Milo forced himself to reexamine his thinking, to explore other possibilities. And that was when he really choked. Because once he subtracted Addy from the equation, there was one target so apparent, so logical, that as soon as he hit upon it, Milo couldn't picture anything else.

"Geez, man, you look like Death eatin' a cracker."

"Then," Milo said, handing Quentin half a sandwich he had bought on the way, "I look a helluva lot better than I feel."

They were sitting in the empty soccer bleachers at Murray Park, splitting a tuna sub. Milo had gotten through morning at headquarters by the hardest, unwilling to approach the Colonel with what was sure to be perceived as his latest bit of fantasy. While he totally believed every word Holder had said, no way could he take his boss some cockamamie story about missing missiles the Pentagon either wouldn't or couldn't confirm, a furtive search for a Company pilot who'd dropped out of sight years ago and hadn't been heard from since, based on a late night phone call from a source he could never identify. All linked to an ex-Special Forces major who was currently serving as adviser to an ultra right-wing preacher with his own religious organization, three members of that same organization who just happened to have disappeared, and a dead nine year old he had no earthly idea how to fit into the picture. Burton Lamann—the quintessential skeptic, who wouldn't believe that fat meat was greasy without a sparerib in hand—would throw him out of the office.

While Q.C. ate, Milo laid it all out. Then came the moment of truth.

"My best guess is, they're going to kill Clinton."

"Say what?"

"That's it. That's what this whole thing must be about. They intend to assassinate the President."

"And that's what this Holder character told you? In so many words?"

"Not explicitly, no. More of a casual reference. But I haven't thought about anything else since he called, and that's the single most likely interpretation. You got a better idea? I'm open to suggestions."

"Nothin' right off the top of my head." Quentin scratched his close-cropped skull. "Milo, you've been sayin' all along that the Tabernacle's dangerous and I take your word for it. But what I don't get is, why call *you*? What does Holder expect you to do?"

"I don't know. Try to stop it, I guess." Milo put his head in his hands.

"Look, Milo, no offense, but couldn't there be some other explanation."

"Jesus, I wish there were. But what?"

Milo wadded up his sandwich wrapper and walked to the end of the bleachers, tossing the crumpled ball into a waste can. He looked around the park. A group of handicapped children was playing in one of the city's barrier-free playgrounds, their bright orange Links paratransport parked next to a pavilion where adult chaperones were cleaning up a picnic. Behind him, an old pickup was backing a dinged-up skiff into the Arkansas River. In repudiation of the forecast, the sky was clear blue, rich as oil paint squeezed straight from the tube.

Dear God, Milo offered up a humble prayer in the outdoor cathedral, *please help me keep something terrible from happening here.*

He sighed, trudged back to join the FBI agent. "You know Quentin, the thing that throws me, the thing I can't figure out is the same thing that's been bothering me all along: what does Addy Willis have to do with any of this? Her death doesn't fit."

"Maybe nothing. Maybe it's like apples and oranges, you can't add 'em up." Quentin paused. "But I don't suppose you'd buy that?"

Milo had reluctantly come to that same conclusion. "Anything's possible."

"Okay, then, so what've we got? I think," Quentin posited, "that whatever is going on comes back to my original question: why call *you*, or anybody on this side of the fence? What's it to Holder and his pals if some group of fundamentalist nuts *does* manage to croak Clinton? The current administration hasn't exactly been enamored with this country's intelligence services. Look at the beatin' we took after Ruby Ridge, not to mention the Waco fiasco. And Justice sicced Kenneth Starr on the White House. Now there's the spy scandal at Los Alamos. Wha'da they stand to gain?"

"I don't know," Milo said, "but I think you're looking at this bass-ackwards. The question is, what've they got to lose? There are still conspiracy freaks out there who think CIA, in collusion with the Mob, knocked off JFK. Now I'm not going to say that theory is entirely without merit; I've got a bridge I'll sell to anybody who believes the Warren Commission's 'one magic bullet' bullshit. But this time they must have clean hands.

"Since the end of the cold war CIA's attracted nothing but negative publicity. Huge slush funds, secret buildings, royal flub ups in Iran and Iraq. And after Aldrich Ames, the Company is about down for the count. There's been talk about dismantling it entirely.

"What I think is, they've gotten wind of something they're afraid of, but can't risk suspicion falling on the Agency or any of its subsidiaries. Holder said he was taking a chance talking to me. From their standpoint he probably was. It's funny, but in the truest sense of the word, Holder *is* a patriot. I think by giving me what he had, he thought there'd still be a chance of preventing whatever was coming down. And, he knew I wouldn't involve him . . . because I couldn't."

"You," Quentin said. "Milo Thomas. You're elected to take care of *It*, whatever *It* is?"

Milo nodded.

"Is there somethin' you haven't told me Milo? You some kinda super, badass hee-ro?"

"No," Milo said. "There are no Jack Ryans. I'm all he's got."

Following his al fresco lunch with Quentin, Milo had just gotten back to the accumulated papers on his desk when the Colonel's secretary called.

"He'd like to see you."

The interview was short and to the point. "It's about time you came back. You get any answers?"

Milo replied truthfully, "Just more questions."

Colonel Lamann looked appraisingly at his chief investigator. "Too bad, Milo," he said dryly. He slid a folder across the desk. "This came while you were gone. You know the drill. Take care of it."

Milo opened the folder, absorbing yet another body blow. There, in black and white, was confirmation of his worst fears: official notification that Clinton was coming to town. In four weeks POTUS, the President Of The United States, would be landing in Little Rock for a weekend interlude in his old stomping ground.

"Sure, Burton," he managed to say. "I'll get right on it."

* * *

In the predawn hours the only noise at the farm was the constant whirring of ventilation fans sucking air through the long chicken sheds. The summertime months of July, August, and September were particularly difficult for poultry producers, when temperatures inside the tin-roofed buildings reached triple digits in the blazing sun. In a non-stop battle to keep thousands of birds from keeling over, the fans ran night and day.

Wendy had grown accustomed to the drone in her weeks of captivity. It was an altogether different clatter and vibration that shook her awake just before four. Her first reaction was that the long predicted earthquake along the New Madrid Fault had finally happened. Rubbing sleep from her eyes, she realized the din was overhead. There was no window in her cell, which was actually Daniel's sleeping niche in the main office. Her only access to the outside world was a high, fixed pane in the adjoining bath. By standing on the toilet seat Wendy could see out. A light wavered over the open space behind the sheds. In the ghostly glare of false sunrise, a black helicopter was slowly settling to the ground.

All Arkansas National Guard AH-1S Cobra helicopters are rigged to carry TOW Weapon Systems (Tube-Launched, Optically Tracked, Wire Command-Link Guided Missiles). Racking for the TOWs (bulkier, heavier, with different triggering and guidance systems than Hellfire), was incompatible with the cult's missiles. Existing rails on the purloined bird would need to be replaced.

When the rotor wound down, Wynne secured the blade, then four men pushed the inert machine into its makeshift hangar through sliding doors wide enough to accommodate farm equipment or a stolen helicopter. They weren't planning to keep the Cobra there indefinitely—just until Wynne could make the necessary adaptations. Then they'd move it to a less vulnerable location. In the meantime, the maintenance facility, which contained a good metal-working shop, would have to do. Up close or from the air, it was just another outbuilding.

Wendy had to get out of there. She'd seen too much, heard too much. Daniel was keeping her alive just to insure Heavy's cooperation. When their mission was over, she was toast. Wendy knew because they didn't care if she heard—fine tuning their plans in the study right on the other side of the door. When the truth had finally sunk in, she'd tried to tell Heavy. He could fix it, he could sneak her away. Big, sweet, lovable Heavy, who'd always taken care of her. But her brother didn't understand. A tear slid down Wendy's cheek. They were all going to die, and a lot more people too.

That cop that had come to Lester's, if only he knew. He'd shown up here asking questions, looking for *her*. Boy had that fried them! How could she have been so stupid? If she'd just told him what he wanted to know, she wouldn't be stuck here now.

Awash in self pity, Wendy crawled back into bed, buried her face in the pillow.

No! She would *not* cry. She would figure out a way. She was clever and conniving and she didn't want to die. There *had* to be a way out. She *was* going to get out.

✻   ✻   ✻

It had been a brutish ten days. Between the regular grind, playing catch up with two weeks' back work, and trying to corroborate Holder's story, Milo hadn't gotten much rest. He had attended a couple of conferences to go over preliminary security arrangements for the upcoming Presidential visit. At no time did he mention to the Colonel or any of the G-men Holder's tip-off about the missiles. He did voice concerns about the Tabernacle and Brother Daniel's anti-government rhetoric. A nudge to the Secret Service couldn't hurt. [Based solely on his denunciations from the pulpit, Daniel would receive the lowest classification in the Secret Service's catalog of potential threats to the Chief Executive's continued health and well being: Class III, someone who might bear watching if conditions changed.]

Milo and Quentin pooled intelligence. Q.C. scoured Bureau files for information on members of the Tabernacle, while Milo sought out acquaintances from the old days, to see what they could dig up on Boyd and Chris Wynne.

One factor in their favor was having access to the President's itinerary. Provided EAGLE were indeed the target, they were able to confine their speculation to scheduled venues. The fact that Hellfires are air-to-ground weaponry effectively eliminated the clearing on Lake Dardanelle as a possible launch site, disposing of Milo's lingering questions about a connection to Addy's murder. It also ruled out an assault on Marine One, the Presidential helicopter. [The FCC maintains a two mile no-fly zone around POTUS at all times, whether he is airborne, holding a town meeting in Des Moines, or tucked comfortably in bed at Camp David. It is curious to note that while a Secret Service agent is stationed in the Control Tower, and air traffic controllers issue stern warnings to keep planes out of the two-mile safety zone, there is no enforcement tool ready to interdict violators. Rather, it is up to the agent on tower duty to relay a warning of infringement to his cohorts on the Presidential Detail. It is then the Detail that must arrange appropriate countermeasures.] Their deliberations ended when the two horrified investigators concluded simultaneously that there was one site that would satisfy even the most obsessive megalomaniac. And they were numb struck.

What neither Milo nor Q.C. had not been able to ascertain was *how* the missiles were to be delivered. And that was a major sticking point.

That morning at nine-fifteen the other shoe dropped.

"Milo, we've got a big problem." Quentin's anxious words rushed at him through the phone line. "The adjutant at Camp Robinson called Roger ten minutes ago to report that a Cobra's missing."

"The hell you say!"

"Now get this. It's been gone for a *week*. A whole friggin' week. They discovered it was gone last Monday, but they spent the whole damn week trying to track it down. At least that's what the man said. But damnit! What'd they think—that it'd just gotten up and walked off? I mean, how do you misplace a helo? They had to have *heard* it, even if they didn't see it leave. I don't believe it. Maybe they thought they could get it back before they had to tell anybody. Who knows? The Army has a mind-set all its own. Anyway, Colonel Stroud finally decided he'd better report the *apparent* theft of one of Uncle Sam's million dollar tinker toys. Shit. If the National Guard couldn't find it, how the hell do they think we can get it back?"

The import was not lost on Milo. "The Tabernacle took it," he said immediately. "Boyd and that Company pilot. *That's* how they're gonna launch the missiles."

"You got it."

"And it's been gone an entire week?"

"Well, he said they first noticed it Monday, but when Roger pressed him, the Colonel admitted it could've been missing all weekend. There weren't any training exercises scheduled so . . . All they're really sure of is it was there on Friday."

"Aw shit, Quentin, why couldn't those fuckin' geniuses have reported it sooner?" Milo fumed angrily, a sick feeling in the pit of his stomach. "After that kind of a head start, our chances of tracking it down now are between slim and none."

"Ain't that the gospel."

"But Christ, Q.C., if we *don't* find that bird, there's no way in hell we're gonna stop 'em."

CHAPTER 18

Milo was running late. Coming back through Jacksonville he had gotten hung up in five o'clock traffic, especially heavy on the eve of the Labor Day weekend. For twenty minutes he chafed, inching bumper to bumper through the mass exodus from downtown. When he eventually turned off the freeway onto Bankhead Drive, a Delta 737 was coming in on final.

He pulled into Short Term parking, lucking into a space being vacated by an exiting Saturn, and dashed for the terminal, dodging a curbside jumble of vehicles. At Security he flashed his shield to circumvent a lengthy line at the metal detectors, and hustled to Gate Three. When he arrived the first deplaning passengers were emerging from the jetway.

Betsy was the fifth person off. She spotted Milo and waved, lighting up like a Christmas tree. "Hi," she said, giving him a kiss on the cheek and a one-armed hug while he grabbed her satchel from the other. "I've flown in here lots of times, but this is the nicest welcome I've had."

He was glad he'd gotten there on time. "Don't tell me all those other bums never met your plane?"

"Other bums my Aunt Fanny," she said. "You know what I mean."

"I hope," he said, "it means you're glad to see me."

"Of course I'm glad to see you. You don't think I'd fly down here on the spur of the moment just to go to the movies or out to dinner."

"Thanks Betsy." He grinned wryly. "Did you check a bag?"

"Nope, I travel light. I've got everything in my carry-on."
"Then let's get out of here."

"You haven't told me," he said over their appetizers, "how's my favorite Basset hound?"

She broke off a piece of French roll, dropping it into what remained of her wild-and-creamy escargot sauce. "Swell. Menga and John Cato both send their regards. Nina, my graduate assistant, is staying with the dogs. She dog-sat for me last semester too, and they're crazy about her. But she spoils them outrageously. I'll have to put them on a diet for a couple of days when I get back." The piece of bread vanished in her mouth. "Me too," she said.

They were sitting in the back room at Alouette's, working their way through a terrific dinner. The conversation remained light throughout: the dogs, her class schedule, who was new on the faculty, the weather, the Razorbacks' prospects—general dinner table chit chat, steering away from what he'd been doing.

After they'd split a scrumptious Grand Marnier soufflé, the waiter brought expressos, and poured them each a tot of fifty year old brandy. Then the hostess appeared with a humidor of cigars. Milo gazed longingly at the contents before declining. He had forgotten about cigars when he swore off smoking. A good corona would sure ease what he was about to do.

Betsy leaned forward. "What a wonderful meal. Thank you for bringing me here Milo," she said appreciatively. "It was every bit as good as Maisonette, and it has four stars."

"I'm glad you enjoyed it." He took her hand. He should have done this as soon as she arrived, but somehow he couldn't bring himself to spoil her innocent pleasure when she got off the plane. Later, at his condo, in the afterglow of their love making, he had willfully kept quiet. Now Milo couldn't put it off any longer. "Betsy," he said soberly, "I have a confession to make. I don't even know quite where to start."

She stared at him with a quizzical expression.

"I'm afraid I asked you down here on false pretenses. This isn't going to be strictly a fun and games weekend."

"It's not?" she raised one eyebrow. "Okay Milo. What's up?"

"What I'm trying to say is, I need your help."

The most logical, and conversely, most dangerous place to stash the chopper—if it were in the hands of Brother Daniel's fanatics as they had every reason to believe—was at the Tabernacle's isolated poultry farm. After that it was anybody's guess.

Betsy had topographical maps covering all of Arkansas. They were prime tools in her work for the Archeological Survey. Milo had looked over some of the charts during his stay at the cabin. When he questioned her she had called them *field quads*, or 7.5 minute grids, covering roughly fifty-six square miles. Blown up to an easily readable 2' x 3' size, they were basically contour maps marked with elevations, trees, and prominent landmarks. Developed by the Geological Survey, it took 970+ individual grids to cover the entire state. But Milo wasn't worried about the entire state. He had dug the point of a compass into a spot representing Daniel's Tabernacle of Divine Redemption and, using a twenty-five mile radius, described a circle extending from Marshall to the Missouri line, taking in parts of four counties. It was an arbitrary decision, but they had to start somewhere. Unfortunately, when Betsy left, the tubes of maps had gone in the back of Homer along with her field notes and photographs.

Betsy knew the terrain in Marion, Searcy, Boone, and Newon counties better than anybody Milo could think of. She had spent her summers for the last dozen years systematically climbing over and through every rock and rill, cave, wood and hollow, probing the land for secrets from the past. If anyone could help them locate the missing Cobra, it was she.

That morning, as soon as Quentin hung up after his disturbing revelation, Milo had e-mailed Betsy's office, knowing she checked her terminal between classes. *Bets, Please call, ASAP or sooner. Milo.*

185

Forty minutes later she was on the line. "What can't wait, Milo Thomas? The house on fire?"

"I'm lonesome," he said. "How'd you like to fly down for the weekend? There's a direct flight leaving Cincinnati at five, gets here at five thirty. I made a reservation for you, just in case."

"You horny fool," she laughed. "Okay, why not? I guess I can swing it."

"Terrific. I'll meet you at the gate."

He hadn't intended to mislead her. God knows his physical longing for her was acute. But he didn't have three days to spare for a romantic tryst. Neither could he go into the problem over the telephone. Well, she had agreed. That was what counted.

Milo next turned his attention to replacing her absent store of maps. The State Police maintains up-to-date, county by county charts of the entire state, showing cities and townships, roads, lakes, rivers, and pertinent geographical features, plus thousands of dots representing rural residences, but they are only larger scale versions of the atlas Milo kept in his truck. They are planar representations, based on extremely accurate, aerial photographs made by the state Highway and Transportation Department.

The Highway Department shoots pictures of every county in Arkansas on a routine basis, updating the film every four to ten years. From these photographs department cartographers produce annually edited surface maps. Milo was lucky in one respect. With the widening of Highway 65, Boone County, in which Turner Falls was located, had been reshot in 1999, as had Searcy County, Newton in 1998, Marion way back in 1996. It would be a big boost if he could get a set of the actual photos.

"What you want," Marilyn told him, "is the Photogrammetry Division of the Arkansas Highway Department."

At the end of ten minutes Milo had found exactly what he needed but was told he couldn't have, at least not immediately —and immediately was the key. An officious bastard let it be known right off the bat that Milo's request would executed when he had time, usually within ten days to two weeks. And that was too late. Way too late. Invoking urgent police business, Milo tried to get the pictures expedited. The fellow was very helpful. He didn't give two dips and a damn that Milo was the law. Nor, he said, would it cut any ice with him if the Governor's office called. He cheerfully informed Milo that only if the head of the Highway Department himself wanted those photos by quitting time would he find a way to get them done. Otherwise, forget it.

Milo phoned Quentin. "Who do you know at the Highway Department?"

"Not a damn soul. Why?"

A short explanation ensued.

"Well," said Quentin, "the world's full of jackasses. It was a good idea but I guess that takes care of that. We'll just have to use what we've got."

"Maybe not," Milo said excitedly. "I just thought of something. I'll get back to you."

What he had thought of were LandSat photographs of his mother's delta plantation, used to figure acreage, set-asides, and crop allotments, before his father sold the land after her death.

It took him two more calls before he reached the right agency. Renamed the Farm Service Agency in 1996, the former ASCS kept aerial photographs of *all* acreage within the bound- a-ries of the United States. There was a six week lag, but for a nominal fee, from their Salt Lake City headquarters the agency would fill orders for pictures of any non-restricted property any-where in the U.S., either from archival footage, or by aiming the best positioned satellite at the specified area and clicking away. That was, if photostatic copies on file at individual FSA county offices wouldn't suffice.

Yes!

FSA administrative offices in Marshall (Searcy and Newton counties), Harrison (Boone), and Mountain Home (Marion and Baxter) would have exactly what he needed. And the scale was even larger than the Highway Department's. He could get four section, 24" x 24" maps where 1" represented 660', or 36" x 36" enlargements, at a ratio of 1" to 330'. Perfect.

Staffers at the three county bureaus went all out to help, and had blow-ups waiting when he arrived to pick them up. It had necessitated a three hundred mile round trip, but when he turned off the ignition and sprinted to meet Betsy's flight, tucked in the back of Milo's Expedition was a thick stack of high resolution photographs covering every square inch of his red-penciled circle.

Meanwhile, Quentin had had a brainstorm of his own. It would mean his job if he got caught, but it just might work.

Roger Teasdale, Quentin's boss and head of the Bureau's Little Rock field office, had taken the day off. When Colonel Stroud's call came the SAIC had just stopped by the office on his way to Hot Springs. Teasdale's oldest kid, a pleasant young man named Ellis, was leaving for the Naval Academy. It was Ellis's third year at Annapolis, and everybody wanted to see him before he left. He'd had sea duty that summer, and he'd only been home a couple of weeks all year, so the Teasdales were having a family reunion at their cottage on Lake Hamilton before Ellis took off.

Quentin looked up the name and number, keeping his fingers crossed that James Fowler, head honcho at Highway, was in. He went through the switchboard and two secretaries before he was put through to the main man. He hoped like hell Fowler and Teasdale weren't friends. If they were he was up a creek.

"Mr. Fowler, Roger Teasdale, bureau chief with the FBI." Quentin held his breath.

"Yes sir, Mr. Teasdale. What can I do for you?"

"Roger, please. Jim, we need your cooperation on something that's come up in the course of one of our investigations. Let me stress, it's urgent. I'm telling you this in strictest confidence, and I'm sure you'll respect that. This is a matter involving national security." That was one thing he wasn't lying about.

"Well certainly, Mr. Teasdale—Roger—anything I can do, anything at all. I'm at your disposal."

A disgruntled Trent Gautier handed over the stack of still damp photographs to FBI Special Agent Quentin Thomasino that afternoon at precisely five o'clock. "I believe this is everything you asked for."

"Thanks a lot. I'm glad you were able to get them done." Quentin took the package and headed for the door.

Mrs. Gautier hadn't brought up any morons. The pictures Trent had just given the FBI agent covered the exact same area that the state cop had inquired about that morning. As Quentin reached the exit, Gautier couldn't resist asking, "You wanna tell me how you managed to do that?"

Quentin didn't bother to turn around. "Not in a million years."

*　　*　　*

"What we think," Milo was explaining to a shocked Betsy as they drew up in front of his apartment where Q.C. was waiting, "is that they're planning to strike while he's at the ball game. Think about it. What could possibly have a greater impact? A nationally televised sports event that's sure to draw a big audience. The President sitting in Hog Heaven. What's to keep them from hovering under radar in the mountains beyond the two mile limit, station independent targeters in the stands or in one of the buildings overlooking the stadium, pop up when the laser designator is locked on, and launch the missiles while the whole thing is broadcast live and in color around the country and around the world?"

While she was still trying to take it in he answered his own question. "Nothing, as far as we can tell."

CHAPTER 19

"Damn," Betsy winced, stubbing her toe and going down.

"You okay?"

"Yeah, fine," she said, dusting off her posterior and cleaning dirt from her hands and knees. "Nothin' broken or sprained except my dignity."

"Okay, so, you guys gonna get movin' or what?" Quentin was bringing up the rear as the threesome maneuvered their way down the ravine. Q.C. had signed on for the duration, but that didn't mean he relished taking a forced march over mountainous terrain. Carrying a heavy backpack.

"Hush, grump," she replied without rancor. "This is a walk in the park."

"A walk in the park my ass," Quentin groused.

"No mine," Betsy retorted. "I'm the one who just fell on her butt."

In fact, while all three had garnered their share of scrapes and bruises over the early going, this last stretch of the hike had been easier. At the top of the gorge Betsy had found a game trail snaking a twisted, but relatively unimpeded path down the slope. They resumed their downward progress in rapidly waning light.

"Ssshh, listen," she cautioned a few minutes later. The tinkle and splash of a brook told them they had nearly reached bottom.

"Hey, cheer up guys. We're almost there." Betsy had the credentials; she held the compass. A hundred yards further on she pointed upstream. "See that clear spot over by the big boulder? Let's angle over there and set up."

According to her reckoning they were now about three hundred feet below, and less than a quarter mile distant from the chicken farm. With only one road in, there was no way to get close to the place undetected except by coming across the mountains, which they had done. From their store of maps Betsy had traced what appeared to be the least hazardous route to their destination, some three miles as the crow flies from a dirt track running along a neighboring hogback, but closer to four or five over the jagged undulations in between. They had left Milo's SUV parked under a tree the far side of Flatrock Creek, shortly after three o'clock, allowing themselves four hours of daylight to get in position. In the flat lands it wouldn't be dark before eight, but at the bottom of the narrow defile, dusk came much sooner.

They could have used more rest, but none of them wanted to hazard the trek at night. Too many things could go wrong. One or two hikers a season fell to their deaths on Petit Jean, and those trails were clearly marked. On this excursion they were relying on Betsy's expertise as pathfinder. Even though the photographs showed nothing in their way except the harsh landscape, Betsy was concerned about stumbling over a booby-trapped marijuana patch. Concealing well defended pot crops in the forest no-man's land was a common practice in those parts. And a profitable one.

As it turned out, the jaunt hadn't been overly difficult. Certainly no walk in the park, as Betsy had teased Q.C., but hardly taxing for someone in reasonably decent shape. They made camp, scouted the path up to the plateau while there was still light, and settled in to wait. Having made it safely to the creek bank and unpacked their goodies, there was nothing left to do but eat a bite and bide their time until they could sneak up to the barn. With little outside help and no legal recourse, night and stealth were their only allies.

*　*　*

They had been up all night, knee deep in photographs spread all over the bed, couch, floor, tables, any flat surface available. As

191

soon as they had come in from the restaurant Milo made hasty introductions, and while Q.C. started unfurling maps, Betsy and Milo shucked their dinner clothes for more comfortable togs.

Since the primary target was the area immediately surrounding the poultry farm and abandoned missile silo, those were the first sets of pictures Quentin dug out of the pile. Silo crews were rotated in for duty from Little Rock Air Force Base by chopper, so if a missile had been interred on the mountain, there would have been a landing pad to service it.

On the monochrome photographs the farm buildings stood out in sharp relief against the cleared plateau, but Milo and Q.C. were having a hard time finding signs of the previous tenant. The passage of years and the government's kept promise to return the site to its natural state had eradicated most traces of the Titan's former home. Betsy was a real help, adept at reading nuances in shades of gray.

"Here," she lectured, brandishing the magnifying glass, "was the silo hatch. See the slight circular depression. It's settled some since it was filled in so you can tell where it was. And over here was the helipad. Look, right behind that barn. If you look closely you can just make out the outline." They couldn't see it, but they took her word.

They had no trouble identifying various components of the farm. It was a large complex, with a manager's house, six long chicken sheds, three sets of cylindrical grain bins, a trench silo, a large barn, and a scattering of other outbuildings—maybe a pump house or storage shed—it didn't make any difference, none of the smaller structures was large enough to conceal a Cobra.

"Do you really think they'd hide the helicopter in such an obvious place?" Betsy asked. "I mean, if they think there's cause to suspect them, wouldn't they figure it'd be the first place anybody would look?"

"Who's to look?" asked Quentin. "We got no cause—we got no warrant. If we had, we wouldn't be worryin' about imitatin' mountain goats."

"You could be right Betsy," Milo said, ignoring Q.C.'s gibe, "but it's a place to start, and we gotta start somewhere. Of all the Tabernacle properties, it's the only one outside city limits. If I were trying to keep a chopper under wraps, a big barn on top of a lonely mountain down a dead-end road would look pretty good to me. More to the point, as far as they know, there's no way to connect the sect to the missing helicopter. And we have not one shred of tangible proof that they *are* involved. It's all supposition on our part, based on the word of one man and what I've dug up in the last month."

"It's a moot point anyway," Quentin said. "We have to check it out if only to eliminate the possibility, so we're goin' in. If it's not there we duck back out and no one's the wiser. Then we have to start looking at alternatives. If it is . . . and I pray to God that ugly mother's sittin' there . . . then we call in some muscle and it's all over. Either way, this expedition is a necessary first step."

On a short list of guidelines, the number one criterion for secreting a stolen attack helicopter had to be isolation. Choppers were not like submarines, rigged for silent running. You could hear them coming miles away. The rotor's ruckus would cause a stir day or night. They ruled out any building within a thousand yards of another dwelling, from cabins and farmhouses to municipalities. They excluded camping grounds, park lands, and any other place with a sizable transient population—hikers, campers, fishermen, boaters, and backpackers. Had all their photographs been current, they could also have discounted the timberlands covering three-fourths of their arbitrary circle. Amid solid tree cover, Betsy should have been able to pick out any clearing large enough for the helo to land—no clearing, no copter. But since their pictures varied in age, the woodlands could, and in many instances would, have changed. This was readily apparent when she compared Milo's AFS prints with Quentin's yield from the ASHD. From her own personal experience Betsy could identify some areas that had come under attack from the loggers' chain saws, but it would take a visual inspection to cover the entire territory. And that would take time.

Next was the size factor. Which wasn't nearly as large as Betsy had supposed. At a height of 13' 6.25", and overall length of 52' 11.5" with the single rotor fixed lengthwise, the helicopter would fit in any type of moderately capacious structure with a big door. And there was always the possibility that the chopper wasn't inside. It could be sitting in a pasture somewhere under camouflage netting.

Throughout the night they had hashed and rehashed, studied the blow-ups, made the arguments. But it wasn't until the wee hours of the morning as she blearily scanned yet another pile of images, eyes tired but still focused, that Betsy realized what Milo and Q.C. had known from the start. If the Cobra weren't hidden at the farm, the odds against their locating it were astronomical.

"Bets, it's time." Milo laid his hand on her shoulder, speaking softly. She was dead to the world, her body catching up on sleep lost the night before. Leaving Little Rock at sunup they had driven to her cabin, picking up breakfast along the way. With their plans laid, they needed rest before starting across country. Quentin took the couch and she and Milo crashed on her bare mattress, too tired to fuss with making the bed. They had set the alarm for one, allowing them a much needed four hour nap before gathering their gear and setting out.

She yawned wearily. "Are you positive? I didn't hear the alarm."

"I'm not surprised with your head under the pillow. I don't see how you could breathe. Then again, maybe you couldn't. **You were really sawing it off.**"

"I was not," she said indignantly. "I don't snore."

"Yes, pretty lady, I'm afraid you do, but I don't mind."

"That's awfully nice of you," she said, sitting up. "You patronizing sack of male chauvinist bullshit. Why haven't you mentioned it before?"

"I never noticed before," he countered. "We were always too occupied with other things."

She threw the pillow at him and got up.

What they hadn't brought with them and she couldn't supply from her store of equipment left year-round at the cabin, they could pick up in Marshall, along with lunch and munchables for the trail. Logy at first, the trio revived with food and drink, but it was the hike that really reinvigorated them.

Once established at the campsite they made the remainder of their preparations and then took turns napping again, stretching out on top of sleeping bags spread on the forest floor. While Quentin dozed Betsy and Milo sat side by side, listening to the brook and contemplating the unlikely chain of events that had brought them together.

"Betsy," Milo said at length, "I have to ask, are you very disappointed in me? I hated having to trick you but there wasn't any time or way to explain."

She brought his hand to her cheek, cradling her head against his palm. "Hush," she said. "Don't you think I know?"

At eleven thirty they rousted Q.C. "Hey, sleeping beauty. Up and at 'em."

This time there was no lingering lethargy. They were keyed up and ready.

Betsy would remain at the creek while Milo and Quentin clambered up the slope. They couldn't conscience taking along a civilian and Betsy hadn't pushed the men to go. She was a good shot, and had brought an old, bolt-action Winchester .30-06 from the cabin. She would monitor the radio, keeping watch over the base camp until they returned.

Milo's watch pinged the magic hour. "All right. I guess this is it."

"Be careful." Betsy kissed Milo, squeezed Q.C.'s hand. There wasn't anything else to say. The off-duty FBI agent and the state cop forded the stream and were gone.

* * *

At twenty-three minutes to one an alarm sounded in the control room of the bunker, startling the drowsy guard and bringing the solitary computer geek up from his terminal and around to the security console. With parameters of sensitivity that would not be set off by smaller nocturnal creatures, and the farm Collie kenneled at night, the watchman assumed that some larger animal, a deer, coyote, or even a bear, had wandered out of the woods and activated one of the motion detectors.

"Shit," the guard cursed, staring at the screen. Right in front of his eyes two decidedly human figures were moving in a low crouch toward the pump house. Commander Boyd had warned them that there might be trouble. The intruders should never have gotten that far without being spotted. Why hadn't he been more alert? If the men were heading straight for the barn it would be a toss up if they reached it before he could summon help. Pressing the button that would waken Mr. Williams in the office above ground, he dialed Boyd's pager, while the computer operator ran up the stairs to arouse McKensie and the other techno-nerds.

After scrambling up the last eighty feet of slope to the edge of the plateau, the investigators were surprised at the brightness of the scene confronting them. Each of the four-hundred-foot sheds' interiors was washed in sodium vapor glare, which spilled through mesh-screened sides, creating clearly illuminated twenty-foot perimeter zones around the six chicken houses. Closest to them the outbuilding was dark, but a yellow insect bulb cast a citrine glow over the door of a corresponding, but slightly larger structure on the opposite side of the complex. A Night Watcher flooded the driveway and gravel parking area.

"Jesus, will you look at that," Milo whispered in disbelief. "This place is lit up like Las Vegas."

"Damn," Quentin swore softly. "Wha'da'ya wanna do?"

They had come out of the woods midway between the farm buildings. Having memorized the layout from the photographs, the men thought they knew what to expect. The lights were a rude shock.

The chicken houses were arranged in parallel pairs, sharing three grain bins between them. Two of the long sheds lay to their right, running north and south, a similar pair to the left. Perpendicular to the chicken houses was an open, block-walled trench, dividing the farm in half. From the aerial view Milo had thought it was most likely a silo, used to store grain. At ground level he could tell from the stench that it contained an amalgam of litter and droppings, refuse from cleaning the sheds between batches of chicks. The organic compost would either be sold raw by the truck-load for fertilizer, or processed and bagged for cattle food. Whichever its end use, it reeked. Backing on the cleared area that had been the Titan base sat the prefabricated metal barn which was their goal. Directly in front of the barn was the last pair of chicken houses.

Milo viewed the collection for several minutes.

"Nothin' stirrin'. Let's head for that nearest building. Maybe we can get a better feel up close."

"How many of them are there?"

"I don't see but two, Commander."

"You're sure about that Tim? You've checked all the sensors? Could there be some more hiding out of sight?"

"Yes sir, I mean, no sir, I mean, right now I think two is all."

"Now look carefully Tim. Where are they going? The house, the barn, tell me exactly what you see."

"Two men, white guy and a jig, no visible identification. Came outta the woods together. Dropped down behind the pump house. That's as far as they've gotten, so I dunno where they're headed. I got everybody up, sir. We're ready."

"Stay there," Boyd barked at the guard. "Do not, I repeat, do not, intercept them. I'll take care of this."

McKensie snatched the microphone out of Tim Oglesby's hand. "Com'on Boyd, let me go," he begged. "This'll be fun."

Boyd almost shouted. "You wanna give the whole thing away? Don't be an idiot. Under no circumstances are you to materialize out of nowhere, you hear me? We don't know what they're doing. Could be just looking for the girl. Now stay put. All of you guys. Harlan and I will sort this out. That's an order."

Totally unaware that they had tripped a motion sensor and were under observation, Milo and Quentin ducked behind the outbuilding and stopped. From its shelter they could survey their target. They felt sure any noise they might have made had been masked by the whirring fans.

"Do you see anybody around the barn?"

"Not a soul. But it's hard to tell. There could be somebody on the far side. Here," Milo handed over the binoculars. "Take a look."

Poking his head around the corner, Quentin trained the glasses on the metal barn, then scanned the rest of their surroundings. "Nothin'," he said. "Let's get on with it."

"Let's separate. I'll go this way, sneak around behind. Can you work your way around to the other side? It would be helpful to know if there's a guard we can't see from here."

"Give me ten minutes or so. To stay outta the light I'll have to take the long way around."

"Keep your head down."

"Don't I always?"

"Not always," Milo said. "You got your neck stuck out about a mile right now."

Milo had nagging doubts about the apparently unguarded setup. Maybe they figured inaccessibility and lighting were all the protection they needed. Maybe he was wrong and the helo wasn't there. Maybe, maybe, maybe. There were a thousand maybes.

Quit worrying and get on with it. He backtracked until he was out of the lighted area, still in the open, but cloaked in darkness. Milo hated having no cover. Staying low, ears straining to catch any sound above the constant drone of the ventilators, he moved to his left. Soon he was hidden behind the sheds. His gait became less tentative.

Harlan Williams hit the floor with a thud, on his feet instantly when the buzzer sounded. He groped around, grabbed his pants from the chair, zipped them up over his pajama bottoms. Reached for his boots. No boots. Fumbled around on the floor. Where the fuck are they? Stumbled over a pointed, steel-tipped toe. Shit, that hurt! *Sat heavily, rubbing his instep. Clicked on the bedside lamp. Picked up the offending boot, cursing.* Calm down, Harlan. You've got to get out there. *Drew his socks out of the footwear where he had stuffed them when he went to bed. Had managed to get one boot on when Boyd's snarl pulled him up short.*

"Turn out the light Harlan. Turn it out now!"

Harlan switched off the lamp. He snatched up the walkie-talkie, furious. "We got prowlers Boyd. Fuck's the matter with you?"

"Listen to me you moron. Leave the lights out and meet me outside when I tell you, not before. You got that?"

"I . . ."

"Just do it, Harlan. And have Flora see to the girl. Now stay sharp and wait until I give you the word."

Quentin was skirting the house when a light popped on in a second story window. He stopped in his tracks, dead still, afraid to move. Afraid period. He couldn't believe he had let Milo talk him into this. They were both liable to get killed. *Christ.* He pushed down the panic. *Steady, Q.C.. Steady.* The light winked out. *Thank God. A trip to the can.* Pulse racing, he moved ahead, swinging out in a wider arc just to be doubly safe.

"Where are they now Tim?"

"They split up Commander. One of them's goin' around back. He's behind Number Six. I lost the other one in front of the office, he must be out of camera range, but if he's tryin' to circle around I'll pick him up again when he crosses the road."

"Okay. Hang on and tell me the second you can see him again."

"Wait Commander. I got him! He's just crossed the drive and is comin' up on your position. The other guy has made it past the litter pile. He's goin' for the barn."

Milo keyed his radio. They were using the same voice privacy model carried by State Police, FBI, Secret Service, and Daniel's troops alike, a Motorola HT 220 hand talkie. The agencies had gone to the voice privacy design to keep anybody with a scanner from picking up their transmissions.

"Betsy. Betsy are you there?"

"Milo? Boy am I glad to hear from you. Are you guys all right?"

"So far so good. It's quiet, nobody in sight. I'm in place, waitin' for Q.C. He should be along any minute."

"Have you found anything yet? I've got so many butterflies in my stomach I could be a belly dancer."

"Now that's a sight I'd pay to see. To answer your question: nothing. Everything's clear. Are *you* okay?"

"Don't worry about me, Milo. Take care of yourself."

Boyd strapped on his 10mm Heckler & Koch while Heavy looked on. "Heavy, you know what to do. Wait 'til I've gone. It's risky, but we can't afford to have anyone find you two. Whoever these guys are, if they're on their own we can deal with them. Right now, we're not even sure what they're after."

Heavy nodded.

"Now pay attention. If this doesn't turn out right, call Brother Daniel right away. He'll know what to do. And Heavy—watch out for McKensie. No matter what Daniel says, he's bad news."

Excitement animated Tim's voice. "Commander, you're in the clear! He's behind Number Two, approachin' the barn."

Boyd was ready. "Harlan, they're going for the barn. Meet me out front in two minutes." Boyd eased open the door, his complexion sallow in the ocher glow. Closed it gently. Striding with purpose, his footsteps muffled by the dirt, the hunter—stalking his prey.

"Ready?"

"As I'll ever be."

There were two doors in the back of the barn: a standard, pedestrian door set in a steel frame, and a heavier, sheet-metal sliding door suspended on rollers above the wider opening. They tried the pedestrian door. It was locked with a dead bolt.

"Must have somethin' to hide. Elsewise, why lock it?"

Milo concurred. He pushed experimentally on the sliding door but it didn't budge. Probing the edges with his fingertips, searching for a catch or clasp, he could find nothing holding it. "Com'on. Give me a hand. Do you think we can get this big mother open without makin' a racket?"

"I guess we're fixin' to find out."

Neither man wanted to force the locked door. If their search turned out to be a wild goose chase, they didn't want to leave any evidence of their uninvited entry.

With Milo one one side of the unwilling panel, and Quentin on the other, they coaxed and cajoled until it moved a fraction, emitting a harsh *skreek* as it broke loose. They stopped pushing, uncertain whether the sound had been audible above the fans. When no bells rang, no extra lights came on, no running feet scrunched on the gravel drive, they shoved again. Milo didn't know what to make of the stubborn door. He wasn't mechanically inclined, but it seemed to him that if it had seen recent use it shouldn't be stuck. Then again, maybe it was just a broken roller. This time it slid more easily, dragging a little but parting a crack without repeating the sound.

Quentin peered through the crack into inky darkness. An oily, diesel smell cut the odor of decaying droppings. "Let me see." Milo put his eye to the slit but couldn't make out a thing. "Okay, one more time." A final push produced an eighteen inch opening. The men slipped through the gap, stopping just inside the door. Milo switched on his lantern, playing its hooded beam over the interior. His disappointment was immediate and acute. No Cobra. "Damn," he swore, crestfallen. "It's not here."

"Hold it right there!" The unexpectd command came from behind them. Milo flinched as the barrel of a shotgun prodded him in the back. Quentin raised his hands. Light flooded the barn as the double-hinged front doors swung wide, and a man with military bearing stepped through the breach.

He walked directly to Milo, looked questioningly at the man holding the gun, who gave a curt nod. "Captain Thomas is it?" he asked sardonically. "I don't believe I've had the pleasure. And who's your friend? And if you don't mind my asking, what are you doing in our barn?"

CHAPTER 20

What could Milo possibly say that would extricate them from this mess? Sandwiched between two men at gunpoint, expertly frisked and relieved of weapons, they were defenseless. Confiscated camera and radios lay out of reach on a grease-caked work bench. Caught off guard, disarmed, his communication link to Betsy severed, Milo's wits had temporarily deserted him. The best he could do was stall and hope inspiration would strike.

"You must be Major Boyd? And I assume, since I talked with him when I was out here two weeks ago, that the man jamming that gun in my spine is Harlan Williams." Milo turned his head gradually, trying to get a better look at the person behind him. "I hope he's not nervous."

"It's *Commander* Boyd, Captain Thomas, and you haven't answered my question."

"Which was?"

"You're in no position to get smart with me mister. Now suppose you tell me what you're doing here."

Quentin spoke for the first time. "Just trying to get in outta the elements, Commander. We were hiking when the storm hit, and this seemed like a good place to sit it out." Stars were shining and there was no hint of inclement weather.

Like the lightning of Quentin's imagination, Harlan whirled. His gun barrel crashed down on Q.C.'s skull, dropping the FBI agent to his knees. Blood trickled from a two inch gash over his left ear. "Shut up boy. Ain't takin' lip off no nigger." The farm manager, showing his colors. Just as quickly Williams returned his attention to Milo, using the gun butt to deliver a savage blow to Milo's side, doubling him over. "You wanna be a wiseass too?"

Milo had to come up with something or the ape would beat them to death. When he could think past the pain in his kidney he straightened, struggling for control.

"Enough," Milo said, ignoring the malicious redneck and directing his words to the officer. "You have the advantage. The truth is, we were looking for Wendy Bolin. When I was out here before, the Williamses weren't very convincing when they denied knowing the girl or her whereabouts. Since I still haven't been able to locate her, I thought she might be here after all."

"You thought we might have a girl chained up in the barn, like livestock? We're not animals Captain Thomas. Now, I'll ask you one more time, what were you looking for?"

Quentin was pushing himself to his feet. Although the cut was bleeding his eyes were clear. And angry. Milo hoped he'd bridle his tongue. Quentin's accent and cheek had already rubbed Harlan Williams the wrong way. Neither man had identification, but if they pegged Q.C. as FBI, all bets were off.

"I swear to you on my mother's grave, I've been looking for the girl. And her brother Heavy. And a computer operator name McKensie. As I'm sure you're aware they're all employees of the Tabernacle and they've all vanished. But not one person seems to give a damn about what's happened to them—not their folks, not Brother Daniel, nor any other members of the Tabernacle that I've spoken to. So with all the big hush hush from you people, I thought maybe there was some spiritual mumbo jumbo going on out here, Satanic dances, or Black Sabbaths, or whatever you call them—involving all three missing people and maybe some more I don't know about. Like ritual sacrifice. Like maybe they're all dead."

"That's ludicrous Captain. You've been watching too many episodes of the *X Files*."

It was pure malarkey but Milo was on a roll.

"You think so? This is a big spread, lonely, off to itself. It's owned by the Tabernacle; it would be a great place to warehouse victims. Then I remembered this barn and I figured if there were some kind of altar set up in here, or even traces of one—candle wax, maybe, or incense, or symbolic writings, or . . . bits of bone, then I'd have proof positive of what's goin' on." Milo squared his shoulders, looked the Commander straight in the eyes. "Because I believe you're all murderers. I think you've got bodies buried out here, maybe lots of bodies, under that big pile of chicken shit, or down in the old missile silo. Who knows? Either those three people I can't find are already dead with their hearts cut out and their blood drained or you've got them stashed on this hilltop somewhere waitin' their turn. Your precious Tabernacle is nothing but a den of sadistic, devil-worshippin' killers."

Without warning a viscious blow exploded the back of Milo's head. He fell hard, face down, nose and forehead banging off the rough floor. Harlan's steel-shod toe cracked a rib. "Shut your filthy mouth you blasphemin' cocksucker. You got no idea what you're talkin' about. We, we, we are *God's* children! *His* chosen. *True Believers!* Righteous inheritors of God's holy grace through his handmaiden Laura." Williams was beside himself. He kicked Milo again. "You lyin', heathen bastard, I'll show you . . ." The enraged man brought the muzzle of his 12 gauge down, rammed the tempered steel into the nape of Milo's neck. His finger tightened on the trigger.

Quentin lunged, knocking Harlan off balance. The shotgun discharged, blowing a ragged hole in the building's metal siding. Milo rolled away, ears ringing. Before the manager could recover Q.C. scrabbled for the gun, frantically to trying wrench it from Williams's clutch. Boyd watched the struggle with a detached air, like a warder who witnesses a fight between unruly inmates and elects not to intervene. Middle-aged and overweight, Harlan was no match for Quentin's Quantico training. Just as the agent was about to snatch the Browning free, Boyd drew his semiautomatic.

"All right gentlemen. I'll take that." Boyd disengaged the shotgun from Quentin and Harlan's grasp, jacked the remaining shells out of the magazine, and laid the gun with the camera and radios. "Okay." He propped against the bench and surveyed the combatants. "Now what do we have here? Captain Thomas, your suggestion that Brother Daniel's followers are disciples of the devil, is, as Harlan has demonstrated, absurd. As is the notion that we might be turning church members into blood offerings." Dismissing Milo's improbable accusations out of hand, he continued, "Let's see if we can come to a consensus. On one hand, *you* are breaking the law, trespassing on private property. Yet I have to admit that Harlan here got a little carried away, although he has every right to protect his premises from strangers poking around where they don't belong. And believe me when I say that it would be unwise to provoke this devout man further; he is passionate about his religion. But none of the persons you seek is here. By now that should be plain to even a hard-headed policeman like yourself, Captain Thomas. If you doubt my word, I think we can settle this issue once and for all."

Harlan glowered at Boyd. Milo and Quentin nursed their injuries, wondering where on earth this was headed. From the look on Harlan Williams's face, it was plain that whatever Boyd had in mind, the manager didn't like it.

"If you two are willing to forget my friend Harlan's impulsive behavior, I think *he* might be willing to have a third, neutral party investigate your allegation that he is concealing a few errant sheep from Brother Daniel's flock on this farm."

Milo was speechless. Quentin, too, was slack-jawed. Harlan stared incredulously back and forth between Boyd and his two battered prisoners.

"Well, what's it going to be? Let's not stand here all night." Casting a pointed glance at Quentin Boyd added, "Besides, I think the rain has let up."

* * *

Betsy was worried. She should have heard from Milo again by now. Thirty minutes ago he had said he was in place, waiting for Quentin. Why hadn't he radioed back to tell her what they'd found? She wasn't supposed to contact the men unless it was a dire emergency. Having no way to predict where they might be or under what circumstances, she was to maintain radio silence until Milo or Q.C. signaled her. Was this an emergency—not hearing? They were using a relatively short range system to communicate with each other, but they had brought a cell phone in case the helicopter were hidden in the barn and Betsy needed to summon backup. Something *must* have gone wrong. Did the men need help now? Should she call the sheriff? *Damn!*

Betsy was afraid anything she might do would be a mistake. What were her options? She was a good three hour hike by daylight from Milo's truck. Or a twenty minute plus climb from the plateau. If she left her post and Milo tried to contact her—what then? If she stayed put and there was still no word, was she dooming Milo and Quentin to an uncertain fate? If she phoned for help and it wasn't needed, they were exposed and probably in hot water. It was an agonizing dilemma. In the end she deferred, putting off the decision a while longer. If she hadn't heard in another thirty minutes, she promised herself she would act.

*　　*　　*

"Jay." Milo shook the proffered hand, wincing involuntarily as his broken ribs sent spasms of pain radiating through his chest and back. "Quentin Thomasino, a friend from Little Rock."

Jay "Bird" Womack didn't miss much. He noted the wince, took in Milo's scrapes and bruises, and registered the crusted cut over Quentin's ear. "Mr. Thomasino."

"Sheriff." A perfunctory nod took care of the introduction.

When he and deputy Truman Sullivan had crunched to a stop on the loose gravel beside the Williams' house, the sheriff had found a strange party assembled on the wide verandah. Four men charged down the steps to meet him before he could get the door open. Swaying back and forth in a rocker on the porch, Flora Williams glared down at them, exuding disdain. With her bulk wrapped in gown and duster, and her puffy face washed out in the cold light from the Night Watcher, Flora looked like a giant, malignant toad. Jay Womack gave thanks he wasn't a fly.

"Sheriff, you know Harlan and Flora. Sorry to get you out at this time of night, but Captain Thomas seems to think that these good people are hiding some folks he's been looking for, and he doesn't want to take no for an answer. He's harboring some very unusual misconceptions about Brother Daniel and his parishioners anyway. Now it's a fact that our brethren at the Tabernacle are all honest, law-abiding citizens. The Captain's allegations are an affront. But *being* good citizens, Mr. and Mrs. Williams would like to set things straight. So, we thought perhaps you could sort this out to everyone's satisfaction."

"That right Milo?" Jaybird didn't know what had happened before his night-duty sergeant got him out of bed to handle this call, but from the looks of the state cop and his black buddy, they had been on the receiving end. Which might account for the cryptic call his dispatcher had patched through to the Jeep fifteen minutes earlier from a woman who refused to identify herself, saying only that there was trouble at the Tabernacle's poultry farm and someone needed assistance. As he was en route to that very spot, it had cost the sheriff nothing to promise to look into it. What the hell had Thomas been up to?

"Yeah, Sheriff. Basically we'd like for you and the deputy to conduct a thorough search of all these buildings, starting with the house. I think Wendy Bolin and her brother Heavy may be detained here against their will. It's also possible you might turn up a missing person named Mike McKensie. That's about the size of it. While you look the four of us will monitor the grounds. That way, no one can escape detection."

Jaybird looked perplexed. With 7,756 residents, Newton was the third least populous county in the state. Aside from domestic disputes and occasional pot raids, crime wasn't a principal commodity of the wilderness region. In any given year there were more accidental drownings than armed robberies. Jay had been reelected sheriff so many times the job was practically a sinecure. Over his long time in office he'd seen some strange things, but this was way off the wall. Why didn't Milo do his own search if the Williamses were willing to accede without a warrant. And why at two-thirty in the morning? And how come this Commander Boyd was orchestrating the whole thing? It was over *his* head.

"Harlan, Mrs. Williams. That okay by y'all? It's your place. You don't have to agree if you don't want to."

Flora rose from the rocking chair. Her scowl would curdle milk. But when she spoke Jay Womack detected an undercurrent more gloat than capitulation. "It's the *Lord's* place, Sheriff. An' if you think we want you storm-troopers trompin' all over you got another think comin'. But Harlan and me ain't got nothin' t' hide. So come on in and let's git this over with."

*　　*　　*

Wendy was waiting when Flora unlocked the door. This was her chance. If she could break away from the older woman, run fast enough, yell loud enough, whoever was sneaking around the farm might hear and rescue her. Maybe whoever it was had even come *to* rescue her. That thought gave her hope.

Wendy had wakened when Lester's pager sounded in the second floor bedroom, goose bumps pimpling her arms. She didn't actually hear the buzzer, but she sat up at the exact same instant as Lester, aroused by whatever extrasensory phenomenon alerts animals to the presence of danger. Guided by a sense of urgency she dressed, making as little noise as possible.

A thump on the ceiling confirmed that one of the Williamses was up and moving around. A short time later Lester clumped down the stairs, sounding like a herd of elephants in his ridiculous boots. He was standing in the dark just outside the office. She could feel him lurking there.

When the third riser creaked under Flora's weight Wendy realized the spiteful old bitch was coming downstairs too. Her throat constricted. Why? Were they coming to kill her? Wring her neck, like the chickens Flora dispatched daily for the pot? Had Brother Daniel told them to wax her in the middle of the night so Heavy couldn't intervene? Wendy was petrified. What was going on?

The answer startled her. Clear as day she heard Boyd say, *"Harlan, they're going for the barn. Meet me out front in two minutes."*

Wendy's heart pounded. Somewhere out there was HELP!

She needed a weapon, anything. She crawled under the bed, snatched the plug of her reading lamp from the socket. Unscrewed the finial, removing the shade, harp and bulb. Wrapped the cord around the base of the brass candlestick. It was the best she could do.

For once Lester left the house without slamming the screen. His boots clattering across the porch and down the outside steps told Wendy he had gone. She flattened herself against the wall, held her breath. In Wendy's heightened state of awareness she could hear Flora's padded house slippers crossing the office floor. Her nemesis paused outside the door. Was she coming in? A key clicked in the cylinder. Yes! Flora turned the knob, stuck her head in the tiny room. Wendy hesitated a second too long before bringing the lamp down with all her might. In that fraction of indecision, Flora caught the girl out of the corner of her eye, registered the downward motion, and dodged. The candlestick smacked into bone, glancing off her shoulder. With an agonized yelp Flora clutched at her collarbone. Wendy rushed through the door, her head lowered, and butted the woman in the stomach. Flora tumbled backwards. Then Wendy was out the front door, racing down the drive toward the barn, screaming at the top of her lungs.

Straight into Heavy's arms.

*   *   *

When the cell phone in her pocket cheeped shortly before four Betsy jumped, pawed for the instrument and popped it open mid cheep. Tears of relief welled forth when she heard Milo's voice.

"Milo! Thank God. Where are you? Are you all right? I've been worried to death."

She sounded so good a lump caught in his throat. "Betsy, it was a fiasco but Quentin and I are all right" Her gasp was magnified by the speaker in the sheriff's Jeep. "No, *really*. We're okay —bloodied but unbowed. But you've been stuck out there for hours by yourself. I'm so sorry I got you into this."

A touch of asperity colored her response. "Oh com'on Milo. All I've missed is a night's sleep. You're the ones who've been in danger."

The sheriff and his deputy occupied the front bucket seats of the Cherokee; Milo and Quentin sat in back behind a wire partition. For security's sake there were no handles, levers, or locks in the rear side panels. Milo's conversation was being conducted on an open, ceiling-mounted mike. Talking to Betsy with the others listening was like walking naked in the park. And while Milo was grateful for the sheriff's intervention, he was not prepared to satisfy his curiosity. "We're with Sheriff Womack now, Betsy. Jay's giving us a ride to my truck. Bets, I hate to ask, but I don't think I can make it back to the brook. Can you get out on your own?"

Sheriff Womack must be eavesdropping. Thank goodness she hadn't blurted out something about the helicopter. At least her desperation call had produced results. (Betsy didn't have any way to know that Boyd had actually summoned the sheriff. Her call had merely served as reinforcement.) And Milo must be hurting worse that he'd let on to ask her to hike out alone. *Damn*. Betsy instantly regretted fussing at him. "I don't see why not. I've been crawling over these hills by myself for years. I'll pack up and start as soon as it's light, and see you back at the truck."

*   *   *

"They did *WHAT*?" Daniel screamed through the telephone. "And you let them go?"

Boyd wasn't intimidated. "Yeah. What'd you want me to do? Let Harlan knock off the state cop. Think of the consequences of that! We'd have the entire Arkansas State Police force down on our heads. You want a hundred troopers going over this place with a fine toothed comb? And we would've had to take out the other guy too. And not only did Thomas bring muscle with him, but judging from the radios we confiscated, he probably had an accomplice or accomplices hidden out of sight. What chance do you think McKensie and his bunch would have tramping through the woods trying to track down a third party?"

"Boyd, you've got to get rid of that meddling sonofabitch. Permanently. Every time I turn around that bastard shows up. Was he lookin' for the helicopter?"

"I can't be sure. He was spouting some crap about the occult and Satanic rites, but that was a smoke screen. My opinion, he's looking for the Bolin girl, pure and simple. We know from what the girl told Heavy, and Thomas's interview with you, that he's investigating the death of that kid McKensie killed. Why he's got such a burr under his tail about that I can't say. But even if he were suspicious, there's nothing here to link us to the chopper. Wynne flew it out three days ago."

"Are you sure?"

"It's over, Daniel, so get off my back. I made a battlefield decision. Heavy hid the girl in the bunker while Harlan and I confronted Thomas and his pal. Now Thomas is convinced the girl's not here. Anyway, the black guy was about to feed Harlan his own gun, so I stopped it. Case closed."

*   *   *

"Nice goin' Milo. I thought we were dead."

"If you hadn't tackled that baboon back there I would have been."

"Shit, man. He was gettin' ready to blow your head off. Those motherfuckers are some *s-e-r-i-o-u-s-l-y* warped jokers."

Sheriff Womack, still flummoxed, had dropped the unresponsive lawmen off at Milo's Expedition. Alone at last, Quentin was driving them to the hospital. If Milo didn't get his ribs taped stat he could wind up with a punctured lung. The cut over Q.C.'s ear had stopped bleeding, but it needed sutures to heal without leaving a bad scar.

"Nothin'. Absolutely nothin'. No helicopter, no captives, no reluctant witnesses hiding' out. Not one friggin' thing outta the ordinary on that whole damn mountain top." Milo banged his fist into the dash board, immediately paying in pain the price for his frustration.

"You're wrong, Milo," Q.C. said, taking a curve too fast.

Milo grimaced, bracing against the door with one hand and holding his ribcage with the other. "Hey! Slow down. That hurts like hell. And this truck's not even a month old."

"Sorry." Quentin eased off the accelerator. "The thing is, how'd they know we were there? The way they bagged us, it was too easy, like they were expectin' us."

"I've been wonderin' about that too." Between disgust at getting caught like rank amateurs and bitter disappointment at coming up dry, Milo's emotions were about as raw as his body. "If Boyd was staying in the bunk house—that's my fault by the way, I should have found out what the other buildings were— and it was clear across the complex, he couldn't have heard us. And did you notice, Williams had his pants on over his pajamas, so he hadn't been sittin' up watchin' out the window. The only real noise we made was openin' that slidin' door, and countin' from then, there was no way they could have set a trap that fast. There had to be some kind of security device. But what? And why? If there wasn't anything to hide?"

Quentin concurred. "And why was Boyd so anxious to show us there wasn't? Why go to such extremes to prove a negative? Even after you diverted his attention. If they didn't have the chopper, *or* the girl, why call the Sheriff in the first place? We'd already seen the barn. It would have been a whole lot simpler just to show us the house and let us go. Not that he didn't do you a favor, takin' ol' Harlan's gun away. How'd you come up with all that hokey Satan shit anyway?"

"Would you believe watchin' reruns of the *X Files*?"

It was the first real laugh they'd had.

At dawn Betsy began the weary trek out of the woods. With only her rifle, telephone, water bottle and walkie-talkie as dunnage, she covered the distance in just over two hours and forty minutes. Twice Milo called to check on her progress and to explain what he couldn't tell her with the perked ears of Newton County law hanging on every word. When she crested the last hill a hundred yards from the Expedition, two taped, bandaged, and depressed agents were waiting to greet her.

She embraced Milo with care and examined the dressing over Q.C.'s ear. Satisfied that they were more or less intact, albeit definitely worse for the wear, Betsy pronounced judgment: "You two are a sorry lot. Com'on. Let's go home. I need a cool shower and a hot breakfast. And eight hours of uninterrupted sleep." A look passed between the men. "Six hours sleep?" She looked at Milo hopefully. He shook his head. "Oh what the hell! Do I at least get to eat?"

"I think," Milo said, "we might be able to manage that."

CHAPTER 21

Sunday segued into Monday, the passage of hours blurred by exhaustion. Betsy had studied the maps and photographs until she was cross-eyed, her flagging concentration jolted at intervals by overdoses of caffeine. The process of elimination was staggering, even without taking into account the ongoing problem of logging. Milo's arbitrary ring, forming a twenty-five mile sweep around the Tabernacle, encompassed 1,963.50 square miles. It was a lot of territory. When she finally threw in the towel and crashed, Betsy had identified ninety-eight possible hiding places, excusing timberland that might or might not have been harvested after the photos were taken. Milo and Q.C. reduced that number to sixty-four. Realistically, the chopper could be anywhere within a three hundred mile radius of Fayetteville—if, and it was a monumental if, Milo were right about the target and when the terrorists would attack. With a cruising range of 370+ miles, the Cobra could be stashed in Arkansas, Missouri, Oklahoma, even Texas, and still remain in striking distance of the stadium.

The other question tantalizing the investigators was why Boyd had gone to the extreme of calling in Sheriff Womack to search the farm. It made no sense at all. The more they talked it over, the more Milo and Q.C. became convinced that far from being innocent, the cult must be harboring some dark secret on the mountain. A secret they would go to almost any lengths to protect. But as intriguing as that line of speculation might be, they reluctantly agreed it had no bearing on their current quest.

For all practical intents, at least where the helicopter was concerned, the chicken farm was out.

It was time to call a halt. Betsy was all in, sprawled across her bare bed dead to the world. Milo's body was stiffening up. He felt every minute of his fifty-six years. Under the adhesive tape, fading bruises from his truck crash were overlaid with a new crop of violet blooms. Every breath was an effort. He was not sure he could mount the steep stairway to the loft, and when he tried to relieve himself, his urine, if it came at all, was stained red from the blow to his kidney.

Quentin too, was asleep on his feet, but younger and more fit, he was in decidedly better shape than Milo. His only visible reminders of the escapade were a shaved patch above his left ear and a bandage covering the stapled cut. On the way to Betsy's cabin he had threatened to shave the rest of his head to match.

Completely drained physically and emotionally, they had to rest. If time permitted, when they awoke they would explore the handful of possible hiding places nearest Betsy's cabin, then take her to the airport to catch the seven o'clock shuttle to Cincinnati. Betsy had classes Tuesday. She had to go back.

"What will you do now?" she asked, as they stood hand in hand at the gate. She had begged him to drop her off at the terminal but he had insisted on accompanying her to the plane. "I truly hate to go off leaving things unresolved like this."

"I don't know," he answered honestly. "We'll check the rest of the places you picked out, but we both know that's a long shot. And we'll go back over the files, see if the Tabernacle has some holdings we don't know about. If nothing pans out, we'll be facing some really tough decisions."

"I don't envy you the next ten days, Milo. If you're right, the country's future may well lie in your hands."

Milo didn't need reminding. He changed the subject, asking shyly, "Bets, will you come back, however things turn out?"

The announcer was calling her flight. She shifted her carry-on, kissed him quickly on the lips. "You betcha," she called back over her shoulder as she hastened down the jetway. Her reply was barely audible over the booming public address system, but he caught the words.

* * *

Totally despondent, Wendy picked at her food. *Eat,* she chided herself. *You're lucky they're still feeding you,* but her appetite was gone, along with the prospect of freedom. She was never going to get away, and her own brother had stopped her. Again. His attitude completely baffled Wendy. What hold did Daniel have on him that he would turn against his own sister? She banged her fork on the melamine plate in frustration. When Flora came back for her tray thirty minutes later, the chicken and dumplings had congealed in the bowl. Wendy had eaten a few bites of cornbread—that was all.

* * *

"What happened to you?" Marilyn asked solicitously when Milo hobbled off the elevator Tuesday morning. "You look like you ran into a buzz saw." She got up and hurried toward him, clucking like a mother hen.

Stiff from head to foot, he moved jerkily, a tin man in sore need of WD-40. Scabs were forming on his nose and forehead, and his eyes, barely visible in pouches of crepe, were bloodshot. Overnight his injuries seemed to have multiplied. Although Milo had deliberately provoked the attack as a means to deter further questioning, his abused body didn't appreciate the sacrifice. He headed for his desk, wishing he were invisible. "You could say that," he said.

"Either that or somebody beat the crap out of you. Is that it Milo?" A different thought popped into her head. "You didn't have another wreck did you?"

"No, Marilyn," he said wearily, sore to the bone. "I did not have another wreck. I had a misunderstanding." By the time he lowered himself into his chair several co-workers had drifted over to check out the freak show.

"Hey Milo, you get the license plate o' that bus?"

"What's the other guy look like?"

"You run into Mike Tyson in a dark alley?"

"All right, already," Milo snapped testily. "Haven't y'all got work to do? Get a good look and shove off." If it hadn't been for the resources available at the office he wouldn't have come in.

Marilyn lagged behind. "I'm sorry I made a fuss. You don't wanna talk about it, that's okay by me. Would a cup of tea help?"

Way to go Milo. Mr. Nice Guy. "Thanks, Marilyn," he said, meaning it. "A cup of tea would be good."

* * *

Had Milo used a fifty mile radius to circumscribe his hunting ground; had Betsy not had to return to Cincinnati; had he and Quentin had more time and more man power to help search— maybe they would have discovered the Cobra's hiding place. Unfortunately, there were too many maybes to overcome. Milo did persuade Terry Weltlich to pitch in, without mentioning the Tabernacle. He told Terry only that he'd had an anonymous tip that the stolen National Guard helicopter might be under wraps somewhere in Terry's territory, soliciting the other investigator's aid in checking out the sites on Betsy's list. In the process, Terry uncovered a flourishing crystal methamphetamine lab, busting brothers David and Donny Hanks, both three time losers, but just as Wendy, Heavy, and McKensie still eluded Milo, so, too, did the chopper and its pilot remain at large.

* * *

Chris Wynne had spent two days as a guest in the bunk- house, overseeing the Cobra's conversion. After midnight on the second night of his short stay, as soon as the work was completed, he flew the bird out to its secret aerie. Initially, only Boyd, Daniel, and Chris himself were privy to his destination, but because Wynne couldn't wrestle the copter indoors alone, and the new retreat required a minor modification, Boyd took Vonnie Lee and Tim Oglesby with him. With Heavy restricted to the farm, Vonnie Lee had inherited those tasks requiring raw muscle power.

Together the men pulled and prodded the chopper into the school. The deserted building made an ideal hide-out. Located in the southeastern corner of Madison county, eighteen miles outside Milo's circle and seven miles from the nearest town, the structure had been abandoned for years. Built in the twenties to educate children of Dempsey Coal Company employees, the eight grade country school fell into disuse when the company went bankrupt. Madison County ore was low grade, but easily mined: there was a whole mountain of it. But what had begun as a profitable enterprise went under when the cost of extracting the coal exceeded its market value.

The company town had dried up with the company, leaving shanties, a general store, and the empty school, wedged between a half-gutted mountain on one side and a mountain of tailings on the other. Rusted coal-car tracks spanned the interval, crisscrossing broken chucks of pavement that had once been Main Street. Ringing the ghost town, skeletons of machinery whose gears had been fused by countless seasons of neglect hulked where they had died. Faded, pockmarked *Keep Out*, *Danger*, and *Condemned* signs dangled at irregular intervals from drooping barbed wire, cautioning sight seers away.

Nature had long since devoured the miners' lodgings. Remnants of the company store still stood, a crumbling wall and chimney, but it was the school, with its concrete foundation and brick exterior that had best withstood the passage of time. All the windows had been broken out or carted off. The interior had been stripped—portable furnishings first—desks, chairs, blackboards, the coal-fired boiler, all sold by Dempsey for what they could recoup. Then the scavengers took over, helping themselves to anything left of value: doors, floor boards, even the lathing that divided room from room had been torn out. Part of the roof had caved in and rotted away, but the external walls were still sound. With a few swings of a sledge hammer Vonnie Lee enlarged the gaping hole that had once held double entry doors, and the Cobra's new lair was ready.

Wynne stayed with the chopper, both to protect the aircraft and to remain out of sight. Visitors to the old mining community were rare. Surrounded by Ozark National Forest, with legal entry prohibited by statute, it was highly unlikely anybody would come poking around.

To guard against that doubtful eventuality, Chris chose a Beretta Model 12 sub-machine gun with forty 9mm rounds in the magazine, plus a box of spare clips. For close-in fighting he preferred a knife, which he could throw with deadly accuracy or use to slit a throat with equal skill. Non-perishable foods and bottled water made up his rations. For company he had books and a transistor radio; a cell phone linked him to Boyd and the bunker. And rocked back on its kickstand under the camouflage netting covering the chopper, a new 250cc Suzuki dirt bike for emergency transportation.

Left on his own, Chris made one perimeter patrol, scoping out the forlorn site by moonlight. When he was satisfied that the helicopter's arrival hadn't attracted attention, he returned to the schoolhouse.

The atmosphere inside the shelter was stale and muggy, like too many temporary refuges from the pilot's past, and smelled of decomposing guano. Unfolding a canvas cot Wynne lay down, dimly aware of bats careering about the rafters and the whispery skitter of mice and rats. Their scrapes and squeaks didn't bother Chris; this was their abode, he the interloper. An errant breeze danced through vacant windows, cutting the sticky air and drying his sweat. Wynne stretched, closed his eyes, and slept.

*   *   *

It was on the verge of his consciousness, something Lester had said just before he bounced Milo's head off the barn floor. In the ensuing scuffle, with a shotgun trained on the back of his neck and death a heartbeat away, what had seemed important instants before had been forgotten. Now, nearly a week later, Milo was plagued by the nagging thought that there was *something* he should remember. The harder he racked his brain, the deeper whatever it was buried itself. Damn. His subconscious would give it up when it was ready. He sighed. In the shape he was in that might never happen.

Sleep had become the enemy. As much as Milo needed its restorative balm to help heal his injuries and refresh powers of deduction dulled by fatigue, when he did sleep, any benefits he might have derived were canceled by the nightmares.

Bagpipes skirled through the swamp, mournful as the deep-throated belling of blood hounds. A woman whose features were blurred by mist slipped a scarf from her head, loosing a cascade of auburn tresses. Her hair smelled of rainwater and patchouli. Milo reached for the square, pulling the woman toward him, but in the way of dreams she metamorphosed into a laughing child with dimpled cheeks and merry eyes. "Come dance with me," she begged, twirling on tiptoe. "I've forgotten how," he demurred. "Oh please! You have to." She grabbed his hand, but her fingers disintegrated on contact, decaying flesh giving way to brittle bone. Milo could not look at her face.

Bourbon, his longtime crutch, didn't help. Nor did Halcion, Elavil, Valium, Prozac, or any other pharmacological remedy. In the mornings he felt worse than when he had gone to bed.

*   *   *

Milo had spent hours and hours going back over everything he had amassed during the investigation: all of the documents, notes, files, newspaper clippings, every single shred of information. On Brother Daniel, Major Boyd, the Bolins, Chris Wynne,

221

the Tabernacle and its precursor, the Foundation of Eternal Life. On Addy. And he was no further along than he had been the day after Holder's call. A goodly portion of his reasoning involved second guessing his own previous conclusions. Had he misinterpreted Holder's warning? What had happened to the missing Tabernacle employees? Where were the missiles? Was the helicopter's theft actually connected to the right-wing sect? And what, if anything, did Addy's murder have to do with any of it?

Faced with no concrete results for all their efforts, Milo was casting about for anything that might help. Lacking just cause for a court ordered wiretap of the Tabernacle's telephones, he and Q.C. planned one more trip to Turner Falls that weekend, but that was clutching at straws. Milo had already acknowledged the inevitable to himself. With the President due to arrive Thursday week, if they didn't come up with something in the next forty-eight hours, he would have to take his unverified and unverifiable suppositions to the Secret Service.

Friday at the close of the workday, Milo and Quentin headed for Betsy's cabin to give it one last shot. They left Little Rock in a downpour, driving north through curtains of rain, with Q.C. at the wheel of Milo's Expedition. Lightning forked across the sky, a dazzling electric crazy quilt, forming and reforming in ever changing patterns to the rolling bass accompaniment of thunder. Despite the pyrotechnic display Milo cat-napped, lulled against his will by the steady drum of rain and metronomic clacking of the wipers. Forty-five minutes later he came to with a start.

"Laura," he announced excitedly.

"Laura? Yo, man. I thought you were in love with Betsy."

"No! Yes! Damn it, Quentin, that's not what I'm talking about. That's what *Lester* said, just before he clocked me."

"Laura?"

"Yeah, *Laura*! Lester said something like, 'God's handmaiden Laura.'"

"You mean *Laura*, as in Laura van Horne?"

222

"Yes!" Milo crowed, his dog-tired brain turning cartwheels. "Quentin, all that gibberish I was spoutin' the other night may not have been so far wrong."

"Now you've lost me."

"Don't you see? Those goons from the Tabernacle have got her body. Laura's body. It's never been recovered, not since the Fed's seized the Redfern compound nine years ago. When they got there the mausoleum was split wide open. Empty. Larry got tipped off they were comin' and everybody figured he had some of his henchmen swipe her coffin before the raid. But that's beside the point. He hasn't got her either! *That's* what those yo-yos are hidin', were so all fired desperate for us not to find. It's not Satan they're worshippin' up on that mountain. It's Laura van Horne."

"Gross. That sounds ghoulish to me Milo, but what difference does it make?"

"I don't know, my fine friend, but it may give us a hook."

Oblivious to the detective's eloquent pleading, Judge Katie Blaine Wainwright remained adamant.

Heartened by Milo's recollection they had made a U turn, speeding back to Little Rock through the waning storm.

"You're wasting your breath Milo. There's no way I'm issuing you a warrant, even if Laura van Horne *is* buried somewhere on that farm. Your best bet is to talk to the daughter. She's filed a civil suit against Larry in Crawford County, trying to recover her mother's remains." The judge looked at Quentin. "What's the Bureau's interest in this?"

He temporized. "Your honor, I'm not here representing the Bureau."

A skeptical frown creased her forehead. "No?"

"No, ma'am."

"Then we have nothing further to discuss. Now if you'll excuse me, my sole *bonne femme* is getting cold. And Milo, the next time you get a wild hair, try not to do it while I'm having dinner at Josephine's." She turned on her elegant high heels and went back in the restaurant.

Crossing the sky bridge to the parking deck, Milo vented his frustration. "Goddamnit! This whole friggin' expedition has been an exercise in futility. Let's face it, Q.C. We're outta options and we're outta time. We're gonna have to have help."

"Who'd you have in mind?"

"The only thing left is to tell the Secret Service. Maybe they can talk Clinton outta comin'."

"Milo, you sure you wanna do that? Those s.o.b.s are fuckin' paranoid." Some of the Bureau's attitude about its sister service had rubbed off.

"It's not a case of *want to*, it's a case of *have to*. I don't know about those assholes runnin' around town from Washington, but Rick Cherry's a good man. I'm hoping he'll listen. Because that's all it's gonna be. Listenin'. We sure as hell have not got one shred of proof." He paused, clicking the remote to unlock his truck. "Well, so be it," he said resignedly. "There's no point in headin' back up there tonight. Come on. If you can't think of anything else, let's grab a burger and go home."

"Don't feel so bad," Quentin offered. "You did the best you could."

"Yeah," Milo grumbled, "big damn deal. That's gonna be my epitaph: 'He Tried.'"

CHAPTER 22

Richard Cherry tore open a packet of Sweet 'n Low, dumping the contents in his coffee. Behind the counter a man in dark glasses and DAV cap inquired, "You want Danish with that Mr. Cherry? I got lemon, apricot, or cream cheese."

"No thanks, Norman. Not today." Cherry laid a dollar in a Lighthouse for the Blind tray. "Here you go. Keep the change." He took the styrofoam cup and went outside to join Milo.

Due to retire the next December, by which time he would have put in thirty years with the Secret Service, Richard Cherry was Special Agent in Charge of the Arkansas district office. At twenty-eight, with a wife and three kids to feed on a Georgia school teacher's salary, he had answered a recruiting ad in the *Atlanta Constitution,* and soon thereafter, found himself on the government roster. It was a decision he had never regretted.

When he needed a break Cherry often walked over to the TCBY Tower to grab a coffee. A steady stream of pedestrians flowed along the sidewalks bordering the sunken plaza, making for interesting contemplation. This Monday morning a brisk breeze was blowing through the corridors of downtown, and the parade of young women clutching at wind-whipped skirts was a pleasant diversion. If he hadn't been so busy Rick would have enjoyed the show, but with preparations for Clinton's homecoming in full swing, he didn't have the time. It was only Milo's insistence that had gotten him out of the office.

"Sure, Milo. What's up? I can make time if you need to talk. Come on down around ten, ten-thirty."

"Uh, Rick, can you possibly get away? Meet me instead? Somewhere close by is fine. Make it easy on yourself."

Cherry had a good working relationship with the veteran investigator and respected his abilities. So here they were. He was shocked at how bad the state cop looked.

"Nice day." Milo inclined his head at the passing spectacle. "Thanks for coming, Rick. I know you're snowed under right now. I wouldn't have bothered you, but . . . there's something you need to know."

Fifteen minutes later the SAIC wished he were anywhere but in Little Rock, Arkansas, with the President of the United States due to arrive in three days.

*　*　*

Reed Sykes-Smythe was an arrogant asshole, his high estimation of himself exceeded only by his ambition. And he had no intention of having his career derailed by some hick cop who probably couldn't find his dick when he needed to pee. Which pretty well summed up Super-Shit's (the nickname was inevitable) attitude toward anyone born outside Boston and educated outside the Commonwealth of Massachusetts. It was unfortunate that Milo and Cherry numbered among the vast unwashed. And it was doubly unfortunate that Super Shit was White House Lead Agent for the impending Presidential visit.

Rick Cherry had been assigned to the Secret Service's Little Rock branch for ten years, SAIC for six, coming to roost in the quiet backwater before *Clinton* was a household name beyond the state line. He liked Arkansas. Being from the South, he spoke the language. In fact, Little Rock had supplanted Macon as home. So much so that when he retired Rick was planning to stay, maybe teach a course in Criminal Justice at UALR just to get him out from under his wife's feet.

Based on his own experience Cherry was prepared to believe Milo. During his tenure in Arkansas he had had his share of run-ins with the radical right. But he sure wished the detective had brought him something more than unsubstantiated rumor and inference. Because the harsh truth was, without tangible proof, they were never going to convince Sykes-Smythe.

Normally, faced with the barest hint of threat, Secret Service mentality assumes that the President is the target. Presented with Milo's theory, the prudent course would have been for Sykes-Smythe to warn the White House, then throw his considerable resources into an all-out, crash effort to locate the missiles. But Arkansas? The WHLA couldn't imagine it. *Deliverance* maybe. He'd grant a certain crude cunning to the yokels, but in a place with names like Toad Suck, Pickle Gap, and Hog Scald Hollow, hardly the sophistication necessary to mount the type of attack this state cop was postulating. Hell, in Arkansas they couldn't rip off the electorate without getting caught. Half its politicians were serving time. Whitewater had become a cottage industry. News organizations kept rooms at the Capitol Hotel year round. This was Clinton territory. He'd come from here for Christ's sakes. Been Governor for God knows how long. These people fucking *loved* him. Super-Shit had no intention of incurring the President's well known wrath by fouling things up on the wild-eyed ramblings of a conspiracy freak. Even one with Cherry's backing.

However, on the extreme outside chance the man was on to something, he'd have to make a pretense of concern—just to cover his ass. This was Cherry's bugaboo. Let him take the flak.

"Ummm, yeah, thanks Richard. I'm glad you brought this to my attention. Based on what you've told me so far, I really don't see going to the AD. I mean, you don't even know that the missiles *are* missing do you? It's all so *tenuous*, if you get my drift. Tell you what. Why don't *you* check around? Get back to me in, oh, say, forty-eight hours. If you come up with anything, we'll give it a spin."

S-S had blown them off like so much dandruff.

"I'm sorry," Cherry apologized as they waited outside his office for the elevator. He glanced back at his door. "They're not all that bad. Washington sends these guys out, most of them are pretty savvy. It's a small service, two thousand agents and not many rotten apples. It's just our misfortune we got stuck with this Yankee bastard."

In fairness to Cherry, Sykes-Smythe's reaction was exactly what Milo had feared; why he had delayed going to the Feds in the first place. "It's not your fault, Rick. I'd be lying if I said I wasn't disappointed, but I know the type."

Cherry frowned, a mixture of consternation and concern. "I guess it's hard for some people to relate," he said lamely. "But damn it all Milo, he should have done *something*." Years of enduring authoritarian bullshit from D.C. hotshots had come down to this: Rick would be happy as long as the President didn't leave his jursidiction feet first. "Look, I'll try to go around him. Take this to the Assistant Director myself."

"Will he listen?"

"To be honest, I don't know. ADs come and go. I can at least ask him to talk to the Bureau, get them to run the names. That alone would provide some corroboration."

Two shafts over the *Down* indicator blinked on. Sidling toward the approaching elevator Milo said resignedly, "Thanks Rick. I hate to put you in a bind. I've got one or two ideas left, but frankly, I'm no magician."

*　　*　　*

C-SPAN I, C-SPAN II, and both CNN news channels lit up the bank of television screens. On CNN's *The World Today* two talking heads were exchanging silent dialogue, backdropped with a shot of rock-throwing Palestinians. Across the room in the White House basement, Secret Service Assistant Director of Investigations S. Clopton Riley was eating a chili dog. The way he was wolfing it down, he'd have indigestion all afternoon. Keeping one eye on the monitors, he bent low over a couple of paper napkins, holding the hotdog away from his tie.

Three telephones crowded Riley's desk. Buttons flickered on two of the instruments but the AD was ignoring them, trying to finish his sandwich. His intercom buzzed. He ignored that too. Then Janice stuck her head in the door. "Will you take a call from Richard Cherry? He says it's urgent."

Riley peered at his secretary over the tortoise frames of his reading glasses, bobbing his head up and down in answer. He hurriedly stuffed the last bite of frankfurter in his mouth.

Jamice subdued a smile. "He's holding on Line Two."

The AD chewed fast, washing the mouthful down with Dr. Brown's cream soda. He licked his fingers and dabbed at a spot on his chin before punching up the call.

"Riley," he burped.

Cherry relayed the bad news.

"No luck, Milo. I talked to the AD and he concurred with Sykes-Smythe. There's just not enough information to revise the President's schedule at this late date. It took some prodding, but he did agree to request a Bureau file check. But I wouldn't get my hopes up. Even if the Fibbies produce something usable, and that's a mighty big *if*, Riley indicated that headquarters would staff any product before taking it to the Director. With time running so short, that's department speak for forget it."

CHAPTER 23

Dan Holman sat at a table in *The Flight Deck*, nursing a cup of coffee and watching the commotion outside the restaurant. He estimated the crowd at over two hundred and growing. As he watched, a mini-van from *Channel 11, Today's THV* pulled into the parking lot behind a pair of similar vehicles from competing stations. A reporter with lacquered hair hopped out and plowed through the throng, trailing a laden camera man. Herded behind a chain-link security fence to await Clinton's arrival, scheduled for seven-thirty, the eager-greeters would be fortunate if EAGLE touched down before nine.

Holman ground out his cigarette and took his cup to the counter for a refill. Inside the Center Flying Service entryway an armed man with restless eyes followed Dan's progress. Next door his duplicate stood guard at the passenger counter of the private terminal. Dan passed into the adjacent room, spoke briefly to the Secret Service agent, and ducked out the back way to Operations.

CFS was Holman's pride and joy, a comprehensive, fixed base operation with eight hangers, offering a full complement of aviation products. Dan and his brother had built the family business into a top-notch facility. A helicopter pilot in Vietnam, Dan served as hands-on administrator, Ray the coat-and-tie money man. Cutting through hanger One behind the passenger lounge, Dan stopped for a second when he noticed Randy still fussing around the new State Police helicopter. Conversion work on the Kiowa had ended for the day, but Randy was preening over the bird like an expectant papa whose new chick has just hatched.

In March the Arkansas State Police had bought two surplus OH-58s at government auction. Dan's crew had finished refitting one of the helicopters and it was already in service. The second, sparkling in a fresh coat of blue and white paint and the ASP logo, still loitered in the shop, lacking only installation of FLIR, an advanced infrared tracking system, before its shakedown flight. The unit had come in minus one vital component, delaying delivery to the police by an extra week. Randy Markovich, one of four Little Rock-based State Police pilots, was fresh out of the military, and hot to get his hands on "his" chopper.

"Whad'd'ya think Mr. Holman?" Green eyed and red headed, with a smattering of freckles highlighting a scrubbed complexion, Markovich was wearing a Nomex jumpsuit, black combat boots, Uncle Buck's cross-body shoulder holster with pistol and extra ammo—the complete regalia. Despite fans circulating air through the cavernous space it was hot in the metal building and rings of sweat stained his armpits.

"We got the part today, Randy." Holman wished he could remember when he had been so young, so gung ho. "This time next week you'll have your bird, maybe sooner."

"Great," Randy grinned. "That's just great. Thanks a lot, Mr. Holman."

"Anytime," Dan said, then hastened on his way. There were always last minute wrinkles that needed smoothing before they rolled out the red carpet.

✻　✻　✻

"Hello." Betsy pounced on the phone on the first ring.

"Hi. Bets?"

"Milo! Hi. Boy am I glad to hear from you! Has anything happened? How're you holdin' up? I've been sittin' on pins and needles all day."

"I'm fine. Q.C.'s fine. And as far as I know, the President's fine too, unless he choked on a piece of steak in the last fifteen minutes. His party was just getting seated at Doe's when I left headquarters. He's running about an hour late, which is par for the course. I've been home long enough to pour myself a drink and dial you. So, tell me, how was my august professor's day?" If Milo sounded sanguine it was a facade. In the interval since being rebuffed by the Secret Service he had called in all his outstanding markers. However this thing played out, he had done everything he could do. Even so, it might not be enough. The thought terrified him.

"Okay. Uneventful. Nothing compared to yours, Milo. As fascinating as you realize my course is, it's hard to stay focused on ancient history knowin' it's crunch time. I'm not at my best when I'm worried about my fella, not to mention . . ."

Milo zeroed in on "my fella," the rest of her answer blurring into white noise as he began to let down. Betsy had become his escape valve, their nightly conversations the release he needed to keep going. He settled as comfortably as he could in his chair. Gulped a slug of Jack Black and felt the whiskey's warmth spread through his abused body. Milo's ribcage hurt still; his face a particolored montage of aging bruises and patches of pink, tender skin where his scabs had sloughed off.

Uh-oh. Betsy had quit talking and he was in trouble. What had she said? He was so tired he had been wool gathering, not paying attention. "Bets? Bets? Are you still there?"

"I'm here."

"I'm so sorry, Betsy. I lost your train of thought. You were saying . . . ?"

"Poor Milo. You're all in aren't you? It wasn't important. Why don't you get some rest and we'll talk again tomorrow."

"Please don't hang up," he pleaded hastily. "I'm listening, I promise."

"Are you sure? I think some sleep would do you a whole lot more good than my nattering."

"Sure I'm sure. Why d'ya think I called?"

"Well, in that case," she said. "Let me see. Oh, now I remember. What I was saying is that the dogs and I care about you more than you know; that we miss you inordinately; that I wish I were there but I'd only be in the way; that what you're doing right now is the most important thing in the world; et cetera, et cetera, et cetera."

In spite of Milo's exhaustion her words provoked a chuckle, lightening his mood. "Well, that makes all the difference. Tell me more."

"No more, you glutton. You've had your daily allowance of ego stoking. Now I really *am* going to hang up. Take two aspirin, go to bed, and call me in the morning."

He laughed out loud. "Yes doctor."

"All right!" Then her voice softened, banter aside. "Good night, Milo. *Please* be careful."

"I will Betsy, I promise. Take care yourself . . . Good night."

He sat in his chair clutching the telephone, long after the line went dead.

*   *   *

More participants attended William Jefferson Clinton's high school reunion than had made up the entire student body of Hot Springs High School when he was enrolled there. Taking into account those class members who had died, or could not otherwise be reached by the invitation committee, every former classmate save one had showed up, plus spouses, children, significant others, and visiting dignitaries, to rub shoulders with their most famous graduate.

A golden September day produced a large Spa City turnout for the Presidential motorcade. Cheering spectators gave their hometown hero a warm welcome as his bulletproof limousine, flown in especially for the occasion, wound up Grand Avenue behind the school band, an equestrian honor unit, and Chamber of Commerce and Rotary floats. Any minor unpleasantness was averted when a band of pickets carrying grisly signs protesting partial birth abortion was, after a brief, but acrimonious skirmish, shunted away from the parade route by local police.

233

For Milo, every hour that passed without a missile slamming into Clinton's entourage was a relief. Because the timing of the attack was a matter of conjecture, as indeed the *possibility* of an attack was conjectural, there was no guarantee *when, where,* or even *if* the Tabernacle would strike. If their goal were simply to assassinate the President, the blow could come at any time, with varying degrees of collateral carnage. Ever since the Oklahoma City bombing, images of broken bodies carried from the ruins of the Murrah building had haunted Americans, never more poignantly than when the cameras focused on injured toddlers. To a sane individual, any loss of life at the hands of extremists was insupportable, but to target those innocent little ones was an indelible stain on the national conscience.

By the perpetrator's own admission, that base act of home grown terrorism had been timed to inflict maximum causalities. *To insure that the government would take notice.* When would Daniel's fanatics strike? Taking into account what he knew of Brother Daniel and the Tabernacle, and all he had learned in the course of his professional life, Milo had bet on the ballgame.

It was a big gamble. If he were wrong, the people of Arkansas, the nation, and by extension, the world, would suffer the consequences. What unofficial resources Milo had been able to muster would barely cover one venue; ergo, he had damn well better pick the right one. It was Milo's call. He had made it.

* * *

Richard Cherry had eaten on the fly—if you could call it eating—a vending machine ham sandwich and a can of Nestea. EAGLE decided to take advantage of Friday's glorious weather, abbreviating his stay at the festivities' afternoon session to get in nine holes before dark. The President's sudden change of plans was a colossal, but hardly unprecedented, headache for his protectors, sending the Secret Service into paroxysms of activity. By the time Marine One landed back in Little Rock, Sykes-Smythe and Cherry, working frantically in conjunction with Milo and

LRPD, had reshuffled and retooled, in keeping with the chief executive's caprice.

With EAGLE coming off the links at Chenal, things got back on schedule. Clinton enjoyed a leisurely dinner at the home of old friends in Hillcrest, and was tucked in for the night, minded by watchers quartered in a rented travel trailer parked in his mother-in-law's driveway. A handful of off-duty agents lounged around Cherry's office comparing notes and shooting the bull. At ten o'clock the SAIC turned up the volume on the TV. Late local news programs were showing repeats of their six o'clock broadcasts: footage from the morning's motorcade, film of the President greeting supporters, and carefully chosen sound bites from his speech. At least they weren't showing scenes of whole-sale death and destruction. Thank God for that. Cherry clicked off the tube. One more hurdle behind them.

*   *   *

In the bunker's ops chamber Daniel was also watching the news. Monitors carried feed from three Little Rock television stations and one in Ft. Smith. "Look at that," he said in disgust. Pictures of cheering crowds along Grand Avenue flickered on two of the screens. Another was airing excerpts from the President's address to his high school classmates, while Channel 7 had switched to sports.

"Motherfuckers won't be cheering much longer," McKensie tittered.

"No," Daniel agreed. "They won't. We're about to strip the wool from their eyes. *Make* them see."

Right.

While Boyd had his own reasons for aiding Daniel's quest for revenge, the evangelist had duped his parishioners with a load of bullshit about waking up the country before it was too late. In truth, those actively involved in the mission hadn't needed convincing. Ideology and suspicion, reinforced by ongoing revelations about the Feds' role in Waco, plus the promise of monetary reward, had seen to that. Nuturing fear was all well and good, but under his self-righteous posturing what Daniel really wanted, had longed for, hoped for, prepared for, even occasionally prayed for, what he *really* wanted was to *get even*, pure and simple. Payback for a lifetime of hurt and rejection. And he meant to do it.

"Too bad that hussy didn't come too," Harlan contributed, probing his gums with a toothpick. "Those stupid buttholes in New York don't know what they're askin' fer. Good riddance, I say. Let 'em have the bitch."

Boyd listened without comment. Daniel's troops were behaving as countless soldiers before them on the eve of battle. If denigrating the enemy helped boost their courage, he had no quarrel with that.

✻   ✻   ✻

Milo stared bleary-eyed as his bedside clock blinked away the minutes. Awake most of the night, at 4:30 he figured he might as well get up. His tongue was coated with the stale, greenish fuzz of nerves, late nights, too much caffeine, too little sleep, and food scarfed on the fly. Zombie-like, he stumbled barefoot into the kitchen. Filled the kettle with tap water and set it on the stove to boil. A black and gold canister held a supply of Darjeeling. While the tea steeped he showered and dressed. He felt older than God. Hopefully the scalding brew would settle his stomach and clear away the cobwebs.

Across town Richard Cherry had also spent a sleepless night. From the beginning the SAIC had given Milo credence, granting from his own experience that the state investigator's theory was entirely feasible. And he gone to the AD, bypassing the chain of command and infuriating Super-Shit. But turned down twice by the powers that be, he had given up. When he tried to close his eyes after slipping into bed beside his wife, Rick was assailed by visions of Oklahoma City. *Why* hadn't he pusher harder? Gone all out? Convinced his superiors to act—before now, when it was almost too late? Tossing restlessly while Dee Dee slept, Cherry realized that he actually *believed* a Hellfire missile launched from a stolen National Guard helicopter was going to crash into Razorback stadium, taking out Bill Clinton and anyone else in close proximity. The death toll could be in the hundreds—or thousands.

He had to do *something* to stop it. He dressed in the dark and headed downtown.

For Richard Cherry there was only one avenue left. Sitting at his desk, queasy and unshaven, he contemplated a smiling photograph of his family. Then he reached for the phone. In Washington it was a few minutes before seven. He would try to catch the Director at home. If he could convince Jason Barksdale, autocratic head of the Secret Service, that the President was in danger, they might still have a chance.

Barksdale was not a benevolent dictator. Brusque, irascible, the Director made no attempt to hide his irritation. "This better be good Cherry."

"Sir, we have a situation here I think you should be aware of."

The Director listened without interrupting. But the force of Cherry's personal conviction couldn't overcome the paucity of hard evidence needed to back him up. Barksdale weighed the SAIC's arguments and found them wanting.

Rick made one last try. "If you won't talk to the President, let me have a little insurance at least. What can it hurt?"

Barksdale growled, "You're sure you want to go ahead with this? Buck Sykes-Smythe and the AD?"

"Yes sir. I'm positive."

"Then it's *your* butt in the sling, *your* pension on the line."

A flash of temper tinged Rick's reply. He was *right*, damn it. "I believe you've made that abundantly plain."

"Okay Cherry, as long as you understand. Now, tell me, if I authorize your request, who going to make the decisions?"

"Since you're holding me responsible, I guess it'll be me."

"All right. You've got what you asked for." The conversation was over. Relieved that he had accomplished something, even if it wasn't all he had hoped for, Richard was about to put down the phone when the Director surprised him, sounding for an instant almost human. "And Cherry, we better all pray you're wrong."

*　　*　　*

Leaving a dust cloud hanging in the still morning air, Terry Weltlich pulled his pickup off Dixon Road and out of sight behind the mobile home. The ground was littered with mast, acorns crunching with small, explosive pops under the wheels of his truck. Terry got out, blew his nose, spat, cursed his sinus drainage, and blew his nose again. A head peered out the trailer's back door.

"Terry? You sound like Typhoid Mary."

"Damned allergies. All this junk in the air." Weltlich kicked at the acorns. "Won't get any better 'til we have a killin' frost. And that's a good two months away."

Terry was running two stakeouts, four men each, one of the Tabernacle and rectory, the other of the poultry farm. Having helped search for the missing Cobra, he was already conversant with part of the story. When Milo detailed his real suspicions, Weltlich had agreed to mount the surveillance. After bleating to the Colonel about Milo's usurping his territorial autonomy, he could hardly refuse. And while he wasn't wild about the *sub rosa* nature of the operation, the specter of Milo's possibly being right was a powerful incentive. If they were fortunate enough to snare someone en route to the chopper, the disaster might be forestalled.

Keeping tabs on the chicken farm was a straightforward proposition. Given its dead-end location, anyone entering or leaving would have to pass his quartet of watchers. Two nondescript vehicles, a tan Ford pickup and a '96 Chevrolet Malibu, had been parked in the yard for covert pursuit. At the moment the Ford was gone.

Surveilling the Tabernacle was more difficult. Positioned on the river bluff, access to the church was off a winding county lane. A vehicle leaving the Tabernacle grounds was free to turn in either direction, one way leading to U.S. 65, the other meandering for miles through scrub country before intersecting Arkansas Scenic Highway 14. Chase cars allocated to the church team included another Ford truck and a Japanese compact. Weltlich was alternating between positions, augmenting their tailing capability.

Terry had rounded up his forces from the far reaches of his jurisdiction, heeding Milo's advice. For the same reason that Milo had refused to satisfy Sheriff Womack's curiosity the night of the abortive raid, he had been afraid that if Terry used local men, word would filter back to Daniel. For OPERATION PREVENT to have any chance of success, they couldn't afford leaks.

The surveillance posts had been operational for close to forty-eight hours, since late Thursday morning, well before the President's arrival. Photographs of the relative players had been secured from DMV and blow ups distributed to the watchers: Daniel, McKensie, Boyd, the Williamses, and all three Bolins—Wendy, Heavy, and Vonnie Lee.

If Milo had hoped that close observation might turn up the missing cult members it was no go; even under round-the-clock scrutiny none had surfaced. Nor had Commander Boyd put in an appearance. The only things of note to report thus far were the movements of Brother Daniel himself.

The cult leader had been observed exiting the farm in a black Dodge Caravan shortly after Terry's men got in place, and they had tailed him back to the rectory. Friday morning he walked over to his church office, working there until noon. After lunch Daniel changed vehicles, driving a Buick sedan to the sect's radio station, where he stayed for over an hour. From there he visited two other Tabernacle businesses, paid a couple of sick calls at the hospital in Harrison, gassed up at Lester's, and returned home. The pastor's next departure from his enclave had not occurred until nine-thirty Friday night, when he had left his house alone, once again in the Dodge. Daniel made a single stop at a Stax in Turner Falls to place a phone call from a public booth (which in itself was peculiar—did he suspect *his* phones were tapped, *and* those at the Pit Stop?), before going on to the farm. He arrived at Flora and Harlan's around ten o'clock.

Weltlich entered the trailer. "Where's Jerry?" he demanded.

"He followed the Williamses to Harrison thirty minutes ago. They're at Wal-Mart, gettin' their tires rotated."

"And the preacher?"

"No sign of him since last night. Far as we can tell, he's still holed up on the mountain."

"Okay." Terry rinsed a chipped porcelain mug in the sink and poured in thick black sludge. He added two scoops of sugar and powdered non-dairy creamer. Regarding the mixture with distaste, he moved to the window, hooked his thumb toward the bedroom. "Erskine, I'll take over. Go get some shut eye. Be fresh when he comes out."

"Thanks, Ter." Erskine got to his feet yawning; cracked his knuckles and stretched. "Best offer I've had all day."

* * *

Milo gunned the Expedition after slowing for a 35mph speed zone through Bee Branch. From there, driving like a bat out of hell, he could make it to Turner Falls in sixty minutes flat.

Milo was wired. He couldn't just sit at his desk while others were doing his job for him. As the morning dragged on he got increasingly antsy. By one o'clock he was crawling the walls. Even the news of Cherry's eleventh hour breakthrough hadn't helped much. It was too little too late—plastering a Band-Aid on a gaping wound—first aid, not surgery.

For the first time in over a month Milo had caught weekend duty. With the President in town, as liaison he was expected to be on hand. But even having set things up to run without him, being stuck in headquarters galled. The problem was *out there*, not in an office in Little Rock. At two fifteen he couldn't stand it any longer.

Milo pawed through his bottom drawer, found a stale pack of Marlboros. "I'm going out back," he said to no one in particular, opening the box and shaking out a cigarette.

"I thought you quit," came from Bigger's corner.

"Yeah, I thought so too," Milo said.

He clattered down three flights of stairs and out the back door. Flipped the unlighted smoke at a trash can. Got in his Expedition and peeled out.

It was a toss up between Fayetteville and Turner Falls. As he sped toward the Conway intersection where U.S. 65 split north off I-40, Milo agonized over the decision. Who needed him the most? Terry was sitting on the Tabernacle. Was the coverage at the University adequate? Who could tell? In any event, it was all he could manage. He decided. He would go to Fayetteville. Milo was accelerating past the Highway 65 turn-off when he suddenly changed his mind, veering across two lanes of traffic to wrench his truck down the exit ramp on squealing tires.

*   *   *

While Milo was barreling up the highway toward Daniel's stronghold, Chris Wynne was packing up. Years of clandestine assignments had taught him to leave no trace of his sojourn in the abandoned school. Each day he had double bagged his trash and buried it well away from the building. The slit trench he had dug for a latrine was filled in, and those stores he had not used would be trucked out when help came to move the chopper. His stay had been uneventful and contemplative. Hardly a garden spot, his quarters, but all in all, not too bad. There were worse places to have spent his last week, if things didn't work out.

*   *   *

On the apron in front of Hangar Number One, the newly outfitted State Police chopper basked in the sunshine. As soon as

241

the ground crew had finished servicing it, Holman's maintenance supervisor had gone over the bird top to bottom for the second time as an added precaution. Smiling with satisfaction, the head mechanic wiped his hands and stuffed the grease rag back in his coveralls. He was proud of his crew. Accustomed to working under pressure, the techs had done a good job getting the thermal imager installed overnight.

His boss emerged from the terminal, accompanied by a man Fred didn't recognize.

"What's the verdict?" Holman asked.

"Topped off and ready to go."

"Anything in particular I should watch out for?"

"Nope," Fred answered. "This baby's clean as a whistle."

Dan clapped his supervisor on the shoulder. "Thanks, Fred. And thank the guys. I'll make it up to y'all." Turning to the man with him, Holman said, "It'll just be a few minutes. I need to do my own preflight check and then we're off. If you wanna wait in the shade, or take a leak, now's the time."

Standing on the blacktop in the afternoon sun was like broiling in a toaster oven, waves of heat radiating off the asphalt, but Quentin declined. "I'm fine," he said. "Let me grab my gear and I'll wait in the chopper."

Holman studied the sweating FBI agent. *We're both crazy,* he thought, *and I'm way too old for this.* "Sure," he said. "That's fine by me."

✻   ✻   ✻

Richard Cherry strapped in as SHEPHERD got airborne. He wouldn't admit it to his colleagues, but his stomach did didos lifting off in a chopper. He didn't get airsick; it was more a fluttering, like being on a roller coaster when the car crests the first loop and plummets down the far side. He'd be fine once they leveled out.

Traveling in a convoy of three helicopters, collectively code named NIGHTHAWK, Marine One, with the President aboard, was second in the formation. For the hour plus flight to Fayet-teville, Marine Two would take the lead, landing first with its complement of press and SS agents to cover the President's ar-rival. Big CH-53As, the helos carried two pilots, two crew, with a seating capacity of ten to twelve in the passenger compartment. Friends, media, attendants, and Secret Service agents were dis-tributed between Marines One and Two. The third chopper, a VH-60 Black Hawk, hastily brought in after Cherry had cir-cumvented the entire chain of command, contained pilots, crew, Cherry, and two CAT teams [Counter Attack Team: a four man, armed-to-the-teeth counter terrorist squad—really *lethal* s.o.b.s]. SHEPHERD would ride herd on the other members of the fleet.

Rick gulped as the helicopter cleared AllTel's new high-rise, then swooped in a graceful arc out over the Arkansas River. The craft righted, soaring above Rebsaman Golf Course, the Little Rock Country Club, and acres of expensive homes in Pulaski Heights. From his window Cherry had a bird's eye view of the zoo and empty War Memorial Stadium. They powered past the State Hospital, Med Center, VA, and Children's Hospital. Un-derneath the State Capitol complex scrolled by, and to the right, the skyscrapers of downtown, largely deserted at five-thirty on Saturday afternoon. Then they were crossing the Arkansas again, north of the Broadway bridge, coming full circle back to River-front Drive and the other choppers awaiting clearance.

What Cherry could not see was Super Shit, seething on Ma-rine One. But Rick's ears, which the WHLA had blistered that morning when the word came down, continued to burn. Sykes-Smythe hadn't taken kindly to having his authority usurped.

"All clear, sir. No visuals and nothing on radar."

"Roger that," Cherry acknowledged. "Let's get this show in the air."

CHAPTER 24

The converted CH-53A flared out at fifty feet, touching down on the practice field as gently as if it were landing on the South Lawn of the White House. As soon as the rotor wound down, a welcoming committee advanced to greet the President. After a cordial exchange with Frank Broyles and other assembled dignitaries, the former U.A. law professor couldn't pass up the chance to work the crowd. Amid the pregame hubbub and bally-hoo, Bill Clinton was clearly in his element. To the consternation of his Detail, and the grumbling of discommoded fans, POTUS glad-handed his way into the stadium, working the rope line and swapping quips about the team's prospects.

During Clinton's slow progression from chopper to skybox, Arkansas had won the toss and deferred to the second half. When the President had settled his tall frame in a plush armchair in Hog Heaven, Sykes-Smythe's thumbs up to the broadcast director was instantly relayed to the TV coordinator waiting on the sidelines. On television sets around the nation Nike's logo was replaced by a close-up of the Hog's kicker standing on his twenty-seven yard line. The camera zoomed out to a wide angle shot of the whole playing field. Cory Carnahan took a running start, and with the wind at his back, booted the pigskin out of the north end zone. Right on time at 7:05, as millions watched across the country, the contest got underway.

At the same time the football was sailing through the air toward the Broyles complex, earpieces from the towers of Old

244

Main and the flat rooftop of Bud Walton Arena to dormitories and fraternity houses overlooking the arena crackled. "EAGLE is in the nest. Repeat, EAGLE is in the nest."

"Alpha clear." Just as quickly the Secret Service counter-sniper teams checked in down the line, until all units guarding the perimeter were accounted for. For the moment, within a mile of the stadium, everything was under control.

It would get harder soon. Circling high above in SHEPHERD, Richard Cherry's eyes strayed to the west, where day was dying a fiery death behind the press box. Streaks of impossible pinks, purples, and oranges ran like water color across the etiolated sky, vivid splashes of sunset no self-respecting artist could ever hope to replicate. Once the sun had gone down, the banks of lights illuminating the playing field would wreck havoc with their night vision scopes.

Farther out, beyond the shooters' range, Milo's recruits manned their posts, the protective network he had hocked his soul to put in place.

"Bud, take a look at this." Charlie Zack was monitoring the radar. Bud Stephens leaned over the scope, the Randall Fighting Knife strapped over his BDUs marking him as an officer with the 39th Arkansas Light Infantry Brigade. On the screen, the blip that represented SHEPHERD was joined by another electronic speck, tracking at the extreme edge of their coverage. "It's another chopper," Charlie pronounced. The two man Stinger crew jumped up.

"Whoa, take it easy guys," Lt. Colonel Stephens cautioned. He fingered his own radio. "INTERDICT ONE to WATCHDOG, come in WATCHDOG."

"This is WATCHDOG, reporting in on station."

"Welcome to the friendly skies."

"Sure thing. Just don't y'all get trigger happy down there."

"Don't sweat it. You're outta range."

"Tell that to the mujahedeen."

"Point taken. Glad to have you, Dan."

Set up on Mt. Sequoyah, barely two miles from Razorback stadium, the four man squad was one of two Milo had used to bracket the University. Four other Guardsmen were positioned across town, on a hilltop west of the U.S. Highway 71 bypass. Armed with LSDIS systems and Stinger missiles, the units were highly skilled air defense teams, equipped with top notch matériel. [LSDIS: Light and Special Division Interim Sensor, a short-range, low-altitude airspace surveillance system consisting of a radar, a commercial 1.5 kW generator, and a FAADC2 interface. With a 360° azimuth and 20 kilometer range at up to 3 kilometers of altitude, the LSDIS is a portable detection device designed to pick up moving fixed- and rotary-wing aircraft, as well as hovering helicopters.]

If securing the field radars had been a bitch, Milo didn't like to think what it had taken to get his hands on the Stingers. His biggest surprise was finding a cache of the missiles in the ammo dump at Camp Robinson. Co-opting their use meant co-opting certain field grade officers who had access to them, since he had not a prayer in hell of talking the military into lending him half a dozen of the shoulder-fired, heat seeking weapons. With enough leverage, this he had accomplished, though it hadn't been easy. Tipping the scales had been the incontrovertible fact of the missing helicopter. According to Stephens, National Guard instructor and combat veteran of Desert Storm, one thing mitigated in their favor. The terrorists had taken a Cobra, which was a fairly easy kill. Thank heavens Daniel's fanatics hadn't swiped an Apache.

"What was that *mujahedeen* stuff about?" Quentin wanted to know. Strapped in the observer's seat in the commandeered State Police helicopter, patrolling an elliptical orbit six to twelve miles out, Quentin was more than a little jumpy.

"Well," Dan Holman replied, "the Army's pretty coy about the Stinger's range. They list it at four klicks. But in Afghanistan, Stingers we supplied to the Muslim guerrillas took out Rooskie aircraft seven to eight kilometers away, firing down on them in mountain passes. And the German Army home page, if you can believe that, says ten thousand meters."

Quentin swallowed. What the hell was he doing up there?

Holman tuned to a different frequency. "SHEPHERD, this is WATCHDOG, do you copy?"

"We read you WATCHDOG."

"Good going, SHEPHERD. We have your six."

When he arranged his defenses Milo had no reason to suppose that Richard Cherry would launch a last ditch appeal for assistance; even less that it would be successful. Now, just because the Secret Service had sent an extra chopper, Milo wasn't about to change his plans. He had told the SAIC that the police helicopter would be up, scanning for intruders. He had told him about the LSDIS systems. He had not told him that Guardsmen armed with Stingers would be deployed with the radars. Even in the hands of friendlies, that would be too much for the Secret Service agent to countenance.

*   *   *

Wendy was freaking out. They had locked her in with a dead woman! She had to calm down, subdue the panic, but it was so unreal. *Get a grip, Wendy. Think! She can't hurt you. She's a prisoner, just like you.* Wendy hugged herself in an effort to get warm, shivering more from fear than from the chilly room. She circled the chamber warily, trying not to look at the woman in the coffin. Being caged in the tiny bedroom off the office was nothing compared to this. And banging on the thick steel door wasn't going to do her any good. She had tried that until her knuckles were raw. She slumped against a carpeted wall, as far from the corpse as the dimensions of the cramped room would allow. She *had* to get out of there.

Her only other descent into the bunker had been the night she tried to escape, when Heavy had hauled her bodily down the ramp and into the computer center to await the outcome of

Boyd's confrontation with the state cop. But that was different. Sure she had been scared then. And frustrated. But she'd also been curious. If she hadn't been so mad at Heavy, and uneasy with that jerk McKensie leering at her, she might almost have enjoyed her interlude with the bunker rats. Confined to the ops level as the struggle unfolded above ground, once her fury died down she had occupied her time memorizing details of the place. If she ever did get away she vowed to tell the authorities every single thing she could remember. When the intruders and Sheriff Womack had finally been ushered off the property, Wendy had been reluctant to leave, knowing she'd have to face Flora's wrath over her smashed collar bone.

But Wendy would take the aggrieved woman's temper any day to the glassy stare of the corpse.

*   *   *

At 8:42, with twenty-seven seconds left in the second period, Alabama scored the go-ahead touchdown on an Arkansas fumble, to lead 14-10 at the half. Speaking into hand-held mikes thrust in their faces as players trotted off the field, both coaches said their teams had to try harder, eliminate mistakes, hold on to the ball. Keith Jackson interviewed the Razorback's Number One Fan for his reaction. Relaxed and smiling, the President predicted an Arkansas comeback in the third quarter; joked with Jackson about their golf swings. Fans called the Hogs. Both bands marched. The only things flying over Razorback Stadium in the crisp September air were pennants of the twelve schools making up the Southeastern Conference. In Fayetteville, everything was normal as nachos from the concession stand.

*   *   *

Tension inside the mobile home was becoming unbearable. Since Flora and Harlan had returned from Wal-Mart with their newly balanced tires and a load of supplies, no one had come into or gone out of farm, including Daniel. With his attention divided between the TV set and the road outside, and his nerves frayed to the breaking point, all Milo could do was wait.

Upon his arrival Milo had sent Terry back to the church, giving the watchers an added pursuit car at each location in the event that Daniel and his henchmen staged a multiple exodus, but with nothing doing, the quiet was eating away Milo's confidence. He paced the shabby room, unable to sit still. By the half Milo was sure they were missing something, since neither stakeout had produced results. Was there another way out? No, he reassured himself, not unless they were going to trek over the mountains, and that was highly unlikely. And where were the Hellfires? With the chopper, which he and Q.C. had proven was not at the farm? Or somewhere he could only guess at? *Face it, Milo, they could be anywhere. A barn, a garage, any of the Tabernacle properties. Anywhere.* It was depressing as hell. Maybe they should storm the farm, arrest everybody in sight, and hold them until the President was long gone.

At 9:18, a few minutes into the third quarter, Arkansas had just kicked a field goal to pull within one when the yellow glare of headlights swept down the lane. Milo snatched the glasses from Erskine's hand. It was the Dodge Caravan, moving fast, followed closely by the Williams' Jeep, throwing up a rooster tail of dust. Milo had only caught a brief glimpse of the van's driver as it sped past in the dark, but he would swear that Daniel was behind the wheel.

"Okay! This is it," Milo shouted as the men raced for their chase vehicles. "Let 'em get by. The first turnoff's a mile this side of the highway. Keep your lights off and stay well back. Follow the dust." He radioed Terry, made an instantaneous decision. "They're coming out. Pull one team off the Tabernacle and send a car to the intersection with 65. See if your men can get there first. There're in two vehicles, so they may split up. Go!"

He punched up Richard Cherry. "They're moving." It was enough. Alerted Quentin and Dan Holman, still circling thanks to the extended range tanks that gave them three and a half hours flying time. "Okay you guys, things are heatin' up. They're on the move. Hang tight and I should have more shortly." Patched through to his strained spotters, cautioning them to look sharp, a totally wasted admonition. Tendons in the Guardsmen's necks were stretched tighter than bow strings.

Reports from the pursuit were coming in.

"Milo, the van's not turnin'. Looks like it's headed straight for the highway. The Jeep's takin' the cut-off to one-twenty-three."

"Okay. Erskine, make the turn. Stay with the Jeep. George, you and Jim follow the van."

"We're on 65 headed your way right now," from Tom Fenton, one of Terry's group, in a Ford Ranger.

"If the van turns right you'll pass it. Keep your eyes peeled Tom."

*   *   *

"Get EAGLE out!" Cherry was arguing with Sykes-Smythe.

"Why? Just because some people what, eighty miles away from here, have decided to go out on Saturday night? Come off it Cherry. You wanna be a hero, do it on somebody else's watch. The President's enjoying the game. You may as well forget it." Speaking angrily into his lapel mike, Super Shit had stepped into the corridor so the Presidential party couldn't overhear. The rift between Cherry and the WHLA had escalated into open warfare. Sykes-Smythe snarled, "Listen buster, you think you're such hot shit, going to the Director. Well let me tell you, I've got your number, and when this thing is over, I will bury you." Quietly he opened the door and resumed his post at the back of the skybox.

"Everything okay Reed?" Davor Papatakis, one of Clinton's Detail, asked.

"No problem," Super Shit assured him.

A roar erupted from the crowd. EAGLE jumped to his feet with everyone else, cheering as D'Shantu Basile scampered down the sidelines, sidestepping the last Alabama defender and diving into the end zone to put Arkansas ahead by five.

Un-hunh, Sykes-Smythe observed the celebration with sat-isfaction. *I'm not frying my ass for some redneck nervous Nellie with PMS.*

✻　✻　✻

When the van hit the highway with one chase car in pursuit, it turned right into traffic, and within half a mile passed Tom Fenton going in the opposite direction. As soon as he was able Fenton executed a U-turn, but by then a mile and a half behind.

From the intersection of Dixon Road and Highway 65 it was five miles to the Tabernacle's turn-off, then three more up the winding road to the church. At sixty-five miles an hour, it didn't take long to determine that the Caravan was going home.

George Wildgen and Jim Burleson, following a couple of pickups back, radioed for instructions. "The van's turnin' off, looks like it may be headin' back to the Tabernacle. What do you want us to do?"

"Let Tom take the van. You and Jim see if you can catch up to Erskine. He's got the Jeep on 123, six or seven miles ahead of you."

When the Jeep had wheeled onto the dirt road that served as a short cut between Dixon Road and State Highway 123, it had spun out, fishtailing on a patch of loose gravel and almost going into the ditch. The driver reduced his speed, traveling at a safer fifty until emerging on the pavement four miles later. Then he accelerated again, apparently unaware that Erskine and King were on his tail.

George and Jim, in the souped up Malibu, rocketed down 65, screeching onto 123 ten minutes behind Erskine. With the pedal down and the speedometer hovering over ninety, they slowly closed the gap.

Tom Fenton switched off the ignition, out of sight behind the barn quartering Terry's Tabernacle stakeout. Over a mile back, he and Marvin hadn't seen the van pull into the rectory's

251

two-car garage, but Terry and the other team of watchers had gotten a good look as Daniel parked, then walked nonchalantly outside through the open garage door.

Terry directed the Ranger, "Don't slow down. He's standing behind the van, watching the road."

Tom continued down the lane, feeling sick. "D'ya think he made us?"

Marvin shrugged indifferently. "Maybe so, maybe no. Hard to tell. Not much we can do about it, either way."

"Shit!"

Five minutes passed before Terry called them back, "Okay, he's gone in and put the lid down. Come on back to base."

Was Brother Daniel in for the night?

* * *

Like the vast majority of Arkansans, James Coltrane loved the Razorbacks. He was glad the Hogs were winning; they just needed to score more. At the end of the third quarter they were on top twenty/fourteen. He'd drawn six and four in the guards' pool. If Arkansas could manage to hold Alabama and kick two more field goals, he'd collect a hundred bucks. Then a sudden thought occurred to him: from whom? Who would be left to pay off?

James was in the kitchen filling his lunch box, a small black and white Magnavox on the counter tuned to the game. He had unscrewed the cap of his old Stanley steel thermos, slipping the foam-wrapped fuse into the cylinder, a carefully measured fit. He jammed the cork in tight and replaced the lid. Hefted the bottle and shook it gently. Hot coffee his hairy ass.

Next he removed lunch meat from the refrigerator, pushing aside blister packs of baloney and olive-pimiento loaf to extract a taped, white butcher paper package from the bottom of the meat drawer. Even that struck him as funny. People were always complaining about plastic sandwiches. Boy, oh boy, wait til they got a taste of his.

He made two Semtex specials, double thick, with mayo and lettuce on Beefsteak Rye. Sealed them in sandwich bags and laid them in the lunch box with an apple and a bag of Fritos. Added a candy bar. He gazed longingly at the rows of beer cans when he put the mayonnaise back in the fridge. Man, a cool one would go down good, but tonight there couldn't be any screw-ups. James grabbed a Dr. Pepper instead and went back to the couch. If they didn't stop the action for too many goddamn commercials, he'd get to see the end of the game before he had to leave.

＊　　＊　　＊

Milo knew something was wrong. As the cat-and-mouse chase down 123 stretched to over thirty minutes, the seeds of doubt that had sprouted during the first half grew to full flower. If whoever was in the Williams' Jeep were going for the chopper, they would have to get there soon or the ball game would be over. It was now mid-way into the fourth quarter, and unless Holder was wrong about the type of missiles taken from Lone Star, once Marine One got airborne, the terrorists couldn't touch it. Equipped with the latest Black Hole IR-suppression technology, it would be difficult to hit the Presidential transport even with SAMs or air-to-air ordnance. Maybe Daniel's group was trying to lull him into thinking he'd been mistaken, then strike at the last minute. Maybe he *had* been mistaken, and the President wasn't the target. Maybe no Hellfires were missing in the first place. Then he discounted that. Someone had, after all, stolen the National Guard helo.

Erskine's voice brought him up short. "Milo, they've turned onto the old Dempsey Coal Mine property. We had to go by. Someone, looked like maybe Vonnie Lee Bolin, was unlocking a chain across the road. Do you want us to go in?"

"Can you tell how many there are?" Milo was raking frantically through his stack of satellite blow ups, but the mine lay outside his circle.

"Naw. We didn't get close enough to take a head count."

253

Milo checked his watch, glanced at the TV. It was 9:51, with 2:56 left in the game. Did rapid calculations. If POTUS spent ten minutes in each locker room, he was what, half an hour from lift off? At a cruising speed of 140 knots, the Cobra could just cover the distance in time. But would they cut it that fine? Not if he could help it.

"Okay. George and Jim are right behind you. Wait for them and go in together. But be careful. I'll call the sheriff, get some backup, but that could take too long. Erskine, if the chopper's there, don't let it get in the air. Do whatever you have to, but *do not let it take off*. You got that?"

"Yeah, Milo," Erskine said, dropping the clip of his Beretta to double check that all fifteen rounds were there. He rammed the magazine home. "We read you loud and clear."

CHAPTER 25

Two things happened almost simultaneously. On the horn arranging reinforcements for his men closing in on the old coal mine, Milo didn't hear the Blazer coming, didn't spot it until it was directly in front of the trailer. He slammed down the receiver and was bolting for the door when the radio came back to life, Terry's excited voice stopping him mid-stride. "Milo, I've got two vehicles leavin' the Tabernacle. We can't tell who's drivin', but the van's turned toward the highway, and the Reverend's Buick's takin' the back road."

"Shit. I'm takin' off after a late model Blazer headed somewhere in one hell of a hurry. Terry, you stay there. Send Fenton with the van. You've got one team left. Put them on the Buick. This command post is off the air . . ."

"Roger that. *Fenton, go! Jason, take the Sentra and follow the Buick.*"

Milo's Expedition shot down the dirt drive. He skidded onto Dixon Road in a cloud of dust, the Blazer's tail lights far ahead. Hit the radio. "Okay, Terry, I'm back. Anything from Erskine and his guys?"

"Not a word."

"Try to raise them, see if they've found the chopper."

"Sure thing, Milo. Wait a minute! Here comes another one. Where's this guy been? It's a . . . what is that? . . . another van? Can't make the type, maybe a conversion."

"Okay, if the second van goes for 65, take it and forget the Buick."

"He's turning . . . yes! *Rouby, you and Jenkins turn around and hit it.*"

Milo wasn't closing on the Blazer. As fast as he was pushing his truck, the margin separating the speeding vehicles seemed to be widening. On straightaways he was only catching intermittent flashes of red. But what bothered him more than the increasing distance was everything coming down at once. No way could the timing be coincidental. "Damnit, Terry. I don't like what's goin' on here. They made us."

"Sure as shit, Milo. Somehow they picked us up . . . Hold on a sec, I'm tryin' to get Erskine now . . ." Terry changed frequencies. "Oh, fuck, the Buick's turned around too, comin' back this way." He flipped channels. "*Jason, you guys watch your back!*"

Sergeant Jason Rouby and Trooper Benny Jenkins never had a chance. When their Sentra roared out of the blind curve a mile below the Tabernacle, the converted van was sideways, blocking the road. Jason stomped on the brake, popping the gear shift in reverse in a frantic attempt to escape, but his reaction was futile; the Buick had come up behind him, sealing off his exit. Jason grabbed for the 12 gauge, pistol-grip Winchester mounted under the dash. Benny ripped his Sig Sauer from its holster, aiming out the window, but neither was quick enough. Before either could get off a shot the windshield imploded. Cut to pieces in a vicious spray of submachine gun fire, the two troopers became the first casualties of the night.

"Was that cool or what?" McKensie was giggling, maniacal, high-pitched laughter that grated on Boyd's nerves like a rasp. "Guess those cocksuckers won't be botherin' *us* anymore."

"No," Boyd said. "Now we'll only have every other cop in the state on our trail."

McKensie snickered, fidgeting nervously at his console. "So big fuckin' whoopee. You think those crackers're smart enough to catch us? No way."

Boyd didn't argue. He'd only have to put up with the warped bastard a little while longer.

*   *   *

When the scoreboard clock ticked down to zero, jubilant Hog fans poured onto the playing field. Arkansas had held off a last ditch drive to defeat the Crimson Tide 23/21. Posted outside the Razorbacks' dressing room while EAGLE congratulated the victors, Reed Sykes-Smythe was smirking. He'd made the right decision, not that hayseed fool who'd tried to sabotage him. S-S had thought all along that all the crap about stolen missiles and missing helicopters was just something Cherry and his crony had trumped up to impress the President. Well, it hadn't worked, and now the SAIC was the one who'd have to face the consequences. After he enjoyed watching Rick Cherry eat crow, Super Shit was going to annihilate him.

*   *   *

Huddled behind the headworks of a collapsed conveyor belt, Erskine and his partner, Abe King, watched as three men piled boxes in the back of the Jeep, pointed toward a ruined building with its headlights on. A fourth stood guard, a submachine gun slung from his left shoulder. They recognized the farm manager and Vonnie Lee Bolin; the other two they couldn't identify, not that it mattered. Even in the dark they could tell from the casual manner he carried his weapon, the one with the burp gun was a professional.

"That's everything," Harlan Williams said, rolling out a dirt bike and rocking it back on its kickstand next to the Jeep.

Erskine prayed Harlan was telling the truth. Maybe the men were retrieving narcotics or hot merchandise and the helicopter wasn't in there. Then they might all get out of this alive. From

257

his crouched position he couldn't see inside, but if George and Jim had made it past the tailings, they should have a better view.

An instant later he knew it wasn't to be.

*   *   *

Milo stared at the riddled Sentra, the bodies of Rouby and Jenkins slumped grotesquely on blood-drenched seats. He had reached the ambush site ten minutes after the massacre, abandoning the Blazer at Terry's shouted warning to his team.

Hearing the fusillade through Jason's open mike, Terry had immediately called for backup and requested a statewide 'armed and dangerous' APB for the Buick and the converted van. Then he had jumped in his pickup and raced down the road, hoping against hope that what he feared wouldn't be there.

The investigators stood side by side, in the dazed inertia of shock. Terry spoke first. "What is this, Milo? I just lost two good men, and I'm not even sure why."

Milo didn't answer; had no answer. It was all out in the open now, the brutal, cold-blooded execution of two state policemen obviating any need for continued stealth. But what, exactly, *was* going on? He looked at his watch. Terry was right. At this late hour, the President couldn't be the target. By his calculations Marine One should be taking off any minute, maybe was already in the air. So where had he messed up? What had he missed?

As Milo groped for an explanation, a vision of Addy Willis appeared to him, her lucent face superimposed on the carnage. And in that instant, the truth finally hit him. He'd had all the pieces, everything, starting with Addy. Her death. The missiles. The Cobra. Everything. But like a fool, he'd left her out of the mix, assembling the wrong picture. Why, oh why, Milo castigated himself, when he had been so obsessed with the little girl, had he failed to realize that she was the key?

"Divert Marine One." Milo's first instinct was to protect the President. If he were correct, after being so horribly wrong before, the entire state was in peril. He had raised SHEPHERD, and was trying to explain. "They're going for Nuke One. You've got to get Clinton out of the state. Divert to Tulsa or Oak City. Have Air Force One meet you, but *do not* return to Little Rock. Richard, I know this must be hard to swallow, but you have to trust me."

"Milo, on your say so I put my ass on the line, and I've just had it chewed up and spit out. Why should I believe you now?"

"Because this time, I'm right."

Betsy had tried to tell him, jokingly, that day in the clearing. He'd even entertained the idea himself, until he'd let the utility brass convince him it couldn't be done. But their denials hadn't been the determining factor. His dismissal of the power plant as the logical target had been less a reasoned refusal than a shying away from the unthinkable. Milo had been unable to believe that any purported Christian organization, least of all one comprised of ordinary *Americans*, would deliberately blow up a nuclear reactor, endangering the population of an entire state, or, God forbid, a whole section of the country.

Was it too late to keep that from happening?

"All right, Milo. I'm in such deep shit now, a little more's not gonna make any difference. We'll head for Oak City. Have Air Force One meet us at Tinker."

One weight lifted. "Thanks Rick."

"Don't mention it."

"Oh. One more thing."

"Yeah? What is it now?" Cherry asked warily.

"If you guys in the Black Hawk aren't too busy, we could sure use a little help down here."

It wasn't the Secret Service's fight any longer, but what the hell. Like he'd said, he was waist deep already. "I'll see what I can do."

*   *   *

"Holy shit!" Abe whispered as the tip of the rotor emerged from the shattered doorway. "The fuckin' copter's really here."

It wasn't supposed to be like this. They were on stakeout, for Christ's sakes. No vests, no helmets or assault weapons. Only their wits and their sidearms to stop a band of assassins. And if they failed, what were the odds the sheriff would arrive in time? But . . . they had to try.

"Yeah," Erskine acknowledged grimly. "It looks that way. Okay, this is our best chance. Let's take 'em now, before they get it all the way out." He whispered in his walkie-talkie, "Jim, close up and cover us. We're goin' in."

The Jeep was between the investigators and the school. They stayed low, darting down the middle of what had once been Main Street behind the protective screen of its headlights. Seeing their confederates break cover, George and Jim moved up behind a crumbling chimney fifty yards away. Daniel's men had wrestled the chopper halfway out the doorway by the time Erskine and King reached the relative safety of the Jeep. Still undetected, the cops split up, taking opposite sides of the Cherokee.

Erskine opened the passenger door, using it as a shield. Stabilized his pistol on the door frame. He was breathing hard, but the command was clear. "Hold it right there. State Police."

In answer a hail of bullets raked the vehicle, smacking into the grill and open door. The first round took out the headlights, plunging the scene into darkness while narrowly missing both policemen. The troopers returned fire, emptying their magazines at the image on their retinas. They were rewarded with an agonized cry as a slug tore into Harlan Williams.

Then, total quiet, the eye of the storm.

"Can you see anything?" Erskine queried his partner, hushed tone barely louder than the pounding of his heart.

Abe peered around the hood. "Not much. I'm gonna . . ." but whatever he intended to do or say was canceled by another fusillade, Abe's skull exploding in a spatter of tissue and bone.

If they were going to help Wildgen and Burleson would have to get closer. They dashed from the chimney, angling toward the corner of the school. In the opaque murk Jim tripped over a rail and went down. George hesitated, dropped into a kneeling position, weapon extended. "Jim?"

Burleson grunted, "Go on, I think my ankle's busted."

"I'm not leavin' you here."

"Go on. You gotta. This thing's goin' down hill." At that moment more gunfire volleyed from the doorway. Erskine had just raised his head after reloading when a Teflon jacketed cop-killer caught him square in the throat, tearing out his larynx before severing his spine.

George rushed for the Jeep. He'd ram the goddamn helo. He might get killed trying, but the murdering bastards wouldn't get it off the ground. That thought must have been telepathic, because at the same instant, the figure carrying the submachine gun broke for the vehicle, squeezing off short bursts to pin George in his tracks. Jim, prone and in pain a hundred twenty feet away, aimed and pulled the trigger. The gunman grunted, clutched his side, and staggered backward toward protective cover.

George scrambled up, raced over the final sixty feet with gun blazing to duck unscathed behind the parked 4 X 4. Then his luck ran out. When he reached for a spare clip, he didn't have one. In disbelief he patted himself furiously, but no amount of wishful searching could conjure one up. Major, *major* screwup. Out of ammunition, he lunged for the Jeep's open passenger door, dived across the seat. Lying face down, he had one hand on the ignition and one on the accelerator when a 9mm Glock poked its evil snout through the driver's window.

Jim Burleson winced at the report. *Dear God.* Now it was up to him. On the range he was a pretty good shot. He had already wounded one of the s.o.b.s. Could he pick off the rest? Or keep them at bay until help came? Were those sirens in the distance? He dragged himself forward, concentration so intense he didn't notice a luminous red dot skipping over the broken pavement until it glanced off his spectacles, coming to rest on his forehead. In the nano-second it took his brain to process the ruby light he realized he was going to die.

Harlan wasn't dead yet, but it wouldn't be long. Propped against an interior wall, Chris, too, had lost a lot of blood but he could still fly. "Hurry," he urged, "there're more on the way."

The faint warble was growing louder. Spurred on by the approaching sirens, Vonnie Lee and Tim Ogelsby, who had escaped without injury, bent to their task with renewed vigor. But as feverishly as the men labored, and as big and powerful as Vonnie Lee undisputedly was, they weren't making any headway. Chris recognized that the problem was the unmanned tail. Without a counterweight to keep its skids level and prevent the Cobra from tipping forward, they were never going to get it out. A change in the Doppler told them the cops had turned off the highway. Fighting nausea the wounded pilot staggered up and grabbed hold. "Try it now." With Chris hanging on, one final, supreme effort freed the caged bird.

"Okay. Help me up."

Vonnie hoisted Chris into the cockpit. There were holes in the plexiglas, and a bullet imbedded in the seat, but the controls appeared undamaged.

Relieved, Chris flipped the toggles. "All right. I'll be okay. Now clear out before the cops get here."

Tim looked wistfully at the Suzuki, but orders were orders. Not until the gunship was in the air was their part of the mission complete. He could see blue lights flickering through the trees. "I don't think so, Mr. Wynne. You go first."

Slowly, then with increasing speed, the rotor began to turn.

"Goddamn. Goddamn bloodbath out here." The last time the sheriff had seen so many bodies was when a truckload of illegals had overturned, strewing wetbacks all over the Interstate. And four of these guys were cops.

"I'm sorry Milo, looks like we were too late. Your chopper took off right before we got here. We got one man in custody, Vonnie Lee Bolin. Everybody else is dead, 'cept one weasel cut out through the woods on a dirt bike."

"Sheriff . . ."

"*Sheriff!*"

"Hold on a sec. *What is it, Langston?*"

"This one's still alive!" The deputy was bent over a prostrate form on the Jeep's front seat. Blood oozed from a hole in the back of the man's head, but he had a pulse—faint and thready, but still a pulse. "Hang in there fella," the officer directed, "just hang in there. We're gonna get you fixed up."

☆   ☆   ☆

"SHEPHERD," Milo's voice was charged with anxiety. "The bird has flown. Repeat, the bird has flown. Shit, Richard, we missed him. They wiped out three of our guys in the process, and another's danglin' by a thread. Where are y'all now?"

" Um . . . about fifty miles northeast of Ozark, comin' your way . . ."

"Good. You're almost here. Rick, I sent everything I had to Fayetteville. Now he's airborne, I don't have any way to stop him. Can you interdict?"

"Let me get this straight. You want us to hit Russellville, find the bastard, and splash him."

"That's about the size of it."

Cherry switched out of privacy mode, piping the conversation through all of SHEPHERD'S headphones. "For the record, you're askin' the U.S. Secret Service and the U.S. Marine Corps to shoot down a National Guard helicopter that may or may not be armed with Hellfire missiles which may or may not be targeted at Arkansas Nuclear One."

"For the record, that's affirmative. Now for God's sakes, step on it."

☆   ☆   ☆

The police copter needed refueling. Before beginning their patrol Dan and Quentin had topped off at Drake Field. The OH-58's extended range capacity of 89.5 gallons translated roughly

263

into three and a half hours cruising time, enabling them to stay aloft throughout the game. But with the departure of the Presidential convoy, both men and chopper were out of gas. Stress from their tense vigil, coupled with relief that no threat had actually materialized, had left Milo's volunteers drained. Having landed, neither man was in a hurry to strap back in, content to relieve themselves and stretch cramped legs while aerial traffic, delayed until after EAGLE'S departure, thinned out.

"Excuse me, sir. Are you with the FBI?" A man wearing a white drip-dry shirt adorned with a plastic nametag hurried up to Quentin. Lounging outside the terminal while a fuel truck serviced the Kiowa, Q.C.'s block-printed windbreaker was a dead giveaway.

"What can I do for you?"

"I'm Kelvin Crofton, the assistant manager here at the airport. If you're Agent Thomasino, there's an urgent message for you."

Quentin found Dan signing the fuel chit. "Let's go," he said, jerking his head toward the chopper. "Milo needs us. I'll explain on the way."

*   *   *

They were converging on ground zero from all directions. Careening down the same deer-plagued short cut he had taken a month earlier, Milo was searching for someone with the authority to shut down the power station. And after eleven on Saturday night, that was proving next to impossible. (In the final analysis, even if he had located someone willing to give the order, shutting down a nuclear reactor is a bit more complicated than pushing the off button.) Steering with one hand, holding his radio in the other, and keeping an eye out for nocturnal fauna, Milo had so much on his mind he didn't have time to dwell on might-have-beens. He had left Terry in charge at the rectory, which, when they had broken in with an augmented force of lawmen from half a dozen jurisdictions, was predictably deserted. Since Milo had fled the mobile home to give chase, surveillance of the chicken farm had been nonexistent, leaving the police ignorant of its current status. Terry was working on a warrant for the Williams' premises when Milo took off.

[Of the four teams on stakeout, Tom Fenton and his partner were the lucky ones. The Dodge Caravan they were tailing contained Daniel's housekeeper, Nelda Abernathy, and her husband Ansel, who had driven to the B.P.O.E. Lodge in Harrison. Arrested and taken to the Boone County jail, the pair steadfastly maintained their innocence. They had fed Brother Daniel his supper, cleaned up, and decided to go into town when the pastor said he would be going out again. What was the harm in having a few beers with fraternal brothers on Saturday night?]

What was he planning to do when he reached Russellville? Milo didn't know. And he wasn't actually going *to* Russellville, rather, *through* it. Compelled by a presentiment he would be hard put to explain, Milo's destination was the clearing, where everything had started. And that seemingly innocuous glade lay more than twenty miles beyond the reactor, through town, across the river, through Dardanelle, and out into the country. He dropped the mike, grasped the steering wheel with both hands, and put the hammer down.

*   *   *

Wendy had examined every square inch of Laura's tomb except the sarcophagus and found no way out, except through the airlock, and she'd given up on that. The room couldn't have been more than eight feet by ten. Furnishings were necessarily spare: a leather recliner, small reading table holding a Bible, lamp, and silver bud vase, and the lidless mahogany casket, nestled inside a hermetically sealed, brass-bound glass vault. Lending an ethereal luminosity to the cadaver's waxy countenance, indirect lighting spilled from a recessed cove. Floor, walls, and ceiling were all carpeted. Under the watchful eyes of the dead woman Wendy had pounded the walls, prodded the corners, tugged the seams,

265

yanked at the ceiling, to no avail. She had turned the chair over; there was nothing underneath. The coffin was the only place left.

When the first wave of panic subsided she had thought about this. Where was the refrigeration unit for Laura's vault? The case was colder than the room, which, more than three stories underground, was cold enough. Air circulating through two 4" x 12" ceiling grills remained a constant fifty-five degrees. Even muffled by the thick carpet, an annoying whine pervaded the chamber, like the humming of a compressor. And compressors had to be vented, and accessible, if they ever needed servicing. Since, on the bottom level of the bunker, the reinforced concrete floor was unlikely, that left only the wall behind the vault, but dear God, she didn't want to disturb the corpse.

Listen to me Wendy, you can do this. It was the woman's stare that got her. Piercingly blue, the Laura's prosthetic eyes seemed to follow her with glassy curiosity as she examined the confined quarters. *Forget her eyes. Just get it over with.*

Projecting into the small space end-on from the short wall opposite the entry, Laura's transparent bier was attached to the wall by an angled brass flange, studded at six inch intervals with polished, hexagonal brass bolts. The shiny finish didn't have a scratch, but anything was possible. Wendy worked methodically, trying each bolt in turn. They were all tight. She took off her tee shirt, spat on the soft cotton fabric to improve her grip, and tried again. Zip.

Next she got down on her hands and knees to inspect the bottom of the case, which was elevated five inches above a recessed toe kick. Plush cobalt broadloom lapped the baseboard seamlessly. No concealed entry there. Starting from the wall, she ran her fingers under the platform's four inch steel lip. She took her time, carefully feeling her way down the length of the overhang, across the end, and back along the far side. Nothing.

Dejected, Wendy was verging on hysteria again. She sank on her heels, pulling on her top against the cold. Rocked back and forth, arms crossed over her chest, sobbing. Tears cascaded down her cheeks, clumping long lashes. *Get hold of yourself, girl. Cryin' won't help.* She dashed at her eyes with the back of her hand, angry at her frailty. *What? Where did that come from?* Her heart quickened a beat, hope a smudge of grease across the tip of her middle finger. Maybe there *was* something there!

Frantically, with no idea how much time she had left, Wendy started over.

The catch was halfway down the near side, flat, indistinguishable from mounting screws that anchored the vault to its base plate, except that the catch had a smooth head. No wonder she had missed it. Saying a prayer, Wendy pushed—hard. Heard a click. To her amazement the whole sepulcher slid forward soundlessly on greased runners, exposing a niche where the case had abutted the wall.

Air whooshed out of the burial chamber like smoke billowing up a giant flue. Wendy peered into the dim recess, where rubber hoses stretched from a compressor to a series of outlets under the body. Ignoring a strongbox secreted in the coffin's false bottom, she crawled over the compressor into the nook. She stood up tentatively, groping around her in the dark. Her hand found a rung. And another. Shivering, this time with exhilaration, Wendy began to climb.

* * *

The dizziness was getting worse. Chris had bandaged his torso with strips torn from his shirt, but his fatigues were sticky with blood. The bullet had gone clean through his side, missing vital organs but leaving a neat entry hole and a larger, ragged exit wound. However the main problem was that the cops had forced him to take off before he was ready. If he flew directly to Nuke One, he'd arrive twenty minutes early. Unaware how badly Milo had misread their intentions, Wynne had every reason to suspect that police defenses would be concentrated around the reactor. He didn't want to expose himself too soon. But with the alarm out, he wasn't likely to find a place to land the chopper while the clock ran down. Well, as long as he could operate the controls he would do his part. His best bet was to keep low, circling over a stretch of Ozark National Forest until time to close in.

*　　*　　*

Daniel whizzed past McKensie's trailer, and a mile further along, the abandoned stakeout. According to the Buick's clock, fifteen minutes would see the culmination of all he had worked for, for so many years. He had to share his triumph with Laura. On this grandest of nights, it was ordained that they be together.

The cleric had gotten such a high smuggling McKensie and Boyd out of the poultry farm under the cops' noses that he had agreed to help spring the mobile command post from their surveillance. It had never been Daniel's intent to become physically involved with the scheme, but Thomas's prying had changed that. What did the meddling detective think? That the fuzz could set up two observation posts in his own backyard and he wouldn't find out? He would acknowledge that being under such intense scrutiny had made things more difficult, but Boyd was a cagey strategist. Daniel smiled to himself, reveling in anticipation. They had a few tricks up their sleeves too.

CHAPTER 26

On board SHEPHERD, circling Russellville midway along the air corridor between Fayetteville and Little Rock, TCAS was picking up a steady stream of aircraft, but nothing that looked like the renegade helicopter. All traffic was keeping well above 2300 feet, the minimum recommended safe altitude for night flight in that sector of the state. Part of a sophisticated collision avoidance system, the proximity radar detected airborne transponder emissions, furnishing details of speed, range, and altitude. The Black Hawk was also outfitted with a thermal imager, similar to the one on the State Police helo, and a Marine technician was studying the monitor for signs of the Cobra. Captain Geoffery Flewellyn, the co-pilot, and a CAT agent in night vision goggles scanned the skies for visual contact.

Chris didn't know that SHEPHERD was lying in wait, but he expected some protective measures around the reactor. Approaching from the same direction as the other planes, he was flying under radar, listening to the chatter of happy Razorback supporters plying the airways above him. The only thing Wynne couldn't hide was the heat from his exhaust, which would show up on infrared, but he wasn't worried about that yet. When he got closer he'd deal with that problem. He was troubled that at intervals he seemed to jerk awake, a warning realization that the loss of blood was making him light-headed, causing mini blackouts. Chris inhaled deeply, boosting his oxygen level and sending a searing jolt through his injured side. That should keep him conscious. Then the lake was coming up, and he would have to ascend to clear the surrounding bluffs, showing up

269

*briefly on commercial radar. Before switching it, on Chris set his
transponder to squawk 1200 [VFR], standard air traffic control
code for aircraft operating in uncontrolled air space, a move that
would ordinarily fool anybody seeing his blip into figuring him for
simply another Hog fan.*

Sweeping through 360 degrees, TCAS caught him seconds
later. "I've got something! This may be our guy," Corporal Breck
Campbell yelled. "Ascending through 1800 feet. Bearing three-
one-five at four plus miles."

Cherry stayed out of the way as the crew's actions meshed
with clockwork precision. Major Bobby Moore banked sharply,
swinging his aircraft on an intercept heading, then reducing speed
so the techs could focus their equipment. Campbell was glued to
the proximity radar. Roger Apted, the FLIR operator, rotated his
scanner, gimbaled beneath the Black Hawk, toward the shouted
coordinates, while the co-pilot and Secret Service agent in NVGs
peered through the darkness for the Cobra.

Carrying four Stinger missiles mounted on external pylons
(and other goodies attested to by assorted bumps and bulges in
the Black Hawk's skin), SHEPHERD had plenty of fire power to
knock Chris out of the sky. With the ATAS [Air-to-Air Stinger]
UNCAGE control on *Auto*, Major Moore flipped the MASTER
switch from *Standby* to *Armed*, activating his missiles' electronic
heat seeker heads, and the hunt was on.

But before any human or technological wizard could verify
the contact it had vanished. Campbell announced bleakly, "Uh
oh, Major, he's gone."

*Had anyone spotted him? Chris turned off the transponder,
dropping like a stone. He leveled out barely ten feet above the lake,
skimming over the surface. September's lingering heat and humidity
enhanced the water's natural ability to mask his IR emissions. Add
false readings from ground clutter, and he might well be invisible.
But flying that low, Chris couldn't afford even a minute slip. He*

took another deep breath, using the pain to force back blinders that had narrowed his vision to a cone.

With a good idea where to look, the FLIR operator found Wynne first. He was there, right there—*on* the water. "Heads up, Major. I think I've got him." Set on wide angle [WFOV] at 1.5x magnification, the four-element mercury cadmium telluride detector "saw" the hot spot, electronically transferring it to Apted's screen as a brighter white bloom against a black and white background. Unfortunately, solar loading made precise identification difficult. Was it the Cobra, or a powerful outboard? Tracking the hot spot with his joystick, Roger switched to recognition mode, narrowing the field of view while increasing magnification, and adjusted the gain level. On 6.5x power, normally he could discern aircraft at three miles. This guy was closer than that now. Two, two and a half miles, and still not clear.

Reflections off the water had exacerbated his vertigo. Disoriented, Chris knew he had to climb. They hadn't planned it this way, but he was losing it. Just a few hundred feet. Easy does it. Okay. He could make out the cooling tower in the distance. Hold it steady. Hold it . . .

The Stingers had found Chris too, but Major Moore didn't want to fire without target verification. Unless someone actually clapped eyes on the Cobra he could just as well be blasting some joker on a speed boat as the chopper. Except he was out of time. Afraid the helo would launch any second, Moore hit the MISSILE ACTIVATE switch at the exact same instant Geoffery Flewellyn bawled, "Confirm. Confirm. I see him, Bobby! Target at twelve o'clock." On the pilot's PDU [heads up display] the acquisition reticle changed to tracking. Flying in the box, the Marine major pressed the TRIGGER/UNCAGE/FIRE button to the first detent, initiating the firing sequence. The missile locked on, and the audio alert began warbling insistently.

"Fire!" Moore depressed the button all the way and held it down. Hovering in a light cross breeze, SHEPHERD shuddered imperceptibly as the Stinger streaked away.

*   *   *

At seventeen minutes to twelve James Coltrane staggered out of the restroom, his face ashen, both hands pressed against his stomach. Reeling into Johnny O'Donnell's office he collapsed in the chair opposite his supervisor. "I gotta go home, Johnny. I'm sick to my stomach and I got the trots. My head's bangin' like a drum."

Concerned, O'Donnell came around his desk and appraised the guard. Coltrane was usually dependable, especially since that wife of his had taken a hike. "You don't look so hot, Slick. You got a bug, or is it somethin' you ate?"

"I dunno," James covered his mouth, suppressing a gag, "but I think I'm gonna puke." He pushed up and lunged for the door.

"All right," his boss said hastily. "Go on. I'll sign you out." James lumbered toward the exit.

Tough, being sick when you lived alone. Intestinal flu was a real bitch. O'Donnell had started after the guard when his phone rang. He called to Coltrane's retreating back, "You know where to find me if you need anything."

James mumbled, "Thanks, Johnny," and escaped outside.

He was pulling out of the parking lot when an orange ball of flame lit up the western sky, followed seconds later by a loud detonation. *What the hell?* James was curious, but he didn't slow down, trying to get as far from the reactor as possible. He had used a twenty minute pencil timer and there were fifteen minutes to go. Part of him wondered if the explosion had anything to do with the mission. Part of him didn't care. All James wanted was to collect his money and get the hell out of Dodge. A Sheriff's Patrol and a State Trooper screamed by him going the other way. In the distance he could see pulsating red and blue lights. James put his foot down and hauled ass.

*   *   *

"We got him, Milo! He's down, splashed, finished, finito!"

Across the river, Milo had seen the fiery flash as he was barreling through the outskirts of Dardanelle, but he couldn't tell what had blown. Was it the reactor, SHEPHERD, or the Cobra? Cherry's exutant transmission provided the answer. Milo pulled into a closed filling station and sagged against the wheel, weak with relief.

"Say again."

"Took the bastard out with one Stinger. We're approaching now, but we can't see much; he went down in the middle of the lake. There's some fuel burning, and a little floating debris, but basically, an oil slick's all that's left."

"What about the missiles?"

"He didn't get off a shot. They're all on the bottom with the mother."

"Thank God for that. We'll send divers down at first light if the Army doesn't beat us to it. But until we locate Commander Boyd and the rest of Daniel's fanatics, we have to secure Nuke One. Who knows what those lunatics might try? The security chief's been briefed. Will your men help hold the fort until the cavalry arrives?"

"Can do. There's nothing left for us here. Dan and Q.C. can mark the site."

Approaching from the northwest at the height of the action, the borrowed police chopper had stayed clear of the fray, following the aerial search-and-destroy by radio. With armaments consisting of a single 30-cartridge, banana-clip CAR 16 from Quentin's duffel, the Kiowa's function had been that of spotter, not executioner. Subsequent to the kill however, Dan took up position over the crash site, enabling SHEPHERD'S heavily armed agents to safeguard the reactor.

*   *   *

She had to get to a telephone. If she could make it to the farmhouse she could warn them. Wendy didn't have any idea of the time but she had to try. She was almost to the top of the shaft. Then her hand encountered a solid object. It was a ventilated hatch cover, raised on metal ribs. *Friggin' bastards.* Wendy clung to the top rung and shoved with all her might. After a second's heart-stopping resistance it gave. She emerged in an unused grain bin. Weak light from the chicken sheds filtered through a port in the bin's conical roof, outlining a small door two feet off the ground. The door had no catch, but when she pushed it swung outward easily on spring-loaded hinges. Wendy had just wiggled through when footsteps crunched on the gravel.

Who could it be? Everybody had gone; that was why Heavy had locked her in with the corpse. Boyd, both her brothers, Harlan, McKensie, Tim the night guard, even Brother Daniel. A geek in the bunker and Flora were the only ones left. Wendy tiptoed around the circular structure, trying to stay hidden but desperate to see who was there. She peered around the bin, stifling a gasp. Daniel was walking toward the shed that concealed the bunker's entrance. Damn. If he went to Laura's room Wendy was dead. He would find her on the surveillance cameras and kill her before help came.

When the door banged shut Wendy abandoned caution, running for all she was worth. Her only chance was to disable Flora and dial the authorities. She had gotten nearly to the steps when lights from three vehicles probed the lane. Wendy dodged behind a bush, flattening herself against the house. Was it over? Had they already blown up the power plant? She cringed, praying they wouldn't see her. Then a Cherokee with sheriff's decals, a State Police cruiser, and a Toyota pickup braked side by side, blocking the drive. Eight lawmen got out, loaded for bear.

"Don't shoot," Wendy begged, crawling out from the shrub with her hands up. "Please don't shoot."

Jay Womack recognized the girl instantly and lowered his pistol. Hadn't he gone over every inch of this same damn farm looking for her in that weird, middle-of-the-night search two weeks ago? "Wendy? Is that you? Wendy Bolin?"

Safe! She was finally safe! With that knowledge a trace of her former bravado returned. "It's me, Sheriff. And," Wendy continued in a rush, "there's somethin' important y'all need to know."

✳   ✳   ✳

"What have you heard?" When Daniel entered the operations room it was seven minutes to twelve. Lanny Shumpert sat alone at the communications console. The rest of the Tabernacle stalwarts had been sent home.

Lanny swallowed. How was he going to tell the preacher that they'd lost the helicopter? "Uh, uh, Harlan hasn't checked in yet, Brother Daniel. But, uh, I, I guess they got the chopper out all right because Commander Boyd reports that, uh, ah, that Mr. Wynne was shot down."

"Commander Boyd told you the helicopter went down?"

"Yes sir. Just now. Do you want me to raise him?"

So Wynne had gotten to the lake. Well, Boyd had said he was good. But having made it, what had happened? There weren't any anti-aircraft defenses around the plant that they were aware of. There weren't defenses of any kind, according to that drunken fool Coltrane. "Yeah, Lanny. Get the Commander for me." Deep underground, mobiles didn't work, so all calls went through the console.

"Boyd, what's going on? Lanny says somebody splashed the Cobra."

"Black Hawk. Don't know where he came from."

A Black Hawk meant the Feds. Daniel didn't like the direction this was taking one bit. Not *another* fuck up. They couldn't have come this far to be denied at the last minute. "Goddamnit, Boyd. Why didn't you kill that cop like I told you to?"

"I haven't got time for this Daniel. The helicopter did exactly what we wanted: drew their fire. Now we're in the clear. I've got work to do. Over and out."

Boyd's preemptory dismissal angered the cleric, but as long as things were still on track, Daniel wouldn't argue. He growled at Lanny instead. "I'm going downstairs."

"Uh, Brother Daniel," Lanny was really miserable. "Heavy, he, uh, he, uh, before he left he took Wendy down there and locked her in."

Heavy. Daniel tensed, cold with rage. Heavy was as devoted to Laura as he. Why would the stupid oaf violate Laura's retreat? Was the big man afraid Flora would take this opportunity for revenge? Double, triple, quadruple damn. He should have let McKensie carve the whore weeks up ago.

Daniel bolted down the stairs. In his fury he dropped his electronic card key. Cursing, he retrieved it, twisting the wheel the instant the light changed. When the door swung outward, the result of Heavy's imbecility—and its implications—stared him in the face. Laura's bier was moved away from the wall and the girl was gone. Daniel bounded across the narrow space. Had she taken it? No, thank goodness the strongbox was still there. He yanked it out. Stuffed the 9 mm Makarov in his waistband and snatched up a handful of bills. When he had filled his pockets he bent, kissed the cold glass. Laura's hyaline stare broke his heart. His hand lingered on the case. "I'm so sorry, my love."

Daniel scrambled back up the stairs. "Lanny, the cops will be coming. You know what you have to do."

The computer operator quailed, plainly terrified.

"It's God's will Lanny," Daniel touched the man's shoulder, "and your bounded duty. *You* were chosen. It's up to you."

       ✻   ✻   ✻

With SHEPHERD'S anti-terrorist squad providing cover for Nuke One, Dan and Quentin on top of the downed Cobra, and Terry in command at Turner Falls, Milo took the opportunity while he was parked to fill in headquarters and set up additional protection for the power plant. Explanations, review boards, and censures would come later. At the moment, apprehending the Tabernacle's zealots had to take precedence.

What Milo would never be able to explain was why he did what he did next. Perhaps it was the conviction that the Cobra aside, Addy's death was inextricably linked to the cult's plan. Perhaps it was because Amy and Addy had become so fused in his subconscious that the midnight pilgrimage was as much to atone for his own daughter as to avenge the murdered child. Or maybe it was nothing more than a sense of foreboding, whetted over years of experience. Whatever the reason, rather than reversing course to join the others, when he exited the Texaco station, Milo continued doggedly toward the clearing.

The moon had come up, a thin sliver of silver, riding pale over the crest of the ridge. Absent the pollution of city lighting, millions of stars glimmered above the barren slope. At five minutes of twelve, monitoring the deployment at the utility on his scanner, Milo had just passed the widened bay when Terry interrupted his musings, more agitated than Milo had ever heard him. "Jesus, Milo, we got a problem."

* * *

"Oohh no, Commander," Heavy whimpered softly, shuffling from foot to foot. "They got him."

Chris had gone down right in front of them. From their vantage on the edge of the bluff Heavy and Boyd had witnessed the whole thing. Boyd had been worried about the law from the moment McKensie killed the kid. Then the state cop had started poking around, and his concern deepened. In his ecclesiastical tower Daniel refused to believe the plan had been compromised, but using Chris as a stalking-horse was cheap insurance. If the police were on to them, they'd almost certainly go for the helo. And in the highly unlikely event an infiltrator had penetrated the Tabernacle's inner ranks, he'd get it wrong too. Which was just exactly how it had played out. The Cobra had served its purpose.

In point of fact, Boyd was surprised the chopper had made it out of hiding. Harlan and Vonnie Lee were such clumsy fools that sending them to move the bird almost guaranteed they'd get caught. Which was, although he and Daniel alone shared the secret, the object. Thinking they'd foiled the plot, the cops would relax. He should have given Chris more credit. The pilot hadn't enlisted for a suicide mission. But granted his evasive skills, going one on one with the Black Hawk Wynne should have had an even chance. Why hadn't he jinked? And where had the Federal helo come from in the first place? And more importantly, were there other defenses that Boyd didn't know about? Surely James would have reported any unusual activity or alerts at work. Boyd shook his head. Too late for second guessing now.

"Yes, Heavy, and I'm very sorry, but Chris accepted that possibility when he signed on, and it shouldn't affect us," Boyd spoke calmly and reassuringly to the big man. "The police don't know we're here. Look, the Black Hawk is leaving. It'll be all right."

Maybe it *would* be all right. While Boyd finished connecting wires the mysterious gunship landed behind the power station, replaced by a police helo, but the cop chopper didn't appear to be armed.

*　*　*

It was easier the second time around. Telephone service to Maybelle's empty house had been terminated, but the main cable was live. McKensie had spliced the wire and was back in the van before the Feds blasted Chris to kingdom come. He had been setting up the laser designator through the moon roof, and had had a ring side seat for the fireworks. *Tough shit, fly boy. This is my show. You were just window dressing.* McKensie watched for a few minutes, grinning evilly until the flames died out, then ducked inside to his keyboard. He'd show these bumpkins a thing or two about computers.

*   *   *

The revelation was worse than Milo could have imagined, spelled out by Wendy in breathless detail. Hurtling down the lane at break-neck speed, Milo's broken ribs grated excruciatingly every time his Expedition jounced over a bump and smaked back to earth. Between impacts he broadcast a frantic, jaw-clenched appeal. "Milo to WATCHDOG. Dan, Q.C., listen up. The missiles are *here*! Repeat. The missiles are *here*, somewhere on the cliff. The Cobra was a decoy. Boyd and Heavy are set to launch at twelve o'clock. You've *got* to stop them. There's no time to get SHEPHERD back."

Q.C. had never taken a course in FLIR operation, but he was adept at video games, having cut his wisdom teeth on *Donkey Kong* at NYU. During the flight to Fayetteville he had practiced aiming, zooming, and tracking with the infrared detector. He was by no means proficient, but he had mastered the rudiments. Dan banked the chopper and started to climb; Quentin switched the FLIR's power control to STANDBY, starting the cooldown sequence. Since it was a brand new unit, it should achieve operating temperature (-196° C) in one and a half to two minutes. They were under four minutes and counting.

And what if he found them? Q.C. had no idea how to keep Boyd from launching the Hellfires. Firing a short-barreled rifle from a moving platform wasn't the easiest way to take somebody out. As far as he could see, that left blocking the path with the chopper, and they could only do that once, leaving three missiles to go and the bastards could still cream the reactor. Or, if he located them in time, he supposed Dan could always fly the helicopter down on top of them. Quentin purely didn't want to be a dead hero, but that's how things were shaping up.

Boyd recognized trouble as soon as the police copter started to climb. "They're looking for us," he informed Heavy matter-of-factly. He didn't know how the cops had gotten on to them, but years in the field told him they were blown. "We have to move up the launch sequence. Get McKensie."

When he was parallel with the top of the palisade Dan leveled out. Quentin clicked the FLIR control to OPERATE, but it was too soon—the gimbal didn't roll out. Shit. This was hopeless. At least his haste wouldn't damage the system. Adrenaline pumping, he checked his carbine for the third time, tapped the monitor, willing it to come on. Still blank. One minute fifty-eight. Seconds later, when the cooldown was complete, a picture formed on the screen. "Okay, we're in business." As Dan maneuvered the helicopter along the cliff face, Q.C. panned the escarpment, trying to keep his hand steady on the joystick. He spotted them right off, barely a quarter mile away.

"I've got 'em," he pointed excitedly at two bright squiggles in the upper right quadrant.

"Right! Try to stay on them." Dan changed pitch and swept toward the points of light.

McKensie had hacked into Nuclear One's operating system without so much as a hiccup, but no one would ever appreciate his finesse. The more successful his intervention, the less chance of its detection: destruction of the reactor would obliterate his handiwork. After the meltdown, when Regulatory Commission analysts tried to determine what had gone wrong, they would only be able to guess at the catastrophic failure *he* had effected. What a shame.

His radio clicked. "I'm ready."

"We're about to entertain uninvited guests, Michael. Do it *now!*"

Goddam cops . . . McKensie reached up, flicked on the pre-positioned GLLD . . . *What the fuck?* . . . stood, staring out the moon roof . . . *Shit! All because of that nigger brat* . . . sneered and hit ENTER . . .

Milo never took his foot off the accelerator, even at the last second. He thundered past Maybelle's going eighty, made the curve, and still gaining speed, plowed into the van head on.

CHAPTER 27

"Fire one!"

The first war head zoomed from the cliff, rose slightly, then nosed down, homing on the containment dome with lethal precision. Lying flat on his stomach, with the designator supported on sandbags, Heavy held the GLLD rock steady, his eyes riveted on the target. Focused on the thermal imager, Quentin saw the missile as a brilliant slash across his screen.

"Sweet Jesus, they launched one! I thought we had another minute."

The Kiowa was almost even with the launch position. "Keep the imager steady. *Don't* lose them," Dan barked.

"I'm trying. Hey! Look out! One of them has a gun."

"Just keep it on them!"

The helicopter was coming in at top speed, four hundred feet . . . three-fifty, three hundred . . . a bullet dinged off the skids . . . *"Hold it!"* . . . two-fifty . . . more shots . . . *"Keep holding."* . . . a shell grazed the rotor housing . . . *"Steady. Steady."* . . . two hundred feet . . . the second missile whirred away . . . *"NOW!"*

Quentin flipped the switch for the Starburst SX-5, flooding the cliff with high intensity white light. Slaved to the FLIR, a fifteen million candlepower beam from the xenon arc lamp hit Heavy full in the face. The big man's hands flew to his eyes, GLLD forgotten. Released from Heavy's grasp, the designator tumbled over the sandbags, landing upside down. Out over the lake, the Hellfire swerved sharply down and to the right, tracking the falling laser, then stabilized as it searched for the lost signal.

Failing to detect one, it continued its altered trajectory, exploding in water five hundred feet off shore.

Boyd had fired all fifteen rounds and was replacing his clip when the search light blazed on. Looking down, he would have missed the full force of the beam except for his wearing night vision goggles. Drenched in light, he was as blind as Heavy. He tore off the glasses and dropped to his knees, scrabbling wildly for the designator.

Before the terrorists could recover, Quentin extinguished the Starburst, casting the scene back to black. Human eyes could not adjust to such violent shifts in illumination.

Timed to fire at eight second intervals, the third and fourth missiles ignited while Boyd and Heavy were still struggling to get their bearings. From its strategically elevated position they left the rack aimed in the general direction of the reactor, cruising on autopilot while the guidance section's electronic brain scanned for directions. Again, without lock-on, the projectiles' course became a function of ballistics, governed by altitude, acceleration, and fuel.

Disregarding the gunfire, Dan had been hovering inside the Hellfire's one hundred fifty meter (500') arming profile. When the last missile soared into the night he backed off a safer margin and Quentin relit the SX-5.

Boyd opted to retreat. Without a scoped rifle he had little chance of hitting the helicopter. Squinting against the Starburst's piercing light, he and Heavy scrambled for the Blazer. That they had a get-away vehicle at all was a direct result of Terry's stake-outs. Using the Tabernacle Grand Caravan, Daniel had sneaked Boyd and McKensie out of the farm to the rectory, where the mobile command post was hidden, leaving Heavy to transport the Hellfires after others had drawn off the police. Milo's unexpected appearance had very nearly tripped them up, but he had broken off pursuit in response to the massacre.

Changing from the concentrated intensity of narrow focus (2°), to a broader tracking beam (17°), Quentin did his best to keep the Blazer in the spotlight. He quickly discovered it was a lot harder to follow a mobile target than a stationary one, especially from a moving aircraft. Thankfully, from the string of blue lights strobing down the lane, it appeared that help was on the way.

Quentin was gravely concerned about Milo; he had been ominously silent since his urgent appeal.

*　*　*

"Clear the building, get everybody out." Cherry was soaked in sweat, his pulse racing. He tore up to Johnny O'Donnell, in conference with Matt Keller, the plant's night supervisor. "We've just gotten word, there's a bomb in the reactor and the missile threat isn't over. You've got to evacuate *now!*"

A look passed between the men, Keller giving rapid assent. "Coltrane," O'Donnell cursed, jogging to a yellow and black diagonally striped box mounted chest-high on the concrete wall. "You lousy sonofabitch!" Ignoring the key, he shattered the glass with his pistol butt, stabbed the button. Instantly a klaxon's frightening blare filled the building.

When the first Hellfire slammed into Nuke One's containment dome Richard Cherry was hustling employees out the side exit. He fell flat as a thunderous explosion shook the structure. They had failed.

Rick jumped up and bolted outside. Anybody left would be barbecue. The parking lot was a pandemonium of smoke, sirens, screams, and people running for their lives. O'Donnell and the supervisor had stayed behind, looking for the charge, and two engineers in the control room were still at their posts, desperately trying to override the computer. Before Cherry could get to the Black Hawk there was another explosion, short of the reactor. The second Hellfire had plunged into the lake, spurting a geyser two hundred feet high.

Rick made it to the helicopter, shouting to Bobby Moore, "Com'on, Major, let's get this thing in the air and see if we can help WATCHDOG." While the pilot was increasing engine rpm the third missile whizzed overhead, detonating harmlessly on a wooded slope across the freeway, followed seconds later by a mushroom of flame as the last Hellfire smashed into an eighteen wheeler. "Good God!" Cherry watched helplessly as an SUV, a pickup, and another semi were engulfed in the fireball. Secondary explosions boomed as their gas tanks ignited.

"SHEPHERD to WATCHDOG, we're comin' your way. Are you guys okay?"

"That's affirmative, SHEPHERD, and thanks, but no need. It was hairy there for a while but we've got things under control. What about the reactor?"

"One direct hit. There's mass confusion and a huge chunk's gone out of the dome, but the good news is, I don't think it was completely breached. We don't know the situation inside."

"God help us if the core's exposed. Has anybody heard from Milo?"

"Not a word."

*   *   *

"Com'on Sheriff, you better see the exit first. We don't want him to escape like I did." Conducting her own gleeful show-and-tell, Wendy led the astonished lawmen to the grain bin. "It's right in there." A trooper with his weapon ready opened the small door and directed his flashlight to the exhaust shaft. "See," she said proudly, "that's how I got out."

They left two deputies guarding the bin. Wendy fairly danced through a sea of clucking chickens to the bunker's entrance. "Y'all aren't gonna believe this!"

Daniel had known they would come, but not this soon. He had one hand on the shed door when he saw the Bolin bitch leading a procession of cops in his direction. Had they seen him? The chicken house was four hundred feet long. He'd never make it to the other door before they got there. Daniel stooped, loping awkwardly back to the lean-to that concealed the bunker's entrance. Drums of disinfectant, push brooms, and rubber boots were stacked against the false panel. He squeezed behind a fifty gallon drum just as the shed door opened.

Pistols drawn, Terry, Jay Womack, and four state policemen descended the ramp, motioning Wendy to stay back.

With Terry covering, two troopers burst through the air-lock, rolling right and left, Glocks extended. A lone programmer sat at his terminal.

"Hands on your head."

The man complied.

Trailed by Wendy, who had edged unbidden down the slope, Sheriff Womack and the other policemen entered the chamber. All six lawmen looked around in amazement. The girl hadn't exaggerated. It was like waking up in a James Bond movie.

Terry quickly shook off the sense of awe. Five men were dead and the whole state in peril. "Where's the preacher?" he demanded.

Their prisoner shook his head.

Wendy crossed the room and pointed down the spiral stair. "He's with her."

Daniel's heart was palpitating. He had to get out of there, fast. As soon as the girl's head disappeared down the ramp he pulled himself up. Running in a lop-sided crouch he made it to the far end of the shed, drew his pistol, and pushed open the door. He didn't see any other officers. They had probably left someone guarding the escape hatch, since that's how the girl had gotten out. With luck no one else was prowling around. Daniel sucked in a lung full of air and raced for the barn.

"Does he have provisions in there?" Terry asked the girl.

"I didn't see any. There was a metal box under the coffin, so maybe he had some cash socked away, but I don't know what else. I

guess there could've been somethin' hidden in the compressor nook, but once I found the shaft, all I wanted was out!"

Trapped in the bunker, Daniel couldn't escape, but how long could he stay holed up with the corpse? If they cut off the power he would suffocate. If he chose not to come out voluntarily they would have to drill the ten inch plate and blast it open. Or drop tear gas canisters down the exit shaft to drive him out. But if the cult leader were half as smart as his setup indicated, he would have sealed that shut. What the forces of law and order did not want was a standoff, reminiscent of Waco or Ruby Ridge.

Terry had seen enough. "Well, we're not gonna get that door open by starin' at it. Sheriff, you and Martin stay here. I'm goin' back upstairs, see if that . . ."

Daniel felt a tremor first. The ground heaved beneath him, swelling and subsiding as shock waves from the blast radiated outward. He pitched down behind the litter silo, short of his goal. Muffled by tons of earth, the rumble was no louder than the passage of a distant jet. Then, as hot gases found the ventilation shafts, feed bins began popping. The roar got louder, bellowing from the hell below as tongues of flame leaped skyward. Shrapnel from the cataclysm decapitated one of the deputies posted at the escape hatch and critically wounded the other. Lying motionless behind the protective silo wall, arms folded over his head, Daniel wept as auxiliary explosions erupted about him and his dream went up in flames.

*　　*　　*

In the control room nothing was working. No one knew better than the men at the terminals what would happen if the core went critical. It would be a disaster of unfathomable proportions, the worst accident in American history. Except this was no accident. This was a cruelly calculated act of barbarism. And despite their frenzied efforts, it was succeeding. Then, miraculously, amid all the noise and chaos, the system began to respond.

Across Lake Dardanelle, the violent crash had ripped loose Mc-Kensie's connection, breaking his hold on the nuclear fail-safes. There would be no meltdown.

It was, however, too late for the men inside.

At straight up twelve o'clock, forty-seven seconds after the first missile rocked the containment structure, the Semtex blew. Superheated water at 620°F under 150 atmospheres of pressure burst from the ruptured pipe in a deadly spew of radioactive steam. Keller and O'Donnell, who had raced onto the floor without protective suits, sustained extensive third degree ionizing radiation burns, making their deaths particularly gruesome. Isolated in the control booth, the engineers were not killed outright. Despite rigorous decontamination procedures, both had received doses exceeding 900 rad, and succumbed to acute gastrointestinal syndrome four days after the attack.

*　　*　　*

Boyd was facing a hard choice. He hadn't been able to elude the police chopper and his one escape route was blocked. With the lake at his back there was no turning around. He stopped the Blazer in the widened bay. "Heavy, your best bet is to run for the trees. If you can make cover, maybe you can get away. I'll try to hold them off."

"No sir, Commander. Brother Daniel tol' me t' hep you. I ain't gonna leave you now."

But Boyd had reached the end of the line. "You have to, Heavy. As your commanding officer, I am ordering you to go. Now hurry, before they get here."

The big man climbed reluctantly out of the cab and trotted off the way they had come. He stopped when he heard the shot and trudged back.

*　　*　　*

When Milo regained consciousness he was surrounded by water. How could that be?. . . wasn't he was sitting in his truck?

He tried to move, but the seat restraint held him firmly in place. Something was wrong . . . the truck was canted at an angle and water lapped at his chin, a filmy white thing floating in front of his face. None of it made any sense.

When he came to again the water had reached his nose and his reflexes had taken over. Milo coughed and spluttered and yanked his head up, trembling as the deliberate collision came back to him. He was astounded he was still alive. Then he realized if he didn't get out of the SUV he wouldn't be for long. The front of his Expedition was completely submerged, and it seemed to be slipping further. The van was nowhere in sight. Had he stopped them in time? The last thing he remembered, trapped in his headlights, was a head protruding through the van's open roof, McKensie's face twisted in a rictus of loathing.

Milo grappled frantically for the seat belt release as his head went under. Then he was free, buoyed over the center console by the rising water. His left leg was useless, crushed from the knee down. His chest was on fire and he could barely breathe; had his splintered ribs punctured a lung? He found the handle and tried to push open the passenger door. It wouldn't budge. Had he locked the doors or were they jammed? Or was water pressure keeping them shut? It didn't matter, in his condition he'd never be able to force one. He half-swam, half-clawed his way over the back seat to a residual air pocket. In wet darkness he managed to locate the storage compartment and extract the tire tool. Then, with every last ounce of strength he could muster, Milo began bashing the rear window.

The injured officer didn't know how many times he struck the glass. Enough. When Sheriff Pressler and his deputies arrived they found Milo face down across the boat ramp. Broken glass, a hubcap, and a mangled bumper were the only traces of either vehicle.

CHAPTER 28

"Bets?" Milo was coming around.

"They tell me you'll live," Betsy advised him cheerfully.

"Are you sure?" Still groggy, he glanced out at the Critical Care station bustling with doctors and nurses. "I thought they'd circled the wagons."

"Pretty sure," she said, "but you *are* a damnably sorry sight. And with all the metal the doctors have holding your leg together, you'll never make it through airport security again."

He frowned, squinting against the bright lights in an effort to recall. "How did you get here?"

"Quentin called me. Something about delirious rantings . . . he said my name kept cropping up."

Milo's memory suddenly improved. "Then Q.C's all right?"

"A real live hero," Betsy assured him, "with the emphasis on *live*. All three of you—you, and Q.C., and Dan, and Rick Cherry and his bunch too."

"What about the reactor?"

"Ah," she said, "that's not quite so simple, but you did good Milo."

It was a near thing. Structural engineers assessing the damage concluded a second direct hit would have penetrated the containment dome, allowing radiation from the ruptured pipe to escape into the atmosphere. Even though the nuclear core remained stable, Daniel's plan would have been a partial success. Internally, clean-up took eighteen months and upwards of half a billion dollars, shared between the federal government and the utility. In January of 2002 the remaining, undamaged reactor at Nuclear One went back on line. There would be no reconstruction. Prohibitive costs and a fire storm of protests from a populace whose confidence in the safety of nuclear power had been severely undermined took care of that.

Milo was fading. On intravenous morphine, tomorrow he'd have no recollection of their conversation. It would be several days before everything finally sank in. No matter. She would repeat it as many times as necessary.

Betsy was relieved he hadn't asked about Terry. Or Daniel. Chances were they'd find the bodies when the excavations were completed. So far they'd only dug down to the top of the bunker.

When she was sure he was out she smoothed back his hair and kissed him gently on the forehead.

Oh, Milo, what am I going to do with you? The first time I saw you you'd just totaled your truck. Now they're fishing your brand new Expedition out of Lake Dardanelle. The next time you might not be so lucky.

✳   ✳   ✳

It took a heavy-duty wrecker to bring up the van and Milo's SUV. Divers had located the vehicles on Sunday, along with the remains of the Cobra, but with the imbroglio in Russellville, it wasn't until Monday that arrangements could be worked out.

[In the immediate aftermath of the attack the FBI assumed control, but the investigation quickly bogged down in high level wrangling over who actually had jurisdiction. Because thefts of the Cobra and Hellfires were part of ongoing military inquiries (albeit in the case of the missiles, heretofore unacknowledged), the Army Inspector General presented a good argument for command. Add the NRC, EPA, ATF, and local law enforcement officials trying to do their jobs, and half the country wanted in on the act. The resulting joint task force satisfied no one.]

Milo's dripping Expedition was towed to a wrecking yard in Dardanelle.

When water drained out of the mobile command post it was loaded on a waiting flat bed and removed under guard to an undisclosed location. FBI experts would spend months analyzing McKensie's handiwork. McKensie wasn't in the vehicle when it was hauled up. Searchers dragging the lake snagged his body with grappling hooks two days later. An autopsy revealed no water in his lungs; his neck had snapped on impact.

* * *

"Aah, y'all are lookin' for James Coltrane, right?"

"Yes ma'am. Who is this?"

"I heard on TV there's a reward."

"Yes ma'am. Two hundred thousand dollars."

"When do I get the money?"

"As soon as he's taken into custody and his identity has been confirmed."

"Well com'on down then and bring the money, 'cause the douche bag's in my backyard, hidin' in the storm cellar."

Lorene watched from the kitchen window as her estranged husband was handcuffed and led away.

* * *

At nine o'clock Tuesday morning following the attack on Nuclear One, while earth movers were tearing away the top of the mountain that had housed the Tabernacle's poultry farm, deputies under the direction of J.J. "Frenchy" DeMoville, Marion County Sheriff, razed the shed behind Mavis Bolin's home and began digging. Thirty minutes later they had exhumed the skeletal remains of her youngest son, Billy Ray. With her two older sons in federal custody awaiting arraignment, and her daughter Wendy missing and presumed dead, the county prosecutor declined to bring charges, saying Mavis had suffered enough.

*　　*　　*

"You gotta eat, chile, you wastin' away t' nothin'."

"Leave me be, Aunt Jenny. I ain't hongry."

"Beauty, this ain't no good. You gotta let it go and start takin' care o' yourself. Look at you. Come a strong wind id blow you away."

It had been on the news for weeks. Reporters had found her and camped on Jenny's doorstep, so that she couldn't go to the grocery store without microphones shoved in her face. When would they leave her alone? Even now, Maybelle couldn't take it in. After all the letters, after Sally Jessie and Oprah, Montel and Larry King, after a personal invitation to the White House from President Clinton, she still couldn't believe what had happened.

Maybelle ate a few bites of mashed potatoes, pushed the pork chop around on her plate, gave up the effort. Jenny was smothering her with kindness, fussing over her until she could scream. Maybelle was irritated with the old lady and irked with herself for being irritated. If she was suffocating in the hot, stuffy apartment, it was her own fault.

Maybelle hated the city. Why had she thought she could start over in the soot-caked, wasted streets of Gary? Nothing would ever fill the hole in her life left by Addy. Nothing. But she missed her home, the open spaces, the fresh country smell of the pasture after a rain. Boo's soft, silky ears. She missed Earl. It was time to admit she had made a mistake.

Contrite, Maybelle spoke softly to the old woman hovering over her. "Aunt Jenny, you're too good to me." Pushing back from the table, she clasped her great aunt's wrinkled hands. "I 'preciate all you done fer me, all you've tried to do, but I cain't stay here any longer, Aunt Jenny. I'm goin' home."

EPILOG

The White House ceremony had been delayed until the end of October so Milo could attend. Occupying a gilded ballroom chair in the East Room, a stone-faced Sykes-Smythe watched as President Clinton paid tribute to the man he had sworn to ruin. Super Shit didn't care that both Feds involved had been reamed and rebushed by their respective agencies for grossly overstepping the bounds of their authority. Public perception was what counted, and to the President and the American public, Richard Cherry and Quentin Thomasino were heroes. Then Dan Holman stepped forward, received his award, and joined Rick and Q.C. on the dais.

Last to be honored was the police captain. When Thomas's turn finally came, the audience, larded with fellow Arkansans, gave him a tremendous ovation. When the applause died down, Betsy pushed Milo's wheelchair to an attractive black woman seated in the front row. The injured officer lifted the medal over his head and handed it to her. His acceptance speech was brief.

"Thank you, Mr. President. Ladies and gentlemen. This is for Addy Willis, an innocent little girl whose callus murder at the hands of terrorists ultimately led to their downfall. And for Jay Womack, Terry Weltlich, Wendy Bolin, and *all* the courageous individuals who forfeited their lives preventing an unspeakable tragedy, I accept this honor on their behalf."

Photographers clicked; cameras whirred. C-SPAN and CNN were airing the ceremony live, while network news organizations were videotaping close-ups of Maybelle's tear-stained face to lead their evening broadcasts.

Off camera, Milo offered his final thanks, silent and heart-felt. *And for you, too, Jessie Holder, you misbegotten sonofabitch. Whatever else your country owes you, this day it is a debt of gratitude.*